Death
of a
Mermaid

Also by Lesley Thomson

Seven Miles from Sydney
A Kind of Vanishing

The Detective's Daughter Series

The Detective's Daughter
Ghost Girl
The Detective's Secret
The House With No Rooms
The Dog Walker
The Death Chamber
The Playground Murders
The Distant Dead

The Runaway (A Detective's Daughter short story)

For Domenica de Rosa

I had an inheritance from my father
As small as the note it came on.
Few words exchanged
In such a long time.

An unwelcome surprise
To walk over familiar ground.
Winter sun clears the mind,
My youthful spirit returned.

Accept, forgive, disappoint,
Who needs to know?
I had an inheritance from my father
And I said no.

Stuart Carruthers
2017

Prologue

Buffeted by the wind, a woman picked her way down the cliff path. A sign on the shingle warned, 'No safe access beyond this point'. Icons showed four kinds of danger. Falling rocks, slippery surfaces, rocky foreshore and deep water with high tides.

The sun had set; the sky towards Shoreham was washed pink.

Four dangers. Or five?

The grille across the entrance to the battery was open. The woman had to look twice to be sure. All her life it had been barred. The Mermaids used to scare each other making up what lay within. They knew the layout from history lessons. Gun chambers off a passage, apertures facing the sea. They'd imagined a skeleton on a heap of ammunition that was used to fire at Napoleon's ships. He would have been a lovelorn soldier who'd killed himself and was never found.

At first the tunnel was pitch black, but bit by bit the woman orientated herself and shapes resolved into doorways into the chambers.

As fast as this vision excited her, it dissipated. She felt the enormity – a plummeting realisation – of her mistake. She was no longer seventeen and in love. The gravelly trawl of the sea ground into her thoughts. If she left now, she'd be caught.

Swiftly, silently, she pulled shut the grille behind her. The padlock hung loose, but in the dusk it would not be obvious that it was unlocked.

She groped back down the tunnel. The walls were wet, not with seawater or rain; neither would penetrate into the heart of the cliff. It was the slime of centuries. She clutched her crucifix and made herself retreat to the end of the tunnel. She hid in the furthest cell. The light was dwindling, the shape of the gun sighting blurred. It was as if reality had retreated with her.

She had come to redress sins. Instead she was skulking in a tomb with her secrets. She crossed herself.

She felt a warm grip around her neck. She tried to shout. Something was stuffed in her mouth. She went to prise off the fingers, but snatched at nothing. She fought blindly, kicking, unable to slither out of the iron-like grasp. Whatever was in her mouth blocked her nose. She heaved for breath but her lungs found no air.

'Where is it?' A grating question like the shingle dragged by the waves.

She had vowed to be unafraid of death. When her time came, she would welcome Jesus. Except…

Not now… not yet…

PART ONE

I

KAREN

'Sort it,' Karen Munday snapped. On her way upstairs, she heard the front door shut. She assumed she was alone.

The bedroom was a heap. Karen picked up a pillow from the floor and then, revved up by the exchange, flung it down. She was within sight of her goal.

That morning she'd bumped into Toni Kemp in the Co-op. Kemp was no better than she ought to be. Just like when they were kids. Acting like she didn't need God. This time, Toni had served Karen gold on a plate.

She retrieved the pillow and, hugging it, sank onto the bed. Her mind travelled back twenty-five years as if the morning in the convent chapel had been just hours earlier. The forty-year-old Karen Munday was a teenager again, sliding along the Mermaids' pew in the hope of sitting close to Mags.

'Sorry, Karen, this is taken.' Mags did sound sorry, but Karen didn't pick it up.

'Then where will I sit?' Karen glared at the crucifix above the altar.

'We don't care, but you can't be there.' Freddy Power's rosary dangled from her fingers. She jerked a thumb for Karen to move away from Mags.

'I was here first.' Although marked with a prayer card, Karen flicked through her missal for the place. Some pages were ripped from when her mum had gone off on one.

'Toni's dad's dead,' Freddy hissed. 'That's *her* seat now.'

'But I'm a Mermaid,' Karen asserted loudly.

'Shut up!' Freddy hissed. Being a Mermaid was a secret thing. '*So* is Toni.'

'Who says?' Karen was stung by this news. You got to be a Mermaid if you liked the Disney film of *The Little Mermaid* or, like Karen, you'd stopped Mags being done over by one of the Dunnings. Karen survived home life by keeping her head down, and school by going in fists first. A face-off with Freddy Power was new territory. Freddy's dad ran the local fishery. Karen's uncle had lost his job for giving Fred Power lip, and Power had seen to it that he couldn't get other port work. The Mundays never again took on a Power. Until now.

A hush fell over the pews. Girls scented trouble. Fights in the convent were supposed to be out of sight, if not from God, at least from the nuns. *And never in a sacred space.* Two sanctions equalled a misconduct mark. Karen had three for sins that involved queue-barging for a second pudding, chewing gum in class and not doing her homework.

'Leave it, Freds,' Mags mouthed at Freddy. Karen was off the hook. Freddy Power always did what Mags told her. Freddy moved up for Toni Kemp and was rewarded by a smile from Mags.

Mass progressed in a blur for Karen. Toni Kemp was a Mermaid, which meant they were no longer a select group of three. As Father George lisped through the 'Gloria in Excelsis', Toni approached the altar and Father George passed her a book. *She was doing the second reading.* You only did that if you'd been very good, could read without stumbling or were Margaret McKee.

Karen swiped through her missal to the Letter of St Paul to the Ephesians. Not a confident reader, she slid her prayer card down line by line to follow.

'"…This you can tell from the strength of his power at work in Christ…"'

Toni had sounded a bit like Karen's idea of God. Surprised by the girl's cool authority, Karen felt a pain as if, like Mr Kemp, she'd got herself stabbed in the heart with a broken milk bottle.

'"…which is his body, the fullness of him who fills the whole creation. The word of the Lord."'

'The word of the Lord.' Karen had raised her eyes. Toni Kemp was watching her. With the twisted perception of a thwarted adolescent, Karen was convinced Toni had engineered her tragedy to worm her way into Mags's Mermaids.

Karen leaned forward in the pew so Mags could see her doing a decade of Hail Marys.

'Holy Mary, mother of God,
Pray for us sinners, now…'
'A-*men.*'

Caught in the tendrils of the memory, Karen spoke out loud in the bedroom. 'At least it's not me whose dad is buried up at Newhaven cemetery.'

Karen had harboured humiliation and the rapier sting of betrayal since the convent. Now she had the perfect means for revenge. That morning in the Co-op, Toni Kemp had not realised that Karen was standing in the sweet section.

When Karen went to the toilet, she didn't hear the creak on the stairs.

2

FREDDY

Freddy Power loved early shifts at the supermarket. The hour and a half before customers arrived when – if you didn't count night staff – she had the shop to herself. Her particular domain was the fish counter at the back of the shop. Although it wasn't why she'd come to Liverpool over twenty years ago – she'd been running away, not running towards – the job was tailor-made for her.

Never overly interested in fashion – at the convent she'd accepted the uniform – now Freddy welcomed the white shirt and black trousers. It made life simple. Shutting her locker, she stepped onto the shop floor. She switched on the fish counter and the oven cooker and like a proud theatre director surveyed the house before the audience arrived. In the fish cooker she caught the aroma of garlic and rosemary from yesterday. At six in the morning the smell was too much for some. For Freddy it heralded the start of a new day.

She admired the sweep of stainless steel reflecting bright overhead lights. Her blank canvas. She envisioned the fish she would arrange there.

Behind the scenes Freddy released the trap in the ice machine and an avalanche of chipped ice shot down into a giant container. She wheeled it through to the counter and hefted it onto the sloping display until it was inches deep in sparkling crystals. Freddy's hands were numb. She preferred contact with her wares. Working with fish, slippery skin, scratchy scales – dead or alive – was about the senses.

In the fridge room, she drew forward the cage of fish that had been delivered overnight. The plastic boxes of fish and seafood reminded her of the fishery when she was young. Yellow, blue and red, filled with fish that needed gutting, filleting, weighing and bagging. Sarah couldn't understand why Freddy loved every minute of it.

Something lay on the floor and she picked it up. Blue beads and a silver chain. Not much of a Catholic these days, Freddy always kept her rosary in her pocket. Mags had bought all the Mermaids a rosary on the convent trip to Notre Dame when they were fourteen. Toni had said Mags only bought it because Freddy was poor and she felt sorry for her. That wasn't kind of Toni, but as she'd got comatose the night before and had a terrible hangover, Freddy forgave her.

Now she remembered that, as the ferry berthed at Newhaven, Toni had flung her rosary into the sea, declaring at the top of her voice that God was dead.

Chilled by the frozen air, Freddy found herself doing a Hail Mary for the Mermaids, wherever they were now. For Mags.

There was a shortfall on her order of smoked haddock. It was a popular day for making Cullen skink, a soupy stew of haddock, leeks and potatoes. She'd be out of haddock by mid-morning.

Annoyed with herself, Freddy set about arranging her stall. Erica had been on the nightshift so all was shipshape, price labels ready, cutting boards scrubbed. Freddy put the previous day's unsold fish at the front of the cabinet, closest to the customers, to encourage a quicker sale. Smoked fish on their left, then breaded fish, followed by a strip comprising tuna, scallops, sardines and squid. Hake, bass and one of her favourites, bream. Lastly, a delicate arrangement of prawns, oysters and mussels around the bags of samphire and parsley and delineated with lemons. The samphire was imported from Israel. As a kid, Freddy used to pick it from the beach at Newhaven, getting out early to beat anyone else who knew where to look. She'd sell it to her dad, leaving a ten per cent mark-up for his customers. Frederick Power had encouraged his eldest child's entrepreneurial spirit. She took after him, he used to say. Before he called her a freak of nature and disowned her.

Freddy speared the labels on sticks into the ice. She walked around to the front to consider the effect from the customer's perspective. When they were trading insults, frequently these days, Sarah said people paid no attention to how the fish were displayed. Freddy said Sarah spending her life with murderers and rapists had killed her eye for beauty.

In a terrible American accent Maxine PA'd that it was 'five to take-off'. Freddy was on schedule.

Last but not least, the knives. From her locker Freddy hooked out a bashed-up leather bag. She had bound the handles with a ring of blue gaffer tape, the colour code for fish, to avoid cross-contamination with the meat section, coded red.

The knives had been a coming-of-age present from Freddy's father when she turned ten. They were, he'd informed her, his mark of trust in her. His father had given him the same gift. She was the next generation. She wished he'd let her stick around to prove it.

She wiped the blades of the knives and placed them on the blue cutting board. She retied her overall and adjusted her net cap. She was all set.

Lift-off, we have lift-off. Maxine's voice crackled over the system. Freddy felt a cool draught. The street doors were open. The first customers were coming her way.

Freddy's phone buzzed. Phones were supposed to stay backstage in lockers, but that morning Freddy and Sarah had had a humdinger of a row.

Today's slanging match had been ignited when Freddy found the front door ajar. *All and sundry could waltz in and murder us.* A realistic possibility; a defence lawyer, Sarah had a few unsavoury clients. OK, so no one had waltzed in, but it came on the heels of Sarah shrinking Freddy's best jumper in the hot wash and buying her five more as compensation. Sarah's behaviour meant Freddy never knew if she was coming or going. *Going, perhaps.*

This has to stop, the text read.

Yes, and? Freddy flicked a look for an approaching customer or for Maxine. When Sarah messed up Sarah usually declared they break up and Freddy find a better person than her. Although she knew that this *was* the answer, Freddy would embark on a round of cajoling, making up instead of giving up.

Another text. A photo of Sarah's bags in the hall. The bags were in black and white, the rest in colour. Upset though she apparently was, Sarah had Photoshopped the snap. Ever consummate with the wordless threat. If Freddy had been there watching, Sarah's packing would have been a hectic affair of banging wardrobe doors and swearing in French. Sarah spoke French fluently and during arguments would rattle off in it to annoy Freddy.

The bags were Freddy's. A new departure.

Let's talk tonight. Heart thumping with misery, Freddy tried to limit the damage. What was there to say?

What is there to say? Sarah fired back.

When they'd got together two years ago, Sarah had declared she was 'in it for the long haul'. She bought Freddy a ring and mooted a big wedding, marquee, band, outfits... Aside from the hard labour implied by the phrase, Freddy was charmed by Sarah's commitment. Used to partners who ran a mile if Freddy suggested they live together, she had embraced the haul, long or whatever. They opened a joint account for bills and discussed getting a pet. Sarah wanted a cat. Freddy liked dogs, so that hadn't come off. Freddy moved into Sarah's big house. Now, pacing behind her array of fish, it occurred to Freddy that the subject of marriage hadn't come up in months.

Freddy was finding Sarah's frequent gifts, the 'date nights' in expensive restaurants, spa weekends, stifling. Her own purse wasn't allowed out; Sarah's Gold Amex covered everything.

Sarah believed Freddy would cheat on her. At first this was appealing and Freddy enjoyed reassuring her. Then Sarah became more exacting about Freddy's movements, which, although typically limited to the route between the supermarket and the house, in Sarah's mind involved clubs, bars and hotel rooms. It was no longer delightful to find Sarah lounging by the plant and flower stacks outside Waitrose, ready to squire her home at the end of her shift.

Last month they'd celebrated 'two blissful years'. The words embossed in gold on Sarah's anniversary card. 'Careful what you wish for,' Toni Kemp would have said. Mags too, except she had never wished for what Freddy wanted. Freddy's long haul had become a life sentence.

Her phone buzzed again. Maxine was making her way up the aisle, stopping to direct a man towards the dental section. Hurriedly, Freddy dug her phone out of her pocket.

It wasn't Sarah. The number wasn't programmed into her contacts.

Your mum is ill. Mags x

Freddy nearly dropped the phone on the prawns. Her hands shook. She grew hot. She hadn't heard from Mags for years. Not since everything went wrong.

'You know better than to be looking at your phone in working hours.' Maxine wasn't admonishing. Everyone liked Freddy.

'Sorry, yes.' It didn't occur to Freddy to tell Maxine what the message had said. She was so astonished it was Mags, her friend – was that the term? – from the convent that Freddy hadn't taken in the words.

'Got any smoked haddock, Freddy? I'm doing a skink. Friday treat!'

'You're in luck, we're a bit low today.' Freddy gave Mrs Wild her best smile and, snatching up a thin sheet of plastic wrapping, slapped an undyed fillet onto the scales.

All day Freddy sold fish. She exchanged banter with customers, remembered the orders of her regulars (ten oysters for Mrs Parker and her friend, three small pieces of cod for Mr Russell's elderly Schnauzer). Upstairs, she plugged the forward orders into the computer.

At three o'clock Freddy came off shift. She caught the bus two minutes after she arrived at the bus stop and got standing space by the exit door. She stared out through the misted panes at Liverpool, her adopted city, full of promise on a winter's night. Trembling as if taking the safety catch off a gun, Freddy opened her phone and reread Mags's message.

Your mum is ill. Mags x

The bus lurched and Freddy was flung against one of the poles. The jarring brought her to her senses. Her mum was unwell. Panicked, Freddy got off the bus a stop early and ran, leaping over puddles and skirting commuters. She had to go to Newhaven.

She slowed down in Sarah's street. How had Mags got Freddy's mobile number? Had her brothers – or her mum? – asked Mags to contact her? Mags had put a kiss – what did that mean? Freddy looked at the screen as she walked, mining the brief message for meaning. How did Mags know her mum was ill? Were they in touch? Reenie Power had always had a soft spot for Mags, a cradle Catholic like herself. She had disapproved of Toni's parents converting to get their girls into the convent. Her judgement softened after Toni's dad was murdered. The irony of Reenie favouring Mags was neon-lit only to Freddy. *Did the kiss mean anything?*

Freddy had dreamt of Mags writing, although the message was different.

The one person from Newhaven with her number was Toni. They were only in touch at birthdays and Christmas and not at all in the last year, when Toni had left London and joined Sussex Police. She was back in Newhaven. Freddy had forgotten Toni's last birthday, Toni forgot hers, but that was normal. Sarah told her not to bother with Toni – what was the point if she never saw her? Did Toni see Mags? Were they still friends? This idea came with a whiff of betrayal. Mags wasn't in touch with Freddy.

Freddy hadn't kept up with anyone from those days. *Least of all Mags.* Sarah scoured Facebook to see what her exes were doing. *It's important to know how the story ends.* Sarah never posted anything; as a lawyer, that would be unprofessional.

Hood up against a rain-soaked squall, Freddy reached the house. A double-fronted affair adorned with railings and a front door with a brass step that some hard-driven maid must have polished in a bygone era. Sarah would employ one now if Freddy hadn't objected.

A Michael Bublé song floated out from the living room. Music Sarah knew Freddy disliked. Sarah would be in there, flicking through a magazine, the languorous pose intended to show Freddy she didn't need her. Freddy would plead for a truce. In bed, in the dark, Sarah would be contrite. It was her fault. Really and truly she would change. Freddy could have her own friends. Go where she liked. Freddy would be faithful. Tomorrow was the first day of the best days of their lives.

Freddy stepped into the light cast by the absurdly grand

chandelier in the hall. Before the Bublé refrain could worm its way into her brain, she extended the case handle and hoisted on the rucksack. Lifting the case over the brass step, Freddy shut the front door. On the road she flagged down a taxi.

'Lime Street station, please.' Dread for her mum engulfed any elation at finally leaving. Fastening her seat belt, Freddy didn't look back.

3

TONI

'The trawler is divided into four main compartments. They cover all that's needed on the boat.' After a year of being in a relationship with him, Toni had finally asked Ricky for a tour of his trawler. Put off by anything on water, she had to admit it was great to see Ricky talk passionately about his pride and joy, bought with a loan from his family's fishery. She had agreed today because the trawler was berthed at the mouth of the River Ouse in Newhaven. Surely nothing could go wrong there.

In the distance the swing bridge was lifting. Damn. Traffic would back up on the ring-road and she'd be late getting to the police station. A large boat – she wasn't good on boats – was being led through by a smaller boat. Toni shivered. The weak sunshine that had cast the slightest sense of warmth had been obliterated by dark clouds coming in from the sea.

'...engine room, cabin, fish hold and the net store where we stow spare netting and nets we're not deploying. It's where we do the repairs.'

'Wow.' Toni knew Ricky, like all the Powers, including his sister Freddy, was a dab hand with a needle. He did his own sewing.

'There are six tanks, for fuel, obviously, and water. We carry at least a tonne of ice when we go out to keep the fish fresh.' Ricky was in his element. Water was his element.

'Wow. Ice.' Toni whistled. She pictured a gin and tonic Feeling guilty for this, she grabbed his hand. 'What happened there?' The tattoo on Ricky's wrist was smeared with blood.

'Caught it on a hook.' He snatched away his hand and rubbed it.

'Careful – you'll make it worse. You don't want it to go septic like Andy's did.' Toni had never got the point of disfiguring your body.

'Do you want a tour?' Ricky sounded irritated; he hated fussing.

'I do. So er, you're up in the, um… cabin?' She indicated a glassed-in structure on the deck.

'The wheelhouse,' he corrected her patiently. 'Done my time in the hold or on the deck. I keep dry unless we hit a problem. Daniel's life is in my hands.' He looked serious for a moment.

'Yes, of course.' Toni preferred the police. Give her toughened criminals over raging seas. However, she liked the words associated with the trawler. Beams, goalpost gantry, derricks, gilson lines and topping lifts. 'Where's Derek?'

Ricky biffed her for her feeble joke.

He yanked a handle on a metal hatch, revealing steps. She followed him down.

Toni was surprised by Ricky's actual cabin, wood-lined walls, leather-padded bench seats, kitted out with food and medicinal supplies. If the boat had been on land, she'd rather like chilling out in it. Although even in port, the creaks and squeaks of the hull and the equipment would make her on edge.

'You down there, Rick?' A man's voice. 'Need to talk to you about upping our bass order.'

'Wait here.' Ricky was up the steps before Toni could say she should leave. Sighing, she remembered the swing bridge. No point; she might as well see the rest of the trawler.

A narrow passage ended in a metal door. Sealed, she guessed, to prevent water getting in or out. Ricky was hot on battening down hatches. She'd noticed that what most people used as clichés or catchphrases – full steam ahead, plenty more fish in the sea – were the nitty-gritty of Ricky's life.

She opened the door and her heart stopped. She was faced with gigantic lumps of metal, a generator, an auxiliary generator, the engine. A puzzle of wires and hoses. Huge pipes, the yellow or red paint stained by rust, snaked above. Narrow pipes ran at her feet. Toni recalled Ricky saying that he and Daniel had to attack the engine with spanners when it stalled in a storm. She could change a tyre, but only on solid ground.

The boat lifted and dropped. And again. She grasped a rail. It would be the wash from the boat that had come under the bridge. She became aware of silence. Of no sound above. *Where was Ricky?*

'Hello?' Calling out by accident, Toni heard the unease in her voice before she felt it.

Toni wove around the maze of components and machinery. She was nauseated by the rank smell of oil and fish.

The massive trawler – Ricky said it was comparatively small – the blue-painted hull, derricks and gantries bristling with aerials horrified her.

The door was locked.

'Ricky!' Toni yanked the handle and, panicking, kicked and bashed the metal.

It burst open.

'All right, hun?' And suddenly Ricky was holding her.

'I was locked in,' Toni mumbled into his chest.

'You must have pulled the handle up instead of down.'

'I have to go. I'm already late.'

That afternoon, Toni was relieved to the point of ecstasy when she got to her office with 'Detective Inspector Kemp' on the door.

The call came in at half past nine. Toni, still working, was spell-checking her report on Newhaven's latest window-smashing spree and picturing her bed.

Uniform had been first on the scene. Answering a 999 from a dog walker. The man reported a bunch of boy-racers 'doing silly buggers' on West Beach. The patrol had found a vehicle crushed against a concrete block. The bunch of kids was just two. A boy and a girl trapped inside the wreckage.

The beach was a desolate reminder of cheery seaside days. A disused refreshment kiosk smothered in layers of tagging. Tracts of concrete were all that was left of the line of light blue beach huts that had long ago succumbed to fire or were demolished for the drug dens they had become.

Emergency vehicles fanned out. Two fire engines, the patrol car and a plain-wrap mortuary van if the kids didn't make it to A and E. Sirens wailed from across the Downs.

The cold air reeked of petrol fumes, and dark, viscous liquid pooled around the front wheels. The ground glittered with glass. The Ford's bonnet was crumpled like a discarded crisp packet. Through cracks in the windscreen, the shadowing shapes of airbags ballooned over the dashboard like the take-home vestiges of a party.

The plate told Toni the Ford – the Grand C-MPV model was brand new. *1.5 EcoBoost, titanium x, four spoke leather steering wheel with silver accents*. A couple of months earlier she'd test-driven a black version before opting for a second-hand Jeep Renegade. Ricky liked that she was a woman who knew her cars.

To Toni, the damage suggested that the Ford had somersaulted, righted itself then slammed into an anti-tank concrete block meant for the Nazis.

Gloving up, she ducked under the tape. She felt a flicker of relief to see the liquid was oil. Not that anyone was off the hook; the incident was still deadly. She stopped short. A boy's face was pressed against the driver's-side window. *Jesus*, he still had acne. What was he doing in a hi-spec motor?

'My initial inspection of tyre marks indicates a swerve, as if the vehicle were avoiding an obstacle.' The PC's face was ashen like someone had turned off his life support, and he was remodelling his gelled hair in the style of Stan Laurel as he talked. 'It's odd, though, ma'am.' He hiccupped and looked briefly panicked. Poor sod, it was probably his first fatality.

'What's odd?' Toni knew his face; she scanned for his

name. She knew Uniform had a shit job, and she always tried to give them the respect they deserved.

'Swerved into the buffer. Like it was deliberate.' The PC pointed at the block, less a buffer than a bloody great full stop.

'That Coastwatch station isn't staffed after sunset. There's a camera facing the beach that operates twenty-four hours. It's up there.' PC Darren Mason – Toni plucked his name from her overcrowded brain bank – nodded at a building up on the cliffs. She knew that most watch stations had been cut by Maggie Thatcher in the eighties. Gradually, with fundraising – Toni had done a parachute jump and raised a grand with Sussex Police – the stations were being reinstated. On a post at the top of the stone steps up to the pier was a camera. She was pessimistic: 'What's the betting it's broken?'

Paramedics hurtled towards the car, the wheels of their gurneys rattling on the concrete.

Sheena, the latest member of Toni's team, a transfer from Police Scotland, appeared over the shingle, as if she'd risen out of the sea. 'The boy in the driver's seat didn't make it. Dead on impact. The girl in the passenger seat has a pulse' Impassive. Sheena would be proving that, as a Glaswegian, she was way too tough for this shite. Toni was struggling with an instinctual dislike of the younger woman based on her – Ricky said it was a paranoid – belief that Sheena wanted her job.

'Thank you, Sheena.' Toni retreated, as if Sheena was actually stepping on her toes. The boy at the wheel would have been high on booze and/or drugs and showing off to his girlfriend. Life – and death – was too damned predictable.

Fire officers were peeling off the Ford's roof like a tin can.

'It impacted at a speed of at least sixty,' Sheena said. 'Suicide by Ford.'

Keen to avoid Sheena's pithy headline patter and keeping clear of the emergency crews, Toni circled the car. A St Jude rosary hung from the rear-view mirror. Last week, Mags had given her a rosary for her new Jeep. Toni had resisted saying seat belts were more effective. Neither of the Ford's occupants had belted in.

A dark object lay in the oil. Toni approached and, bending down, she extracted it. Avoiding drips of oil, she held it to the headlights of the patrol car. A passport. Most likely an ID for a night out, though she supposed they could have been headed for the Dieppe ferry. She examined the pages, grateful that the oil hadn't seeped between the covers. Daniel Tyler. Blond hair, pouty lips, butter-wouldn't-melt brown eyes. Distinguishing feature: birthmark on right buttock. That would have attracted a few laughs. Although, with the looks of a teen idol, Daniel would have ridden them. Sweet sixteen. By that age Toni had done it with Martin Gilbert in the men's toilet of the Hope pub metres from this beach. Back when she was a good-time convent girl and Mags despaired of her. Sixteen was too young to be behind the wheel of a car. It was too young to die.

'We've got the ANPR.' PC Mason joined her. 'The boy wasn't the owner. It's registered to a Karen Munday, 23 Seaport Road, Newhaven.'

Karen Munday. Toni would never forget Karen's first day at the convent. Karen bloody Munday.

'Daniel Tyler works for Ricky,' she blurted out. Since

getting back to Newhaven, Toni's past had confronted her at every corner. Newhaven was a small town and the Catholic world smaller still. If you were a Catholic girl (or pretending to be), you went to Our Lady of the Immaculate Heart.

Until that morning Toni hadn't spoken to Karen since leaving the convent. In her years at the Met in London she'd almost managed to forget Karen Munday existed.

Toni had gone into the Co-op to stock up on chocolate. She'd glanced to her right as she was taking a Snickers bar. Karen Munday was watching from the end of the aisle.

'Is Karen Munday a friend of yours?' Mason broke into her thoughts.

'Not any more. No, never, not at all.' Darren Mason was looking at her strangely. 'I mean, not since school.' The bullying felt as real as yesterday. Karen had nicked stuff from her bag, shoved her, punched her if they were alone and, a more subtle tactic, stared at her in Mass, which distracted Toni when she was doing a reading. From the way Karen had fixed on her in the confectionery aisle, Toni could tell she had still not forgiven Toni for taking her place in the Mermaids.

When Ricky apprenticed Daniel Tyler on his boat last year, it had taken a while before Toni made the connection with his mother, Karen Munday, who ran the Power family's fish round. Ricky had been sympathetic when Toni confessed – paradoxically, she was ashamed to be a victim of bullying – but he had no say in who got employed.

As she took in the wreckage in which Karen Munday's son had died, for the first time in her life Toni felt sympathy for her old enemy. Never in her most darkly vengeful fantasies about Karen had Toni dreamt up this punishment.

Toni longed for them to be wrong. But the address in Daniel's passport matched the one registered to the Ford. Ricky would be in bits; he rated Danny as a skilled fisherman even at sixteen. Toni regarded Daniel's pretty-boy mugshot. She felt winded with sorrow for the life wasted. Rage welled and she imagined accosting Mags:

Tell me exactly for what purpose your God whipped up this carnage? These babies have hardly got going.

Mags would say something about free will...

'Nice-looking lad,' Sheena remarked over her shoulder. 'Shame we can't dish out cautions to this teenager for joyriding in the family car. Give his mum a ticking off and tell her to take better care of her car keys. Word is you know her?'

'I did once.' *Was it karma?* Toni banished the horrible notion in case it showed on her face.

Daniel Munday's body was extracted from the Ford, zipped into a body bag and slotted into the mortuary van. Toni's gaze tracked the van along the beach until the turn onto Fort Road. It was followed by an empty ambulance.

Toni could have tasked a colleague with informing Karen Munday her boy was dead. But she decided to do it herself.

Recently, with Ricky away more frequently and in a bad mood when he was on shore, Toni had begun to question the wisdom of her move to the coast. She valued London's anonymity over the seaside town of best-forgotten faces. The answer lay in the darkness beyond the beach. As the crews worked on in comparative silence, Toni caught the hush and push of the tide. She smelled seaweed on the swift breeze. She'd been lured by another kind of siren to the blues and twos. The sea had called her home.

★

Newhaven was at the mouth of the Ouse, a tidal river that ran into the English Channel. One bank was lined with timber-clad townhouses and glass-balconied apartments. The other was untouched by regeneration. Portakabins, breeze-block lock-ups. A down-at-heel pub jostled with a sprawling estate of warehouses.

The town ended with a pebbled beach, the port at one end and Tide Mills, the ruins of a Victorian village, at the other. When the river was rerouted, the old outlet became a graveyard of urban junk, supermarket trolleys, oil drums, car engines, tyres and traffic cones. Stretching away were tracts of coarse grasses hiding treacherous pools of brackish water.

Driving towards the beach, Toni shuddered; in the last vestiges of night, it seemed to her that the unforgiving landscape belonged to the dead.

Seaport Road was one of several little streets of flat-fronted houses around the harbour. Some were boarded up, others curtained with England flags. One was behind rusting vehicles resting drunkenly on perished tyres being slowly strangled by triffid weeds. This area, where an unwanted sofa was as likely to be parked outside as a car, was yet to be snapped up by descending middle classes in search of a bijou Victorian bargain.

Toni drove past Karen's house and U-turned at the bus garage, where, behind a metal stockade, double-deckers had been corralled for the night. She idled for a moment to muster courage. Destinations promised seaside cheer: Brighton, Eastbourne, Worthing, Hastings. Each bus was named for a notable Sussex resident – Dora Bryan, Ivy Compton-Burnett, Virginia Woolf – none of whom, Toni was sure, would be seen dead in Newhaven.

There was a space outside Karen's house the size of Karen Munday's Ford. Unable to quite fit the Jeep in, Toni left it nose out.

With twenty years in the job, Toni could do the death knock. This was different. She should have delegated to Sheena. Or better, Malcolm, her DS, would have struck the right note. Grief took people in many ways. Toni didn't fancy finding out how it would take Karen. Lulled by the heated seats, she didn't move.

As the past came back to bite her, Toni couldn't know that only an hour earlier Karen, too, had been gripped by memory.

'Give it back.' Toni reached down but the hand had already whipped her bag through the gap under the toilet door.

'Tampons,' Karen chanted. 'Sister Kemp's got her period.' Her name for Toni since her dad had died. She heard sniggering. Karen's Minions, Freddy called them. Four tough girls who were rather nice to Toni when Karen wasn't there.

Toni could stay in the cubicle until the next lesson. But Karen didn't care about missing lessons. She'd be happy to keep Toni prisoner. Toni pulled the chain and drew back the bolt.

Karen had unbuckled Toni's briefcase. Her dad's case. Everything would spill onto the revolting wet floor. Toni lunged, but Karen was quick. She started singing Take That's 'It Only Takes A Minute'. The Minions tapped their feet. If Toni hadn't been frightened out of her wits, she'd have been impressed that they could keep time.

'Give it to me.' Toni was furious about her tears. Even when the police officers had told them about Dad and made her and Amy drink hot chocolate she hadn't cried.

'Only if you do what I say.' Karen spoke so only Toni could hear.

'What?' *Inside her dad's case was the lock of his hair Toni took everywhere and slept with under her pillow.*

'Make me a Mermaid again. I was one before you. They listen to you.'

'No, they don't.' Then it dawned on Toni that it was true. These days, since her dad died, everyone listened to her.

Toni Kemp had joined the convent in the second year when friendships were already cemented. She had gravitated to Mags McKee and Freddy Power, but didn't care for Karen, who told her that four was a crowd.

Then her dad had died and everyone wanted Toni to go round with them and share their lunch boxes. This she often accepted, because, with her dad dead, her mum mostly forgot to pack hers.

One day, Toni had sat with the Mermaids beneath the Mary statue where they hung out. Toni knew they were Mermaids because Karen had told her. She'd have got the idea anyway, because they told each other stories about living under the sea away from rules and nuns. Karen made it clear that Toni would never be a Mermaid when she said that she hadn't seen Disney's *The Little Mermaid*. It was all kids' stuff compared to her last school, where Toni had been the official supplier of cigarettes – shoplifting them from Sainsbury's and selling them at an attractive discount to the older girls. She wasn't interested in King Triton's creepy relationship with Ariel. She suspected Karen of setting her up. No way would she seriously be a Mermaid.

Arms resting on the steering wheel of the cooling Jeep, Toni struggled to recall how the toilet thing had ended. Karen had once stuck chewed gum in her bag, but that was another time and another bag.

Opening the car door, Toni heard the question as if Mags had been waiting for her on the pavement.

'D'you want to be a Mermaid? You, me and Freddy.'

'And Karen,' she had reminded Mags.

'Not any more.' Mags had looked strange.

'OK.' That had changed things. 'Yes. Great. Thanks.'

A few months older than Toni, Karen was forty. Ricky had gone to her beach party – fireworks and a Spice Girls tribute act. Toni could have been Ricky's plus one but, pleading work, had skulked at home watching wall-to-wall *Gilmore Girls*.

Crazily, it occurred to Toni that Karen's boy had died on the same beach where Karen had danced under a silvery moon to the Spice Girls. Standing on the pavement outside Karen's house, Toni wished she had gone. Were it possible, it might make what she had to do less awkward. Maybe Karen would have gone easier on her in the Co-op. She couldn't think about that.

Ms Munday? Karen. Hi. We've found your car... maybe you didn't know it was miss— Get to the point.

Karen, I'm so very sorry to say that a boy fitting...

The door was open.

'Karen?' Toni edged inside. 'Anyone home?'

Switching on her Maglite, Toni revealed a poky lounge. Leather sofa, mismatching armchair, massive wall-mounted telly above a flame-effect gas fire. A half-eaten box of Maltesers lay on the sofa. There was a pet cage on a table by the window. Here, too, the door was open, the cage was empty. Toni fastened it shut, although the horse – hamster or whatever – had bolted. No water bowl, food dispenser empty. Toni mentally stored the observations and continued into a galley kitchen.

'Hello? Karen? Police,' she called. 'Are you OK?'

A pan of stew was on an induction hob. Toni brushed the steel with a knuckle, already mindful of leaving prints. It was warm. The stew had been heated some while ago and, going by the full pan, no one had taken a helping.

'Karen, it's me. Toni Kemp.' *Like it would be good news.* She mounted the stairs. The main bedroom was empty. The untidiness was not the kind Toni constantly fought in her flat when she was too tired to hang things up. The room looked ransacked. Twisted and tumbled bedding; a pillow lay at her feet on the floor. Pieces of broken glass were scattered by a bedside shelf; the dark patch on the carpet signalled a spilt glass of water.

Karen Munday was slumped on the toilet, trousers and knickers around her knees, her head against the wall. She didn't stir when Toni approached.

'Karen.' Toni knelt down by the toilet brush. She put a finger to Karen's neck. She felt warm. *Like the stew.* No pulse.

Karen Munday would never know her son was dead.

Punching 999 into her phone, Toni flipped through possibilities: heart attack, stroke, drugs? Were the deaths linked?

As she called it in, Toni took a closer look at Karen's body. It was none of the above. There were marks on her throat.

Karen Munday had been murdered.

4

MAGS

'Newhaven Public Library. How may I help?'

'You didn't see my text.' Ricky sounded accusatory.

'We're not allowed phones at work,' Mags said.

'Couldn't you keep it on silent?'

'It's not about being quiet, these days libraries are noisy, creative spaces, it's so that—' Mags stopped. Cut Ricky some slack; his mother was dying.

'Andy said could you come? Now?' Ricky sounded as if he was pleading.

'Is Freddy there?' Since she'd texted Freddy the morning before, while convinced she wouldn't come, Mags had been watching for her.

'You're kidding me. She doesn't know.'

'Tell Andy I'm on my way.' Mags hurriedly replaced the phone before Ricky asked if she'd told Freddy. Lying would be a gift for the devil.

Twenty minutes later, having told her boss she didn't feel well – true, after last night's brandies, she had a headache –

Mags was with Andy Power as he made tea in his mother's kitchen.

'I'll do that. You go up to Reenie,' she said again.

'Glad of the excuse, to be honest.' Andy filled the kettle to overflowing. 'I can't take much more.'

Andy was the eldest brother. Since Fred Power's death twenty years ago, Andy had taken the reins of Power's fishery aged just eighteen. Ricky, four years Andy's junior – Toni called him her 'toy boy', although at thirty-four Ricky was grown up – had joined from school. Toni maintained that Fred Power's death had strengthened his iron grip on his sons. Mags tended to agree.

'Not long, the nurse said.' Mags could say this to Andy. She was careful around Ricky. The last to leave home and super-protective of his mum, Ricky dissolved if she so much as hinted that Reenie wouldn't survive her latest illness.

'Yep.' Andy was checking his phone. The fishery was essentially twenty-four/seven. 'Ricky's going out on the boat tonight.'

'Not if Mum's like this.' Ricky had a habit of sneaking up. Unfair, Mags remonstrated with herself. He had a light step.

'No, of course.' She touched her crucifix.

Ricky had been reading Reenie *The Little Mermaid* from the Kindle on his phone. He said she had responded. She'd read it to him when he was young. At the convent, Mags had got the impression from Freddy that Reenie had only read it to her eldest child. It was their thing, Freddy used to say.

'Doubt she knows.' Andy mashed the teabag against the side of Reenie's 'I ♥ Lourdes' mug. 'It'll be fine if you go out. Mum would want us to keep the business going.' He handed Ricky a mug of tea.

The brothers exchanged a look that Mags didn't understand. She was intruding on a family's grief.

'That's Mum's.' Ricky scowled. 'Don't bother for me.'

'You need to get several hauls in tonight.' Andy began cleaning the counter with the dishcloth. 'We've got orders to fulfil.'

'Maybe not tonight?' Mags knew she should keep her mouth shut, but Ricky would never forgive Andy – *or her* – if Reenie died while he was at sea. 'I was wondering, should I call...' she clasped her crucifix, 'if we should tell Freddy?' At the convent it had usually been Toni who sought permission to do something she'd already done. Her head was pounding. She must have what Toni called a stalking hangover; you woke up thinking you'd got away with it and as the day progressed it caught up with you. This one was fast overtaking.

'No!' The brothers rounded on her.

'Over my dead body.' Ricky seemed to blanch as he heard himself.

Mags changed the subject. 'Did you manage to speak to Danny about Karen's fish van?'

'*Shit*,' Ricky snapped, his face to the ceiling. He'd agreed to remind Karen, via her son Danny, not to sound her horn in Reenie's street.

'Karen's due.' Facing Freddy would be bad enough; Mags didn't want to deal with Karen Munday again. Last week had been excruciating.

'Reenie's ill,' she'd told Karen, although she had to know.

'I *forgot*.' Karen had pantomimed horror for leaning

on the hooter and handed over a bag of fish. 'Forty quid, please. And make sure Andrew reimburses you! He can be a slippery customer.'

Mags had given Karen two twenties from her purse.

'Please could I have a receipt?' *Why had she asked that?* She'd never ask Andy to reimburse her.

'I don't do them. Too much faff.' Karen had sucked her teeth as if with regret. Tipping back her baseball cap, Karen had asked carelessly, 'You ladies still Mermaids?'

'No, we're not.' Mags had been firm.

'You hear anything from Fred-er-rica?' Karen had freighted her question with disdain. 'She'll want to say goodbye to her mum.'

'Freddy doesn't know Reenie's ill.' Mags had regretted saying this. The less Karen knew about Freddy, the better.

'No *way*!' Karen had looked genuinely shocked. 'What, she doesn't know? That's not good.'

'I expect her brothers will tell her.'

'They hate her. I'm surprised you haven't. You're her friend. Isn't that the job of a Mermaid?' Karen's sarcasm failed to mask her hurt. Mags had felt herself redden.

Andy was holding out the tea – the Lourdes mug – to her.

'Don't worry, I'll handle Karen when she turns up.' He pushed off the kitchen counter. 'It's my fish. That reminds me, I must pay you for last week.' Andy peeled forty pounds from a roll in his trousers. 'You're a saint the way you've cared for Mum, but don't be out of pocket.'

Accepting the money, Mags took a sip of tea.

They trooped up the stairs. Crossing herself, Mags took the dressing table stool in a corner. She prayed it would be soon; the family was suffering. The brothers kept vigil either side of the bed, clasping their mother's hands. The only sound was Reenie's ragged breathing.

Mags listened for a taxi. *Surely Freddy would not come?* Watching the wisp of a woman in the bed, Mags recalled. Luke said, *...even sinners love those who love them.* It was too late to say sorry, but Mags had accepted that Karen was right. It had not been good to leave Reenie's eldest child unaware that Reenie was gravely ill. Now it was Freddy's choice if she came or not. *She had not said Reenie was dying.*

Ricky's knuckles were white; he was gripping Reenie's hand too tight. Andy glanced at his watch. He'd be fretting about getting back to work.

Mags's challenge was to love her enemies. She'd go into the church on her way back to the library. She'd have to get back to her own work; she couldn't wait for Reenie to die.

The second hand ticked on. It was faster than Reenie's hard-won breaths. *In. Long gap. Out. Long gap.* Like a pump, in the last throes the body returned to basics.

What would that new priest say if he heard what you and Freddy Power got up to? Like Toni had, Mags should move far away from anyone who remembered. Toni had come back.

The buzz of a phone. Ricky scowled across at Andy. No mobiles at the deathbed had been Andy's rule.

'It's Kirsty. Must be to do with the kids.' Andy let go of his mum's hand and without a backward glance trotted downstairs. Reenie hadn't cared for Andy's wife – she'd been sniffy about her boys' girlfriends. As for Freddy...

After a moment, muttering about fish orders, Ricky kissed Reenie's fingers and went after Andy. Mags took Andy's seat and, hesitating, rested her fingers on Reenie's hand. The old woman's skin was cold. Suddenly, Reenie's eyes snapped open.

'Reenie, it's me, Mags.' Astonished, Mags said the obvious.

'Do what I—' Reenie squeezed Mags's fingers with surprising strength for a dying woman.

'Reenie, I—' Mags made to get up. She had to fetch Andy and Ricky. Reenie's fierce stare stopped her.

'Fred...' A clattering gasp. *Silence.* Another gasp. Silence. Yawning silence.

Nothing.

From the kitchen came low, angry voices. Had Karen come? Dreading meeting Karen almost more than the news that she had to break, Mags went down the stairs and into the living room to give herself breathing space. For some weeks, the boys had been snappy with each other; they were beyond stressed. Mags's own parents had died five years ago in the same week. Hr father of heart failure while her mother was under anaesthetic for a minor operation from which she never awoke. Mags had been spared prolonged sick-bed visits.

Sunlight filtered through the turquoise and emerald plastic strips stuck on the window. Someone had turned on the lava lamps; they glowed green and blue. Muted light from a blue lampshade mingled with the aquarium's pink heat light. With its shell-patterned carpet and fish wallpaper, the room had always resembled a seabed grotto. The blue-tinted mirror over the fireplace finessed the subterranean effect. Toni always said Freddy had got her dream of living beneath the sea at Reenie's knee.

The statue of Mary hadn't been on the window sill when Mags had last been there. Was it her own statue? In a panic, she snatched it up. The cheap plaster figure was hollow, the empty cavity furred with dust. It was empty. Not hers.

Freddy and Mags had each bought an icon of Mary in Paris on a school trip. Freddy had given hers to Reenie.

'...why didn't Toni ring me?' Ricky's raised voice suggested it wasn't the first time he'd asked. No Karen, Mags decided with faint relief.

'I guess she wanted me to tell you. Away from Mum.' Andy was placating his brother.

'Tell me what?'

'Keep it cool, mate, but Danny's dead.'

'What do you mean?' Ricky shouted.

Mags hurried in. 'What's going on?'

'What do you mean, what do I mean? *For God's sake.*' Andy glanced at Mags and shook his head. He looked pale.

'Who's Danny?'

'Danny Tyler, Ricky's apprentice on the trawler. Seems he's crashed his car and died.' Andy smacked a hand on the tap. 'Bloody waste.'

'Danny doesn't have a car.' Ricky would be snatching for proof Andy had it wrong. If Andy was pale, Ricky's face was stark white. *Neither man needed this right now.*

'He stole Karen's Ford.'

'Karen Munday's son?' Mags whispered. That was why there'd been no fish van. Karen would be coping with the terrible news that her boy was dead.

'No question it was suicide. There was a witness,' Andy said. 'He slammed into concrete on the beach.'

'*Crap.* Why kill himself? I'd just made him permanent crew.' Ricky bit at the side of his hand.

'Listen,' Mags said. 'Andy, Ricky—'

'My guess is Daniel found Karen in bed with her new man. It's always been Danny and Karen.'

'I'm calling Toni.' Ricky was prodding at his phone.

'Ricky, stop, please!' Mags shouted. 'Both of you.'

From the living room behind her, Mags heard the bubbling of Reenie's fish tank.

The blank sorrow on Andy's and Ricky's faces said they knew their mother was dead.

5

FREDDY

Freddy got to London too late to catch a train to the south coast. She booked into a hostel in Victoria for backpackers who were clearly on one long party. Sarah claimed Freddy could sleep through a riot. However, the raucous belting of 'Down Under' had her cycling around the narrow bed until around five. Eventually dropping off, Freddy was woken by a text at 10.58 a.m. *Where are you?* Mags? No. Sarah had launched her ninety-ninth making-up campaign.

Ignoring it, Freddy flung herself through the shower, dressed and reached Victoria station in time for the 11.47 a.m. train. Freddy had been so intent on the journey that it wasn't until the train was passing above the back-yards of south London terraces that she let herself think how her mum would greet her. What would it be like? She fretted in a corner seat. She wasn't heading to some tear-jerking family reunion. Her mum had had over twenty years to get in touch. Toni had always known Freddy's address and number. What if her mum told her to leave? She couldn't bear that.

Her mum hadn't asked for her. Mags had texted. Why wasn't she going back to Newhaven?

Your mum is ill. Mags x

Freddy stumbled off the train. On the platform she stared, utterly directionless, at a heap of croissants in the window of a refreshment bar. The croissants and aroma of fresh coffee reminded her that she hadn't eaten. Freddy was about to go in when a man, dashing for the train, jolted her shoulder; he shouted an apology. As if caught in his slipstream, Freddy chased after and clambered back on board the train as the whistle blew.

It was two thirty by the time Freddy reached the little house which, for her first eighteen years, had been her home. She bit back emotion at faint footprints in concrete from where her dad had replaced the coal hole cover. She'd been seven and Andy had been five. She had thrilled with excitement as first she then Andy (he'd been scared) placed their feet onto the damp cement. Freddy knew why Andy had been scared. Their dad was always much harder on him.

The plain wood front door needed a varnish. It looked smaller than in her memory. Freddy trembled. She heard her father's voice.

You will leave this town and never return. I can't even look at you, the sight makes me sick. You're damaged goods. A freak of nature.

A sporty Mazda with spoilers was parked at the kerb. Who was visiting? She forced herself to step up to the door. Her dad was dead. He was not there. She imagined a home-coming.

'*Hi Mum. It's me. Let's tuck up on the couch and watch* The Little Mermaid.' The line belonged in Disney; it was saccharine. Reenie had watched the film to escape. She had taken her little girl with her under the sea and left her forever disappointed with real life.

Someone opened the door.

'I got the text.' Freddy gaped at the thickset man in T-shirt and jeans, a scar like a lightning flash pale against his unshaven chin. Was he the owner of the Mazda?

'You're twenty years too late.'

'Ricky,' Freddy gasped. The last time she'd seen her youngest brother he was thirteen. 'I can't believe it's you.' She stared at the tattoo on his bare forearm. The last time she'd seen Ricky he'd been too young for tattoos.

'Why the hell not? This is my home.' Ricky slapped the edge of the front door.

'You're still living here.' Not really a question; Ricky hadn't been old enough to leave home when she'd last seen him.

'Of course not, I meant it's where… What text?' Ricky demanded.

Mags hadn't told Ricky she'd sent Freddy a message. *Her mum had not asked for her.* Freddy felt a crushing pain. She could have expected her dad to be unfriendly – or worse – but never Ricky.

'Andy texted me.' *Jesus.* Ricky had only to ask Andy to know it was a lie.

'Why did he do that?' In her day, even with their dad making Andy's life a misery, for Ricky, his older brother's word had been gospel. Not any more, it seemed.

'So that I could spend time with Mum?' Mustering

outrage she didn't feel, Freddy barged past Ricky and dumped her case and bag in the hall.

Fred and Reenie Power had stayed living in the cottage even when the fishery took off and they could afford something bigger. All the same, in the years she'd been away Freddy had imagined her lost home as vast, with high ceilings and spacious rooms. The aquarium endless. As a toddler, her tiny fingers had picked at the shells in the carpet pattern.

The living room had shrunk. On Freddy's walk from the station a watery sun had penetrated streaks of grey but, inside, her mum's coloured windows and lamps illuminated the room like an underwater cave. The statue of Mary – with the space in which Toni had made Freddy smuggle a pack of Gauloises cigarettes back from France – was still in the window.

'You can turn around and leave.' Ricky followed his sister into the front room. He stood in front of the fish tank as if she might try to take it.

Freddy breathed in smells that were in her DNA. Stale cooking, wood polish, washing powder and cosiness. Most of all, she had remembered that. Too cosy when her mum kept the heating on into summer for the small animals. She drifted through to the kitchen, where her mum had always been when Freddy got home from school.

That you, Freddy, love?

'She's not here,' Ricky said.

'Hey, Freddy.'

Toni Kemp. Long, glossy hair swapped for a shorter, cool, copper's cut, the jeans and sweatshirt she'd lived in beyond the convent replaced by black jacket and trousers. Freddy's best friend from then, if you didn't count Mags – *you did count Mags* – was grown up. Awkward, Freddy stepped forward but she stopped when Toni, didn't reciprocate. Ricky stood close to Toni, as if he was now guarding her.

'Thanks for being here, Tone.' *Mags must have asked Toni to be there for her. Where was Mags?* Freddy glanced past Toni to the door; she was expecting Mags.

'Freddy. I'm afraid your mum has died.'

The statue of Mary seemed to shimmer in the fusty gloom. The aquarium pump grew deafening, the noise all around her.

'No. No. *No.*' Freddy put her hands up, as if the ceiling was coming down on her. *I can't even look at you, the sight makes me sick. You're damaged goods. A freak of nature.*

'It was very peaceful. She didn't…' Toni trailed off.

'Andy shouldn't have texted.' Ricky sounded on the verge of a tantrum. Freddy had forgotten about them. Ricky's 'terrible twos' had lasted for years.

A creaking. Freddy looked up. It came from a cage beside the aquarium. A hamster was galloping on its wheel, going at a rate of knots. Freddy felt a flicker of happiness at the sight of it. *Her mum had still had her small animals.* She had still had the fish. Freddy treasured the times they went down to the pet shop and chose another species and a new ornament for the aquarium. Only ever Freddy, not the boys. She and her mum had divided feeding between them and every Christmas they added another ornament.

'Toni isn't here for you,' Ricky snarled.

'Not now, Rick.' Toni took his hand. 'Darling, it's Freddy's mum too.'

'When did she…? When did Mum…?' Saying the word

'Mum' made Freddy choke. She forced herself to breathe. She needed Toni to let go of her brother's hand. Why was she on Ricky's side? Freddy was being stupid. Did she think her brothers would care about her?

'At 10.49 this morning.' Ricky let go of Toni and folded his arms. Triumph mixed badly with his own grief.

If Freddy had left work then and there, she'd have made it in time to see her mum alive. *Mags had not made it seem urgent.*

'Andy shouldn't have messaged you at all.' As if Ricky could see Freddy's thoughts cross her face. She'd forgotten her lie about Andy.

The doorbell rang. The same Dalek *drrr* of her childhood. But nothing could comfort Freddy now.

Hushed voices. *Mags.* Freddy's heart punched her ribs.

'Hello, Frederica. I gather you're Reenie's eldest.' He reached out a hand. 'I'm Father Pete. Frederica, I'm so *very* sorry for your loss. Reenie was a special woman. Such a loss.'

Freddy burst into tears and fell into his arms.

When Toni had told Freddy that her mum had died, it hadn't occurred to her that her mum's body was still in the house. Reenie Power lay upstairs. When Father Pete suggested Freddy say her goodbyes, she'd nearly rushed out of the house. Ricky's angry face made her hold fast.

'Yes, that would be good, thanks.' Refusing Father Pete's offer to accompany her, Freddy plodded up the stairs. She'd have liked Toni with her, but Toni was with Ricky on the couch, sitting close, like she'd arrested him.

Freddy knew every whorl and knot in the banister, the painted over dent on the skirting board. Outside the door she lost her nerve and it was only to infuriate Ricky that she eventually twisted the handle and went in.

Someone had lit a scented candle, but for Freddy it didn't disguise the dull odour of the disease that had killed her mum.

The woman in the bed was a stranger. This woman was older than her mum's sixty-six years. Thinner, the shape beneath the sheet inconsequential. Her mum would be down the town, getting romances from the library, veg at the market stall.

Freddy recognised the wedding ring. Not bought when her parents got married and lived on a shoestring. Freddy had been ten when her dad said they should renew their vows. The fishery was successful; he could afford white gold.

'You can't renew something you've lost,' her mother had groused to Freddy before the ceremony. The only proper glimpse Freddy ever got into her mother's thoughts about her marriage to Frederick Power.

Cancer had eroded the plump cheeks and, without her false teeth, her chin met her nose. The hands with crabbed fingers were the colour of alabaster. Someone had placed them like a saint on the duvet. Her mum's hands had never been still. Reenie Power equated doing nothing as collusion with the devil.

Tentatively, Freddy touch the ringed finger. It was cold. Stiff like a twig. She should have come straight to the house yesterday.

Freddy knelt on the carpet and, her eyes screwed up against tears she couldn't risk, whispered a prayer.

'Eternal rest give unto her, O Lord, and let perpetual light shine upon her. May she rest in peace. Amen...'

When Freddy got up, her mum's features made sense. She felt a punch in the chest. Her mum was dead and they had never made up. Freddy crossed herself and her own face twisted with pain as she stooped and kissed the unyielding forehead.

When Freddy returned to the front room, Father Pete was leaving. She was politely non-committal when he invited her to pop into the church any time during her stay. 'If you want to talk or simply to pray.'

Toni and Ricky were still on the couch so Freddy saw the priest out. On the doorstep he clasped her hand and, like a magician, palmed her his card. *Jesus, it was business cards now.* Freddy accepted it, although no way would she be praying in the church, and worse still, *talking* with him.

'Thanks for coming, Toni.' Freddy hovered in the doorway. Gripping the handle on her case, she waited for Toni to say she'd leave with her. *Why hadn't Mags come with Toni?* Freddy could answer that herself.

'She's not here for you.' Ricky was up like a coiled spring. As a kid, he'd kicked and flailed like a fireball when he hadn't got his way. Her mum had said he was a Power while Freddy and Andy were Lynches. Reenie had believed her side of the family were a cut above.

'Ricky, don't,' Toni murmured.

'I want to go to the funeral,' Freddy said.

'No. Bloody. Way.' Ricky's chin jutted. Freddy felt a glimmer of warmth for the little boy she had looked after.

'Freddy will be there if she wants.'

Everyone turned. Andy pushed shut the front door, a

bunch of keys in his hand. Twenty-two years telescoped. Freddy might have seen her favourite brother only yesterday. She knew the very bones of him.

'All right, sis?' Andy rested a hand on her shoulder and Freddy tensed against another tearful collapse.

Andy was bronzed, even though it was early spring. His weathered features would be from foreign holidays, not night fishing – like their dad, he hated the sea. He wore jeans and a blue fleece jacket with 'Power Fisheries' within a fish-shaped logo. Fred Senior never bothered with 'fripperies'.

'Mum didn't want it,' Ricky stormed.

'It's up to us. Freddy has the right to pay her respects.' Andy edged around Freddy so that he was blocking Ricky. Did he think Ricky would hit her? Freddy felt her stomach shrivel.

'So, our c-word of a sister dumps us in it when we're kids and thinks she can waltz in now and pick up where she left off?'

Ricky's voice was rich as chocolate. Sarah had just joined a choir – their resolution to have separate hobbies – and ridiculously, Freddy pondered that he'd be a great baritone.

'Why the hell did you tell her?' the baritone demanded.

Shit. Freddy froze.

'Because she's our sister.' Andy didn't miss a beat. Freddy felt his fingers tighten on her shoulder. It had always been her and Andy.

'I'll go.' Freddy nodded at Toni. *You coming?*

Toni didn't move. She had an odd expression. Guilt. What was she guilty about? The question had barely formed when she saw Ricky coil his arm around Toni's waist like a boa constrictor.

She's not here for you.

Darling, it's Freddy's mum too.

Toni wasn't there to support Freddy. How could she have known Freddy was coming? She had come with Ricky. Toni was *with* Ricky! Although Freddy knew it was unreasonable, she felt betrayed. Deeply and profoundly betrayed. She picked up her suitcase and left.

A Volvo estate was parked behind the Mazda. Andy was less ostentatious in his choice of car than their little brother. The Mazda expressed a side of Ricky that, having left before he could drive, Freddy couldn't have seen. Flashy and fast.

'Hang on, Freddy.' Andy caught up with her. 'Listen, ignore Ricky, he's upset.'

'He's right. Mum didn't ask for me. Me being here is not what she wanted.'

'Mum never knew what she wanted. It was always Dad's gig. *I* want you here.' Andy hadn't contradicted her. 'Where are you staying tonight?'

'I hadn't...' Was Andy going to invite her to stay? Freddy had no idea of his circumstances. Ricky had referred to their mum's house as his home. Did Andy live there too?

'There's a Premier Inn opposite our house in Lewes. Reasonable rates. I'll come in later and see how you are. I'd drop you now, but I've got to wait for the undertakers. Can't leave it to Ricky.' Andy gave her a peck on the cheek then, suddenly, he was hugging her.

Freddy let go of the case and put her hand on his back. She had missed him.

'Welcome home, Freddy.' At the front door, Andy turned. He brushed his forehead with the back of his hand and Freddy saw how exhausted he was. World weary. She could only guess the strain their mum's illness, and her death, had put on him. She hadn't been there for Andy when he needed her.

'Who texted you?' Andy asked.

'Mags,' Freddy told him.

At Newhaven Town station, Toni eyed a bunch of boys in ratty school uniforms, ties loosened and shirts untucked, clustering like heroes right at the edge of the platform. They hooted at some crude teenaged joke, tweaking crutches and doing high fives. Four girls leaned on the waiting room wall with expressions of contempt. 'Wankers,' said one. The others nodded. Not convent girls; Sarah – in one of Freddy's childhood cyber-stalking sessions – had discovered that the convent had closed: cuts or something.

The girls might have been her, Mags and Toni. Karen too. Freddy felt a twinge of regret for what had not been. Where would this scornful quartet be in twenty years' time? Regret became envy for the girls they had all been. The Mermaids were long gone.

Freddy boarded the Lewes train and found a seat away from the kids. Andy hadn't invited her to stay with him. She was welcome, but not that welcome.

Before her courage ebbed, Freddy sent a message to Mags.

Can we meet? Fx

Outside the train window, the silhouette of Lewes Castle rose above the curve of the Downs. The town of Lewes itself was nestled in a dip between the hills, a sketch of rooftops visible through threads of rain-laden mist.

6

MAGS

Can we meet? Fx

The text was in her phone in the staffroom, but the words had wormed their way into Mags's head. She was trembling so much, it took three goes to swipe the audiobook's barcode. She'd apologised to the woman – her library card said she was Mrs Barker – the heating had packed up hence the staff were in their coats and scarves. Mags saw Mrs Barker spot her hands shaking; she'd have Mags down as a functioning alcoholic. Elderly, grey hair stiffly set, Mrs Barker gave the stack of books she was borrowing proprietorial pats. Her strong resemblance to Mags's late mother didn't help the headache. Maureen McKee had drummed it into Margaret that *Wine was for Communion*.

Mags taunted herself with a rerun of the brandies she'd drunk the night before. The first downed in one, the others in rapid sips in an attempt to obliterate everything. Her statue of Mary glowed white and recriminatory from the alcove.

In bed, Mags had tossed and turned – she had imagined Karen Munday standing over her demanding reinstatement as a Mermaid. Or Mags would burn in Hell. When it wasn't Karen, Reenie Power was filling her with secrets.

It's all I ask, Mags, love…

Then, that morning, Reenie had died.

Returning to her flat at lunchtime, Mags had found her copy of Mother Julian's *Revelations of Divine Love* open on the duvet. She must have resorted to it to ward off the ghosts. In a quavering voice Mags had read aloud from a passage: '"Everything other than the cross was ugly to me, as if much crowded with fiends…"'

As if Julian herself had spoken, Mags was soothed. It wasn't up to Reenie. And now Reenie was dead. Mags's duty was to God, not Andy or Ricky. Or Freddy.

'What needs doing?' Edward was the part-time librarian recently transferred from Lewes who had too many cigarette breaks and not enough initiative.

'Have you finished the audit of the inventory?'

'No.' His expression implied that the task bored him.

'Maybe do that?' Mags wrinkled her nose at the reek of smoke from his latest cigarette. It took her back to the convent, when Toni and Freddy would slink out of the convent garden after having a fag. They thought Mags didn't know. Mags should have minded their duplicity, but Toni and Freddy's ability to be what Sister Agnes called 'rascally' impressed her.

'He needs a rocket up his backside,' Mrs Barker remarked with pursed lips.

Mags nodded vaguely. She had taken Freddy's number off Toni's phone one time when Toni was in the loo. She'd never used it. Until yesterday. With Julian beside her, Mags had texted, *Your mum is ill. Mags x*

In her flat earlier, Mags had knelt by the alcove and prayed to Mary for forgiveness. Had she opened a can of worms?

Returning to work, she'd processed parking tickets and loans and drifted between the stacks, more of a zombie than Edward. Toni would tease her that paracetamol couldn't touch a stalking hangover. Mrs Barker was speaking.

'Sorry, pardon?'

'Bad behaviour catches up with you.' Mrs Barker's eyes glittered.

'I don't see it as bad.' *How could Mrs Barker know?* Mags had taken life into her own hands. Her teeth chattered. She gripped the counter.

'I was looking at *Breakfast*, doing my list of chores. Ned had his coffee. Suddenly there's Newhaven. *Where I live.* Police swarming everywhere.' Mrs Barker tapped her intended loans. 'One lad dead. A girl fighting for her life. When I was young boys were tearaways. Apple scrumping, chicken and knock-knock ginger. Not stealing cars. That poor girl's parents.' As Mags processed each volume, Mrs Barker placed it into her tartan wheelie trolley. 'Well, I never...'

'I haven't seen the news.' The brandy had made Mags paranoid. Mrs Barker knew nothing. Ginger and chicken? Jamming her cold hands under her armpits, Mags couldn't contemplate food.

'A teenager stole his mum's car.' Mrs Barker was beside herself at recruiting new blood. 'He only goes and crashes it on West Beach. Dies instantly. His girlfriend – she's fifteen, little mite – is hanging by a thread in the Royal Sussex.'

Tipping into the present tense with the skill of a reporter, Mrs Barker slotted her library card into her purse. 'My husband says it's a group mentality. You get a ringleader and the others follow like lambs to the slaughter.'

'You said there were two.'

'Double trouble; they egg each other on. It only takes two.' Confirmatory nod. Mrs Barker was neatening the opening times leaflets. Mags wanted to slap her hand and toss the leaflets up in the air.

It takes two... She heard the song in her head, and allowed herself to be transported for a moment. She and Freddy, dancing to Marvin Gaye in her bedroom, the CD on repeat. They were seventeen. Only five months left at Our Lady before freedom. Fred and Reenie were down the social club. After they'd danced, they'd dropped, exhausted, onto Freddy's bed.

'... the dead boy is Daniel Tyler, son of a single mother. You all right, dear? You're as white as snow. They should send you home in this temperature. There's no limit for heat, but when it's this cold, you've got rights. Oh.' Mrs Barker clapped a hand to her mouth. 'Did you know those kids?'

'No.' Mags didn't know any kids. Unless she counted Andy Power's three, who she'd seen at communions and at their nana's house. She knew the 'single mother'. It was Karen Munday.

'Well, I'm sorry to spoil your morning, but there we are.' Mrs Barker didn't look sorry at all. She brandished the Ruth Rendell audio *The Best Man to Die*. 'This'll cheer me up over the ironing.'

After the heating was restored, Mags remained cold. The hangover was a raging migraine. She alphabetised the books on the returns trolley. She flicked them out and fitted them in the right place with speed: *One Pair of Hands* by Dickens – Monica not Charles; Thomas Hardy's *The Return of the Native*; three Ruth Rendells and the last two Sue Graftons. She began pushing the trolley around the stacks, reshelving the books. Freddy Power's return to Newhaven was like the native in Hardy's novel, the traveller coming back to the home from which she'd fled in search of a better life. It was a story that belonged in the nineteenth century.

She rubbed her temples as she returned the books to the shelves. She trundled her trolley around to the military history section and stopped with a biography of Napoleon in her hands like a votive text. The shock of Karen losing her son mingled with the guilt she had never quite shaken off from their childhood. She was the one who had invited Karen and Toni to be Mermaids and who, later, as if from paradise, had expelled Karen. She had played God. It was her fault Karen had hurt Toni.

When she had caught Karen tormenting Toni, she had hissed at her that she was no longer a Mermaid. Karen had not argued. She had turned the other cheek. At the door she'd said, 'See you all later, yeah.' She had seemed timid.

Mags recalled Mother Julian's words.

... *those who deliberately occupy themselves in earthly business, and are constantly seeking worldly success, find no peace from this in heart or soul...*

Mags was desperate for the medieval anchorite to drag her back over the centuries to her own time. To before,

DEATH OF A MERMAID

when, like Judas, Mags had betrayed Karen Munday. And lost all peace in her soul.

Her head pounding, Mags shoved Napoleon into the bookshelf. At the desk she called out, 'The library is closing. Please pack up your things, everyone.'

She looked again at the text on her phone. *Can we meet? Fx*

She should not have sent that text to Freddie. She was still playing God... Poor Karen.

7

FREDDY

After picking over a burger and chips in the restaurant below the hotel, Freddy was in her room. Resting her forehead on the window, she gazed down at a car park below.

Her mum hadn't wanted Freddy at the end. Nor had Ricky or Andy asked Mags to contact her. Ricky hated her as much as the day he'd accused her of killing their father. Sarah had said it was a feat since she wasn't there when he'd died. It was enough to Freddy that she'd planned to surprise her dad at his sixtieth party. Nothing Sarah had said could convince Freddy that she wasn't guilty. She had killed her dad.

Now it seemed that Mags had texted off her own bat. This was bad and good. *Mags had thought of her.* But Mags hadn't been in touch since the first text, although she knew Freddy's mum had died. She hadn't said how ill her mum was. Why bother to text and not give the full picture? Was she hedging her bets by leaving it to fate? Freddy had been scared that Mags wouldn't reply if she texted back. Now she felt angry with Mags for leaving it to her, as she always had. She felt angry for so much.

Freddy wandered from the window over to the bed. The king-size mattress was firm – at least she'd get a good night's sleep for her money. She would have it all to herself. The shower wasn't up to Sarah's multiple power jets. Freddy felt a moment of poignancy that this was her past. She reminded herself that the split was overdue. Freddy was deleting Sarah's hourly texts without reading them. She had ignored her calls. She'd personalised the notifications to avoid the moments of hope that Sarah's texts were from Mags. Something Sarah had always wanted to do. '*Give me a special signal.*'

Within twenty-four hours Freddy had walked out of her job and left her longest-lasting relationship of two years. Her mum was dead.

Becalmed in Premier Inn limbo, Freddy appreciated the anonymous generality of the room. A nowhere place, it cleared her mind. She would not go to the funeral. Ricky might cause a scene. He would say it was hypocritical to be a mourner at her mum's grave when, in the last twenty-odd years, Freddy had never come home. He'd be right. From his vicious greeting Freddy knew that her dad had never told them the real reason why she'd left. He wouldn't be the only one to accuse her of wrecking her parents' lives. Why was Andy being so nice? Rinsing her teacup under the bathroom tap, Freddy reminded herself again that he hadn't asked her to stay with him.

When she left she wouldn't come back. On the train to London she'd let herself concoct a fairy-tale return to her home town. Tears and forgiveness. Love and warmth. The reality had been very different. There was nothing for her in Newhaven.

An hour later she was startled by a tap on the door. *Mags?* Freddy peeped through the spyhole. Andy had come.

'All right, Freddy?' Andy Power wore iron-creased slacks and a golfing jumper over a polo shirt. Bare feet in yacht shoes, short hair damp from a shower.

Freddy scoped the room for discarded knickers after her own shower. Thankfully, intending now to leave in the morning, she'd packed everything away. Not that it mattered; it was like twenty years meant nothing: loving siblings, they were at ease with each other.

'We caused a stink when they wanted to build this place. The first design was crap; this is more in keeping with the town.' Andy flung himself into the armchair, manspreading, hands behind his head. Casually pointing out the window, he said, 'We're over there.'

'Over where?' It was nearly dark. Beyond the room's reflection Freddy saw only the lights of cars parking below and a row of tall houses.

'We've got one of those wharf buildings.' He yawned.

'What, those huge ones?' Freddy remembered Andy had said he lived opposite the hotel. She hadn't supposed he meant literally. She gaped with astonishment at the glass-balconied, clapboard houses designed in the style of the wharves they'd replaced. Their dad had hated show. Success for him had not meant money; like his name, it had meant power. 'You used to say Lewes was for snobs in fancy dress and bells.' Andy had become Rotary Club Man.

'Like Dad always said, I came out with stupid things.' Andy did a bright smile.

'Dad was always wrong,' Freddy told her brother. 'So, the fishery is paying then?'

'We scrape a living against the odds of the politicians.' Andy felt in his back pocket and passed her a card. 'There you go.'

'"Andrew Power, Chief Executive, Power Fisheries." Brilliant, Andy.' Freddy sat on the edge of the bed. On their second anniversary, Sarah had given her a silver card holder which was still empty. Sarah hadn't packed it in Freddy's case or she could have put the cards she'd been given today, for a priest and a chief executive. Who knew?

'The staircases in my house are lit under the treads, like the Starship *Enterprise*.' Andy squinted across the car park at his glass palace. 'We've got triple glazing and a dumb waiter.'

'Oh.' Feeling dumb herself, Freddy needed Sarah – she'd be impressed enough to say the right thing.

'Sorry about earlier; Mum's illness and death have hit Ricky hard. It's been a long road.' Andy pulled out a vape pipe and, flicking it on, sucked on it as if it was his last hope. A scent of strawberry tinged the air-conned air. 'I go out on the trawler with him sometimes, keeps me fresh and Ricky on the straight and narrow. You should come with us.'

'I've got my marine qualifications.' Freddy felt excited at the idea, then she came down to earth. 'Ricky would love that. He always was *so* good at sharing. Not.'

Their baby brother had been a pain. Yet she had adored him.

'Do you remember the time we bunked off school? We arranged it in the morning. I sneaked out after dinnertime and met you at the convent.' Andy puffed steam above his head.

'We went to the old Rex cinema.' Freddy grinned. 'I can't remember what we saw but it had to be illegal. I was about thirteen so you were nearly twelve.'

'Yeah, it was. A rerun of *Jaws*, some over sixties thing. God knows how we got in. I was scared out of my wits. Who'd be a fisherman?'

'You never let on.' The treat was meant to make up for their father hurting Andy's arm. 'How did we get in?'

'Through the fire exit. We crept up to the back. It was half empty, no one noticed us. Massive place, over five hundred capacity, shame they knocked it down.' Andy opened the minibar. 'Fancy a drink? They've got Jack Daniel's – is that still your tipple?'

Freddy started to refuse, but decided she did fancy a Jack Daniel's. *Andy had remembered it was her drink.* She watched while Andy prepared it, quelling the fear that any minute their dad might walk in and have a go at him.

How long was Mum ill?' Freddy wanted Andy to say it was quick, her mum was diagnosed and dead within a week. Like the Waitrose customer who never picked up her salmon order. It would explain why no one had told Freddy until yesterday.

'Five, maybe six months.' Andy tipped a miniature bottle of Scotch into his glass and then another. 'She was in hospital a couple of times. At least she got her wish to die at home. Mags was great. I don't know how we'd have coped otherwise. Mum treated her like a daughter...' He rapped a tattoo on the arms of his chair as if to scare off the elephant in the room.

'No one let me know.' Struggling with tears that, since Father Pete, were close to the surface, Freddy got off the bed and began leafing through the folder of the hotel's services on the table as if for information pertinent to the stilted exchange.

'No. Well.' Andy regarded his vaper. 'You know how it's been.'

'I don't, actually.'

'*Sláinte.*' Andy used their father's old toast as he raised his glass to her and drank.

'Cheers.' Freddy knocked her glass against Andy's with a little too much force.

'After you went, it was tough.' Andy emitted steam out of the corner of his mouth. All he needed was a gentlemen's club, Freddy noted. 'We were kind of lost without you.'

'I'm sorry.' Her mum hadn't once asked for her. *She had Mags.* Freddy gulped the Jack Daniel's.

'So, Mags told you.' Andy swirled Scotch in the glass. 'I didn't realise you guys were in touch.'

'We're not.' *Mags and Toni had said nothing.* The words repeated in her head.

Freddy returned to the bed and propped herself on a bank of pillows. A couple of sips in and she mellowed. She was glad to see Andy. Eleven months apart, they'd once been close. As kids, Freddy had protected Andy. One of Andy's legs had grown to be slightly shorter than the other. His right shoe had a lift incorporated to redress the balance. In compensation, Andy had hurtled everywhere. In addition, he'd been clumsy, tripping on his loose shoelaces, which, when he was very little Freddy had tied for him, and bumping into furniture. At school he got vilified for missing football penalties and letting go of the cricket ball too late when he bowled so that it tore the grass feet away and Andy fell on his face. Aside from his leg, Andy was diagnosed as dyspraxic. The neurological disorder explained his clumsiness and reading difficulties. Infuriated by anything that implied imperfection, Frederick took Andy out of school at sixteen and set him to work in the fishery, packing and loading and swabbing down floors.

Freddy, netball team captain at Our Lady, led her team into the county league more than once, amassing silverware and her dad's respect. Top of the class, she sat at the front of the room in lessons. She'd left the convent two years after Andy with straight A's and three university places. None of which Fred Senior let her accept. His first-born, and his favourite, Freddy was heir to the Power throne. After Ricky came along, Andy wasn't even the spare.

Freddy had tried to counteract Frederick Power's contempt for Andy by diverting him from taking anything and everything out on Andy. She taught Andy everything about the fishery that she learnt from Fred until the day when her dad chucked her out of the house. A year later Fred was dead and Andy had, it seemed to Freddy, finally come into his own.

'Please come to the funeral?' Andy asked.

'So that Ricky can rip me to shreds? Not the best idea.'

'The cancer played with Mum's mind.' Andy downed his drink. 'Or she'd have asked you. *Dammit*, Freddy, I won't plead.'

'She didn't want me at Dad's funeral.' Freddy was pushing him. If she kept going, Andy would feel compelled to lie and say she'd changed her mind at the end. Freddy would save them the embarrassment. She'd check out in the morning and go far away from Newhaven.

'That was different. She was in shock. He died at her feet.' Andy swung his legs over the arm of the chair, a relaxed boyhood pose. Freddy guessed it hid that he was tied in knots. She gulped the drink, to quell a sob in her throat.

'Funerals are for the living. It's one day,' Andy cajoled.

'I'm lapsed.' Freddy was raising obstacles for Andy to surmount. She wanted him to plead. For decades no member of her family had wanted her. She finished her drink and, clambering off the bed, looked in the fridge for another. The idea of staying was attractive. As Andy said, it was one day.

'Another?' She held up the remaining little bottle of Scotch.

'Oh, go on. Kirsty's not here to count.' Andy guffawed.

'Kirsty?'

'My wife. We've got three kids – little tearaways – a little girl and two boys, like us.' Andy beamed. 'Didn't I say?'

'No, you didn't.' Freddy had even less to say than about his fancy house. She felt stunned by news which in another life would have been joyous. There was even more family from which she was excluded.

'Kirsty Baxter was at the convent, the year below you. She's got the same birthday as Mags. That came out last year when they were talking round at Mum's. First of May.' Andy held out his glass for a refill, 'She's Kirsty Power now. Obviously.'

'Lovely.' The girls in the lower years at Our Lady had been a blur. Freddy had never heard of Kirsty Baxter and felt nonsensical outrage that the woman had her surname.

'What about you? Kids? Married?'

'Neither.' Freddy tossed the empty bottle in a bin under the table.

'Oh, one thing,' Andy gave his thigh a slap, 'Mum's will.'

'She left a will?' Reenie Power was a housewife; her earnings had been pin-money. Fred Power had hated his wife having her own business. Freddy was surprised there was a will; Fred Power didn't put up with anything he didn't like.

Of course, her mum had inherited the fishery when Fred Power died.

'The estate is split between Ricky and me,' Andy said.

'The estate?'

'The business and the house.' Andy sucked on his vaper. Puffing steam into the air, he drank the Scotch in one and, lunging across, slammed the glass on the tray of tea things. It tilted on a used teabag which Freddy had forgotten to throw away. 'Mum never got over you leaving.'

'I didn't *leave*.' Her drink tasted sour. Her mother hadn't left her anything. It was as if she didn't exist. Freddy didn't care about the money. All she wanted was a token, something that told her that in the end her mum was on her side. At times, over the decades, Freddy had indulged in wishful thinking that her mum missed her. She never lost the hope that a message would arrive, asking her to come back. Cross with Sarah and astonished by Mags's message, she now realised she had misinterpreted the text. Her mum had left her nothing.

'I'm sorry.' It seemed she hadn't lost the habit of rescuing Andy.

'Me too, because, obviously, that's that. Legal restrictions, and we must respect the wishes of the deceased. Mum.' Andy fiddled with the tassel on his shoe. 'Kirsty would kick off. She fights tooth and nail for the kids, she's like Mum.'

No one was like her mum.

'It's better I leave.' Her outer layer flayed, Freddy stung with hurt. She rearranged the bottles in the mini-fridge. Why had her mum cut her out? She understood about her dad, but her mum? Was she frightened he could get to her from beyond the grave?

'*No*. Hey, listen, I've got an idea,' Andy said. 'We've lost our lady mobile fishmonger. Bloody tragedy. She was murdered by her own son. Toni Kemp told Ricky. Dan crewed for Ricky; a good kid, we thought. Seems he got off his head on drugs and strangled her in cold blood.' Squinting through narrowed eyes, Andy looked out of the window at his house. Every window was lit. To Freddy, in the growing dark, it could be an office block. 'Total shock. What with Mum. I wonder, would you take over Karen's round? Until the funeral. Then you'll want to go. With your experience at the fishery, it'll be like getting back on a bike.' Almost as soon as the words were out of his mouth, Freddy had the vague sense Andy regretted them. He'd be feeling guilty about the will.

'Karen?' Freddy felt the alcohol curdle in her stomach. Lots of women were called Karen.

'… you could stay at Mum's.' Andy clicked off his vaper and got up.

'You should run it by Ricky?' Freddy felt sympathy for Andy. As her dad's favourite and her mum's only daughter, she had had the edge. Andy had been a cautious boy, he looked before he leapt and, being frightened of heights, mostly didn't leap at all. When Ricky had come along, barrelling into danger, afraid of nothing, their dad had loved the bones of him. Freddy couldn't blame Andy for holding on to what their parents had left him. Anyway, she didn't want a share in 'the estate'.

'Thanks for thinking of me,' she said. 'But really, it's not worth the aggro.' It hurt to refuse. She was looking through thick glass at the perfect life. Why had she never thought to be a mobile fishmonger? She could have set up on her own.

'Would you at least stay at the house for the funeral? I'll sort Ricky.' Andy rattled change in his trouser pockets like their dad. Fred Power had been reminding them who paid the bills, and himself that he had sway. Andy would be nervous.

'OK, yes.' Freddy couldn't help her mum, but she would do anything for her favourite brother. She would go back to the house on Beach Road. 'Thanks, Andy.'

When Andy had gone, Freddy took his chair by the window. After a few minutes she saw him, lit by thin lamplight, striding across the car park to his personal castle. She knew it would matter to Andy to have got his own family. Freddy pressed her face to the glass. She had two nephews and a niece who she'd never even seen in a photograph. She was overtaken by a wave of sadness.

A text from Sarah jolted her mood. *We'll make it work. We're so good together.* Sarah would not give up. Freddy would have to reply. But if she did, then they'd be like the guinea pigs her mum looked after, trundling round and round on a wheel. Making up, arguing, breaking up, making up... With nowhere to call home, it was tempting to slink back. Sarah had wanted to be all the family Freddy needed. A notion that made Freddy short of breath, like having a pillow over her face.

Freddy opened Google Maps. Newcastle, Grimsby, the

north coast of Scotland. She zoned in on Bristol, the city where her mum had been born, but to which, once she'd married, she had never returned. It was a city without an ex. Maybe Freddy could start a fish round there. At the least, there'd be a supermarket with a fish counter.

Andy had said he'd drop her mum's house key into reception on his way to the fishery. 'You're doing me a favour; the house needs looking after,' he'd reiterated outside in the corridor. Fancy Andy talking that way about bricks and mortar, Freddy thought now. Perhaps he, too, thought of it as home.

Freddy was filled with the impulse to text Mags again. She opened her phone and pricked with embarrassment when she saw the text she'd sent from the train.

Can we meet? Fx

Mags hadn't replied. Perhaps Freddy could say she'd be staying at her mum's house from tomorrow. Freddy put this, then hastily scrubbed the message, as if Mags would read the words without her having sent it. Mags might take the message as a hint that Freddy wanted her to visit. Which it was. Freddy's stomach clenched. Mags liked honesty. Or so she'd said. *Please come to my mum's house. I'd like to see you.* Freddy smarted at the words and deleted it. If Mags refused to come, it would be worse than silence after Freddy's earlier text. Freddy tossed her phone on the bed.

Would Andy be angry with Mags because she had told Freddy? She could send her an apology for dobbing her in. More likely, Andy would thank Mags and relate to her how Freddy had got there too late. That would make Mags contact Freddy.

Freddy stared over at her phone, praying for it to ring.

It beeped. Sarah again. *I love you.*

It was the first time Sarah had said that. Automatically, Freddy made the sign of the cross and, her cheeks wet with tears, muted her phone.

Outside, the car park emptied. A light shone in the top window of Andy Power's house. The rest of the row was dark, yet to be sold. Beyond, the River Ouse flowed fast, black and slick, to the sea.

8

TONI

'Andy, I know it's a crap time.' Bit of an understatement, since his mother had died hours ago. 'This is a murder case. Every minute counts.'

The minutes – days – were slipping away. If the preliminary time that the pathologist had given them was right, Karen was murdered somewhere between six p.m. and ten p.m. on Friday night. Forty-eight hours later they had nothing from the first round of door to doors or the press conference. Circumstantials pointed at Karen's teenaged son, Daniel, but Toni considered the obvious last. Whatever, she needed something solid soon or Chief Superintendent Worricker – dubbed The Worrier – would have a view.

Like Ricky's trawler, Toni had avoided the fishery; the glassy eyes of dead fish staring from the crates gave her the creeps. But when she'd rung Andy to tell him about Karen and Daniel and ask for an interview, he'd said he'd be at the fishery at six for the Monday morning market.

'Not a problem, we've all got jobs to do.' Togged up in yellow wellies and a long white plastic apron, Andy gesticulated at a woman in an office overlooking what was called Market Hall, a vast space crowded with buyers and sellers of freshly caught fish. Not the best place to talk, but Andy had to monitor the sale of the night's catch. Ricky had gone out on his trawler the night before. They had fallen out. Toni had been aghast that Ricky would fish on the day his mother died. He had said the sea stopped for no one. *It won't stop for you if you go and make a mistake.* He'd hired a last-minute crew – which meant second-rate or they wouldn't have been available – and gone. One stupid decision, because Ricky was desperate for a decent haul, could mean death.

He must be late landing. That was why he wasn't in the hall.

'I need a complete list of Karen Munday's fish-round customers.' Toni had to shout over the auctioneer. 'Until we rule them out, they are all suspects.' She had ruled out Daniel's dad, Karen's ex. He'd been in McDonald's with his wife and two daughters. The poor bloke had gone green when he had to identify his son. By the looks of things, when Daniel Tyler died, he took a big chunk of Tom Tyler with him.

Men were still carrying crates of fish. Cards were tossed in with the produce, identifying it: sole, bass, plaice. Where was Ricky? Toni tried to keep her mind on her questions.

'I'll get it run off for you.' Andy nodded. 'This is crazy. It can't be murder. If Karen had heard about Danny's death—'

'No doubt about it. Anyway, she died before him.' Toni cut him off. Although Andy was sort of family, he, too, was a suspect. *So was Ricky.* She could rule him out in principle.

Plus, he had an alibi. Ricky had lost a valuable crew member in Danny and, being out with his boat, had had little to do with Karen.

She spotted Ricky. He was listening to the auctioneer, willing the price to go up. She let herself breathe. Who'd go out with a fisherman? She hoped to God Ricky would get a good sum. His mood was bad enough without being in debt. She had never asked Ricky what he earned. A decent amount, going by his Mazda.

'Did Karen report any difficult customers? You know, made a pass or harassed her? Or, for that matter, has someone complained about her?' In a lapse of generosity, Toni thought this probable. Through a gap in heavy plastic drapes she could see through to the fish outlet, where a middle-aged man in a trilby and George Smiley glasses was buying a large bag of cod roe. *Yuk.* She shadowed Andy as he inspected price labels tossed down on sold catches.

'Kaz wouldn't let them touch her.' Andy nudged a crate of sea bass in line with others. The trawler's name, *Jacinda II*, was embossed on the sides. What had happened to *Jacinda I*? Toni blinked. Two men had drowned off Beachy Head last year when their trawler had capsized.

'Sorry?' Andy had said something.

'Didn't Karen give you a hard time at the convent?'

'Sort of.' It was a bad idea to return to your roots. You could trip up on them.

'Last week, a man in Ringmer answered the door bollock naked!' Andy gave a mirthless guffaw. 'Karen is clutching his dabs and fishcakes and has to watch while he pats himself down for his wallet.' Andy was back with Karen telling the story. Abruptly, he snatched off his fish-shop panama, bashed it and put it on again. 'The chap was eighty-five with dementia so you can cross him off.'

'Enemies?' Toni asked.

'What, apart from you?' His eye on the loading bay where the buyers were backing up their vans, Andy frowned. 'Karen was popular. Except with Ricky.'

'Why not with Ricky?'

'He didn't give her the time of day. For your sake. Otherwise, she was a hit. Kaz could sell oysters to vegans.'

Ricky had never told Toni that. Filled with love for him, Toni kept a stupid grin off her face. She cast a glance over to where, now by the loading doors, Ricky was counting a wad of notes. Inscrutable as always, he gave nothing away.

Naked Man might not be a killer, but he was an example of a customer crossing the line with a woman who sold fish on the doorstep. In a fish shop there were generally witnesses. A lonely man, dependent on who delivered the mail and a newspaper, might buy fish to grab two minutes of Karen's time. *And her.* If she rebuffed him, then what?

'How does your mobile service work? Are orders booked in advance or did Karen sell on spec?' Toni was distantly ashamed she'd never asked Ricky about the brothers' business. Much as she loved him, she couldn't get excited by a fish's journey from sea to plate.

'Either. Karen carries – carried – a selection of the night's catch, including Ricky's. Usually the more popular species – bass, skate, salmon.'

'Did she have regulars?'

'Yes, although some punters don't buy for weeks. Plus, she'd be flagged down by a random customer and, like as not, add them to her round for the future. Karen had the gift of the gab.' A grimace flitted over his face. Toni reminded herself that Andy would be shocked. To be fair, so was she.

'Karen's round was restricted to residential?'

'Yes.' Andy corrected himself. 'No, she carried a few commercial pre-orders, for restaurants, office canteens and the like, bagged up and handed over.'

'Was that usual? Don't businesses come here to buy in bulk?' Toni nodded at men – there were a couple of women – lugging crates out of the market. 'You've got a national delivery service, haven't you?' This was about as much as she'd gathered from Ricky. Not that he knew the first thing about the Police and Criminal Evidence Act, so she shouldn't feel bad.

'We do, but Karen did some local stuff. Her idea, saves everyone time,' Andy said.

'Sounds like she cared about the work.' More shame, Toni had warned Ricky that Karen would rip them off.

'She was on a bonus, it was worth her while.'

'Who will take over?' *Would you kill to run a fish van?*

'Toni, know what? I have no idea.' Andy took off his hat again and smoothed his razor-sharp haircut. Unlike Ricky, his dark, unruly hair forever storm blown, who lived in jeans and fleeces, Andy kept himself Paul Weller smart.

'Tough call.' Toni mustered herself. 'Andy, sorry, mate, I have to ask. Where were you on Friday night between the hours of half five, when Karen was seen in her car on the ring-road, and twelve fifteen, when I found her body?'

'That's easy,' Andy said. 'I was in the fishery until six then I went up to the golf club. I bought a drink or ten for Jerry Ross, a councillor who I thrashed in a game last week. Left about...' he ran a hand over his cropped hair, 'it would have been close to seven thirty. Tons of people saw me; the club will have Jerry's address, or the council. I got home about seven forty. Me and Kirsty were in all night.'

'Thanks. And Ricky was on his boat, I know that.' Toni pulled a face. These days he was always on his trawler. 'A couple more things. Have you noticed any strangers hanging about? Might someone have clocked Karen on her round and followed her? Checked out where she lived? She was attractive and strong-minded. Some men hate that.' Had Karen been strong-minded? Toni hadn't considered this before. At school she'd called it nasty.

'She'd have told me.' Andy was firm. 'Or Danny would have told Ricky.'

'Karen might not have known she was being followed.'

'True,' Andy agreed. 'We get the odd druggie wanting free cockles and all the cash from the till, but it's a schlep down here so that's rare. Karen was mostly out in the van. I suppose she could have been followed in a car.'

'Did you say about the dashcam?' Ricky materialised by her side.

It was all Toni could do not to ruffle his hair, pull him close and breath in the sea smells that had become him. While she disliked the fish and diesel stench of the trawler, she couldn't get enough of them if mingled with the scent of Ricky's weather-beaten skin.

'There's a camera on the van?' She felt a spark of hope; so far this case was what she and Malcolm called Wi-Fi. No leads.

'It's broken.' Andy opened a door marked 'Freezer Room'. Out came a mechanical roar that bounced off the breeze-block walls.

'What is that?' Toni shouted. It wouldn't hurt to show Ricky how very interested she was in all things fish. Actually, Toni found she was intrigued.

'Fish go in one end and come out frozen the other. Dad got it off a frozen-food company. Clarence Birdseye invented the quick freeze tunnel in the twenties. She's about forty years old, our faithful old beast.' Ricky was positively elegiac. Toni knew he'd be glad to change the subject from Karen and Daniel.

'That's amazing,' Toni marvelled.

'Isn't it?' Ricky batted her on the shoulder. For the first time in – weeks, it seemed to Toni – he was smiling. 'Like you care, Antonia Kemp.'

'I *do* care.' Stepping out of role, Toni reached down and took hold of his forefinger.

'Don't be nice,' Ricky said under his breath. He had the same expression as Freddy had when she burst into tears because Father Whatsit had been kind to her.

Toni squeezed his finger and let go. Andy was watching a man packing up frozen fish coming off a belt from the freezing tunnel. Fleetingly, Toni considered how efficiently the monster machine – the size of a small bus – might render a human corpse as stiff as a board. She jumped aside for a man wheeling a stack of blue and red crates. She'd rather underestimated the Powers' fishery. It was an efficient and complex outfit.

'Karen was going to sort it,' Andy said.

'Sort what?' Toni had forgotten the question.

'The dashcam.'

'When did it break?' Toni sensed a clue uncoiling. 'Was the damage caused by vandals or specifically targeted?'

'Karen broke it, she said it was by accident— Keep those prawns back, Chris, I've got a woman coming in for them later.' Andy broke off to shout across to a man arranging stock for freezing. He got a thumbs-up sign.

'Did you doubt it was an accident?' Toni asked.

'What? No, I'm sure it was.' Andy appeared careless, but Toni wasn't convinced. She knew Andy liked his gadgets. Had Karen disliked being, effectively, monitored by her boss? A reminder that she was only a cog in the Powers' wheel.

'Andy said you have Daniel for it,' Ricky said. 'That's crazy, you do know that, don't you? He couldn't murder his own mother.'

'It's too early to close off possibilities. It's an option, that's all.' *When I tell you how to trawl you can run a murder case for me.* Toni's burst of love for Ricky dissolved. The personal connections in this case were starting to hem her in. Maybe the Chief Super had been right and she should give it to Malcolm.

'Ask me, Dan walked in on Karen with her man and went ape. Think if that was us.' Andy returned to the market hall and began sluicing water over the bloodied tiles from a hose in the corner. Toni guessed Andy's hands-on mentality – Ricky said Andy worked all hours – was why the fishery was so successful. She suspected Ricky was raking it in, but to hear him, he was nudging bankruptcy.

'Karen didn't have a boyfriend,' Ricky said.

'How do you know?' Toni retorted. *Shit.*

'Says who?' Andy swished a mop at their feet. The searing smell of disinfectant blotted out the stench of raw fish. Toni disliked fish, raw or cooked. Not great if your boyfriend was a fisherman. 'Karen kept it private; she didn't need Tom Tyler getting wind. He'd jump at the chance to stop forking out for Danny.'

Karen had obviously confided in Andy. Freddy Power used to say her brother could get an oyster to give up its pearl, unlike their father, Fred Power, who would have smashed the shell. Criticism of Fred Power was off limits for Ricky; he worshipped his dad and blamed Freddy for his death. Now he had Reenie's death to contend with. He'd said it made him feel 'wobbly, like the flu'. And then he had gone out on the boat.

'All right, love? Are we friends?' Toni asked him once Andy and his mop were safely on the other side of the room.

'Of course. I'm back on the boat for three nights, did Andy say?' Ricky spoke as if the decision was out of his hands.

'No, he didn't. Do you think that's a good idea?' She kept her temper.

'Got to meet targets.' A year ago, if anyone had suggested she'd have a relationship with a man who risked his life so Mrs Smith got her bass fillet, Toni would have told them where to shove it. It was safer being a copper. Trouble was, Ricky was too damned attractive. Not just that, he was a decent bloke.

'Danny hated blood. No way could he kill,' Ricky said.

'There was no blood – she was strangled – and anyway, like I said, it's one avenue of possibility. Daniel Tyler was a fisherman. He killed thousands of fish every trip. Like you.' Toni lost it.

'That's different. Danny said fish die so we can live. He was a natural, he was practically born with sea-legs. He did what I asked, he knew what needed doing. So, he hated the gutting, he never got used to it, even when he got to be a master at it. We would get through a haul in record time, fastest deckhand I've ever had.'

'Yes, I know.' Toni had been irritated by Ricky going on about his apprentice, but the description of Danny Tyler hating blood and guts was out of kilter with a kid strangling his mum. Or not? Strangling was clean. It was also an intimate way to kill. Up close to his mum, Danny would have had time to change his mind.

'If I get my hands on who killed Karen and Dan, I'll—' Ricky scratched his unshaven cheek.

'Leave it to us,' Toni said. 'At this point Daniel Tyler's death was an accident.'

'You said suicide.' Andy and his mop were back.

'I said we have not drawn a conclusion. Andy, Ricky, please, guys, don't go spreading rumours, it will really stuff up my investigation.'

'Say Danny's high, gets in and finds Karen with her kit off. He's shocked and slams out. He snatches Karen's keys from the hall and takes off in that spanking-new Ford. She only got it last week. She loved that car – what better revenge?' Andy rested on the mop handle.

'Why would Danny want revenge on Karen if he'd killed her?' Toni pointed out.

'That's why you're a detective and I'm a businessman.' Andy tipped his cap at her. He went on with his theory. 'Him and his girlfriend head for the beach. He floors the Ford and *bang*. Danny loved his mum. It's tragic. I guess he couldn't live with what he'd done.'

Ricky looked fit to punch Andy. 'How would he be

high? Dan didn't drink. He was keen to make something of himself. He was a decent lad. If Karen was with a bloke, he'd have been glad for her.' Toni believed that Danny was the little brother that Ricky, the baby of the family, never had.

'Hey, what about CCTV? Coastwatch has a station up there,' Andy said.

'We're waiting for it.' Not true. The camera on the pier had been smashed, and the Coastwatch station's primary purpose was looking out to sea, not at land. Unfortunately for her team, Danny had crashed by the harbour, near the lighthouse pier. The view of the Seaford-facing camera was blocked by jutting headland. Besides, it only operated in daylight. So far, all they had to go on was a dog walker's testimony, tyre skids and the impact damage to the vehicle. Toni kept what she did know to herself. Andy was a sociable chatterbox. If he knew, Lewes golf club and every fisherman between Hastings and Southampton would be all the wiser.

Andy appeared to accept this. He wandered across to a whiteboard scrawled with the names of boats. *Patricia M*, *Jubilee Sun*, *Kestrel X*.

'What's happened to your hand?' Toni saw Ricky worrying at a cut on his palm.

'Caught it on a lever when I was hauling a net.' He was dismissive. 'She never asked for me.'

'Who didn't?'

'Mum. She wanted to see Andy on his own. And Mags, but not me.'

'She never asked for me either.' Ludicrous response; Reenie hadn't disguised her disapproval that Toni was with her baby boy. 'It doesn't mean she loved you less.' Reenie and Fred Power had not treated their kids equally. Freddy had been the favourite until she suddenly was not. Toni's parents had been scrupulously fair with her and her sister. Not that Andy had ever been top dog, Ricky was the golden boy. Toni decided not to remind him. It was the worst time to set up a wedge between the brothers.

'Andy won't tell me what Mum said.' Ricky was glum.

'Reenie probably tore a strip off Andy for walking his muddy football boots through the living room. You said she kept saying stuff as if you were kids and she couldn't tell dreams from reality.' Toni kept to herself that she was less upset by Reenie's passing than by the murder of Karen Munday. Whatever Karen had done to Toni when they were girls, she hadn't deserved that death.

Watching the stiff frozen fish drop out of the tunnel onto the belt encased in plastic like a body bag, Toni vowed that, however long it took, she would find Karen's killer.

9

MAGS

Hands clasped, Mags fixed her gaze on the body of Christ on the cross above the altar and, fingers busying through her rosary, she prayed for forgiveness.

No guidance was forthcoming.

Can we meet? Fx

Until the reply came in yesterday, Mags had been pretending that she hadn't sent the text to Freddy. She should go to confession, but devout though Mags was, at this moment she could not forget that she would be talking to a flesh and blood man. Father Pete – she couldn't call him Pete as he'd suggested – would know. *God knew.*

It was raining when Mags emerged from the church. She pulled up her hood. A figure raced up the steps. Involuntarily, thinking of Karen, Mags shielded her face against harsh words.

'Mags, it's me.' Toni peered around Mags's hood.

'What are you doing here?' One place Mags could be sure not to find Toni Kemp was the church.

'It was you, wasn't it?' Toni ignored the question.

'What was me?' Mags knew.

'You told Freddy about her mum.'

'It was a mistake.' Mags zipped up her anorak.

'Well, good for you, whatever it was. I should have done it months ago. I was putting off telling Freddy about me and Ricky. Effing idiot.'

'It will open old wounds.' Mags fastened the Velcro strap under her chin, as if, cocooned, she would be safe.

'Ricky's furious. Another reason I said nothing. It's so crap for Freddy. I'll never forgive myself.' Toni shot a look at the church, as if she might unburden herself to Father Pete.

'Did she go to Reenie's?'

'Of course she did. Unfortunately, she got there too flippin' late.' Perhaps seeing Mags's shocked face, Toni added, 'She did at least *see* Reenie, you know, pay her respects. Job done, our Mags.' She patted Mags's arm. 'The undertakers came ten minutes after Freddy left. We both know that Reenie would have sent her packing if she'd had enough breath in her body.'

'Did Freddy tell Ricky it was me that told her?' They did not *both* know that.

'Ricky thinks it was Andy, so no.' Toni gave a sudden laugh. 'Same old Freddy, covering our arses. Don't worry, if Ricky finds out Freddy lied, I'll say it was me. He's already cross I didn't see Ma Power while she was conscious. He should be grateful. I'd have hastened her death if I'd gone. That, or she'd have rallied and reiterated in detail why I'm not nearly good enough for her boy.'

'Actually, Toni, there was something I—'

Toni's phone beeped.

'I'll have to go. I can't tell you everything, but something awful's happened.'

'I heard a boy crashed his car.' Mags remembered Mrs Barker in the library. She hadn't turned on a TV or radio since Reenie died. 'How awful for his parents.'

'His mother was Karen.' Toni's face was tight.

'Karen Munday?' Mags went cold.

'Yes. And it's looking like he murdered her and then crashed his car.' Toni ran down the church steps, raindrops bouncing off her police-issue jacket. She looked back at Mags. 'I found her the night before Reenie died. It's been crazy. I can't get the image of Karen dead out my mind.' Toni suddenly looked lost.

'Oh goodness. How?' Mags retreated within the shadow of the porch. She didn't want to hear.

'I shouldn't say, but I can trust you. She was strangled. In her home. On the toilet.' For a moment Mags saw that same stunned expression Toni had worn after her father was murdered.

'Oh.' Mags felt winded. 'So why are people saying it's her son?'

'That's not been confirmed. But he was in a car crash soon afterwards. It looks like he meant to crash.'

'Is it OK for you to run the case? What with us being...' Seeing Toni's face cloud over, Mags tailed off.

'It's work.' Toni pulled her collar up against the sea breeze and the police officer was back.

Beyond the masts of boats on the marina, the sea was gun-metal grey flecked with white horses. The scene, filled with light, space and lush colours on a summer's day, was, this April afternoon, drab and bleak. Although Mags was close to a house of God, she sensed the proximity of evil.

'Stupid way to go,' Toni said, more to herself. She took a breath. 'No one deserved to die like that. And, to answer your question, no, it won't affect my judgement. Like any murder case, I work for the victim. Karen Munday is no different.'

'I'll light a candle.' Mags was stunned beyond belief. 'Two candles.'

'She always wanted to be your friend,' Toni remarked, as if it was hardly important.

'I don't know if that's true.' Mags flushed at the lie. Karen had been her friend and Mags had got rid of her.

The grey was lit up by a blinding flash. A second later, right over their heads, came a tremendous clap of thunder. The sky opened and rain pelted down, fat drops bounced off the car roofs and in seconds a stream raced along the gutter.

'Bloody great. Catch you soon, Mags. I've got a hospital visit to make.' Toni raked sodden hair out of her eyes and, dodging puddles on the pavement, raced towards the town centre.

As she watched her friend battle through the downpour, Mags was overtaken by amorphous grief.

She opened her phone and answered Freddy's text.

Meet at lunette battery. 7.30pm. Mx.

Then Mags pressed delete.

For as long as she lived, Mags would regret she had not sent the message.

10

TONI

Toni hated the smell of hospitals; a miasma of antiseptic, meds and baseline fear. Her job meant she was too often in A and E attempting to get sense out of some traumatised victim or a drug-hazed perp. It was where her dad had been declared dead. Whenever she was at the county hospital, Toni caught herself wondering in which emergency room her dad had been treated.

'We're here to see Daisy Webb?' She raised her badge to the young woman at the desk in the ICU. The nurse flipped up the watch on her tunic, as if that would have a bearing on her reply.

'Can't you lot leave her alone? She's been through enough.' A man, his bloated belly to the fore, barrelled towards them, his grey hair aging-rocker style, the leather jacket and jeans confirming the image. He stopped toe to toe with Toni. She caught a whiff of stale tobacco. A lace of one of his trainers was undone; it was tempting to tell him, but that would be unkind.

'Step back, sir.' Toni was aware of Malcolm closing in.

'And you are?'

'Daisy doesn't need you barging in upsetting her. Tell them.' The man appealed to the nurse.

'Daisy tires easily.' The nurse obliged.

'I'm her uncle. Bill Webb.' He yanked up his sleeves, exposing pale, muscled forearms. 'We nearly lost our little girl. She's hanging on by a thread.' He went puce with the effort of trying not to cry.

'Daisy is the surviving witness to a fatal vehicle crash, sir.' Toni kept her voice level. 'I'm afraid we do need to talk to her.'

'You could tip her over the edge,' Webb spluttered. Toni felt for him, but right now empathy was a hindrance. She strode past. Malcolm kept close; it wouldn't be the first time a distraught relative had taken a swing. Toni was slight, not quite five foot one, but she'd done enough karate to toss Bill Webb face first onto the shiny floor if he cut up rough. Though that, too, would be unkind.

Toni bit the inside of her cheeks as she entered the dimmed room. *It's not Dad. It's not Dad.* Tubes, monitors, bleeps. A woman by the bed, her face ravaged by lack of sleep and torment, gazed listlessly through them from an armchair. Her fingers fluttered over her daughter's bandaged hand as if she was unable to touch her and unable to leave her alone. Her varnished nails were bitten, lifeless dark hair framed a face that would have been unremarkably attractive on a happier day. Josie Webb's every available sense was attuned to the girl in the bed.

In contrast, Daisy – hydrated and oxygenised – had colour in her cheeks. Her glossy long hair was coiled around her neck brace. Her eyes tracked them, unblinking.

'Hello, Daisy. How are you doing?' Toni went for official but friendly. Daisy's gimlet stare said she didn't suffer fools.

'She's just woken up.' Josie Webb might have been talking about any teenage lie-in. 'Can't you come back later?'

'I'm afraid not, Mrs Webb.' Toni introduced herself and Malcolm. 'Daisy may have useful information to give us about the crash.'

'You've got five minutes.' A tall black nurse in her fifties was taking Daisy's obs. Her name badge read Annette, and her facial lines suggested she smiled more often than Toni.

'I can't tell you anything.' Daisy sounded bored, as if some promised treat had fallen short. Toni hoped it was a sign she was returning to herself.

'What do you remember? What stands out for you?' Toni tried a different angle.

'What else do you need?' Josie Webb bristled. 'That boy did it. He's dead. You can't punish him.' Her tone said, had Daniel not paid the ultimate price, she would be first in line to punish him. Toni had seen the look on her own mother's face when the police told them her dad was dead. *If looks could kill.*

'Hush, Josie.' Annette patted Mrs Webb's arm.

'What? Dan's dead?' Daisy's hands shot up, wrenching at a cannula.

'You've upset her.' Josie Webb moved aside as Annette readjusted the tape securing the cannula. 'Poppet, try to relax. We'll have you out of here soon. Daddy's on his way. Don't be upset, poppet.'

Toni's envy for those with dads had never lessened. Even though, as Daisy was intubated and bandaged in a hospital bed, there was little to envy her for.

'Is Dan dead?' Daisy asked Toni.

'Yes, Daisy. I'm afraid he is.' Toni ignored Josie Webb's *Don't say!* semaphore. Her daughter would have to be upset sometime.

'I told him he was going too fast.' Not the response Toni had expected. *Anguish and tears*. 'His mum's to blame.'

'You remember Dan was going too fast?'

'He was showing off to me.'

Time after time Toni saw examples of girls being way ahead of boys. It would have been bloody tragic if this particular immature boy had taken this perceptive and sensible girl with him, never mind Karen Munday. 'Daisy, did Dan say anything to you? How he came be driving his mother's car?'

'The little liar. He said it was his.' Daisy's eyes narrowed. 'Whatever, she deserved it.'

'You don't like Daniel's mum?' Toni leaned forward.

Initial findings suggested the driver had taken avoidance action which had placed the Ford in the path of the concrete. Toni put that down to one hell of a distressed kid. But that Daniel had lied to Daisy and that Daisy didn't like Karen changed the picture of the loving mum and perfect boy she'd gathered so far. 'Had Daniel argued with his mum, do you know?'

'She was a cow.' Daisy scowled.

'Darling, this isn't like you.' Josie Webb looked terrified. Toni guessed that her girl coming over as a bitch herself suggested Daisy's head injury had had character-changing consequences.

'Was?' Toni winged in.

'*Is*. What are you, my teacher?' Doubt shadowed Daisy's face. '*Is* a cow. She makes Dan's life a misery.' She put a hand to her neck brace.

'Daisy, darling, don't talk like that.' Josie Webb had probably heard Karen was dead.

'I'll talk how I like,' Daisy mumbled.

'Do you remember what Dan said about his mum?' Malcolm asked.

'No. I already said.' Daisy shut her eyes. 'Mum, my head hurts.'

'*Enough*.' Josie reached for the communication cord. 'You've had your five minutes, please go.'

'Poor kid isn't out of the woods yet.' Out in the corridor, Toni pressed for the lift. 'No mother should have to be at what could well be her child's death bed.'

'No, she shouldn't.' Malcolm checked his hair in the lift's mirror, a thing he did when he was upset. He caught Toni noticing and dropped his hand. 'I wonder if it's a coincidence that Danny nicked the car. Had he perhaps always intended to take Daisy out in it? Pass it off as his own motor, bought on his wages.'

'Good point. There are, after all, simpler ways to kill yourself. Unless they had a suicide pact, why pick up Daisy then write himself off at the beach?'

The lift stopped on the second floor. Two porters trundled in a gurney on which lay an elderly man, his mouth open as if gasping for air. Toni was thinking he was dead when his eyes snapped open. He beamed at her. Toni hoped she was smiling back.

Daniel had driven to Daisy's – how he'd got past Josie beat Toni – then played the big man out to impress his girl by exceeding warp speed. Open and shut. Yet doubt niggled.

Sometimes it was the open and shut cases that were the hardest to close.

'Karen comes out of the kitchen from cooking the tea. She goes upstairs to relieve herself.' Malcolm led them back through the living room, past the couch – the box of Maltesers was bagged as evidence or Toni would have been tempted to finish them – and paused outside the lavatory. 'Karen pulls down her trousers and sits on the pan.' In another context Malcolm's 'I followed her in a westerly direction' tone would have cracked Toni up.

'Her assailant follows her. Or he's already upstairs. He steps forward, catches her by surprise. Before she can defend herself, he has her by the throat. Like so.' He made a grabbing motion. 'Karen loses consciousness, tips half off the pan and empties the rest of her bladder.' He indicated a stain by the toilet. Malcolm backed out onto the landing.

'Cold-blooded,' Toni breathed. 'Karen went to the loo with the door unlocked. She must have known her murderer pretty well. Or maybe she believed she was alone.'

'Not Daniel then?'

'Don't be a plonker, Mal. He was her son. She'd been peeing in front of him all her life.'

'My mum locked the door.' Malcolm flapped his choirboy hair. All his own, it had the look of a wig. Toni suspected him of being in a roundhead enactment group, but he'd never said.

'Not like my dad. Mum said when he went to the loo, we

were privy to the privy.' Toni coughed. She hadn't meant to go there.

When Sergeant Malcolm Lane had joined her team a year ago, Worricker had marvelled at how bright he was – a first in astronomy – and hinted that one day he would step into his shoes. Worricker never suggested that Toni might land in his footwear.

Toni had been primed to hate the fast-tracker who would know the difference between a star and a planet, but from the first day he'd asked Toni astute questions like where to get good coffee and – knock me down with a feather – what did Toni need from him. It had taken less than a week for Toni to develop a grudging liking for the thirty-eight-year-old beanpole (too tall to fit into the ACC's shoes) with a haircut that owed much to a seventies André Previn, if not the roundheads. Six months in, to Toni's irritation – she hated Worricker to be right – she thought Malcolm a better detective than any she'd worked with.

'This is where me knowing the victim's character comes in handy,' she said. 'At the convent Karen was first to pile into a fight. She could wind you up to a blind rage.'

'Did she wind you up?' Malcolm eyed her steadily.

'Me? *No.*' He wouldn't get her on subjectivity. 'I was terrified of her.'

'It looks premeditated – if only by minutes. He must have come upstairs and opened the door.' Malcolm rolled his eyes. 'Unless it was open.'

'We can't rule that out. Danny's were the last fingerprints on the handle, but they would be.'

'Boss, you all right working this? You know, with Karen Munday being a friend?'

'She wasn't a friend.' *Here we go.* Toni had headed off Worricker; she should have bargained for Malcolm. 'It's twenty years since I knew Karen. I've seen her a handful of times since. The last one was in the Co-op the morning she died.'

'Did you?' Malcolm failed to hide his astonishment that Toni had kept this from him. 'What did she say? How did she seem?'

'We talked about chocolate,' Toni said airily. 'She was the same as usual. I have told Worricker, so keep your hair on.' Hair reference. *Damn.*

'Besides, as you must be discovering, round here it's hard not to have an acquaintanceship with those we serve.'

'Shout if it gets too much.' Malcolm headed down the stairs. He knew better than to push Toni.

Toni contemplated the toilet. What a place to die. She hoped that Mags had remembered to light a candle.

She found Malcolm outside the back door. The yard was tiny with most of the space taken up by plastic bins. The only greenery was ivy on the rear wall. Toni wandered over.

'This is ripped.' She lifted up a tress. 'This was his – or her – exit.'

Malcolm didn't need to stand on tiptoe to see over the wall. 'There's an alleyway here. He could have gone either way to reach the street. But if it was Daniel, why not just go out of the front door?'

'He didn't want to be seen?'

'But he'd be seen coming around from the alley.'

'Maybe this was his usual way out if Karen had grounded him? That's his window there.'

'That makes sense. I did that.' Malcolm nodded. 'I broke the trellis.'

'There you are then.' Toni was pleased to hear Malcolm had not been perfect as a child.

'Whoever did it was agile.' Malcolm ducked back into the house. He was constantly ducking.

'If he did go out over the wall, it suggests that he had some wits about him.' Toni hoped it wasn't Daniel. Ricky would be very upset. 'Andy Power suggested there was a boyfriend.'

'Did he know his name?' Malcolm looked animated.

'No. Karen might have told Mo, her sister. We'll talk to the neighbours. In case they saw anyone.'

'They start a row down here. Maybe he says something that riles her, or vice versa. Karen leaves the room. I *hate* it when Lizzie walks out on a row.' Malcolm ground to a halt. Toni hoped he didn't have too many rows; she relied on Malcolm's domestic bliss for the ecology of her team.

'Karen was strong, she'd have fought like a tiger,' Toni said. 'The best way to get her was on the loo, hobbled with her pants down.' She heaved a sigh. A dead boy and his murdered mother. It had got media attention, which meant Worricker was slavering for a quick solve from a skeleton team. 'Would you strangle your mother on the loo?'

'No, but then I wouldn't strangle her anywhere.' Malcolm was tracing a finger along his scar; a line from his lower lip to under his chin, it resembled a dimple. She had noticed he did it when he was thinking. The two men in her life had scars. Ricky had been hit in the mouth by a swinging derrick or beam; she should know which. She hadn't asked Malcolm how he got his. It looked relatively recent. *Not her business to dig up painful memories.* She had enough of her own she wanted kept buried.

'It's an intimate way to kill someone, and especially in that situation.' Toni rubbed her neck then snatched away her hand as she caught herself.

'What if she calls out to him as he's leaving that she's got a new man? He comes upstairs and Karen's on the loo. She laughs at him for minding, or some such. Daniel loses it and lunges at his mum. Like we said, he's already planning to take Daisy for a drive. Karen loses consciousness and he panics. He rushes out, drives to Daisy's. She thinks he's showing off – but really he's lost it.' Malcolm sounded sad. Like Toni, he'd prefer that Karen's murderer be a bad stranger. Not a pissed-off hormonal teenager with an Oedipal complex. If it was Daniel, whatever way you cut it, the case was beyond terrible.

'What about this boyfriend?'

'He's a suspect.' Toni nodded. 'He's also a myth until we find out if he exists.'

'Karen's hubby, Tom Munday, is alibied, and so is Andrew Power; his golf club visit checks out and his wife, Kirsty, was at home with him all night. Besides, he has no motive. You corroborated Ricky's alibi. He was preparing his boat and then went out to sea; he was literally on the radar,' Malcolm said. 'I'll have another chat with Mo, her sister.'

'Mo was the nice Munday. Never said boo,' Toni remembered. 'You could argue I have a motive, but thankfully I was in the station until the call.'

'Yes, or you'd be the prime suspect.' Malcolm did his blank stare.

'Anything from customers on her round?' Toni asked.

'Not so far. Sheena's onto it. She says they're shocked. One bloke asked if Sheena was taking over the round.'

Toni resisted applauding the idea. She was finding Sheena a handful. An idea occurred: 'What if Daniel didn't pick up Daisy?'

'We know she was in the car.' Tactful, Malcolm would be resisting pointing out the bleedin' obvious.

'We're putting Daisy as a witness to the crash. Could she have been a witness to Karen's murder?'

'Or her murderer?' Malcolm said.

'*Jesus*. This case has as many holes as a fishing net.' Toni scowled at the marine analogy.

'We need Daisy to get her memory back.'

'If she ever lost it,' Toni said.

'You think she's faking it?' Malcolm stopped at the Rottingdean lights. He looked at her.

'I'm not a doctor, but I'd say Daisy doesn't have amnesia. Her recollections were selective.'

'She referred to Karen in the past tense. She could know Karen was dead. *Is* dead.' Malcolm was watching the traffic lights; he'd have challenged himself to be off the second they changed.

'No chance. Josie Webb has her girl in solitary, she's clearly sick with fear about how Daisy might take anything,' Toni said. 'More likely the slip means Daisy met Karen in the past, not that she knows she's dead. I don't see her killing Karen – you'd think she hadn't had enough time to find her a pain in the arse. That said, it is odd.'

The sun had come out while they were at Karen's house. The sea was a band of glittering silver. The appetising aroma of fish and chips wreathed in through the open window. The shop was next to a beach-supplies on the lane down to the sea. Ten past three. Toni hadn't had breakfast, never mind lunch. She was about get Malcolm to do a right when the light changed and he accelerated up the hill to Saltdean. *Damn*.

'Guv?' Malcolm asked. 'What's odd?'

'What? Oh, Daniel and Daisy were an item for a matter of days, yet Daisy has a negative opinion of Karen.'

'She said he talked about her. When you're in love you open your heart. You swap stories about family and your past.' Malcolm spoke with feeling.

'These are teenagers, Mal. Kids don't open their hearts, they act cool.' Toni never had heart to hearts with Ricky. 'Actually, Mal, could you do a U-ie? I fancy chips and a pickled onion.'

11

FREDDY

The living room was cold. The blue gleam of the aquarium increased the chill. On the window facing the street the blue and green plastic which Freddy had once helped her mum stick onto the panes had blistered and cracked. Darkness filled the gaps, like lead in stained glass. Freddy switched on the lava lamps and the bulbs of oil began to stir like exotic marine creatures. Sometimes, lying on one of Sarah's huge leather sofas – with reclining and massage features – in her vast new-build house in Liverpool, Freddy would recall her lost home as a grotto on the seabed.

As she'd trundled her case back down Beach Road, Freddy had regretted that she'd given in to Andy's request to stay at her mum's. She could be on her way to Bristol. She had enough savings for a B & B until she got a job. She could have returned for the funeral. Or not.

Reenie had put in a new kitchen. In her day, her dad had refused to change anything in the house in which he'd been born. She approved of the IKEA oak veneer. Sarah's kitchen, sheets of stainless steel, hooks for pans, owed a lot to a pathologist's mortuary. Freddy guessed that Andy, a driver of progress, had persuaded their mum to splash out. She checked the cupboards. Tins of beans, sweetcorn, a couple of soups: tomato and chicken. Packets of Uncle Ben's rice. She hadn't thought to bring food because she hadn't been hungry. Nor was she now, but she felt empty. Freddy was eyeing the tin of tomato soup when it occurred her that everything in this house belonged to her brothers now. She would take nothing from Ricky specifically.

On the greying white walls in what had been her bedroom, Freddy saw the ghosts of Spice Girls and *Little Mermaid* posters. The photos of trawlers she cut from *Fishing News*. Above her bed had been a drawing of a humpback whale that Andy had done for her. All gone now. In this room, Freddy was aware of the emptiness, the stillness; her mum was dead but so was the little girl who'd slept there.

A book on a chair by the bed was not a ghost. Malcolm Saville's *Seaside Book*. Freddy gasped. It had been a present from her dad for her eighth birthday. What was it doing here? Fred Power hated reading, so Freddy had been surprised when he'd given it to her. Her mum had said, *Don't thank me, I had nothing to do with it.* As if the sight of it made her cross. Freddy had devoured instructions on choice of bait and where to fish. It was meant for boys, but she didn't care. Her dad had said she was as good as any boy. The slim hardback, the cover scuffed and torn, was as thumbed as, she remembered suddenly, Mags's *Revelations of Divine Love*.

Memories swooped around Freddy like bats as she roved through the house. Ricky sulking in the dark on the stairs because Andy had accidentally knocked over the boat he'd built with his bricks. Her mum making fishcakes in the kitchen.

The fish swam amidst the ornaments. Her mum still kept two species of tetra: the penguins were black and silver, and she counted four serpaes. A Siamese fighting fish flitted about Princess Ariel perched on her rock. A second ornament featured the little mermaid sat in a boat, her saucer eyes willing the prince to kiss her. Toni used to scoff, 'Don't wait, *kiss* him or dump him.' Was she like that with Ricky?

Freddy had never understood why Ariel longed to leave her idyllic palace beneath the sea. The tank, furnished with crumbling arches, shell-encrusted grottos and scattered with sundry starfish and seahorses, was Freddy's door to a magical world. As a little girl, home from school, she'd sit cross-legged on the shell carpet and gaze into the tank. 'Better than the telly,' her mum had said. Freddy was the Mermaid and Flounder her best friend. At the lunette battery with Mags on that summer's evening, Freddy had confessed that Princess Ariel was her first love. Ariel had made a bargain with the sea witch and won. She had imagined that if she was under the sea with Ariel, the princess would never have wanted the prince.

Although Toni always took the piss out of the little mermaid in the boat, it was she who had given the ornament to Freddy. She'd nicked it from the pet shop, her gift to the Mermaids when Mags asked her to join. Freddy had blinked with shock. As nice Mr Carter wrapped up Flounder – bought with the money Freddy had saved from her Saturday job at the fishery – Toni pocketed the boat. Outside the pet shop, Freddy had been horrified.

'What if you'd been caught?'

'I'm never caught.' Toni had sailed about the pavement to Take That's 'Could It Be Magic' on her CD Walkman.

'You've done it before?' Freddy shoved the ornament into her bag. Biting back tears – of shock – she had vowed to save up and pay Mr Carter back.

'Loads.' Not a boast; Toni dealt in facts. 'What else d'you need for your fish?'

'It's a sin!' At thirteen, Mags was going to be an Anchorite like Julian. 'Thou shall not steal.'

'Now she's got the boat, Freddy can get something else next time,' Toni had explained. 'Two for the price of one.'

'What about Mr Carter?' Freddy had cried. 'He's sold one thing for the price of two.'

'I don't think that's right.' Mags was good at maths. 'He's got half the money he'd have had.'

'He's got a whole shop of stuff.' Toni had danced off down the street.

Mr Carter never got his money. When Freddy had earned enough to pay for the boat, she spotted a barnacled shipwreck in the window and temptation got the better of her. Like Toni had said, she could have two ornaments and pay for one.

Freddy had grown to know the signs. They'd be in a shop. Toni would go still, a cat about to pounce, and, unable to bear the suspense, Freddy would flee. Eventually Toni made her stay, because Freddy acting strangely would attract suspicion. The trick, Toni said, was never to glance about. Always buy something. In addition to aquarium ornaments, Toni stole sweets, accessories, bracelets, socks, keyrings, fish hooks. Anything she could hide in a pocket.

Forced to accompany Toni to the till, Freddy would die of terror while the legitimate item was rung up. She'd be close to a faint as Toni prolonged the agony with inconsequential chat about the weather and the times of the tides.

Toni had peaked with a pair of shoes which she wore out of the shop. She bought a scarf to match. Presumably the shoplifting had stopped when Toni became a cop. They'd all moved on since they were Mermaids.

Freddy wouldn't turn on the heating and give Ricky another fit. She went out to the little garden and found wood in the old outside lavatory. The logs were veiled in cobwebs. It would have been some time since her mum got downstairs.

Freddy lugged an armload into the living room and built up the fire. She got one of her mum's *Daily Mirror*s from a pile under the stairs in the kitchen. *Lady Lucan The Final Tragedy*. Freddy scanned the story. In 1974 Lady Lucan had survived an attempt to kill her. She alleged the culprit was her estranged husband, Lord Lucan, who had immediately disappeared and had never been caught. Locally, the story had gained the status of folklore because Lord Lucan's car was found in Newhaven. He was rumoured to have jumped off the Dieppe ferry. Now, wrongly believing that she had Parkinson's, Lady Lucan had committed suicide. Not *now*, Freddy realised: the paper was dated January 2018. Had her mum been ill that long? More likely she'd burned more recent newspapers. Freddy slotted screws of paper within her wigwam of logs.

She went out to get more wood and, distracted, wandered up the narrow strip of grass to a shed at the bottom. With everything that had happened over the last couple of days she'd forgotten about the small animal hotel. The sign on the shed read:

Sunnyside Hotel, for anyone with fur or feathers
smaller than a cat.

Freddy was unprepared for the pain. It was almost worse than seeing Reenie dead. She leaned on the shed. Her mum had run a service minding household pets while their owners went away. It was the only work Fred Power had allowed his wife to do.

Freddy had been Reenie's deputy. She'd cleaned out hamster cages and rabbit hutches, filled water bottles and feeders and restocked with hay and food. Guinea pigs, a parrot called Marcus, cockatiels, gerbils, rabbits. Freddy fussed over the guests in the hope that they would want to come again. She had been shattered when Reenie broke the news that Mr Bun, a brown rabbit who had hopped after her in the house, had died. Freddy had let rats named Pinky and Perky sleep in her bed. They had weed on her duvet, which had driven her mum spare.

Freddy crept inside the shed and was enveloped in a sweet mix of hay, seeds, feed and warm fur. She must have imagined the smell of fur, though, because the cages and hutches would be empty now. *This was where her mum could be found.*

She groped for the switch. Light bounced off the silver insulation lining the walls. During the day, in the summer, furry guests were settled in caged runs on the lawn, each with a 'room' lined with hay for them to snooze in and to nibble. Tubes and toys kept them stimulated. Reenie Power had been before her time in attributing hopes and feelings to her charges. She'd kept carrots as a treat long before vets warned of the high sugar content, and had understood the nutritional quality of hay. Owners planned their holidays around availability at Sunnyside Hotel. The waiting list stretched into the years ahead.

On a shelf beside a stack of care and feed forms were blank postcards of Newhaven harbour, the breakwaters encircling the sea like loving arms. It had been Mags's idea to send cards to owners, as if from their happy pets.

Dear Sybil, I'm having a whale of a time. My friends are guinea pigs called Spice and Sugar. I tell them to 'Buck up and seize the day.' I hope you're enjoying your well-deserved holiday, love Marcus x.

Writing the cards had become the Mermaids' 'job'. Toni got banned after including the awful news that Mrs Prior's cat had gobbled up Fancy the gerbil.

Freddy picked up one of the postcards. It would never be sent. How long ago had her mum shut down Sunnyside?

With an armful of logs, she stumbled back to the living room. The lava lamps were warm, the green and blue glo-bules morphing from one shape to another. Freddy sat on the couch, elbows on knees, her face cupped in her hands, her gaze lost in the flames. She felt a flash of contentment before reality swooped in. *Mum is dead.*

Who would take the fish tank? Neither of her brothers had been interested when they were boys. Perhaps Andy's kids would like them. Was his daughter like Freddy? *Idiotic.*

Why would she be? Freddy hadn't thought to ask their names. You couldn't envisage people without their names.

She was startled by a rap on the door.

'Dolly's all ready.' The woman thrust out a carrier.

'Who?' Freddy was face to face with a cockatiel.

'Two weeks bed and full board. Don't let her stay up late with the telly.' The woman, in her seventies with long, yellowed hair, laughed then sobered abruptly. 'How are you, lovey? It's so sad about your mum. Reenie was a lovely lady. Dolly will notice. I haven't broken it to her. Sunnyside's her high spot.'

'Thing is—'

'Don't let her chew her bars. A nasty habit, she'll ruin her beak. It's not a holiday, I'm having my fireplace taken out – fibroids are the devil – I'll be in the Princess Royal should Dolls think to write one of her little cards.' She winked at Freddy.

Before Freddy could speak – and give Dolly back – her owner had gone.

Freddy placed the carrier next to the cage she'd seen yesterday. The hamster was standing up on its hind legs. A small animal guest was residing in the middle of the front room, yet Andy and Ricky had forgotten about their mum's Sunnyside Guest House. Freddy was about to ring Andy when the door went again.

This time, Freddy was unsurprised by the arrival of an elderly woman introducing herself as Mrs Nowak. Bent with scoliosis, her coat reached to her shoes. She passed Freddy a cage from which peeped a small white rabbit.

'Lovely stay for Mikolaj,' Mrs Nowak crooned in a Polish accent. 'My son-in-law will fetch Mikki.' She told Freddie she was taking her daughter to Lublin. 'She never went before.' On the doorstep, Mrs Nowak grasped Freddy's arm. '*Ci biedni chłopcy*. Those poor boys. No mother to love them.'

'What about me?' Freddy told the closed front door. The outburst caught her by surprise. She never felt sorry for herself. With great care, she lined up Mikolaj's carrier beside Dolly the cockatiel. With three cages and the fish tank the room was cramped. She couldn't house them in the shed; it needed to be heated through.

Her mum used to say things happened in threes.

A man in his sixties introduced himself as David Bromyard. His hearty tone suggested she should know him. This made Freddy nervous. So far, the pet owners hadn't given any impression they knew her before she left home.

She inspected the mouse-like rodent – Roddy – who was too intent on a leaf of iceberg lettuce to notice that he'd been in transit. She felt Bromyard watching as she positioned Roddy's fancy wooden cage on the table by the couch. He passed her a sheaf of instructions that carried over from the usual care-sheet. 'It's not that my wife doesn't trust you, it's just she's very attached to Roddy.' The paperwork said Roddy was a degu. Small and quick, a degu guest had once escaped when Freddy was doing out her cage. It had taken two hours to find it. Freddy's heart sank.

'She says he's more of a husband to her than I am.' David Bromyard pulled a weird face.

'I'm sure that's not true.' Freddy was only being kind. She knew full well that many of her mum's pet owners were more attached to their pets than the humans in their lives.

Hovering by the television, Bromyard showed no signs of

leaving. If he came out with anything about poor Andy and Ricky, she might hand Roddy back.

'I knew your dad. He was a lovely man.' Bromyard looked embarrassed.

'Yes?' Freddy steeled herself for a lecture on what a cruel daughter she had been. *Lovely* was one hell of a stretch, but it didn't surprise Freddy. Outside the home, Fred Power had taken care to be charm itself.

'I used to see you. You came on my boat. You were about three, do you remember?' He looked earnest, as if he really hoped that she did. *Jesus wept.*

'I don't.' Freddy was knocked off course. 'But if I was three...'

'I took you out on my beam trawler.' Bromyard had short brown fluffy hair. Now that she looked properly it was his original colour. She'd put him at over sixty, but the fact that he was a fisherman explained the reddened sandpapery skin. He might be younger. He was overweight, but his size and height allowed him to carry it. 'With your dad.'

Bromyard laughed, too heartily she thought. 'Of course, I couldn't cope with you by myself. I had a three-man crew back in the day to get in the catch. He loved the sea, Fred. He'd have run his own boat if he hadn't been sickened by quotas.'

'Quotas?'

'It's the limit set on a species to conserve the stock, so the government says.' Bromyard pulled a face.

'I know what it is,' Freddy snapped. 'What did it have to do with my dad? He didn't run a boat. He got seasick.'

'Freddy never did!' Bromyard ground a meaty fist into a palm.

Freddy. No one had called her dad that. It proved Bromyard had hardly known him.

'I think you must be mistaken.' It didn't matter but, fazed by the changes to her family, of this at least Freddy was certain. 'Dad hated being on the sea.'

'He loved it.' Bromyard seemed to stop himself from saying more. Likely he wouldn't want to argue with the woman who was going to look after his wife's precious degu.

'He got seasick,' Freddy repeated. She knew she should leave it. If this big, burly bloke attacked her, she would only have a few rodents and a cockatiel on her side.

'It was a life he denied himself. But that was him all over.' Bromyard looked sad. It shocked Freddy that anyone should miss her father.

'Right,' Freddy conceded. She'd had enough.

'It's nice to meet you.' Bromyard made to go. He hesitated, perhaps to mend the awkwardness. 'You look like him.'

'How long have we got your pet for?' Freddy nearly shouted the question.

'A month.' Perhaps seeing horror in her face, 'Andy said that was OK. I hope it is?'

'Andy should know.' Freddy raised a hand to guide Bromyard to the door.

When she returned to the room, she was shaking. With cold and something else indefinable. She tossed another log onto the fire and raked the ashes. Bromyard was definitely familiar. But if she had been out on his trawler, so had her dad. And that didn't make sense.

She remembered a night at the fishery when she had been around fifteen. It must have been the holidays because she'd been working full time. She was on her way home when she realised she'd left her knives behind. Her dad got angry if she left them, which meant she couldn't ask him to bring them home with him.

Karen's uncle was driving a delivery truck out of the gate when she went in. Dave Munday leered at her out of his cab window and licked his lips. He gave Freddy the creeps. Light from her dad's office spilled over the tarmac.

When Freddy had retrieved her knives, she'd stopped by his office. After seeing Munday, she didn't want to walk up the road in the dark.

Fred Power was slumped at his chair, the order book out on his desk.

'All right, Dad?' She was gripped by sudden fear.

'Seasick.' He'd looked at Freddy as if she was an intruder. His skin was white and shiny with sweat, like Ricky when he had the flu.

'Have you been out on a trawler?' Power's Fishery didn't own a boat. Let others do the drowning, her grandfather used to say. Her dad couldn't even swim because he hated boats.

'I'll gut you if you breathe a word to your mother.' He had glared at her.

'Why did you go on the sea? Whose boat were you on?' If her mum had been there, she'd have signalled for Freddy to shut up.

'What did I say?' He'd come at her as if he might hit her. He sometimes hit Andy, but never her. Maybe this occurred to him, because he halted in the middle of the room and, waving a hand, mumbled, 'It's business. Forget it. Too many pints at the Hope.'

Now Freddy saw her father's expression as clear as if it were he, not Bromyard, who had been in the room. Fred Power's expression had not been anger. It was like he'd been nervous. Was he nervous that his daughter would judge him for his weakness? After all, strong fishermen didn't get seasick. Freddy hadn't cared; she'd just been surprised that her dad had gone out on the sea at all.

Now she reasoned that her dad must have wanted to check the man was legal. Fred Power was picky about his suppliers. Odd that Bromyard thought Fred had loved the sea, but then he could say what he liked; the dead don't argue.

Freddy got up from the stool and opened a drawer in a sideboard opposite the window, the gloomy oak accentuated, rather than offset, by a lace runner. Where her mum had always kept it, among elastic bands, pens, redundant keys and other odds and sods, was the Small Animal Register.

She leafed through the death notices, copied across from the previous book; the list grew each year. The fact that Reenie had known the names of their deceased pets reassured the owners. Bert, white canary – 2002. Fanny, lovebird – 2001. Mr Bun, brown Nederlander rabbit – 1999. Her mum's handwriting blurred and swam. Freddy dashed at her eyes. *Don't cry.* Not for Mr Bun. Or her mum. Her grief was deeper than the sea.

Freddy ran a finger down the dates. The most recent guest – Brad the hamster, who'd run on his wheel yesterday – had arrived three days ago. *Andy knew the guests were coming.* Andy had known that once the pets arrived Freddy could not turn them away. She sighed; he must have remembered how much she'd loved looking after them. She resolved to stay for the funeral. She would run her mum's hotel. Filled with sudden excitement, she bent and released Mikolaj the white rabbit from his cage.

'Have a trot about,' she told him.

The visit from David Bromyard still nagged at her, but she pushed him to the back of her mind and returned to the guest list. Brad was due to be collected today. Freddy felt ice creep down her spine as she read the booking information, not in her mum's handwriting. Brad belonged to Karen Munday. She would not be coming to pick him up.

Freddy was digesting this grim information when there was another knock at the door.

12

TONI

'What do you want?' Freddy was gruff.

'I came to see how you're doing.' Toni tried for a friendly smile but guessed it was more of a wolfish smirk. Freddy had kept her on the doorstep. To the point that when she opened the door, Toni was about to go.

Freddy glared at her.

'You know, after yesterday.'

'Yesterday? Oh, you mean when my mum died and my brother tried to chuck me out of this house? Yes, well, I'm fine. Why wouldn't I be?' Freddy's sarcasm failed to mask her hurt.

'Can I come in?' *Damn.* Never ask a question that leads to a dead end. Toni, a skilled police interviewer, never made that mistake on the job.

For answer, Freddy shrugged and wandered off into the lounge. Toni scuttled in after her before she could change her mind. Freddy had got a fire going. Toni gravitated towards the grate then saw a creature on the sofa. *A bloody hamster.*

'*Oh*. My. *God*. You've taken on Reenie's Hotel. Did Ricky and Andy sell you a sob story?'

'Their sob story is mine too.' Freddy scooped up the hamster. 'Andy asked me. Until the funeral.'

'Couldn't you stick a "No Vacancy" in the window?' Toni had sworn not to resort to jokes. It never worked with Freddy.

'We have rooms,' Freddy said.

Freddy sat in her mother's old chair. She played with the hamster's ears, and Toni felt a wash of sadness for a time long gone.

The room felt warm and homely. Reenie had always skimped on wood even after her husband was no longer there to ration her. There was a movement out of the corner of her eye and Toni spotted a white rabbit preening itself under the television. It was like old times.

'Have you come to gloat?' Freddy stroked the hamster.

'About what?' Beady little eyes watched. A white bird about a foot in height was perched on the wall clock. Toni, familiar with Reenie Power's creatures, identified it as a cockatiel. The rabbit was eyeing her too. 'I just came to see you.'

'About Ricky getting half the estate? He's welcome to it. They both are.' She softened. 'I mean it, they've been there for Mum all these years.'

'Excuse me?' Toni got a nasty feeling.

'Didn't your *boyfriend* tell you?' Freddy spat out the word. 'Mum's will says Ricky and Andy get the lot.'

'You are *kidding*.' Toni was aghast. 'No. Ricky didn't say a bloody word. He does have other fish to fry, so to speak, but all the same. You get nothing?'

She'd been ready for flak from Freddy about Ricky. At some level Toni did feel she'd betrayed her old friend by being with her brother. But she hadn't anticipated this.

'Yours truly has been cut out.' Freddy sounded strangely sanguine. 'It goes to the boys. Andy was embarrassed, Ricky not so much, I'd imagine. Stick with my baby bro, he's *rich*.' As if gifted with a sense of drama, the cockatiel did a fly-past, swooping low and landing back on the shelf.

'That's total shit.'

'What did you expect?' Freddy put the hamster down and whistled at the cockatiel. He flapped over and teetered on her arm as she steered him into his cage. Freddy looked thoroughly at home.

'I'd assumed, if I thought about it at all, you'd each get a third.' Reenie had dubbed her a cradle-snatcher, although Toni was only five years older than Ricky. But she hadn't been a vindictive woman.

'When I started seeing Ricky your mum asked if I was in touch with you. I said we'd texted. No point lying, Reenie would have known.' A multicoloured fish darted around an ornamental starfish. Toni wondered if Freddy remembered that she'd given her the boat with the princess and the prince.

'What did Mum say?' Freddie asked.

'She started on about the ironing or some such. It's a shame you didn't make it to your dad's funeral.'

'A shame? It was a bit more than that. Dad forbade me to return. If I'd shown up, my brothers would have killed me.'

'No way.' The Powers might not stretch to murder, but things would have got ugly.

'You saw Ricky yesterday. I'm the devil.'

'He came on strong. I'm sorry.' Toni snatched at the vestiges of their friendship.

'Don't apologise for my brother.'

In the silence the fish tank bubbled.

'How did you know I was here? Andy said he wouldn't tell Ricky.' Freddy spoke first.

'Andy texted. Coming back here. It must be painful.'

'Less painful than spending my savings at the Premier Inn. Andy's offered me work. Without asking Ricky, so if you tell him, prepare for a fit.' Freddy bared her teeth. 'The pet hotel and the fish round. No doubt he feels guilty; very Andy: he won't go against the will but can't bear that I'm done out.' Freddy cuddled the hamster. 'He told me about Karen.'

'It's shocking. Who would do that to her?' Toni was relieved not to have to break it to Freddy.

'Andy said it was her son.' Freddy tapped the hamster's nose.

Toni pulled a face. 'The lad's dead too, we can't ask him.'

'That is awful.' Freddy let go of the hamster, grabbing it before it headed off her lap. 'They were both murdered?'

Tension between the once best friends eased. Murder was safer conversational ground.

'No, Daniel smashed his car – Karen's car – into a barrier on the beach the same night and nearly took his girlfriend with him. He worked at Power's – maybe Andy said?' Freddy gave a slight nod. 'Ricky's devastated; Danny was something of a protégé, he was developing him into a skipper.' Toni didn't admit how it had annoyed her that

Ricky had treated Danny like a son. Guilt, perhaps, for her drawing a line at them having children.

'Karen Munday made your life a misery. Did it piss you off, my brother putting himself out for her son?' Freddy always hit the spot.

'I wished her dead a few times at Our Lady,' Toni agreed. 'I used to wind Mags up saying that, remember? She was worried God would lose patience with me.' If Toni felt guilt, it was for that. Mags had stuck by her when Toni took the piss out of her faith. 'My dad used to say that my mum's side of the family bore grudges so, when it came to Karen, I supposed I was a chip off that block. But seeing her dead, if I could have one wish granted, it would be to see her driving her fish van. It's one of the most upsetting murders I've seen, which is saying a lot. Not gruesome. Calculated, nasty. Personal.'

'If it was her boy, he must have hated her,' Freddy mused.

'Ricky says Daniel couldn't stand the sight of blood. Karen was strangled, which would figure.'

'Mags wanted us both to go to confession, to be proper Catholics. Remember when we pretended to go in and slipped out the back?' Freddy frowned, as if the memory was bad. 'We were only fooling ourselves.'

'A sin shared is a sin doubled.' Toni snorted at their old joke. A rat-thing was gnawing at a bar in its cage. The name tag said 'Roddy'. 'Bless her, Mags hasn't given up on me as a lost cause.'

They went quiet, perhaps both considering that Mags had given up on Freddy.

'Terrible if Daniel did kill Karen,' Freddy said. The rat stopped working at his cage and glared at her.

'It's not definite Daniel's the perp. There's no compelling motive.' Toni stuck a finger into the rat's cage and clacked her tongue.

Don't!' Freddy shouted. 'Roddy's care sheet says he bites if you haven't introduced yourself.'

'I'll pass, thanks.' Toni snatched away her hand. 'Daniel was a teenager. All it might have taken was Karen telling him to tidy his bedroom to send him ape.' Here she was, chatting with Freddy Power as if nothing had happened since they were Mermaids. It felt good.

'I can't get my head around it,' Freddy said as she left the room.

'Andy's theory that Daniel caught her doing it with a bloke doesn't stack up. There's no evidence, nothing in Karen's phone records or emails. We're asking her neighbours and customers.'

'Why does Andy think there was a man?' Freddy returned with a box of 'tasty mix' for rodents. She tipped some into a dish decorated with nibbling creatures and placed it in Roddy's cage. From the speed with which Roddy scuttled over, he didn't need formalities to crack on with supper.

'Karen was a catch, he reckoned. Your brothers put everything in fishing terms.' Toni shot a look at Freddy. 'The clothes in her wardrobe have to be worth about ten grand and she didn't get that kind of dosh from a fish round.' Watching Roddy reminded Toni she hadn't eaten. She felt in her pocket. 'Want half a Snickers?'

'No, thanks,' Freddy said, so sharply that Toni expected her to ask if she'd paid for the chocolate. 'Finding your mum in bed with a stranger, or with anyone, would be horrible. Could it be Andy? I never asked, why *did* he employ her?'

'Andy is Mr Family Man. Did he say he's married to Kirsty Baxter from school?

'I'd never heard of her.'

'She was a friend of Amy's – nice girl. Still is. She could handle your mum, which is more than I did!' Toni risked a jibe at the all-wonderful Reenie Power. 'Kirsty has the same birthday as Mags. Younger, obviously. Proves astrology's nonsense; they're not a bit alike. Mags is passionate about the church; Kirsty is passionate about *Strictly*.'

'How're things with Ricky?' Freddy didn't need to expand. Ricky was the subject that, so far, they had avoided.

'The third person in our relationship is *Teresa-Mary*.' Seeing Freddy's quizzical expression, 'His trawler. He's out fishing most nights.'

'Is that OK with you?'

'If he did a nine to five, we'd have broken up by now. Keeps it fresh.' Her moaning about her boyfriends and Freddy sorting her out, now it really was like the old days.

'Could Ricky have been with Karen?' Freddy never had minced words, but Toni hadn't expected her to suggest her own brother for murder. Freddy must be very annoyed that Toni hadn't told her she was with Ricky. Toni felt hurt. Freddy had never been petty. 'If he and Daniel were close, might Daniel have gone nuts when he found them? It happens. When Andy got pneumonia and Mum sat up nights with him, Ricky smashed up a dinner set because she wasn't there for him.'

'He was a kid. I nicked money out of my dad's wallet to buy him a birthday present,' Toni snapped. 'That scenario puts Ricky in the frame as much as Daniel.'

The goodwill between them evaporated.

'Maybe you're the wrong person to head this case,' Freddy said. 'Ricky's my brother, but I'm willing to accept he's not perfect.'

'So am I. But that doesn't make him a murderer. What does he have to gain? He's lost a crew member.' Toni balled up the Snickers wrapper and tossed it in the fire. They watched as it burnt blue and green, like the lava lamps. 'If Ricky murdered Karen, don't you think he'd work out it wasn't in his interest? Don't answer that.'

'Fishermen go on about how poor they are, but it's a decent living.' Freddy seemed to be out to needle Toni. 'Sounds like Daniel's not your only suspect.'

'It's too early to close off possibilities.' Toni wished she hadn't come. Mags had known to keep away. The past was the past. The Mermaids were finished. 'Andy was at home with his wife. Ricky was fishing.' *Why had she said that?*

'Not great alibis.' Freddy scattered a pinch of fish food into the tank. 'From his wife. And why wasn't Daniel on the boat with him?'

'Day off, or he threw a sickie.' Toni offered an olive branch. 'Listen, I'll talk to Rick about you, make him see—'

'Don't bother. After the funeral, I'm gone. I don't need his charity. Or you pleading for me. Long ago I learnt that if you don't rely on others, they can't let you down.' Freddy was expressionless. In their Mermaid days that meant she was upset and keeping it in.

'*Jesus*, Freddy.' Toni lost it. 'If we're talking about friends, where have you been over the last twenty years? Is the odd text your idea of a Merma— of friendship? While you were living your new life, Ricky and Andy slaved their guts out, and I mean *slaved*. Fred Power worked them like mules; he paid a pittance. Then he dropped dead. Don't get me wrong, that's a happy ending. At last the boys got to run the place. All I'm saying is so what if Andy does feel guilty about the will? He's a decent bloke and loyal to his sister, so don't diss him for reaching out—' She stopped. Freddy had gone red. She was no longer blank; Toni had said too much.

'*Ci biedni chłopcy,*' Dolly screeched.

'It's Polish.' Freddy was trying not to laugh. The rabbit ventured out from under the television and gave a few hops towards the kitchen. Damn thing knew where to find the lettuce.

The aquarium gurgled. Fish whisked and darted around the prince and princess in the boat. Roddy had left off grinding at the bars of his cage and was preening himself. Freddy petted the hamster on her lap. Domestic bliss in another life.

'I miss the Mermaids,' Toni heard herself whisper.

'Me too,' Freddy said. 'Karen never got over being chucked out.'

'Yes,' Toni said. 'Mags went a bit over the top, perhaps. She was sticking up for me.'

'Brad belonged to Karen.'

'Who's Brad?'

'This is Brad.' Freddy lifted the hamster and gave it a kiss. 'Karen brought him to stay at Sunnyside.'

'You're kidding. Why?' Toni sat up. *Was Karen planning a holiday with a mystery man?* Seeing Freddy's face, 'No, I mean, obviously, this is a nice place for animals, but why did Karen need Brad to stay anywhere? She didn't go anywhere.'

'Maybe she wanted Brad to have a break?' Freddy looked dumbfounded that a hamster wouldn't want to stay in the animal hotel. At another time this might have been funny.

The silence was broken by a mournful sound. The foghorn. Bad weather was forecast. Not a night to be at sea. Ricky had fished in worse conditions. *Ricky.* Although Toni didn't owe Freddy an explanation, she offered it anyway.

'I bumped into Ricky on Piccadilly Circus. He'd come up to see the sights, he said.' She laughed heartily at the memory. 'Madame Tussaud's, the Science Museum and finally the lights. He was sitting on the steps at Eros.'

'That doesn't sound like Ricky.' Freddy looked puzzled. 'Although he did like books on how things work. But the waxworks?'

'He said you and Andy went with your mum, but he was too young.' Toni took a breath. 'I think Ricky often felt left out around you and Andy. You were very close.'

'He was younger.' It was difficult to work out whether Freddy was reminding Toni of her and Ricky's age difference. Toni remembered that the Power family had a tough reputation.

'So, well, a drink in a pub segued into a burger and chips, and then, crazy, since I was a couple of years shy of forty, we went on to a club. We ended up at my flat.'

Freddy was silent, and Toni ploughed on.

'I know I should have told you, especially when I moved back here. To be fair, a fisherman could hardly work in London. When the DI job came up in Sussex and with no openings in the Met, I returned. I bought one of those new apartments on the Quay.'

'That bit I knew. You didn't mention shagging my baby brother.' Freddy was still cross.

Toni was fed up of feeling guilty. 'I should have done. But you were getting on with your life, and none of what happened to you was Ricky's fault.'

'Have you seen Mags?' Freddy changed the subject and dribbled Brad back into his cage.

'What? Yes. Mags nursed Reenie; she was brilliant.' Toni hadn't meant to rub it in. Her mobile rang. Malcolm.

'Guv. It's Daisy Webb, they've found a blood clot on her brain. She's in a coma.'

13

MAGS

Mags had prayed that Freddy would not reply to her text. It was hardly a prayer God could answer. He forgave a sin, but didn't reward the sinner.

… while a man or woman loves sin, if there be any such, he is in pain that surpasses all pains…

Tuesday morning. Cold and dull. Mags was at her sitting room window, staring out. Through a gap between the new houses she saw a snatch of the river. Yellow-grey, sluggish. It mirrored her mood.

She went over and touched her statue of Mary. *Keep it safe.* Her intention is in Mary. She recalled the words in her diary. Reenie's wishes were her sons' command. Silently, Mags crossed herself.

Ever since Mags heard that Freddy had arrived in New-haven, she had been a bundle of nerves. Freddy had come, but she'd been too late to see her mother. Mags's mother had told her – many times – *if you do a thing, do it properly.* Mags had done this far from properly.

She could not answer Freddy's text. She would not meet

her.

Sin upon sin.

Unbidden, Mags's mind drifted to an evening long ago. A memory that until now she'd battened down with the rest.

They were going to Sammy's nightclub in Newhaven. Toni's dad was in hospital, but she'd sneaked out of the house. She needed some fun, she said. Mags had agreed to high heels and a make-up session with Toni. Freddy wore the leather jacket she'd bought in Brighton. They'd jostled in front of Freddy's parents' full-length mirror, checking their hair and executing dance moves.

A boy Toni knew got them into the club without ID. They'd had a last 'titivate', as Toni called it, in the loos. The man Toni fancied – called Steve – was on the decks. He'd played Aerosmith's 'I Don't Want To Miss A Thing' for Toni. She'd given it everything, miming the song to him, writhing and coiling under the glitter ball. Decor the Mermaids had declared totally naff but Mags thought magical.

Mags danced with Freddy, pouting as if to a *Top of the Pops* camera, fingers admonishing, palms gliding from faces, hips and shoulders jerking in sync. Then everyone gave them the floor, egging them on. Mags took off. The lights, the sound, the heat dissolved her senses. She danced for Freddy.

It was 1998, before mobile phones were common and a while before they had cameras – no one was filming. But an ambitious cub reporter from the Brighton *Evening Argus* – never off the clock and dreaming of a front-page story – had taken shots of them. Planning a story of underage drinkers, she couldn't have guessed her snaps would illustrate the paper's headline story the next day:

Teen's joy turns to heartbreak.

Karen Munday had broken them up. She'd marched onto the floor and made for Toni. Freddy and Mags had closed ranks.

Karen had yelled in Toni's ear. Mags couldn't catch it, but she saw the effect on Toni. She stopped stock-still, her hands reaching for the glitter ball. In the strobing lights, Toni was spectral. It hadn't been hard to lip-read Karen:

'*Your. Dad. Is. Dead.*'

'Shut up, Karen.' Freddy was squaring up to Karen.

'Her dad's dead. And she's dancing with you two lezzies.'

The word scalded Mags as if Karen had dropped liquid metal on her chest.

The music stopped. Lights went up. Everyone drifted from the floor, leaving the four girls beneath the slowly revolving glitter ball.

Footsteps clacked on the parquet. Sister Bernie and a uniformed police officer, his helmet under his arm. Sister Bernie had her arm around Toni. She led her away. Sister Agnes had told everyone to return home to their parents. Funny thing to say, Mags thought. You didn't go home to your parents. You just went home. Despite everything, Mags's lingering image was of the nuns in the nightclub.

It turned out that Karen was telling the truth. Toni's dad was dead. He'd been murdered. Toni was driven off in a police car like a criminal. The lezzie bit was wrong, though. Mags knew it was a sin to love a woman. *Like that.* You might not know a sin until you had committed it and your life was ruined.

Leaving the statue of Mary, Mags got her coat. Outside, rain clouds formed. Grabbing her bag and keys, she stepped out on to the landing. The lift was there, but Mags was trying to get her Fitbit steps.

And now Karen Munday had been murdered. It was mad. As mad as the fact that Freddy was in Newhaven.

14

TONI

'It was a man; the way he walked wasn't ladylike. At that hour an' all, no decent girl would be out by herself.' Mrs Haskins puckered her lips in disapproval.

'Can you remember what time this was?' Malcolm was scribbling in his pad. Toni gave him credit for patience. She'd boxed off the elderly woman as a ghastly succubus who fed off the weird and twisted problems of others. They had interrupted Mrs Haskins slavering over a reality show that involved someone having custard poured over their head. Toni doubted Mrs H had much to offer them; she'd be after a speaking part in their case.

'Half past ten.' Mrs Haskins was glued to the screen.

'That's precise.' The woman's age would not deter Toni from arresting Mrs Haskins for wasting police time. She was already doing a good job of wasting her own.

'I always heads up to bed after the news,' Mrs Haskins confided in Malcolm. 'I was shutting the curtains when I saw him.'

'That must have been only a glimpse. Did you see his – or her – gait?' Toni was deliberately obtuse.

Malcolm winged in, 'How did he walk? With a limp? Was he rolling from side to side, walking fast or ambling?'

Yes, all right. With their star witness comatose and the visit to Freddy, Toni's patience was in tatters.

'It was a proper look. I knew you lot would ask.' Mrs H nodded at Toni. 'I sneaks downstairs and, sure I'd be murdered, I goes and opens the door. I was scared out of my wits; suppose he was waiting to get me?' She clutched at her chest and looked out across the small, cramped, overly hot room as if she was in a TV studio trying to impress an audience. 'He was sneaking away. Got what he came for, mark my words.'

'You knew we'd ask?' Toni said. 'What led you to think the police would be involved? Did you hear an argument? Raised voices?'

'It was a matter of time. *Mrs* Munday was up to all sorts when her boy was out. I felt sorry for the blighter.' She gave a sniff.

'You're suggesting Karen Munday was seeing men. For money?' Malcolm asked pleasantly. He could be having tea with an aunt.

'How else did she get that car? Not on what them Powers gave her! Not for what she said she did for 'em.' Mrs Haskins leaned into the television, where the words, 'I admit I cheated on you with a woman half my age' bannered the screen. A man of about a hundred and ten, craggy features making him a body double for a risen corpse, grinned to camera. Not cradle-snatching, Toni noted; the woman must be long pensionable.

'Did you recognise him?' Saint Malcolm asked.

'They don't come in daytime. She does *fish* selling then.' As if 'fish' was a dirty word. 'She's in that van with no one to keep an eye.' Mrs Haskins upped the TV volume; the police were wasting her time.

'No love lost there,' Malcolm said when they were in the car. 'I talked to Karen's colleagues at Power Fisheries.' He consulted his notebook. 'One said, "Karen Munday had a dry sense of humour; never mind who she upset, Karen'd always speak her mind." Another woman, Shirley Vance, said, "She touched our lives like no other." There's more, all nice enough, although no one mentioned a boyfriend.'

'Perhaps because none of them were real friends. It seems like she only really had her sister, Mo.' Toni wondered who would claim to be her friend when she died. Not Freddy. Mags?

'It surprises me, guv. Karen's son is killed. She's murdered. People usually fall over themselves to claim they were mates, to speak well of the dead, but only her boss, Andrew Power, seemed upset. Richard Power was tight-lipped about Daniel. We all show emotion differently.' His hair flopping like a mushroom, Malcolm was keeping it formal. 'Mo told me that Karen's favourite meal was mac 'n' cheese and that she'd wanted to work for British Airways and travel the world. Facts that, while they might not lead us to her killer, give a glimpse on who Karen had been. Did you know any of this?'

'No.' Would they lead them anywhere? Usually the business of a detective on a murder case was to get to know the victim. Understand the measure of the loss. The human behind the body. Freddy couldn't bear these small proofs of Karen's humanity. It told her what she, too, had missed out on. Karen had only ever wanted to be their friend. Would Karen Munday be remembered as a murder victim and a school bully?

'Ricky keeps his feelings under wraps.' Toni cleared her throat. She wouldn't tell Malcolm Ricky had broken down. He had raged like a mad bull in her flat; he was beyond comprehending that his mum and Daniel were dead. His own life had been torpedoed. 'Any joy from Karen's fish-round customers?'

'Could Karen have been offering more than sea bream?' Malcolm stopped at the Brighton Road lights. 'Like Mrs Haskins suggested?'

'If you're thinking sex-worker, I don't see it. Selling drugs from the van is a possibility, I suppose. It would explain the car and the clothes.'

At school, Karen Munday's devotion to the Trinity had been real enough, although when she had contemplated being a nun it had been when Mags had briefly flirted with the idea. Where Mags went, Karen went. Toni frowned. She hadn't thought of that before.

PART TWO

TWO WEEKS LATER

15

FREDDY

Freddy paused in the church lobby and, automatically – she called herself lapsed – making the sign of the cross, dabbed holy water on her forehead. 'The Father, the Son…' She pattered down the aisle and, a hand brushing the side of the pews as if for reassurance, approached the altar.

The coffin rested on a trestle beneath the wooden carving of the Passion. It had been brought in the night before. The frailty of Jesus's prominent ribcage always struck Freddy as undeniably human. He had suffered. The stiff, ruched skirt fitted around the casket was too short, revealing the iron supports beneath. The effect was like a pantomime horse. Hysterics threatened. Then, as abruptly, Freddy didn't feel anything but sorrow.

In the last fortnight Freddy had not gone to the library where Mags, apparently, worked. She had set out twice, but her courage – and her legs – failed her. She told herself she'd hated it when Sarah turned up at the fish counter. She wouldn't do it to Mags. Deep down, Freddy knew the real reason was she was scared. What would she say? Supposing

Mags ignored her?

Four tall candles in gold holders burnt at the corners of the bier. The smell of hot wax took Freddy back to childhood. Confirmation, preparation for marriage... Mass after Mass. She complained, but it was reassuring. A place to belong. She didn't belong with Sarah. She had nowhere to be. She gazed at Jesus. This was a place to be.

Andy had been an altar boy. Ricky, too, but it was Andy to whom her heart had gone out. Making his way down the aisle, holding the thurible or the cross, trying unsuccessfully to disguise his shorter leg, limping all the more. Their dad had looked furious.

'You were proud of him, Mum,' she whispered.

It had been Freddy and Andy against the world. Against their father.

Freddy shuddered. She had a vision of the fishery. She was about ten so Andy must have been nine. They were meant to stay in the staffroom kitchen. They had brought toys: Freddy had a doll, Andy had a red car that was missing a wheel. They'd gathered up odd bits of Lego, which had made nothing worth making. They were bored. Freddy dared Andy to leave the room. *Run across the car park and touch that post.* Andy took every opportunity to run; he believed it would make his leg grow. When it was Freddy's turn, she did it twice to show who was in charge. Still bored, the children tiptoed out of the kitchen into the fishery.

The descaling room was empty. So was the shed that housed the freezer tunnel. The catch had been processed and the fishery had been sluiced down. Freddy was explaining how to gut a fish to Andy when they heard footsteps. They knew they were not meant to be in what was called the factory. She grabbed Andy and dragged him behind a tower of fish boxes.

Men's voices. One was their dad's. Freddy felt sick with terror, even though she knew it would be Andy who got told off. She couldn't place the other man. Risking everything, she peered around the boxes. Her dad was talking in a funny voice. The men's faces were close, like they were telling secrets. The man wore yellow oilskin trousers reaching to his tummy and held up by straps. Freddy recognised him as the fisherman who was always nice to her, who had once told her a story about a girl called Freddy who ran a trawler and caught more fish than anyone in the whole world.

Freddy saw her own fear in Andy's eyes. They kept still. After a while her dad and the fisherman went away. The journey back to the kitchen was one of the scariest of Freddy's life. Although she couldn't put it into words, Freddy believed her dad would have killed them if he'd caught them watching.

The fisherman was David Bromyard. What had he and her father been whispering about?

'Hello, Frederica.' It was Father Pete.

'Hi. Hello.' Flustered by his silent entry.

Father Pete smiled. His eyes were solemn. 'Welcome.' At their last meeting, she hadn't noticed his slight Irish burr. Freddy knew that it was hard to 'get the staff' these days and fewer men were opting to be priests. A leaflet by the door said that Father Pete had lived in Mexico for twenty years and now oversaw three parishes: Newhaven, Peacehaven and Haywards Heath. Sundays must be a whirlwind tour. Andy had confessed – his word – that he went less often, since the times of Mass changed and didn't fit with the fishery hours. Andy worked Sundays – unusual; traditionally, many fishermen were Catholics and, like their father, observed the Sabbath. A lot had changed since the day her father had dropped dead.

Despite his youthful looks, Father Pete must be middle-aged. *Pete.* Freddy trusted the matey ones the least. He was flesh and blood, with no special power. Yet, in the steady candlelight, with Mum's coffin inches away, she felt in awe of him.

'Thanks, I popped in… to…' Her eyes burnt. She dug her fingernails into her palms to stop more tears. Why had she been stupid enough to think she could do this?

'My mother went before I got to see her.' Father Pete's eyes flicked over the coffin. 'It's been eleven years. I still grieve. The pain will ease. You will find your way of living alongside it.' He touched the coffin. 'The manner of our death is not the sum of our life. Reenie was at peace when she went.'

'Good.' *Did she ask for me?*

'… I'm glad to hear you've stayed,' Father Pete was saying. 'It's a blessing for your family that you're keeping Reenie's home warm, alive somehow. For yourself, too, perhaps, it's a comfort?'

'I'm there until just after the funeral,' Freddy hastened to explain. After the end of the week, the house would be empty. She felt a stab of dismay. In the two weeks she'd been caring for the various pets – like her, they were due to return to their owners – she'd grown used to the routine. She'd found peace in returning to tasks she hadn't done for over twenty years.

'Reenie would be pleased.' He said it so quietly Freddy

wondered if she'd heard right. Had her mum confided in Father Pete? A priest's real power was in the secrets he held.

'It is *your* home.' He fingered his cross. 'Reenie was a brave soul, loyal to her principles. It's a rare gift to put principles before love for God.' He implied this was a good thing while surely it wasn't. 'Please be in touch whenever you wish, Frederica.' His gaze moved to the Passion carving and, with a sigh, he said, 'When our parents go, we're freed to live.'

Freddy nearly retorted she'd been freed long ago, but it would have been rude.

The coffin, solid and definite, expressed the finality of death more than her mum's body in her bed had. Her fingers busy with the rosary she'd long abandoned, Freddy whispered a prayer.

Hail Mary full of grace,
the Lord is with thee,
blessed art thou among women
and blessed is the fruit of thy
womb, Jesus.
Holy Mary, Mother of God,
pray for us sinners now,
and at the hour of our death.
Amen.

Working her way through the rosary, decade upon decade, Freddy came full circle.

Her parents may have gone, but Freddy did not feel free.

16

TONI

The hearse stopped beneath the arch spanning two chapels. Four limousines moved around the bronze statue of a boy reaching a burning cross up to a cloudless blue sky. In turn, like a sundial, the statue's shadow travelled across the gravel, shortening and lengthening with the hour.

On the narrow road that wound out of Newhaven, the queue of mourners' cars up on the grass verge outside the cemetery was causing a mid-afternoon jam.

Fastening a jacket button like a politician, Andy Power leapt out of the first car before it braked. He leaned in and helped out his wife, Kirsty, and their three Sunday-best-clad children. Toni squeezed Ricky's hand. Having sorted out his immediate family, Andy was bearing down on their car.

'Richard, old son, look alive!' The door was flung open. In comparison to Andy's bright and bushy-tailed efficiency, Ricky looked terrible, bags under his eyes and, of all the days, he'd cut himself shaving. He had never believed his mother would die. Nor had Toni imagined her dad would suddenly not be there. But she was fourteen and her dad had been murdered. Toni wanted the old Ricky back, the one who was on top of things.

She hustled Ricky onto the drive and, Andy on his other side, they walked up to the hearse. It had been Andy's idea that he and Ricky be pall-bearers. Toni reassured herself – again – that Ricky was used to hauling crates; he wouldn't drop his mother. As he approached the hearse even Andy seemed to falter. Toni left them in the care of the undertakers, who surely were used to mourners wanting to join in.

Irene Power's casket slid off the rails onto a gurney. Toni ground her teeth as, initially out of sync with the professionals, Andy and Ricky each shouldered their share of the weight. The six men began a slow tread up the long incline to the waiting grave at the top of the hill. Toni held back to let Kirsty, her children and Freddy pass. She'd seen Andy introduce his family to his sister before the funeral Mass, which was held at the Catholic church in the town. Beyond tight smiles, there had been no further interaction between the two women, and the younger generation of Powers showed no curiosity in their long-lost aunt.

Spring sunshine picked out the graves. Wild flowers flourished between the headstones. Aside from the pall-bearers' steady plod, there were discreet coughs, cars rumbled by on the C7 below, and from a stand of trees separating the cemetery from fields came the piercing call of a blackbird.

Andy and Richard relinquished the coffin, the task achieved and confidence restored, their arms folded as if their next role was to ensure that the undertakers paid out the straps and lowered Reenie Power's coffin into the family plot in a seemly fashion. Men. Toni was sure she glimpsed

Fred Senior's coffin: dark, rotting wood. *He deserved to rot.* More likely it was earth sodden by the recent rain.

The priest's voice rang out, 'All praise to you, Lord of all creation. Praise to you, holy and living God…'

Andy scooped up soil and dropped it onto the wood. Kirsty slipped her hand into his and pulled their kids close.

Ricky was in a bloody trance. Toni stepped forward, grabbed a handful of soil from the displaced mound by the hole and practically threw it at him. She could feel his emotion, like electricity thrilling through him. Poor bloke. You couldn't blame someone for something they couldn't manage. Freddy was the last. She took her time. Sprinkling the earth as if it were seeds onto her mother's grave. Ricky stiffened and Toni hoped he wasn't going to lose it. Perhaps a disadvantage of having known your boyfriend when he was a kid was that she had witnessed Ricky's fits. She had teased him about them, but since they'd been together, he had never lost his temper. Until Freddy came back. As Freddy and Andy had expected, he'd been livid that Freddy was staying in their old home. It hadn't helped when Toni had pointed out that, as the eldest, Freddy had lived there first.

'…let us take leave of our sister Irene. May our farewell express our affection for her; may it ease our sadness and strengthen our hope… joyfully greet Irene again when the love of Christ, which conquers all things, destroys even death itself…'

Someone was scurrying along one of the paths back towards the chapel. Short hair, trouser suit. It was Mags. She always wore black so today had been bang on message. Toni saw Andy look as concerned as she felt. Was Mags all right? Andy had covered every aspect of today. He'd emailed lists, issued black-bordered invitations, bamboozling Ricky with timings and cars. Now Mags was rushing off early. That would not be in his schedule.

There was another figure on the path. Shading her eyes, Toni squinted in the sunshine. She sucked in her breath. Freddy. At the church, Toni had seen Mags avoid Freddy. She'd be trying to go before Freddy could speak to her. Freddy was gaining on Mags. Toni dreaded what would happen next.

17

MAGS

'Mags! Wait. Stop.'

Cursing her heels, Mags gave up. 'I have to go.'

'You didn't answer my text.' Freddy didn't sound accusatory. Mags felt worse.

'We're short-staffed...' She couldn't finish the excuse. Sin upon sin. But for some lines like a veil draped over her face, Freddy looked the same. Her eyes narrowed, she would be puzzling to make sense of Mags, her mum, everything.

'Don't do this, Mags. After all this time—'

'After all this time there's no point. I have to get to work.' Mags resisted the sudden urge to pull Freddy to her. 'I have to go.' She made for the statue of the boy as if he would save her. *Nothing would save her.*

'Can we at least meet? I'm going back home soon.' Freddy caught up and stopped her. She put out a hand, but must have thought better of touching Mags; it fell lifeless by her side. 'Thank you for caring for Mum. Andy said you two were close.'

'It's what anyone would have done.' Mags could not say

how being with Reenie Power had brought her closer to Freddy. When Reenie smiled it was Freddy's smile; when she held her hand it was Freddy's hand. The hand that was inches from her now.

'I don't think so,' Freddy said.

A beam of sunlight caught the bronze statue and the glare shone on Mags as if from God.

'It's not a good idea.'

'I want to say a proper goodbye.' This time Freddy brushed the sleeve of Mags's jacket. A moth's touch. 'You told me about Mum. You asked me to come. You knew I'd come.'

'There's nothing to say.' Mags had wished with all her heart that Freddy would come and had prayed that she would not. It was costing Freddy everything to plead. She heard Freddy's words from twenty-two years ago. *You love bloody Mother Julian more than me.*

'Did Mum say anything to you about me? I know she didn't put me in her will. I'm OK with that. I don't care, I only care—' Freddy's face tightened. She would care. She would cling to anything that showed Reenie had thought about her. Mags forced herself to harden her heart. She couldn't deal with Freddy in Newhaven.

'I can't do this.' Mags was pleading. Then, suddenly, 'Karen's dead.'

'I know.' Freddy subsided. 'It's terrible.'

'It's my fault.'

'What? That's mad.' Freddy grabbed her shoulders.

The crunch of gravel.

'Not mad. I didn't mean that.' Freddy smacked her forehead. 'You can't take it all on; it was me too. I could have been nicer.'

'Hey! *Guys.*'

Andy Power strode down the hill, clutching his jacket, jabbing his sunglasses over the bridge of his nose. The grieving son. The businessman who got things done.

'Seven thirty at the battery. Tomorrow night,' Mags breathed.

Mags turned her ankle as she hurried to the bus stop. She greeted the hot pain as a gift from God. Another gift was the bus coming down the lane.

Julian's *Revelations* fell open at the page. As the bus ground to a halt in the car park behind the library, Mags dwelt on every word.

18

FREDDY

'I invited her to come in one of the cars. She refused.' Andy looked desperate. Like when they were kids and he'd failed – *again* – to score a goal or clean the fishery floor to their dad's impossible standards. Shattered by the funeral and the snatched moments with Mags, Freddy pulled him to her.

'Did Mags say anything?' Andy held onto her.

'We're meeting at the battery tomorrow night. I'll ask.' Freddy was furious with herself. Sharing the information made it seem less precious. *Mags would not want anyone to know.* Tough. Freddy was fed up with secrets. 'Listen, I'm going on Sunday. There're no more animals coming for a week. If any do arrive, could one of your kids feed him?'

'You could *have* the hotel. Rick won't do it. I don't have time and my brood have school.' Andy hadn't asked if she had a life elsewhere. It was like he knew she didn't. 'The offer's still out there for the fish round. It's commission, but Karen made it pay. Once you got into the swing, you would too.'

She shook her head. 'Thank you, Andy.' Why not? Her

parents were dead. Her dad couldn't stop her. She'd tell the truth about why she had gone when they were young and never come back. Andy would understand.

'Andy—' Freddy stopped. *Mags and me, we loved each other. I've never loved anyone as much before or since, she was my soulmate.* It wasn't only her secret to tell. Besides, Andy might not understand. A cool-headed businessman with a wife, kids and a position at the Rotary Club, his world wasn't so different to their dad's.

'Coming to the wake? I'll sort Ricky.' Andy spun on his heel, the host, mindful of the mourners.

'Best not. Not being funny, but neither of us could sort Ricky.' Freddy planted a kiss on his cheek. 'Mind yourself, bro!'

At the gates she glanced back. Framed by the arch, sharp-suited with shades, amidst the sprawl of gravestones, her brother cut a lonely figure.

Freddy had meant what she'd told Toni: she didn't want charity from either of her brothers. Her mum's will had respected Fred Power's wishes. Reenie Power had punished Freddy for falling in love with a woman. Or she would have changed it.

Father Pete's words came back to her. Freddy was freed. She would say goodbye to Mags at the lunette battery then leave Newhaven. For ever.

19

TONI

Toni was driving past the church when she saw the woman in a vivid purple anorak coming out. She was struggling with the door in what was building to a gale. Yesterday, Mags had left Reenie Power's funeral before Toni had a chance to speak to her. She'd seen Mags talking to Freddy. If they were talking, maybe they could all get on. Toni lowered the passenger window and leaned across the gearstick.

'Confessing your sins!' From Mags's expression Toni saw she'd hit the wrong nail bang on the head. *Shit*.

Mags seemed inclined to ignore Toni, then changed her mind. She came over to the Jeep. 'I'm on my way to the library.'

'Hop in. I'll give you a lift.' To Toni's surprise, Mags did so.

'I've been to confession.' Mags shut her eyes and rested her head against the seat.

'Oh no! I mean, I hope it... um, worked.' Toni let go of the ignition key and sat back. At the convent, on Freddy's suggestion – Toni claimed to have nothing worth confessing –

149

Toni had told Father George she'd shoplifted. Disgusted, she discovered that absolution depended on not nicking again.

'Have you seen Freddy?' Mags asked.

'She's not cool about me and Ricky.' Toni watched a man lifting a ladder off the roof of an alarm installation van and manoeuvring it up the steps of a house. Idly, she wondered at the need for a burglar alarm if you lived next to a fire station and a church.

'Why not?' Mags sounded surprised.

'I think mainly because I never told her. And Rick's being shitty with her, treating her like a gold-digger.' Toni swivelled to look at Mags. 'I saw you guys talking in the cemetery. Did you make up?' Idiotic phrase.

'She wants to see me.' Mags was clasping a small volume. Toni knew without looking that it was Julian of Norwich's *Revelations of Divine Love*. At the convent Mags had experienced the discovery of Julian (a female saint) as her own revelation. Her crush on the fourteenth-century saint could have won Mags *Mastermind* with Julian as her specialist subject. Not that much was known of the recluse, whose text was considered the earliest by a woman writing in English. The *Revelations* had struck Toni as far-fetched and unnecessary agony for Julian, but in Julian Mags had found a soulmate. Toni admitted to herself now that while she'd furiously questioned the dogma of the faith imposed on her by her parents' decision to send her and Amy to the convent, she did at least envy Mags's devotion. After her dad was murdered, Toni had been rudderless. She sometimes envied Ricky's Catholicism too. He went to Mass before every voyage.

Toni never commented – whatever kept him safe. What Toni did miss in her life was the Mermaids.

'Are you going to see Freddy?'

'Yes.' Mags opened the book and Toni saw scribbles and underlines. Mags had got A for Religious Studies and, by practically bashing Toni over the head with her missal, helped Toni scrape a pass.

'You and Freddy, you were… good together.' Toni risked it.

'I have done her harm,' Mags said. 'I've hurt her.'

'I'm sure it's not that bad.' Toni was unnerved by Mags's vehemence. She knew that being gay wasn't the deal it once was, at least in Britain. But she also knew from hate-crime statistics that in many places it was still a bad idea to kiss on a bus or walk down a street hand in hand. *Being a Catholic didn't help.*

'I must tell her.'

'You could tell me, as a kind of rehearsal.' Toni meant it, but she heard the nosy detective within.

'I have to go.' Mags flung out of the car as if ejected and hurtled off down the street.

'Julian, you have a lot to answer for,' Toni breathed. She debated warning Freddy of the divine revelation heading her way. No. Things were bad enough between them.

The church door opened and the priest came out. Toni knew Father Peter slightly from meetings about supporting the community and crime prevention. He'd been hearing Mags's confession. If only witnesses would open up to detectives as easily as parishioners to priests.

★

'We have no corroboration for that door-to-door witness who claims to have seen a man leaving Karen's house at half ten one night. Mrs Haskins.' Malcolm scooted his chair across to Toni. He rarely put his feet on the floor in CID, instead whizzing about with the alacrity of a kid in a baby-walker. The other day Toni caught herself cautioning him about the perils of lack of exercise. God knows why she went mother hen on Malcolm. Probably selfish – she needed Malcolm fit, healthy and happy.

'Doubtless, Mrs Busybody's mystery man is a figment of her twisted mind.' With no air-con, CID was stuffy with a miasma of takeaways and overworked humanity. The heat outside and a case which, like Daniel Tyler's car, had hit a block, had landed Toni with a stonking headache. Most people were loving the record-hot temperatures that signalled the end of the world. Fair-skinned and too busy to lie in the sun, Toni wasn't one of them.

Malcolm's phone rang. He zipped back, putting out his hands to buffer the chair from hitting his desk, and lifted the receiver. He nodded as he jotted down whatever the caller was telling him on his pad, finishing, 'That was the lab, some fibres on Karen's clothing match the jumper Daniel was wearing. They'll have the report over later. That partial print—'

'So, Daniel comes home, finds Karen in bed and goes mental.' Toni massaged her temples. 'Man scarpers and is spotted by Old Mother Haskins. Daniel has a row with his mum and steals her car. He rounds up Daisy Webb and drives them to Kingdom come.' She hadn't wanted Andy to be right about there being a man. She hadn't wanted a boy to have killed his mother. It was a rotten outcome. She clutched her head. No, the timing's wrong. Mrs H saw the bloke at half ten.'

'There's more.' Malcolm was munching. No point in reminding him that he came out in blotches when he wolfed a packet of Starburst. 'We got the lab results, finally. That partial print in the toilet? It brought up a match.'

'And?' Toni's mouth watered at the idea of a strawberry-flavoured Starburst. It could pass for supper.

'Richard Power.' Malcolm read from his pad, although he didn't need the prompt. 'Ricky's on the database from that business—'

'Jesus, Mal, *say* it. You mean when Ricky lost his licence for being pissed and parking the fish van on the Beddingham roundabout.' Toni took her anorak from the back of her chair and hauled it on.

The incident had happened before her time. But police memories are long. When she'd started seeing Ricky the team were merciless with jibes about parallel universe parking, puns involving sea creatures and the highway code. Google flung up links of headlines in the *Argus* and the *Sussex Express*. Andy had made a cack-handed attempt to render rubbish PR into wine by leasing a hoarding outside Lewes station. A photograph of the van marooned in the middle of the A27 with the words 'Power Fishery' on the side. Reenie had sent him to confession. The all-purpose cow.

'What was he doing in Karen Munday's toilet? No, Ricky didn't play away with Karen Munday.' Toni blew off Malcolm's scaredy-cat look. 'Actually, no surprise his prints are there, he sometimes took Daniel home after a trip. Let me tell you, for my sins, the clown loves me.'

20

MAGS

With the spring came the motorhomes; fold-up tables were erected, picnics spread. The occupants sunned themselves in deckchairs facing France. But it had been an unseasonably cold day, and a biting wind ruffled detritus – empty cans, plastic bottles, twine – on the shingle. The hollow boom of waves hitting the cliff face might be gunfire from the lunette battery warding off enemies, Napoleonic or Nazi.

From the cliff, Mags surveyed the deserted beach where, two weeks ago, Karen Munday's boy had crashed and died. It was the day before Reenie Power died. Mags passed a hand over her eyes but still saw the image of Karen sobbing, *Please let me back in*. Mags slammed shut her mind. Toni would say Mags wasn't that powerful, but Mags couldn't shake off her belief that everything, all three deaths, were her fault.

The only sign of the tragedy now was a length of crime tape whipping like a windsock from a life-ring post and oil stains on the concrete.

Mags knew that a girl was still critically ill in hospital. Mrs Barker had been back in, full of how the poor mite wouldn't walk again and was in a coma. Unlike Freddy when Toni's dad had died, the tragedy didn't jolt Mags's faith. Jesus died for the pain of humanity, he wasn't responsible for our actions. Mags had schooled herself to forgive evil. A forgiveness that stopped with the Australian cardinal, Pope Francis's number three, who had been jailed for abusing choirboys. Mags drew the line at child abuse, but these men were not Catholicism. Mags had confessed her sins to Father Pete. One step towards renewal. She opened Julian's *Revelations of Divine Love* and in the dimming light re-read, *The Holy Spirit leads a man to confession to reveal his sins willingly...*

Was she willing? The drop to the beach, not sheer like at Seaford Head, was still precipitous. When they were Mermaids Freddy had met Toni's crazy dare and clambered down to the beach at the steepest point. Halfway, she'd skidded on loose chalk and tumbled the last ten feet. She'd lain still on the shingle. Rushing down the same way, Mags had fallen on her knees beside Freddy. She'd kissed her, stroked her hair and prayed to God to save her. She'd told Freddy that she loved her. Freddy's eyes had snapped open. *I love you too.*

Mags had worried that Toni would feel left out, that the dynamic of the Mermaids would be besmirched. Toni was generous, she was good. Thinking of this now, Mags saw that Toni, the fervent unbeliever, had been closer to God than any of them. Toni had been pleased for them. By then she had a steady boyfriend. The Mermaids were perhaps less important to her.

They had swapped what they loved about each other. Mags loved the way Freddy walked as if she was always in a hurry and was in charge. How she narrowed her eyes when she was thinking. Freddy couldn't take her eyes off the sweep of Mags's thigh when she crossed her legs and the faint ripple of muscle on her forearms. Mags had been unnerved and excited by Freddy's intimate observations. Freddy saw the whole of her. And then it was over.

Freddy was due at the battery in five minutes. From this perspective, Mags would see her arrive. There was time to leave; she could go over the hill, past the fort and out through the nature reserve. Perhaps, like Mags, Freddy would have second thoughts and not come. Mags had wanted to cancel. But Julian had made her stick to the arrangement. She must face Freddy. She must tell the truth. All of it. Her life was not worth the price of evil. Mags was a Mermaid. She would do it for all of them.

Buffeted by the wind, Mags picked her way down the cliff. A sign on the shingle ridge warned, 'No safe access beyond this point', with icons depicting four kinds of danger. Falling rocks, slippery surfaces, rocky foreshore and deep water with high tides.

Who is the fifth danger? Freddy. Always Freddy.

The sun had set, the sky towards Shoreham was washed pink. Over the lighthouse, clouds darkening the cliffs gave Mags a bad feeling as she fumbled her way along the bottom, uncaring of falling rocks.

The grille across the entrance to the battery was open. Mags had to look twice to be sure. All her life it had been barred. The Mermaids used to scare each other, making up what lay within. They knew the layout from history lessons. Gun chambers off a passage, apertures facing the sea. They'd imagined a skeleton on a heap of ammunition that was used to fire at Napoleon's ships. He would have been a lovelorn soldier who'd killed himself and was never found.

Should she wait for Freddy? How much more exciting to greet Freddy as a guide already familiar with the battery's secrets. With Julian's book for courage, Mags ventured into the dank dark. At first the tunnel was pitch black, but bit by bit shapes resolved into doorways to the chambers and she orientated herself.

As fast as her mood had soared, it evaporated and Mags knew that she'd made a terrible mistake. *Foolish*. She was not seventeen and in love. She bumped into cold stone. She could not see Freddy. What had she been thinking? If she left now, she'd meet Freddy. She had sworn to be honest, not to play childish games and mislead her. Tell the truth. She'd been mad. *She could not see her*. There was a way to avoid her. Mags felt her way to the entrance and pulled the grille to so that it appeared closed. The padlock hung loose, but it was nearly dark, Freddy might not notice it was unlocked.

Mags crept back into the tunnel. The brickwork was wet, not with water but with the slime of centuries. Her heart in her mouth, she forced herself to go the end of the tunnel. If Freddy did come in, she'd never go that far. Inside the cell, dwindling light crept through the gun sighting. Mags had come to redress her sins. Instead, here she was, skulking in a tomb.

Mags felt warm fingers around her neck. She tried to shout. No sound came out. She went to prise off the fingers but snatched at nothing. Her arms were pinioned. She fought blindly, kicking with her feet, but she only aided the dragging into swimming darkness. Something gagged her, blocking her nose. She couldn't breathe.

'Where is it?'

She had vowed to follow Julian's example and be unafraid of death. When her time came, like Julian, Mags had longed to be with God. She would go gracefully. Except.

Not now… not yet…

When she came to there was something floating before her. *Mary*. Mags pictured her icon. *Intention*. It was the crucifix.

Mags felt a firm push. The ground was cold and hard, but she barely felt it. The cross resolved into a gun slot. She was still in the lunette battery.

'What have you done with it? Where is it?' That grating voice again.

'I don't know. I don't understand what you mean.'

The cross vanished.

21

FREDDY

Dolly's owner had been late and then in no hurry to go. She'd lamented what a loss dear Reenie was and what a wonderful daughter Freddy was to take over the hotel. *And look at how happy Dolly is – she's smiling.* Freddy couldn't see that the cockatiel looked bothered one way or the other but agreed for politeness's sake. She and Dolly had not quite hit it off. Freddy did not add that Reenie's wonderful daughter would be hightailing it out of Newhaven as soon as the last guest checked out.

She raced along Fort Road; it felt as if she was running the wrong way on a travellator, past the morgue, the fire station and the church. Mags had been reluctant to meet so she would not wait. Perhaps Freddy would catch Mags coming back. *Not if she goes by the nature reserve.*

She was running into the wind, her lungs molten. Freddy missed owning a car. Not that she had owned one; Sarah had bought her a Toyota Aygo for her last birthday. But of course, she'd left that in Liverpool. She would take nothing off Sarah.

By the time she passed the pub Freddy had slowed to walking, crippled by a stitch. The sun had set, and a luminous light picked out the shingle, the cliffs. There was no one waiting outside the battery. Freddy stumbled to the ridge, her effort doubled on the loose stones. She looked out over the beach. The sea was like glass, insidious as ice. The beach was in shadow, but Freddy could see there was no one down there. Freddy's feet were leaden, her boots heavy, as she struggled back up the bank to the battery.

Mags was there. Freddy nearly cried out with joy. The wind making her ears ache, she staggered towards her. Mags was peering into the gate erected by the council to prevent the battery from being used as a drug den. She must have been behind Freddy on the road. When Freddy had assumed she was running towards Mags, she had been running away from her. This idea cut her to the quick.

'Freddy, thank *God*. When I got here and couldn't see sight nor sound of you, I was beside myself.' As if the last two weeks had never happened, Sarah pulled Freddy to her.

'How did you know where to find me?' Freddy would have collapsed if Sarah hadn't been holding her. Tight.

'Didn't I say you, should install Find my iPhone on your phone?' Sarah murmured.

'I didn't install it.' Freddy had ignored what had been posed as a suggestion but was in fact another of Sarah's rules.

Sarah wasn't Mags.

'No. But lucky for you, *I* did. I checked it after I reached your mum's house and got no answer. Otherwise, I'd have been stumped.'

'I might have been at the Fishery,' Freddy said, for

argument's sake. What the hell did it matter where she might have been? Mags had not come.

'I did have a quick scout about the fishery. All those shipping containers. What a dump. It's a goddamn shanty town. Your brothers are running the place on the cheap. I can see why you hate your family.'

'I don't hate…' Freddy felt a paralysis take hold.

'I put in your number and, hey presto!' Sarah linked arms with her. 'This is a godawful dump – what are you doing here?'

'I was…' *Mags had not come.* 'I came when I was a Mer— when I was young.' Freddy craned her neck to gaze up the cliff. Was Mags up there watching? Freddie was clutching at straws. Mags had never intended to come.

Sarah guided Freddy away from the battery and past the section of beach where Karen's son had died. Outside the Hope pub she asked Freddy, 'While I think of it, how is your mama?'

22

TONI

'Where were you between the hours of 18.00 and midnight on Friday nineteenth of April?' Malcolm asked.

'I'd need to see my diary,' Ricky barked. 'In my line of work, it's hard to distinguish days. When we're at sea they merge.'

'According to my information, you were fishing that day; you lifted anchor at eight. You had come ashore the day before after a five-day trip.' Malcolm was pleasant. 'You do a lot of fishing.'

'We don't call it that.'

'Sorry?'

'We didn't lift the anchor. We were in the harbour. We use ropes.'

Toni tossed down her pen. She yelled at the monitor, 'What Malcolm is asking is if you strangled Karen Munday to death because she threatened to tell me you were having an affair.' Horrified, she checked the CID room. She was still alone. The interview was meant to be routine, but Ricky was turning it into a shit-show. She herself had given

Ricky his alibi. She had assumed that after she left him on the trawler he was there until he left. A stupid mistake that Malcolm was, thankfully, overlooking or Worricker would hang her out to rot.

'…where were you?' Malcolm's light tone was a prelude to the *Jaws* music. Toni longed to haul Ricky across the table by his T-shirt and yell at him. That she might actually do this was precisely why she was sitting this one out and watching it on her laptop. She dragged the headphones to her neck and massaged her scalp. She had another headache. Not helped by Ricky wilfully inserting himself in the frame for murder.

'I went to the fishery around seven.' Perspiration on Ricky's forehead and his ruddy cheeks (from being outdoors) made him look as guilty as sin.

'Can anyone verify that?' Malcolm was scribbling on his pad as if Ricky had given him vital information. An obvious tactic to unnerve Ricky, which Toni knew would go over his head. She wished she could whisper in his ear, *Sit back, breathe. Act like you have nothing to hide.* She could whisper in Malcolm's ear. She spoke through the mic. 'Ask about his phone, the alarm system, CCTV… anything that places him on the trawler.'

Malcolm frowned fleetingly. He wasn't short of interrogating experience; she had doubtless taken the words out of his mouth. Toni muted the input.

'What about your security system? Would there be a record of when you logged out of your computer, for example?' He was genial.

'I wasn't *on* my computer. I was mending nets.' *Play nice.*

'Can you prove it?' Malcolm wasn't smiling now. A signal that he was taxiing to the killer question.

'I was on my own until we went out. The stand-in was late. I didn't think I had to prove where I was, so no. I already gave a statement.'

Malcolm slid a photograph across the table.

'Your fingerprints were found in Karen Munday's toilet.' He tapped the picture. 'Can you explain why that would be?'

Ricky was still. Toni tracked the second hand on the clock above the tape machine, five... six... seven... *Come on, Ricky.* There were men serving life sentences for being unable to prove they were somewhere other than the crime scene.

'I can't understand it,' Ricky said on the count of ten.

'Why would you be at Karen's house?' Malcolm was patient.

'Listen, mate, do you honestly think I strangled Karen and left my fingerprints for you to find?' Ricky fired a look up at the camera. Toni shrank back, as if he could see her. Ricky didn't know how Karen had died. They'd held it back.

You lot. She puffed out her cheeks. Ricky was binding his own noose. She batted at the keyboard and accidentally minimised the window showing the interview. She restored it. *Had she told him?*

'Why do you think we found your fingerprint in the Mundays' house?' Malcolm repeated the question.

Yes, why in actual hell is your fingerprint in Karen's toilet, Ricky? Toni silently asked.

'I often drop Dan off after a trip. ' Ricky stuffed his hand between his knees. 'I've gone in sometimes.'

'You remember that now? I was disappointed for a moment. Guys like you, every step has to be considered. Weights, water-line, weather.' Malcolm the poet. 'Forget anything and you're in trouble, I'd think.'

'Yes. No. That's the only explanation, isn't it?' It wasn't the only explanation. Malcolm let this fact hang in the air between them.

'Have you used Karen's toilet?'

'No.'

'You are sure that you have never gone into the toilet?' A leading question. She should tick Mal off for that, but she was grateful.

'*Christ.*' Ricky shook his head. 'Maybe, yes, I must have. It's not something you remember, is it?'

Toni would remember. But she could imagine Ricky forgetting that he'd needed a piss. Ridiculous, but she minded he had been upstairs, that he had gone to her toilet. Ricky would have asked her permission. Karen would said something like 'Help yourself' with her wicked laugh. It felt like a kind of intimacy. She hoped that was all it was.

'Did you use the toilet the night Daniel died?' Malcolm was asking.

'I didn't see Daniel that night. He rang in sick. So, no, I didn't.'

Toni sat up properly. *Daniel Tyler had not been with Ricky on the boat.* She had forgotten that.

'Danny lied to you?'

'I wouldn't call it that. Dan was an honest lad.' Ricky stared up at the camera, perhaps hoping for a message from Toni.

'I'm here, darlin',' she said without thinking.

'... Look, Danny wanted to get on. He was focused on the job. He wouldn't have done anything to mess it up.' Ricky ground to a halt.

Tick. Tick. Tick.

'Daniel Munday lied to you and then he stole his mother's car,' Malcolm said.

23

FREDDY

'It's amazing you all lived in here, it's so poky.' Sarah was cradling Brad the hamster on her lap. He lay on his back like a baby. 'Why didn't your parents move when their business took off?'

'Dad was born here, and my grandfather. He'd say if it was good enough for them, then...' The shout when Reenie had brought up the idea of buying one of the new houses nearer town popped Freddy's eardrums, as if her parents were in the room. Ricky had cried, Andy's hand had found hers, they knew to be silent. Freddy had told Sarah about why she'd gone, but not the rest. Not how Fred lost his temper at the drop of a sharp knife, how he had once grabbed hold of Andy so forcefully he had sprained his arm. 'My son's so clumsy,' he'd laughed as he charmed the hospital staff. Freddy had held her dad's other hand, forcing herself to suck on the lollipop he'd bought her to shore up the image of a loving family man. Now Freddy stole a look at her phone. No text. Had Mags seen her with Sarah and gone away? Better that than Mags had stood her up.

'Those fish are gorgeous colours. What will happen to them now your ma is dead?' Sarah was behaving as if all was normal – death was just another day – a ruse that experience had proved would work.

'They'll go to one of my brothers.' Freddy could return with Sarah to their spacious house on the gated road with Victorian lamp-posts that defied time and the hoi-polloi. She hadn't resigned from Waitrose; she could go back to her beloved fish counter. Many settled for a compromise that lowered the tidemark of happiness but was better than nothing.

'What did you get?'

'Get?' She didn't want Ricky to have the fish. Nor Andy.

'I'm being practical, girlfriend.' The street accent ill fitted the privately educated lawyer. 'Your mum's will – what's your share? Don't tell me the fish tank.'

'Dad disinherited me.' Freddy didn't say how she'd dared hope her mum would call her home. They would sing songs from *The Little Mermaid*, go to Mass on Sea Sundays, dive and soar with the fish in the tank. Freddy had never said how, when Sarah and she were sipping wine on the box-hedge-delineated patio, she'd longed for this grotto. Seabed light drifting through the coloured plastic, the morphing glow of the lava lamps. She and her mum dwelt under the sea in a shell-encrusted world without Fred Power. When the film ended, they'd be sad, as if seeing it for the first time, when Princess Ariel chose to live on land. 'Stupid girl,' Reenie Power would sigh. 'Stupid, stupid girl.'

'You are kidding me?' Sarah broke the reverie. 'You said your father cut you out, but it's your mother who's died.'

'It's what Dad wanted. Mum didn't go against him.'

'That's outrageous. *Stupid woman.*' Sarah put up a vaguely apologetic hand. 'Seriously, we'll contest. Especially if it's an old will and there are no accompanying notes giving any reasoning for the disinheritance. Does it say, "My daughter is a raging dyke so gets nothing"? Mind you, that crap wouldn't be a first,' Sarah raged at Brad the hamster.

'I told you. It was when I came out. Mum was a strict Catholic. Dad used it when it suited him. Give Brad here.' Freddy took the small creature. Animals were promised a tranquil stay at Sunnyside.

'Je-*sus*! Being gay is *not* reasonable? This is *insane*. We could go for the house, a chunk of the business, maybe loss of earnings for the last twenty-two years.' Sarah was off the blocks.

'I don't want to live here.' Freddy nestled Brad in the crook of her neck. He was definitely low, no doubt missing Karen and Daniel. She had always believed that the creatures knew when their holidays would end. Did Brad sense that his family no longer existed?

'Naturally not,' Sarah purred. 'But you could gut it, remodernise and let it to get the costs back, then sell.' She arched her eyebrows at the covered windows. 'We'll argue that your mother should have made reasonable provision for *all* her children.'

Sarah's favourite theme was for Freddy to stop working – as a partner in a law firm, Sarah could support them both – but not to be a housewife: they had Ocado and a cleaner. *Go to uni, use your brain.* This prospect diluted by the stream of spa vouchers, *treat yourself to a massage, it's what you deserve, babes* and the gym membership on birthdays. Sarah wanted a trophy wife, Freddy would tell her when they argued.

'I won't contest the will.' Freddy followed the progress of a rainbow fish. It flicked and darted about Flounder. She wanted to be among the rocks and ornamental sea creatures. This time it wasn't Fred Power she would be escaping from.

24

TONI

Toni stopped outside the Co-op and nearly fell out of the Jeep when a squall of spitting rain whipped the door from her hold. She went into the shop.

The woman on the till had eyes pinned on the lads fussing around the offy section. None looked old enough to brush their teeth on their own, but Toni knew they would be debating which of them got to slip a bottle of spirits down their boxers. Idiots. Their future was clear to see. Off duty, she dipped down the confectionery aisle.

Mars? Snickers? Faced with the array of sweets, she blanked. Crunchie bar? Her blood was zinging, heart rate increasing, practically punching her ribs. The *best* feeling. Toni knew there was a camera above the chiller cabinet that pointed at the sweets. She was blocking its view. From where she stood, she could see that the cashier was concentrating on the kids, who were too stupid to see the CCTV focusing on them from the till. Or that a copper had just walked in.

Since Karen Munday's murder, despite the police with-holding their suspicions, rumour was rife that Karen's son had killed her. All Newhaven's teenagers were deemed the Devil's foot-soldiers.

Toni hadn't waited for Ricky to come out from the interview. She had left before the end. They had him at the crime scene. Either Ricky had gone to the loo or he had murdered Karen. Toni's money was on the former. She trusted Ricky.

Toni was sure Ricky had not touched Karen. The motive simply wasn't there. He had nothing to gain and lots to lose. Ricky had been a natural fisherman, and they didn't grow on trees. Or among the seaweed. That Daniel had become skilled at gutting and scaling didn't go in his favour; although the murder was strangulation, it showed the boy had no difficulty killing and dismembering a creature. Of course, Ricky had that against him, too, but Daniel had motive. Toni wished she could have coached Ricky for his interview. Obviously, he was innocent, but almost because of that, he was wide open to looking as guilty as hell. Malcolm had said everything you did was out of character until you did it. Murder was no exception. Unfairly, she felt cross with Ricky.

Three months off forty, Toni had accepted she'd never do the marriage and kids thing. Not that she'd ever wanted it. You didn't bring a kid into this harsh world and then expose it to grief. Then Ricky Power rocked up. The little brother of one of her best friends had turned into a young Jack Nicholson. Two years in, he'd just broached the idea of living together. She'd said she'd think about it, but both of them kept forgetting to give it airtime. If Toni was honest with herself, she might say that Ricky Power was the best thing to happen to her. But Toni was rarely honest with herself.

Toni opted for a Snickers. Turning her shoulder to the camera for a split second, she took two bars, the action so nifty it was as if the Snickers defied gravity. She flicked a wrist to check her watch and propelled one bar down her sleeve, nearly to the crook of her elbow. She faced the camera and then, on an apparent whim, snatched up a Mars bar. She returned the Snickers in her hand to the shelf in full view of the lens. At the till the woman, labelled 'Trish', was still glaring at the boys.

'Just this.' Toni dropped the Mars bar onto the counter by a charity box for lifeboats. She gave Trish the right money, chucked a couple of pound coins into the box and flashed her badge at her. 'Let me sort this.' She sauntered over to the group.

'If you're planning to wait until you come of age to get that vodka, you've got years yet. Bugger off home to bed, lads.' Toni flipped open her badge wallet.

'You going to arrest us?' The kid could be no more than thirteen, but a knowing look in his eyes and the set of his jaw gave him another decade.

'If you *do* that Smirnoff, I will bang you in solitary until you learn how to do up your shoelaces.' She gave an obese boy – the one she guessed had been nominated to conceal the bottle – a death stare.

He went a dangerous red colour. 'We ain't done nothing.'

'Let's keep it that way.' Toni circled around them as if they were sheep and herded them to the exit. 'It would spoil my evening to have to process you lot down at the nick.' She put her hands on her hips to make the most of her well below intimidating height.

When the kids had gone Toni hung about and exchanged

a few unpleasantries about the youth of today with Trish. Back in the Jeep, she shook her sleeve and palmed the stolen Snickers. She unwrapped it and, eyeballing the boys, still loitering on the corner of Gibbon Road, took a generous bite. Revelling in the sugar rush, she texted Mags, *I've got chocolate.* Then, thinking to appeal to Mags's ever-present guilt, *It's freezing!*

Five minutes later, Toni was trying the bell of Mags's second-floor flat on Fort Road. A light was on.

The Newhaven ferry was in, a giant office block resting on its side, sparkling with lights. Giving up at last, Toni got back in the Jeep. Ricky had texted. Malcolm hadn't charged him. He had to stay in the area in case Malcolm needed to speak with him again. A sad-face emoji. Toni knew that Ricky wasn't a person of interest but, irritated by his unhelpful attitude in the interview, she wasn't ready to put him out of his misery. She called Malcolm.

'If it helps, I believe him, boss. It's a bit staged. If Ricky had murdered Karen, he'd have cleaned the loo handle.'

'In the heat of the moment he might have forgotten?' Toni hazarded.

'From all accounts, Ricky is a thorough man?'

'Yes, he is.' Toni dislodged a chip of peanut from between her teeth. 'Talk to Mo Munday again. What hasn't she told us about Karen? Something trivial she forgot. Track Karen's every step since the convent. Regardless of Ricky, Karen was certainly murdered by someone who knew her. A boyfriend, or more likely Daniel, possibly with help from his girlfriend, Daisy Webb.'

'I'll do it now.' Malcolm was at home; she heard the TV and clattering plates. His eagerness would be relief that, having hung her boyfriend out on a rack, Toni was still speaking to him.

25

FREDDY

'You can't stay here,' Freddy told Sarah.

'Of course not. Let's stay in a hotel tonight.' Sarah looked appalled at the notion that Freddy imagined she'd want to stay. Then, forever the literal devil's advocate, 'Why not?'

'It's my mum's house.' Freddy's solar plexus swooped. God would punish her if her female partner (her *ex*, she reminded herself) slept with her in her parents' home. Her parents, who were *sickened* when she told them she was gay. *I've spawned a monster.* Freddy could hear her dad's shout.

And within days of her mum's burial.

'Your mum is dead. By rights this house is partly yours,' Sarah said.

'It's not right.' Although she had felt flayed by their blinkered – her dad's cruel – response, yet Freddy was bound by their memory.

'Look, I get you feel odd about it. Like I said, this place is a mousehole. We'll go to the Hotel du Vin, there's one in Brighton. I'll pay.' *I'll pay.* Freddy had gone two weeks without hearing those two words.

'There's a Premier Inn at Lewes. It's closer.' Freddy was surprised at herself; faced with a chance of leaving, she felt reluctant.

'OK, we'll go there. Tomorrow I'll dictate Ruth an opening salvo to your brothers. Show them you're not taking this shit lying down.' Sarah's snappy efficiency had been one reason why Freddy had fallen in love with her. Ominously, perhaps, it had reminded her of Fred Power. Unable to sleep upstairs – in her old bedroom – and so curling up with a sleeping bag on the couch each night, Freddy imagined snuggling down in the hotel bed she'd slept in on her first night in Sussex. They could wander into Lewes for breakfast. Then she remembered, 'I've got the pets. Andy asked me to care for them.'

'Tell Andy you've changed your mind. Is the loo outside?' Sarah was making a point. Or no, she seriously thought it was.

'No, upstairs.' Sarah had tracked her to the beach. Freddy imagined what Toni would say about that. Mags too. Freddy checked her phone again. No text. She had the urge to sink her phone in the fish tank but remembered that Sarah had bought her a waterproof device so it wouldn't kill the signal. She could turn it off but then she wouldn't know if Mags had texted.

Sarah's bag lay on the couch. Had she taken her phone to the toilet? Sarah was on twenty-four/seven. Freddy heard the flush go, then the pipes rush with water. She tipped out everything. The phone was last.

Sarah had got herself a personalised phone cover of Freddy licking an ice cream, hair blowing in a breeze. Freddy prayed that Sarah hadn't changed her password. She put in her own birthday and, her heart missing a beat, let her shoulders drop as the home screen came up. Another picture of Freddy. She was freewheeling a bicycle down a country lane with no hands. It was a long time since she'd felt that brilliant.

She heard the lock slide on the door as she located the Find My iPhone app. She bungled the first attempt to delete her number. The door opened as she succeeded. Hastily, Freddy shovelled everything back in her bag. A lipstick rolled onto the carpet. She bent to get it but heard Sarah on the stairs. She had to leave it where it was, in full view under the fish tank.

'Brad has nowhere to go. His owner was – she's died – I'm *not* coming with you.' Nerve-wracked, Freddy was blunter than she'd intended.

'Haven't your brothers inherited your mum's hobby along with rest of her estate?' Sarah peered into the tank as you would into a cesspit.

'It's not... it wasn't a hobby, it was – *is* – a business.'

'At this point, until we get to work, it's not *your* business.' Sarah's shoe was an inch from the lipstick.

'I'm looking after Brad.' Freddy couldn't begin to express how she owed it to Karen to care for her pet. Nor that she cared not a jot about her mum's money. She had to stay to see Mags.

'Don't expect me to stay with you.' Sarah would turn an argument on its head so that, if Freddy wasn't watchful, she'd be fighting in the wrong corner. Was it coercive control? Sarah had described the characteristics during her defence of a woman in a divorce case. The man managed his wife's bank account, made friends with her boss and found fault with her friends so that she stopped seeing them. Sarah hadn't done that. Freddy hadn't made friends, not ones like Toni. When other relationships had ended, their friends had taken her ex's sides. Freddy handled her own money, at least when Sarah let her spend it. Freddy could stand up for herself.

'Don't do anything about the will until I say so.' Under cover of being nice, Freddy came over to the aquarium. As Sarah put her arms around her waist, Freddy kicked the lipstick out of sight.

'Can I do a little draft?' A baby voice. They both knew Sarah didn't need Freddy's permission.

'Don't do a bloody thing.' Freddy lost her cool.

'I'm on your side, babes. We compensate for each other's weaknesses, remember? It's why it works.' Sarah stroked Freddy's hair from her face. Over Sarah's shoulder, Freddy saw Sarah's phone half out of her bag.

'What are your weaknesses?' she said quickly.

'You.' Sarah hugged her closer.

'Apart from me.'

'I can't swim?' Sarah was having trouble – weaknesses were not her strong point. 'OK.' She snatched up her phone. She was brisk. 'I'm out of here.' She let go of Freddy and strode across the cramped room, narrowly avoiding stepping on Mikolaj the rabbit nibbling a carrot by the couch, grabbed her bag and swung it onto her shoulder. 'I'll make it work, I promise.'

'Yes, I know you will.' Euphoric at having got away with it, Freddy babbled the opposite of what she meant.

And, as she closed the door on Sarah, she wistfully recalled their life. Her regulars at Waitrose's fish counter, the Sunday brunches in the deli, evenings with the telly, *Poldark*, *Gentleman Jack* and reruns of *E.R.*

Freddy was startled by a knock. She flipped open the pet register. No one was expected. Had Sarah discovered the phone tampering?

Was it Mags?

'Hello, you. I'm betting it's still your favourite.' Toni was brandishing a bottle of Jack Daniel's. 'I seriously didn't expect you'd be here. Weren't you leaving after the funeral?'

'I'm leaving when the animals are sorted.' Freddy made the decision then and there. She got glasses and poured drinks. 'Or rather when Roddy goes home.' Freddy glanced at Roddy. He was basking in the underwater glow of the room in his cage. Unnerved by David Bromyard, she'd paid him little attention. 'When I've found a home for Brad. Do you think Mo Munday would have him?'

'I'll get Malcolm to ask.' Toni tilted her glass at Roddy. 'And I know what you are, not an effing degu, Fred. What about that time one escaped while you were cleaning out the cage? Took us flippin' hours to catch him. Then the bugger bit you. Seriously, what is the point of a pet who won't be cuddled and flies about like a racing car? Ricky wants a dog, but he's away too much to make it work.' Freddy saw Toni regret mentioning Ricky. However, since Mags had failed to show at the battery that evening, Freddy no longer minded about her brother and her friend.

'He belongs to a creepy friend of my dad.' Hardly fair; Bromyard wasn't creepy. Or was he? She had a sudden flash of her dad and Bromyard, whispering in the fishery. 'It's weird because this man – David was his name – claimed me and Dad went on his boat when I was little. I do have a half-memory of going out on a trawler once, but Dad said he got seasick.'

'Seasick?' Toni was ogling Roddy as if daring him to escape. 'Ricky has never said. Odd for a man whose whole life revolved around fish.'

'If it was true.' Freddy surprised herself.

'Why lie?'

'So he could meet people secretly on a boat.' A theory around quotas began to form. Far from feeling guilty, Freddy felt excited now that she had told Toni.

'Oh what, an alibi in reverse? Whatever happened aboard a trawler couldn't have been your dad because he'd have been hanging over the side?'

'Maybe.' Freddy could tell Toni wasn't interested. Her eyes glittered like one of her dares.

'Have you seen Mags?'

'We were supposed to meet at the battery earlier tonight. She never came.' Freddy felt herself flush, Toni had come to check on Freddy's plans. *For Mags.* Freddy felt a rush of misery. With Sarah there she'd not had a chance to feel the weight of the reality. Mags had not wanted to see her.

'Oh, I'm sorry.' Toni was a proficient liar – she always convinced the nuns she was a good Catholic to get out of a scrape. 'I dropped by this evening; her light was on, but no answer. I didn't call first and we both know Mags hates the unexpected, more so than ever, I'd say. She seemed a bit out of sorts when I saw her yesterday.' Toni dipped a finger in the Jack Daniel's and licked it, an old habit. 'It's weird, though, she was definite about seeing you, said she wanted to tell you something.'

'Tell me what?' Mags *had* intended to come. Freddy felt elation. You should never rush to judgement.

'Believe me, I tried to worm it out of her. Mags had been to the church. I made some lame crack about confession which, turned out was what she'd been doing. Classic Antonia.' Toni sucked an ice cube. 'Wish I'd pushed her now. Silly Mags, she's always feeling guilty about something.'

Freddy felt ridiculously happy. Toni wasn't there as a spy for Mags. She must be there for herself.

'She never did want to meet.' Freddy woke Brad and extracted him from his cage, nestling him against her chest. Mad to hope that Mags felt guilty that she hadn't left with Freddy when they were eighteen. Freddy downed the Jack Daniel's.

'Are you still interested in her?' Toni seemed untypically tentative.

'I'm in a relationship.' Freddy poured herself another drink, although her glass wasn't empty. She tipped the bottle at Toni, who shook her head. Her glass, hardly touched, was on the fish-shaped table Andy had made in woodwork. She hadn't taken it in until now. That he'd been skilled with wood had meant nothing to their dad.

'Good for you. That's great.' Toni looked disappointed. Not that good a liar, it seemed. 'I suppose that stuff with Mags is water under the whatsit now.'

'You just missed Sarah.' Freddy ducked the question. She wondered again how it was for Toni when Freddy and Mags got together. Had she minded being left out? For Freddy they were still the Mermaids; nothing had changed. *And everything had changed.*

'Sometimes I can barely manage to be civil to your bro, let alone an ex.'

'Mags wasn't an ex. We never had a relationship,' Freddy reminded her.

'You were in love, you did the deed – how was that not a relationship?' Toni's cool attitude had normalised Freddy's passion for Mags. She had made it possible for Freddy, if not finally for Mags. Freddy felt bad for not being nice about Toni and Ricky. She owed her. 'Mags didn't call it a relationship.'

'Well, see, Mags is one tortured soul. Faced with a choice between you and God, she chose wrong. That Julian of Norfolk, half dead and hallucinating, has a lot to answer for. Mags still reads her. But for Julian, you and Mags would be married.' Toni came over and began stroking Brad.

'Norwich.'

'Granted.' Toni grinned at her.

'You think we'd be married now?'

'Totally. You are made for each other. I thought so then and, honestly, I still do. Mags needs you. You would give her a spark she's never dared have for herself and she'd keep you grounded, secure. If you could only keep that Julian from sticking her wimple in.' Toni gave a hearty laugh.

'Thanks, Toni.' Freddy was stunned; it meant everything that Toni thought this. And she was spot on about Julian of Norwich. At the convent Freddy had been jealous of the medieval saint to whom Mags had been unashamedly devoted.

'Andy made that, didn't he?' Toni was looking at the fish-shaped coffee table.

'Yes, he was brilliant with wood.'

'I know. Remember that time he brought home a little stool he'd made for Ricky? He was showing it to your mum when your dad blew in, raging, wanting to know why Andy hadn't cleaned out the crates like he was supposed to. I've never been so scared in my life, which is saying something.'

'He burnt it,' Freddy said quietly.

'Jesus.' Toni looked away. 'Ricky doesn't really talk about all that stuff.'

'Ricky was probably in bed. Besides, Dad was always nice to him.' Freddy sighed. 'Andy offered to rent this place to me. Let me do the fish round. I said no.'

'If it's because of Ricky, I can talk to him.'

'I need to get away from here.'

'I get that.' Toni continued stroking Brad.

'Yup.' Freddy rubbed her hands with cold. Although the flames had dwindled, the room was hot and stuffy. Flounder was gazing at her from his rock in the fish tank. 'I wouldn't mind keeping the fish, though.'

'The fish? You should get a share of the damn fishery! And this place.' Toni slapped a hand on the couch, startling Brad. 'Your father should never have cut you off and your mother should have changed her will the minute he died!'

'You said yourself it's Andy and Ricky who've slaved in the fishery. It's not fair to waltz back as if I was never away.'

'Fred told you never to darken his door. What choice did you have?' Toni had got out a Snickers bar and was pecking at it as if she didn't really want it. 'You know Fred Power told Ricky that you didn't give a toss about your brothers, that you thought the fishery was beneath you and you wanted a better life?'

'He lied! I never said anything like that.' Freddy's eyes pricked. She didn't want to cry in front of Toni.

'Well, I know that.' Toni's cheek bulged like Brad's. 'But I couldn't tell Ricky the truth, could I? Not without asking you first. But it makes me angry. Catholicism has a lot to answer for. Refusing to grant happiness to anyone who isn't straight. The church of the poisoned mind.'

'Don't blame it on religion. Dad could have been an atheist and he'd have still been a bigot. He couldn't face that I was a lesbian and therefore, in his eyes, far from perfect. Mum wouldn't have cared except that she was frightened of contradicting him.'

Toni screwed up the chocolate wrapper. 'I wish you'd tell Andy and Ricky the truth.'

'I thought they knew why he kicked me out, and they just didn't care.' All those years, Freddy had believed her brothers had abandoned her. She had assumed that her father had at least told them the truth. But it was the other way around. She had abandoned them.

'No. They never knew.' Toni kept her eyes on Brad. 'Who is this Sarah?'

'My partner.' A couple of hours ago she'd told Sarah it was over. Did Sarah keep her grounded? Secure? 'Sarah's a defence lawyer. She wants to fight my case and get me a share of the fishery.'

'From a saint to the Devil.' The profession was not a good fit with a police detective. 'Sarah has a point.'

'I am not suing my brothers.' Freddy splashed in Jack Daniel's and again offered the bottle. Toni put her hand over her glass.

'At least tell them the truth. You owe them that.'

'I don't know, Toni. It's not only my secret. There's Mags. Maybe it's best if they keep thinking I left for my own reasons.'

'You don't have to name names.'

'Andy would guess. Ricky would ask you and, if he did, would you lie to him? I wouldn't want you to.'

'At least let me put in a good word for you with Ricky.' It was brilliant that Toni wanted to fight her corner. *Toni was still a Mermaid.*

Freddy smiled and tipped her glass at the tank. 'Get Ricky to let me have those fish and your job is done.'

'I could have a word with Mags too.' Toni was on a roll. She got up and paced about the room.

'No, leave Mags.' The drink had kicked in and Freddy felt jaded. The Mermaids were three women who'd chosen different seas.

'There it is.' Toni paused by the television. 'Reenie always made Andy's kids watch it.' Toni waved a copy of *The Little Mermaid*. A DVD, not the video of Freddy's day; the tape had snapped after so many plays.

'It bored them silly, no sex and no violence.' Toni was at the door. 'But really it was just an excuse for your mum to watch it. She told Mags it reminded her of us three girls and when you were small. How we Mermaids invented a new ending where she doesn't kiss that dim prince but continues to live under the sea with Flounder and Sebastian. That's why I'm gobsmacked Reenie didn't change her will.'

'Was Mags really here a lot then?' Freddy felt woozy; she rarely drank.

'She did lots round the edges of the care. The commode, concocting tempting suppers, washing. Made me look like a right bitch. I'd turn up empty-handed and be out in five! Kirsty was as bad, thank God.'

After Toni had gone, Freddy poured another drink. She could consign herself to oblivion. She prised open the DVD cassette. It was empty.

Freddy knelt by the DVD player and pressed 'eject'. Out came *The Little Mermaid*. Pushing in the tray, she bundled Brad up to her cheek, her nose buried in his sweet hay-scented fur, and settled back to watch.

26

FREDDY

Despite dating from the Victorian era, Newhaven cemetery wasn't an ivy-clad jungle of Gothic statuary and chunky mausoleums. It covered an open hillside, shaded by one yew tree beyond which swathes of grass awaited the dead still living. Ranks of low-slung headstones, heart-shaped, teddy-bear-shaped, some with photographs of those within the grave. Others scattered with toys and ornaments, windmills, gnomes, miniature picket fences. All reminiscent of a sprawling yet homely suburbia.

Toni left the car by the statue of the boy and, skirting the chapel, made for the far reaches of the cemetery. There, most graves dated from the early twentieth century, with row upon row of war graves, the light sandstone contrasting with the dark marble of civilian monuments. Toni stopped by a lone headstone in the shadow of a beech tree. An outpost of the dead.

Nicholas Kemp 1948–1991

Forever in our hearts
Safe with Jesus

Flaking stone had erased the capital N of Nicholas and
the J for Jesus.

Thirteen-year-old Toni had kept it to herself that she had
wanted *Come Back* on her father's epitaph. Safe with bloody
Jesus – what sort of God had let her dad be killed like that?
At the time, Mags, desperate to bring Toni back from her
living tomb, said it wasn't simple. God created humans who
sinned and could be forgiven. For Toni it was simple. Jesus
suffered on the cross for our sins, so why didn't that let her
dad off? She wanted no one forgiven. What was simple was
that there was no God.

Mags had assured her that God would remain with her
until one day her belief would reignite. This had been during
Mags's insufferable period, when, as if she had a direct line
to the Almighty, she spouted pious crap.

Toni did not believe in God, but she had grown to be
grateful for Mags's assurance that Nicholas (Nicky) Kemp
was in Heaven. A better vision than that his flesh was rotting
under the ground. Seeing Freddy make the sign of the cross
over Reenie Power's grave, Toni had wondered if Freddy's
faith (lost when she came out) had reignited. But her visit to
her last night had put her straight. Freddy's only faith was
in Mags. Unfortunately, Toni thought as she knelt at her
father's grave, that faith might be misplaced. Toni doubted
that Mags would ever come to terms with her feelings for
Freddy. Her Catholicism was entrenched; it was too big an

obstacle. She appeared to have stood Freddy up the other night and was probably avoiding her until Freddy finally left Newhaven.

Nicholas Kemp 1948–1991. Two police officers had sat Toni and her sister, Amy, in the living room and given them mugs of hot chocolate, like they were kids. Toni had been outraged, but unable to resist the rich chocolatey smell.

'Antonia, you must be very grown up and look after your sister and your mum…'

Toni had been aware only of the sickly-sweet drink scalding her tongue and the blue of their uniforms. A Pavlovian moment because in her last year at the convent, drinking a hot chocolate in a café, she'd determined to join the police.

'Hi, Dad. Remember that girl at the convent?' Toni checked she was alone. She was in the habit of telling her dad (a criminal lawyer) her latest case out loud.

A grassy mound with no flowers or plants, the grave was low maintenance. Toni left the few flowering weeds, which her dad, a hiker over the South Downs, would have appreciated. Her dad's final resting place on a hill above the sea had, over the years, lessened the memory of his violent end. The milkman had stabbed him through the heart with a broken milk-bottle. All because her dad had queried the order.

Toni removed a pot with a dead azalea she'd brought for his birthday in January. She was Nicholas Kemp's only visitor.

Burial hadn't been the Kemp family's preferred method of interment. Appalled by his murder – for the price of a gold top – the community had collected for a lavish interment with a double grave so that one day the grieving widow would be reunited with her husband. A day unlikely to come. Katy Kemp had remarried and moved to New York with her American husband. Toni's sister, Amy, was a Buddhist in Scotland. In between her sports massage practice, Amy went on so many retreats that, Toni quipped to Ricky, soon she'd disappear.

'If you remember, I was at school with Karen. She was a bitch... that's not swearing, she was. Teacher's pet with Sister Verruca. She got away with murd— all sorts.'

In the sun's glare, Toni saw someone under the chapel arch. She scrambled up and hid behind the tree, although from this distance it was unlikely that she was visible.

As she watched, the person took the central path, coming closer but still a good hundred yards from where she stood. Toni disliked being seen at the cemetery. Her grief was private. Then the person – a man, she thought – moved away, crossing the rows of graves diagonally. He was heading for the top of the hill, where the graves were sparse. He was going to where Reenie Power had been buried.

Close to the boundary hedge, Toni kept parallel. She drew closer and, when she was as near as she dared be, she opened her phone's camera and took a photograph. She enlarged the image. She could make out Reenie's plaque on the temporary cross and the wilting bouquets clustered on the heaped earth. And Ricky.

Toni felt a rush of love. She started towards the grave. When Ricky had asked her to come with him to his mum's grave, she'd reminded him she had a murder case on and suggested he went on his own. Which, on reflection, had been unkind. She'd seen he looked nervous. Here he was, actually shaking with grief, holding onto the cross as if he might fall over otherwise. She blundered over the grass towards him.

Because he was out on the trawler day and night, the tips of Ricky's dark hair had been bleached auburn by the sun. She often teased him about his expensive highlights. Toni stopped. The man now openly weeping by Reenie's grave had short dark hair. It was Andy Power.

Throughout his mother's illness, Andy had been Mr Practical, covering all angles, booking carers, liaising with the hospice and with Mags. He'd set up a visiting rota. He'd been one step ahead, even organising her funeral before Reenie died. A step too far, Ricky said, although Toni was with Andy on that one. All the time Andy kept the business going, Ricky was the one who seemed to be falling apart.

Now, Andy was sobbing his heart out over his mum's floral tributes. Any other place and Toni might have applauded the fact that he wasn't made of stone and, like Ricky, missed his mum. All she knew right now was that Andy must not see her. Andy could provide the sympathetic shoulder, but he'd be mortified if it was the other way around.

She backed away, willing him not to turn. She skirted the hedge and headed back to the safety of her dad's grave.

When she finally reached the car, Toni swore under her breath. Andy would have seen it. There couldn't be many with a nearly new Jeep Renegade in the area. Andy had said at the time that she'd wasted her money. But surely if he had seen the Jeep and thought she was in the cemetery, he'd have left.

Malcolm's call came in as Toni was pulling into the police station car park.

'Guv, we've got a witness, lives on the other side of Karen's house. She says she heard Daniel and his mum going at it hammer and tongs on the night they died. Apparently, he called her a whore.'

'Why didn't she come forward before?'

'She said they were always rowing so she thought nothing of it. Although he'd never used, as she put it, such filthy language before, it never occurred to her that Daniel was a suspect.'

'Even though the local paper was calling him "the Boy Killer"?' Toni never ceased to be amazed by Other People.

'I got the impression she doesn't go out much. I went to her house; there's no telly and more books than a library.'

'Did she notice any strange men? Any men at all?'

'A man whose description fitted Ricky. She said he never got out of his car, he was dropping off the nice young man, as she put it. No one else, but I didn't get the sense she's the nosy neighbour type.'

Toni took the stairs two at a time. Bursting into CID, she got Malcolm in stereo – over the phone and in front of her, where he was hunched over his desk. '...It's pointing towards Daniel. We have him at the scene and it explains his crazy driving. Yes, there's Ricky's fingerprint, but he had a reason to be in the house.'

'This case is closing itself,' Toni agreed. Malcolm swivelled around in his seat and chucked down the phone. 'Daniel – and perhaps Daisy – administered their own capital punishment.'

'Wouldn't you say that Ricky was scared in that interview? Innocent scared not guilty scared. I don't think it's him.' Malcolm continued, 'Daniel murdered his mother in what amounts to a glorified domestic. A cliché of a tragedy.' He abruptly zipped his chair across to the murder wall and, rising, tore down Daniel's boy pop star picture. He sat looking at it.

'I can see it.' Sheena got up from her corner. 'He bears her a grudge, grumbling away at him. Probably something stupid like wanting driving lessons, or to sleep with his lassie. His hormones are raging. Against his mother, against his boss. Sorry, guv, but being realistic, maybe he wasn't as happy working with Ricky as Ricky was with him.'

'We get used to seeing all sorts in the force.' Toni's lips pursed to stop the words *Shut up, Sheena* escaping. The woman got to her.

'It's a terrible thing for a boy to go to the bad like that.' Malcolm was still looking at Daniel's picture. Toni remembered that, while looking like a teenager himself, Malcolm's own son was Daniel's age.

A speedy wrap-up was good for the team. Good for her record too. Later, when Toni was booking the pub's function room to celebrate the end of the case, she reflected how, once upon a time, she'd have thought the world a better place without Karen Munday. Now, she would give anything for Karen and Daniel to still be living in that little house by the port.

27

FREDDY

A wave smashed against the stone pier, the explosive spray obliterating the lighthouse and sending pebbles spraying like bullets over the esplanade. In gaps between onslaughts came the cry of the wind. A seagull blown off course recovered itself and swooped away over cliffs. The horizon was fuzzy grey. Sky and sea the same.

Extreme weather inevitably attracted amateur photographers to the coast willing to dice with mortality for the perfect shot. Today the only person braving the beach carried no camera. They stumbled blindly in the lee of the cliffs.

Freddy avoided the chunks of chalk that signalled the likelihood of more rockfalls. She'd put Sarah off for two days with the excuse that she needed space. She'd expected Sarah to argue – turn up on the doorstep – but Sarah had said she'd use the time to catch up on work. If she hadn't been relieved, this might have roused Freddy's suspicion.

Freddy had come back to the battery. She hadn't admitted – it was, after all, absurd – that she harboured the hope of finding Mags. Toni's visit on Saturday night had brought alive their Mermaid days at the convent. That easy camaraderie, shared humour, shared experiences. Freddie didn't have to describe her dad to Toni. She knew.

Freddy couldn't leave Newhaven until she'd seen Mags. That morning she had plucked up her courage and gone to the library to suggest they have lunch. Only to find it was closed. She'd peered in at the glass doors either side of the building but seen no staff inside. Mags hadn't answered the buzzer to her flat either, even though Freddy was sure that she could see a light on inside. Neither had Mags replied to Freddy's texts. Freddy couldn't face the possibility that Mags's silence meant she wanted to be left alone.

Freddy gravitated to the lunette battery because, apart from the church, where else could she go? She had not gone to the church for fear of having to explain herself to Father Pete. The battery was where, in the dusk of a summer evening twenty-two years ago, she and Mags had done, as Toni had put it, the deed. They'd consummated their love. Freddy winced. *Love?* The last thing Mags had said to her on the day she'd left Newhaven was that they had committed a terrible sin.

In daylight Freddy could see pools of brackish water on the floor of the battery. The walls were slimed with seaweed. Pressing her face to the grille, she found some shelter from the deafening tumult. As a girl, Mags had imagined the wind's shrill whistle was the song of mermaids. Toni had said surf booming against the wall was the Devil's drumbeat. Toni always brought the Devil into it.

I love you, Freds. Mags had cradled Freddy's head in her lap, stroking her hair, while Freddy pretended to be dead.

No one else called her Freds. From that day, their friendship had segued into being lovers. At first, necessarily clandestine, it had been exciting. The heightened emotion dictated by secrecy was a drug of which Freddy couldn't get enough. Without external opinion, their relationship was free from expectation; there had been none of that awkwardness with Rob from the youth club when each date was expected to end with clumsy kissing and groping. Had Mags been a boy, Freddy's mum would have approved of their old-fashioned courting. But the fun of the hidden wore off and hindsight had shown Freddy it was toxic. A love kept secret feels barely true.

That summer, the landscape golden in the setting sun, the sea a deep azure, Freddy's life changed for ever. When she saw her for one last time, Freddy would ask Mags how happiness could be a sin.

Something lay on the pebbles beyond the battery. A baby seagull storm-tossed from its nest, wing flapping. Freddy swallowed hard as she struggled towards it. She hated creatures to be hurt. Nearing it, she saw it wasn't a bird, but a takeaway wrapper.

Ever trying new apps, Sarah had added a litter-spotting app to Freddy's phone. You snapped discarded crisp packets and uploaded the location onto a nationwide database. The idea was to shame manufacturers into reducing their plastic packaging.

Eyes smarting in the salty air, Freddy was bent on achieving one good deed. It didn't measure up to working in a soup kitchen, but might at least make her feel better. Freddy pushed against the wind, willing the rubbish not to whirl away before she reached it.

Freddy crouched on the wet pebbles. It wasn't rubbish. It was a book, pages flapping in the wind, not a broken wing. *Revelations of Divine Love*. Freddy knew the author only too well. Julian of Norwich. The saint who Toni reckoned Mags had chosen over Freddy.

Pocketing her phone, Freddy gingerly examined the book. It was the same as the edition given out at Our Lady which Freddy had inadvertently abandoned on a train while they were still at school. Not exactly beach reading, and not in a ten-force gale. Who had dropped it? Several pages were mended with Sellotape, which had cracked and yellowed. The pages, damp and crinkled, bulked up the slim volume. If it had been washed up on the tide, it would have fallen apart. A hardback, it must have been dropped near where Freddy had found it, beyond the reach of the tide.

There were initials on the fly leaf. *MPTM*. Freddy sat back on the shingle heavily. Margaret Pauline Theresa McKee. It was Mags's actual copy. The paper was damp. Not wet.

Mags must have dropped the book recently.

An elderly black woman was replenishing the votive candles. Freddy could see at once that Mags wasn't in the church, but it felt rude to walk straight out again. She wandered up to the altar, suddenly aware of all the times she had come here. The lingering smell of incense, the musty prayer books – the place was part of her. How often had she received the host and felt blessed by the warm touch of the priest's finger on her forehead? She recalled the sensation of her dad holding her up to kiss the feet of Jesus on the cross held by the priest. Her mum forbade her to kiss the wood because of germs. When Freddy was a teenager, a deacon was ready with a disinfected cloth to wipe after the touch of the congregation's lips. Freddy and her mum kept to air-kissing.

The confessional was no longer used – for safeguarding reasons – but Freddy still imagined the dark box, light filtering through the grille, where every Christmas and Easter she confessed how she hated Ricky for messing with her make-up or her dad for hitting Andy. She made up false sins for Andy so he had something to tell the priest, usually Andy refusing to share sweets. Andy shared everything with her and had nothing to confess. But that would have made Fred Power even more angry with him.

Newhaven had a long Catholic history. A couple of saints' relics were locked away and brought out on saint's days. Statuettes of saints and tableaux illustrating the stations of the cross were fixed to the walls. This was where Freddy would find Mags.

The woman, in her sixties, her greying hair trimmed short, nodded a greeting at Freddy. She placed a last candle in the rack and, taking a container holding spent night-lights, went off to the vestry.

Two candles were newly lit. One was burning down. It could have been because Freddy was in the church where she'd spent her formative years or that she was clutching the damp volume by Julian of Norwich, but she was prompted to light a candle. Dropping a couple of pounds in the box, she took a wax spill, held it to the flame of one of the lighted candles and put it to the wick of another candle. It was for her mum. She executed the sign of the cross and blew out the spill.

She sat in the front pew and, hands clasped, gazed up at the carved rendition of the Passion.

'It's good to see you again, Frederica.' It was Father Pete. Perhaps seeing Freddy's expression, he said, 'I'm sorry to interrupt, I keep doing this.'

'I'm not really... no, you don't.' Ludicrous to say she wasn't really there. Nor could she tell him that her faith was battered. She was only there to find the woman she used to be in love with.

'You're reading Mother Julian.' Father Pete indicated the book on her lap. Was there astonishment in his tone?

'No!' Freddy slapped the cover. 'It's not mine. I mean, I have my own copy – *had*. I lost it.' She felt herself redden. *What the hell.* Father Pete was an ordinary bloke in his fifties, not God himself. 'I was looking for Mags, Margaret McKee. She goes to this – comes to this church.'

'I know Mags,' he said.

'She's not at work. Or her flat. We arranged to meet and she never came.' Freddy blurted it all out.

'Are you worried about her?'

It was polite of him to take her seriously, but Freddy was embarrassed. Mags had been living happily for over twenty years without her. Why be worried? Mags must be in her flat and was ignoring the door and Freddy's texts. Mags was probably wondering what more she had to do before Freddy got the message.

'No. Yes. Well, it's not like her.' *What was Mags like?* 'I heard she came to confession. I hope... hope she's all right.'

'If you'd like to talk any time, you know I'm here.' He gave nothing away.

'I'm fine. In fact, I'm leaving in a couple of days. Like you said, I'm free to go where I like.' Freddy thrust out the book. 'Please, could you give this to Mags? It was on the beach. Where we were going to meet. At the lunette battery where we used to... Please say I found it. No, don't say that. Please would you return it?' Flustered, she got to her feet and did something between a curtsy and a stumble as she left the pew.

'Why don't you give it to Mags yourself? When you see her.' Father Pete didn't take the book. 'It would be a reason to talk.'

'Did she mention me?' Freddy was so surprised by his last comment that the question shot out. 'Forget I said that.' She hugged the book.

'I hope you'll come again. Perhaps with Mags?' he said.

With Mags. *Did he know?*

Outside, a stiff breeze off the River Ouse lifted her fringe. There was a salty tang in the air. She looked up at the church. Yes, the pinkish roof tiles and decorative motifs around the porch were a kind of home.

She had Julian's *Revelations of Divine Love*. She wished Father Pete had taken the book; it felt wrong to keep it, as if she'd stolen it. Freddy no longer knew Mags and, unless they could meet, had no way of getting to know her.

A seagull's call was answered by the desolate hoot of the ferry plying the heavy swell towards France.

Freddy separated the damp pages, careful not to tear the paper. Sentences had been highlighted, no surprise; as well as devout, Mags had been a bit of a swot. At random, she read one of the highlighted passages:

For since I have set right what was the greatest harm, it

is my will that you should know by this that I shall set right
all that is less harmful...

Had Mags caused harm? Freddy could answer that.

28

TONI

Toni carried the glasses to the table to the usual steady handclap from her team. Three pints of Guinness, two lagers, two glasses of red and six bags of crisps, the last held between clenched teeth. With a skill born of practice she put down each glass without spilling a drop.

'You're too cool,' Malcolm shouted over raucous cheers. He tossed her a five-pound note and, raising one of the lagers, drank it long, to more handclaps. Toni was relieved when he stopped after half of the pint. Malcolm Lane wasn't one of those blokes and she didn't want him trying.

The team were in Tarring Neville instead of their local in Newhaven. Toni reckoned it more sensitive, in a town grieving over two deaths in one night, a mother and her son, to drink a glass or ten in honour of closing a case in a village a couple of miles away. She'd put her card behind the bar and got in orders of ribs, fresh fish and bowls of chips.

'To good old-fashioned coppering!' Malcolm bellowed. Toni sipped her Merlot.

'It might not have been Daniel Tyler,' Sheena piped up.

'Meaning?' Questioning the solve was step one in sending Sheena right back to Police Scotland.

'Meaning *nothing*.' Malcolm would guess that Sheena was pissing off her boss. He knew more than anyone that, with a few drinks inside her, Toni's charm could go walkabout.

'We never got a bead on that man who visited Karen late one night.' Sheena was fearless. A quality Toni admired, just not now.

'You seemed pretty sure earlier,' Toni reminded her.

'I am sure, just raking through the coals.' Sheena gave a lazy-cat smile over the rim of her large glass of Malbec. 'All the same, if you believe that witness, Mrs Haskins, Karen had a new man every night. But what if there was a man? If that's what drove Daniel nuts. And if she did have a bloke, then who is he?'

'We can't chase ghosts, we barely have the resources for positive sightings.' Toni took a gulp of wine; ignoring her dentist's warnings of staining your teeth, she held it in her mouth, savouring the rich, mellow taste. They had chalked up a solve in record time. Sheena wasn't going to put a damper on things.

'Good work, everyone.' Eyes on Sheena, Malcolm clashed his half-drunk lager against her glass. 'Sheena, you going back to that second neighbour clinched it.'

'Thanks, sir.' Sheena sipped her wine.

The next hour passed in a cheery blur of small talk – footy, kids, Sheena's passion for off-road cycling – with glasses never allowed to stay empty.

'Toni.'

Toni twisted around in her chair. Freddy Power was at the door.

She pushed aside chairs to get to her, disasters unspooling in her mind. Ricky was fishing. The weather was terrible. She hadn't wanted him to go.

'Is Ricky here?' Freddy scowled at the room.

'He's out on the boat. Why, what's happened?' Toni felt the floor tip. The wine was acid in her stomach. She hated it when Ricky was at sea. He diced with death every time he raised the anchor. Or loosed the rope.

'That's good. He would tell you not to listen to me.' Freddy looked wild, her hair mussed, cheeks blotched with the cold. 'It's Mags. She's missing.'

'Take a breath, Fred. Missing how?'

'Missing as in not *anywhere*. What other kind is there?' Behind her Toni was aware of a lull in the chat. 'She hasn't replied to my messages. I've called round to her flat.'

'Did you try the library? Or maybe she's gone away.'

'Yes, of course I did: the library, the church, her flat – if she'd gone on holiday, she'd have told you.'

'I doubt it. Mags has always been a devoutly dark horse.' Toni was sorry. After all that, Mags had bottled out of seeing Freddy.

'You're thinking Mags doesn't want to see me. But she didn't open the door to you either.' Freddy thrust out her hand. 'Then I found this.'

'*Revelations of Divine Love*.' Toni read the book's title, although she'd seen it only last Friday and knew it from the convent.

'It belongs to Mags. I found it at the battery.'

'She probably dropped it.' The floating sensation

increasing, Toni leaned on the back of a chair. It was a while since she'd put so much booze away. She brushed at Freddy's coat. 'Freddy, maybe let Mags sort herself out, yeah? Give her space? Tell you what, come over and have a drink with the guys. We closed the Munday murder this afternoon. You'll hear soon enough, her boy did it. Be great to introduce that lot to my oldest mate.'

'You're not listening.' Freddy could be scary when riled, but Toni – and Mags – had always been impervious. 'We were meant to meet. Mags didn't come.'

'Yes, I know, but well…' How to put it? *You stir up too much stuff that Mags doesn't want to face.*

'It's got Mags's initials. See?' Freddy stabbed at the writing in the book with a finger.

The letters swam. Just how pissed Toni was sank in. Sheena's doubt about the case niggled. Mentally, Toni ticked off the evidence. *The solve was solid.*

'Toni?' Freddy shouted above the hubbub from the table. 'Are you listening?'

'What do you want me to do?' The only other time Toni had been this drunk was after her dad died. She'd drunk the rest of his whisky and been sick in the garden.

'What do you usually do when someone goes missing?'

'It depends on their age, if there's a threat to life… Look, it's far more likely Mags'll have gone away.' Toni caught sight of Julian of Norwich's face on the book. Mona Lisa lips, eyes inviting salvation. 'Maybe to Lourdes.'

'It's not funny!' Freddy thundered. 'If you won't do anything, I *will*.' She pivoted on her heel and left. Toni was about to follow when Malcolm called.

'Settle this for us, guv!'

'What?' Toni went back to the team.

'Where is Kiev? Sheena says it's in Russia, Tommo reckons Romania. I've got a fiver on Poland. Winner takes all.' Malcolm raised his eyebrows at her in case she'd missed his hint to say Poland. Toni wasn't in the mood to lie.

'Ukraine.' She reached over Malcolm for her coat. 'I'm done in, going to hit the sack. Good work, y'all. Add that to my winnings.' She tossed in fifty quid and went to the bar to settle up her card.

Occasional headlights on the A26 pierced the darkness. Sobered by the fresh air and unwilling to call a taxi, Toni set off along the verge, the glow of the Newhaven incinerator her lode star.

29

MAGS

'"...all grew dark around me in the room, as though it had been night, except for the image of the cross in which I saw a light for all mankind..."'

The voice in her head broke off. For the first time, Mother Julian offered no comfort. Mags couldn't embrace death as Julian had. She did not want to see Christ. She wanted to be in her living room, warm and safe. Tears coursed down her cheeks. Fear, a terrible gnawing, tore up her insides and strangled the breath from her. *Freddy.*

She lay on her side, her face against rough stone floor. Her hands and feet were bound tightly. Shapes floated in the darkness. The air was cold and damp. She smelled the sea. Heard waves smashing on the beach. Groggily, her head hurting, her cheek pressing down, Mags pieced together snippets of memory. She had been meeting Freddy. She had hidden in the battery. She had had something to tell Freddy. *What was it?*

That was it. She was in the battery. She had gone inside to hide. She had slipped and been knocked unconscious.

Freddy had come and, not finding Mags, gone away. *Why had she wanted to hide from Freddy?* Cowardly. She couldn't have been hiding from Freddy. She had wanted to tell her that what she had done – or not done – had been for the best. The best for who?

Mags had lost track of time. How long had she been there? Who had shut her in? She had never imagined it was possible to be frightened and feel sorry for yourself at the same time. She should not feel sorry for herself. She had meddled where she had no business. This was her punishment.

She succeeded in lifting her head and felt something drop. The merest sound, a chink. She shuffled into a sitting position and, leaning back, managed to scrabble with her fingers. She felt a tiny, hard object.

It was her crucifix. Her captor must have ripped it from her neck when he overpowered her. Mags was overwhelmed with devastation. God had abandoned her.

Freddy wouldn't know that Mags had wanted to see her. That Mags had got to the battery early. That she'd wanted to tell Freddy everything.

Freddy couldn't know how Mags was sorrier than she could ever say. Mags didn't have Mother Julian's fortitude. She wasn't ready to die.

Mags tried to stand, but her ankles were bound. She wriggled on the cold, damp floor, but was helpless. The stuff had been removed from her mouth, which was a relief, but tightly gagged, she couldn't call for help.

Who had done this to her? Mags trawled through her life. If she knew who it was, she might be able to persuade them to let her go.

An angry library user? Had she upset someone? She'd had a spat with a young man standing for the council who had leaned right over the counter when she was ordering his parking permits. Last week the would-be councillor had been unpleasant when she wouldn't let him display his leaflets. Toni would want motive. Was it a reason to kidnap her? Who would vote for the councillor if they found out? *If anyone ever did find out.* Articulating the word 'kidnap' horrified her. A word that had nothing to do with her.

Countless people got cross with her. The librarians were on the front line for complaints about cuts to opening hours, cuts to jobs, the television licence fee. Some of these complainants battled with mental illness, but few were threatening or violent. Unless she counted the elderly man who'd thrown red paint at the crime books section, yelling *Murder!* Luckily, he'd missed. She'd calmed him down until the police came. Had that made him angrier? Was it him? If it was, what did she have that he wanted?

Mags felt the panic return. Her young assistant, Edward, had been made redundant. When she told him she was sorry, Mags had been shocked that he called her an old cow. She should retire and give the next generation a chance. What had Edward expected her to do? She was only forty, for God's sake.

'*Do you not think that the number of times you've been late over the last year and all that texting your friends in work hours might make you easy pickings?*' Mags had loosed both barrels. Could it be him? It could. Where is it? The question that might have been in her head haunted her. Where was what?

Freddy. The sound came from far off, like a remembered

voice in a reading. Had she shouted? Mary held custody of Mags's sin.

Mags's head hurt, as if her skull was an eggshell held together by her scalp. The pain had a sound; it was the jangling of a gaoler's keys. Discordant. Unremitting.

Gradually, Mags understood that what she could hear was not in her head. *Edward, please.* But the gag meant no sound came.

Mags's scrabbled the crucifix and the chain into a bundle. Her mind blank with terror, she was blindly aware that she must leave something for Freddy.

30

FREDDY

The harbour glittered with lights. The ferry was in, car passengers long disembarked; little traffic was coming out of Newhaven. The incinerator glowed like a spaceship landed within the darkened downland.

Freddy stormed along the road. The faintest glimmer on the tarmac showed her the way. Embroiled in a mental shouting match with Toni – she'd been prepared to do eff-all about Mags – Freddy was oblivious of where she was beyond keeping off the verge to avoid tripping in a culvert.

She should have known Toni would refuse. Mags was a forty-year-old adult with no apparent threat to her life. Had she gone on a pilgrimage? But then, why agree to meet? Revenge? For what? Freddy had done what Mags wanted and left town. Her dad had sworn her never to tell a soul and that had suited Mags too. Only Toni knew the truth. And she hadn't even told Ricky.

As she blundered along, the road a fuzzy strip tapering away, Freddy's fury with Toni meant she heard the noise behind her before she registered that it was a car. The hiss of tyres skimming the tarmac, the drone of the engine. She tripped on a stone. The hedges and tarmac were bathed in pale light. Behind her, the car advanced. The road was wide, there was no other traffic, she marched on, her mind on Mags. The car rounded the bend. Freddy was startled by the headlights. Her shadow elongated before her on the road. Spinning around, she was caught in the glare. The driver must have seen her.

The night was so quiet that Freddy could clearly hear the rising hum of the accelerator as it gathered speed. It took her a few more moments to comprehend that the car wasn't swerving. It was coming right at her.

Freddy dived for the verge. Wheels bumped up onto the grass. The scrape of metal on stone. The car had hit the kerb and left the road. It was coming after her. With a final effort, Freddy pushed into the hedge; brambles scratched her face and ripped her jeans. She tumbled out into the field beyond and, her legs jelly, crawled, pushing with her arms, along the earth.

The car was so close that exhaust fumes enveloped her. Coughing, Freddy sat up and peered through the hedge. Brake light further along the verge. The driver was stopping. *Fuckwit*. He must be pissed – he'd pinned her in his headlights. No way had he not seen her. The lights went out. Darkness and silence.

Then the black shape revved. The bastard. About to shout, Freddy stopped. Did she want to confront a maniac? Her eyes readjusting to the dark, she watched in a kind of limbo as the car, lights back on, sped away towards Newhaven. He'd doused the lights but even so she couldn't read the registration plate or see the colour of his car.

Freddy felt a tickle on her cheek; her finger came away wet. Her cheek stung – she would be covered in scratches. Either side of the road were fields; the nearest sign of life was in Tarring Neville, where there was a pub full of drunk police detectives. Freddy knew already how helpful they'd be.

Her phone vibrated. Sarah must have surfaced. She'd have checked on Freddy and discovered she couldn't track her. Freddy felt the pull. Sarah would rescue her. She'd get there from Lewes in fifteen minutes. Warm car. Cosy room with a drink. A hot bath. A comfortable bed.

The text was from Mags: *I'm walking on a pilgrimage. Leave me alone.*

The fishery was in darkness. The high galvanised fence appeared to glimmer phosphorous grey in the moonlight. The wind had died down. All was quiet.

Too quiet. Although the tracts of boggy land thick with reeds, the railway bridge stark against the velvet sky and the endless hush of the tide were familiar, tonight everything had an eerie, unsettling quality. The incident with the car had frightened her more than she realised.

Freddy had come to the fishery because she couldn't face her mum's house. There was no logic in the decision, and it now struck her as idiotic. At her mum's she could have locked the door and been safe. At nine at night, there'd be no one in the fishery. Why had she come here?

Freddy turned away and the movement activated the

security system. The car park was flooded with bright light. A door in one of the cabins opened. A man was coming across the car park.

'Christ, *Freddy*, I could have killed you.' Andy Power rested the flat of the blade against his thigh.

'That would be the second attempt tonight.' Freddy breezed past him. 'Am I glad to see you!'

'What do you mean, the second time?' Andy followed her into his office.

'I think someone tried to kill me.' Freddy grimaced; the idea was new. She pulled out Andy's chair and collapsed onto it. 'For God's sake, put down that knife.'

'Self-defence, I wasn't expecting a visitor. It's too early for the delivery vans.' Andy slid the knife into his desk drawer. 'Who tried to kill you?'

'I was nearly mown down. On the Newhaven Road near Tarring Neville.' Freddy hugged herself as she started shivering. Sarah would say it was shock. So would Freddy, for that matter. 'Any chance of tea with lots of sugar?'

'Did you get the reg plate?' Andy checked the kettle had enough water.

'It was too dark.' Freddy gave her brother a blow-by-blow account. She missed out the bits about Toni and her worries about Mags. Andy would be angry that Toni hadn't helped her. And Mags, well, she knew where she was now.

'It sounds like kids off their heads. There's been gangs of vandals and hooligans smashing windows, wing mirrors, nicking stuff. Not forgetting Daniel Tyler killing Karen.' Andy pumped hand cream into his palm from a bottle and briskly kneaded it in. Freddy wondered when he'd started caring about his skin. She could imagine what their dad would have had to say about that.

'It was deliberate, the car veered right at me. Karen's son murdered her. A tad more serious than breaking a window.'

'You should tell the police if you're sure. Are you sure?'

'Yes. No. How can I know? It slewed out of control. It was like the driver didn't expect a pedestrian.'

'You know the A26 is the devil. Foreigners off the ferry driving on the right and Brits pissed on duty free. They don't know which side of the road is right, or wrong.' Andy mashed the teabag on the side of the mug and added milk and sugar. He passed it to his sister.

'So, did you call the police?' Andy was opening a stack of envelopes.

'They are useless.' Fred wrinkled her nose. 'I didn't see anything – what could I give them?'

Safely in Andy's office, the tea warming her while Andy dealt with his mail, Freddy reflected that maybe she was being dramatic. How much more likely that it was a kid on vodka behind the wheel of a stolen car. Or, as Andy said, someone used to driving in Europe. No one wanted to kill her. She took another slug of tea and changed the subject.

'Global Ghost Gear Initiative – are you involved in that?' Freddy spotted a branded mouse-mat as Andy reached the last envelope.

'We're also in the Sustainable Seafood Coalition. We recycle tons of end-of-life netting each year.' Andy sounded proud.

'Bit different from Dad's day. I don't remember him giving a toss about anything except the profit margin. Least of all fish stocks.' Freddy doubted that, in the end, Andy did either. He would have a firm eye on the bottom line.

'Lots of things are different.' Andy crossed his legs at the ankles. 'If I didn't get involved, my kids would kill me. They're all for saving the planet.'

'Good for them.' Freddy recalled the three shiny-haired, rosy-cheeked keepers of the environment at the funeral. Dry-eyed, seemingly little moved by their grandmother's death. Regal and confident, they had stepped from the car with the air of those who know that, whatever state it got in, the world was their oyster. Andy must have done well with the fishery. She asked, 'How come you're here so late? Are you doing the night orders?'

'Yes. We're short-staffed since… since Karen and Daniel.' Andy fiddled with a broken stapler, catching staples as they fell out. 'I was at her grave today.'

'Karen's?'

'Mum's.'

'Oh. How was that?' Freddy hadn't thought of going to the grave.

'I kind of expected she'd be there.' Andy looked sheepish.

'Wasn't she there?' Freddy was horrified. Had someone vandalised their mother's grave?

'I mean, I had this crazy hope that she'd be alive. You know, on a bench waiting for me.' Andy rubbed at the back of his neck. 'Insane. How can Mum not be here? I never felt this way with Dad. Mum, I thought, would go on for ever.'

'Yeah. It is mad.' Freddy leaned down and gathered up the staples that Andy was dropping without noticing.

'You planning to hightail it out of Newhaven again?' Andy opened the last letter and scanned its contents.

'Actually, no. Not for a bit. I wondered…' Freddy shoved her hands in her anorak pockets. 'That job you mentioned, the fish round? If the offer is still on, I'll do it.' She hunched in the chair. 'I could stay on at Mum's and run her small animal hotel. Maybe instead of rent?'

'You've got some front.' Andy was thunderous. Of all the reactions Freddy might had expected, this was not it. He waved the letter that he had just opened at her.

'Is your little plan for the court's benefit? Get a foot in the door and then prise it open?'

'The fish van was your idea!' Freddy was dismayed. What was the matter with him?

'I offered you that *before* I got this.' He flapped the letter. 'What is that?'

'You know damn well what it is. Only a letter from your super-posh solicitor threatening to take us to the cleaners.'

'What the hell?' Freddy jumped up. 'I didn't send you that.'

'What do you call this then?' Andy flicked at the paper with a finger and tossed it on the Ghost Gear mouse-mat. 'Nice as pie to my face. Coming here claiming you were run over, assuring me that you don't want a share of this place and all the time getting your lawyer on to us. Nice move, *Fre-der-ricah*.' He gasped for breath.

Freddy snatched up the letter. She smacked it open and read it. She had to go over it twice to understand it.

'It's a joke,' she said finally. Nothing more plausible occurred to her.

'Do you see me laughing?'

'No. It's in poor taste.' Freddy felt her way. She couldn't tell him about Sarah, not yet.

'Once your feet are under the dashboard of the fish van, you're in. Is this the advice you paid your lawyer for?' He snatched the letter off her. 'You must be doing OK to afford one. You're not at the mercy of shrinking fishing quotas and endless red tape.'

'Andy, I'm sorry.' Shocked by a mess not of her own making, Freddy babbled. Sarah would have no idea about quotas beyond a vague notion that they were a good thing for fish. 'I'd been drinking. I was upset. About Mum. You know how I used to play practical jokes, hiding Ricky's clothes at the pool, and that time I moved Dad's car and he thought it was stolen?'

Andy gave the slightest nod. 'He let you get away with anything. If I'd done that, he'd have had a fit.'

Freddy winced. She knew the outcome of her father's fits. 'Well, once, I pretended to Mags I was dead.' Freddy laid the letter on Andy's desk. 'That wasn't funny either.'

'A posh firm like that would charge a hundred quid easy to send these to us. Got money to burn, have you? Or is it no win, no fee and you're offsetting the bill against your winnings? You think we're idiots?' Andy gestured at what must be Ricky's desk. 'He's got one as well?'

'It's not like that.' *My ex-girlfriend runs me. I didn't pay a penny for the advice. Unless you count being tracked every hour, never being allowed to buy my own clothes, posh meals out when I'm dead on my feet...* 'I am *so* sorry, Andy.'

Andy sighed. 'So, do you still want the fish round then? Why?'

'So that I can mind the hotel. You never cancelled the animals. I'll do it for Mum. Like I used to.' Andy looked as if he didn't believe her. Freddy didn't believe it herself. 'A month, or until you find Karen's replacement. Until all the booked-in guests have had their holidays.'

Andy appeared to be considering it. Freddy prayed inwardly. Then she counted to five.

'A month. But only if your claim,' Andy indicated the letter, 'goes in the bin.'

'Of course.' Freddy snatched up the letter and began ripping it up. 'Thanks, Andy.'

'Don't thank me. You're on probation. I'll destroy Ricky's letter. If he sees it, there's no deal.' Andy retrieved an envelope from Ricky's desk and ripped it in half. 'Although, Freddy, no offence, but Karen bust a gut to make the round work.'

'Dad said I could sell fish to fishermen. But if you need to talk to Ricky…' Freddy opened the door, letting in a blast of freezing air.

'I'm the boss on land.' He waved a hand. All his good humour was gone. Their rapport had burnt out.

'Andy, one more thing.' Looking back into the dimly lit office, Freddy noticed how tired her brother looked, with dark circles under his eyes. For all the money he was making, the office was basic, a picture of his wife and kids on his desk, schedules on the wall. It was a cheerless place. 'One of the animals belongs to Karen Munday. A hamster. How come he's there – was Karen going away?'

'She hadn't asked for time off. Mags took that booking, check with her.'

'Mags is away.' Freddy remembered the text.

'Oh, right, I forgot. She's walking on one of her pilgrimages, to get over Mum. One thing's certain,' Andy tossed the stapler onto his desk and shot more staples onto the floor with a sweep of his hand, 'Karen's not going to pick up her pet up now.'

In tentative rapprochement, brother and sister exchanged a grim smile.

Outside, waves breezed over the shingle and from somewhere at the back of the fishery a vixen screamed.

A car was parked by the gate. Freddy recognised it. She'd seen Ricky's Mazda outside the house the day her mum died. The engine was ticking. Had the Mazda been there all along? Freddy touched the bonnet. It was faintly warm. The front bumper was dented.

31

MAGS

Her captor came in the dark. She couldn't see who it was. She scuttled into the corner; the wall behind chilled her bones. A figure stood against a black sky. She saw real stars. Whoever it was had a radio, or maybe a phone. The radio was playing a French station; she recognised the voice of Edith Piaf. Toni would tell her it was *to drown out any external sounds*. Silly if so, because she knew she was in the battery. She had no idea of time. She could have been there days or since yesterday She couldn't tell if it was a man or a woman. She assumed a man, but then she wasn't sure. A sack was dragged with care over her head. Hands fumbled inside and carefully removed her gag. An alien-sounding voice told her to put the sack on whenever she heard a knock. Mags had had to ask some kids to stop playing with a voice-changer app on their phone in the library so she knew that these were pre-recorded instructions. Whoever it was had gone to great lengths to disguise their gender. Surely it was a man; no woman would treat another woman this way. *Don't shout or I'll kill you. Cover your face when someone comes.*

Inside the bag, she had nodded to each of these. Shuffling. The door clanged. Piaf left her alone. Gingerly, Mags felt about and found a bottle of liquid. After sniffing it and pouring some into her hand, she decided it was water. When she had first tasted it, she recoiled and spat it out. Acid. In the morning, with sufficient light, she saw it was sparkling mineral water. She dared risk it. She had been left a cheese sandwich. Home-made, going by the uneven slices of bread and lumps of cheese. Not so much lack of skill as that someone was in a hurry. She managed half before fear closed her throat. Was it, she would ask Toni, a good sign that she was being kept alive? Toni didn't reply.

She fixed on Edward, her jealous colleague. Edward, who had said she was too old to work. He had looked at her with hate.

The drawstring bag was made of brushed cotton like the bag Mags got with the shoes she'd splashed out on as an early fortieth-birthday present to herself before Reenie died. She had agonised about buying those shoes and, true to form, felt guilty afterwards. Was this her punishment? *Don't be an idiot,* Toni would say afterwards. Would there be an afterwards?

She had always believed that you were never alone if you had faith. God was always with you. But, cold and frightened, she couldn't form the words for a prayer. It was thinking of what Toni would say that brought her some scant comfort. As if Toni was in there.

The bag gave her hope. Toni whispered that if kidnappers planned to kill you, they didn't bother to hide their faces.

She had been obedient. She hadn't shouted or screamed. She had put on the bag every time he or she bought her food. She was mortally afraid of angering whoever was keeping her prisoner. On their last visit, when her captor had tripped and dropped her bottle of water, Mags had wondered if he – or she – was as scared as she was.

32

FREDDY

Freddy was parked by the mouth of the River Ouse. It was eight o'clock in the morning and she should have been starting the fish round.

As she'd left the fishery that morning, she'd seen the square shape of the ferry coming in from France. She'd driven around to the car park on the opposite bank to watch. Ahead of her on the other side of the river she could see Power Fisheries, a grey huddle of buildings and ranks of rusting shipping containers that Sarah had called a dump. Misted rain blurred the view, so Freddy flicked on the wipers and the radio. 'That will be yours one day, my darling,' her dad had said to her as, when she was thirteen, they'd sat in his truck on this very spot, looking at his kingdom. 'You're the only who can carry on the Power dynasty. Ricky's a baby and Andy's a cripple.' Freddy had vowed to herself, and to God, that she would share it with her brothers. There were three of them in the dynasty.

Seven years after that day with her dad and two years after he'd chucked her out, aged twenty, Freddy had worked in a fishmongers' in Liverpool. Being close to the sea, it was rare to buy in from suppliers down south. But a fire at the local fishery meant that for a couple of months her boss bought from further afield. One day, in December 2002, Freddy came into work to find Ronnie, one of her dad's delivery drivers, unloading boxes of fish. He told her Fred wasn't the same man since she'd left. *He mopes about, shouts at your brothers. Between you and me, I think he's too hard on Reenie. Come home, lass, we need you. Christ, girl, you were the bass and sole of the place!'* The old joke.

Ronnie told Freddy that Reenie and Fred's brother were throwing a surprise party for his sixtieth. *If you pop out of the cake, he'll be made up.*

She spent her savings on a brass nautical survey compass with a leather case. Fred would love it. She prided herself that no one else would have thought of it. The event was to be upstairs at the pub on the corner of Fort and Gibbon Roads. Fred's local.

Her legs shaking, Freddy had arrived. The barman knew her and greeted her warmly. He was so sorry. *So so sorry.* He insisted she had a drink. *Jack D, isn't it?* Gradually, it sank in. There was no party. Her dad had died of a heart attack a month ago. He'd been taken to Eastbourne District Hospital but died in the ambulance before he got there. He'd left the fishery to his wife and sons.

Freddy had taken the train back to Liverpool, the compass in her bag. No one had got a message to her. No one had told her Fred Power was dead.

The *Seven Sisters* had reached the river. As it glided by, slow and majestic, Freddy became aware that dreamy music on the radio accompanying a trailer for Steve Wright's

'Sunday Love Songs' programme fitted the ferry's elegiac progress up the river. The ferry was vast in comparison to the moored trawlers and skiffs. The regular chock-chock of wipers beat time.

'*Go to Facebook, search for BBC Radio Two, leave your requests under the Love Songs post...*'

Freddy composed a message. *Mags, this song is for you. I will always love...* She couldn't finish. She'd choose 'Un-Break My Heart'.

An old-fashioned bike with a leather saddle chained to railings was a static contrast to the *Seven Sisters* as she went past, while a motorhome, miniature against the ferry, appeared to slide backwards. The ferry glided towards Newhaven port, her orange funnel bright against the greys and greens of the beach and the sky. Freddy wept.

The rain had eased as she reversed the van away and drove into town to begin the round. She consulted the map Andy had given her and pulled over in a street off Meeching Road. She sounded the horn. A cringeworthy fanfare that announced her arrival. She stayed at the wheel, checking her phone to give the impression she didn't care if she sold fish or not. But mostly to see if Mags had replied to one of her texts. When she'd returned from the fishery after seeing Andy that night, she'd texted Mags to find out where she was walking on her pilgrimage – odd phrasing – and reassured her that *I will not try to find you.* Freddy tried to work out which pilgrimage Mags might be on. There were more than she'd expected. One to Germany, another to the Holy lands at the end of the month. Lourdes seemed obvious and one had begun two days ago and lasted a week. The longest was a fortnight. Most were sold out months ahead so Mags would have had difficulty booking at short notice. *Had Mags known she would be away when she arranged to meet?*

Whichever pilgrimage Mags was on, she should be back soon. Freddy would see her then.

Meanwhile, she had Sarah to deal with. In the last few days, Freddy had swung between never wanting to see Sarah again and imagining telling her exactly how she'd messed up Freddy's relationship with her brother. Andy would never trust her again. Probably guessing Freddy was furious, Sarah had maintained digital silence; perhaps she'd gone back to Liverpool, tail between her legs. Freddy tried not to picture the dent on Ricky's Mazda. *It could have happened anywhere*, Freddy muttered again as she waited for customers to crowd around the fish van. Hardly.

The morning passed in a blur – literally, as rain lashed against the windscreen faster than the wipers could clear it – and few customers braved the wet. Hour after hour, Freddy chugged the van up and down Newhaven's streets, the cheery music on Radio Two deepening her gloom.

Freddy was beginning to see what Andy had meant. She was barely scraping a living. If it went on like this and Mags didn't return soon, Freddy would pack it in. The saving grace was that Andy had – *Don't tell Ricky* – given her a cut of the large pre-orders to local restaurants and a couple of market stallholders which she loaded onto the van each morning. The lowest-value order was £200.

She wondered if he'd offered this to Karen too. Freddy had to hand it to Karen – she must have gone all out to make the kind of money that had bought her car and posh clothes. Unless maybe she'd had a rich lover? The Karen Munday she'd known at the convent would not suffer anything approaching a sugar-daddy. Karen would need to be boss.

She'd had a couple of oddball situations on the fish round. A woman calling from an upstairs window with the code to her key safe because she was locked in. It had taken ten minutes because the woman insisted on giving clues to the numbers, which Freddy couldn't get. 'Tusks of an elephant' had been two. She was told to post the keys through the letter box so that the woman could open the door. The woman had taken another five minutes to put on make-up. At last she'd emerged and asked for two skate. Freddy had no skate because Andy had advised they were expensive. Another woman was cross that Freddy had no live lobsters.

'Did you use to have them when Karen was here?'
'Never.'

A thump on the window. The other night's near miss on the A26 still fresh, Freddy jumped with fright. Her terror wasn't diminished at the sight of a man in a tight vest and shorts which might have passed for sexy on a Seventies heart-throb, but on a reptilian old man waving an Illy coffee tin was repulsive.

Gingerly, Freddy opened the van door, tempted to whack it aside when the man was slow to move out of the way.

It was nearly eleven and the man's Illy tin reminded Freddy she was gagging for a coffee; next week, she'd bring a flask. She bet Karen Munday had handled difficult customers with her eyes shut.

'You got my bream, dearie?' Mr Reptile stroked a brush

moustache that owed much to army blokes of Freddy's dad's generation.

'Yes.' Freddy raised the back hatch and again felt pleasure at the sight of her display. That morning in the fishery, she'd shovelled ice from the trolley onto the shelf. *Big enough to hide a body*, one packer had said. Fretting about Mags, never mind Rick, Freddy hadn't seen the joke. As if back in Waitrose, she'd lovingly arranged her stock. Plaice, salmon, bream and bass fillets, an array of dabs and, today, prawns fresh off Ricky's boat. Salmon steaks at the front for colour for the outlying villages. Freddy knew from Waitrose that salmon was a favoured easy meal of the middle class. *Wrap in foil, squeeze a lemon over, add a couple of heads of dill. Decorate with lemon segments. Pop in the oven for twenty minutes.* She had the patter. Packets of the smoked variety lined the back wall of the 'shop'.

Andy had stowed the pre-orders in polystyrene boxes in the hold beneath the counter. The weighing scales fitted into a cubbyhole, along with knives and a wireless card reader. The fish van had been upgraded since her uncle Ray operated it in the eighties. The service had stopped when Ray Power, like his older brother, Fred, had died of a heart attack.

'Red or black bream?' That morning she'd taken a punt on the red; the quota was fixed low, making it expensive.

'I'm white inside and out.' He twitched his moustache. *Fascist.*

'Red or black?'

'Steady on, girl. Keep your bra on. *Red.*' He unscrewed his coffee tin and tipped out a heap of coins and notes into his palm. 'You're not as amenable as the other lady, are you? Karen knew what I like.'

Freddy had learned to button it with revolting customers. The advantage of a sole operator (ha ha) was you could drive away.

'What did you do to Karen?' He leered at her.

'I think we're done here.' Freddy slapped the bream back onto the ice and prepared to shut the van.

'You can't do that!' he bleated.

'What can't she do, Alistair?' A woman, a little older than Freddy, blow-dried hair swished in a side parting, a dash of red lipstick showing off white teeth, mauve puffa jacket slung over her shoulders, clutched a Mulberry purse. She was as put together as Alistair Moustache was falling apart.

'She's refusing to serve me.' A spray of saliva came with the words. 'Karen was a different kettle of fish.' He laughed through his nose.

'What about that time she stuffed a lemon sole down your trousers because you asked her to come upstairs?' The woman widened her eyes at Freddy. 'At least this way you don't have to wash your smalls.'

'Red bream. One.' The man folded his arms as if a show was about to begin.

'For goodness' sake.' The woman snatched the ten-pound note off him and passed it to Freddy. 'Please would you deal with me? I'm Rosie, I'm Alistair's human translator. Welcome to our street.'

'Thanks.' Freddy bagged the fish, ran it through the sealer and handed it to Rosie, who handed it to Alistair.

'That wasn't difficult, was it?' Armed with his fish, Alistair was himself again.

'Alistair, if you want your box ticked next week, try being civil to the community in which you hope to serve.' Rosie dug around in her purse.

'What about my skate? And I wanted turbot.' His eyes were like dead fish.

Freddy's heart sank. She couldn't choose her customers any more than at Waitrose. Alistair was what Andy had called a pre-order. These were phone messages from local restaurants. Freddy found his fish at the bottom of a box at the back. She could feel him about to suggest she learn her routes and packed accordingly. Andy had fulfilled the list and stowed the stock on the van for her. There was a small quota for skate and turbot, both large and expensive fish. Freddy had one of each species on display in the van. Judging by the size of Alistair's pre-order, most of the skate and the turbot that the fishery stocked had been reserved for him. Freddy was surprised at the low price. Alistair could spot a bargain. She took three twenties off him. No change; Andy had said pre-orders were rounded prices. Freddy bit her tongue to hide her grimace when she brushed Alistair's fingers.

'Karen *did* refuse to serve him,' Rosie said when Alistair had gone back into his house. 'He's standing as an independent councillor. Being free of morals or a drop of the milk of human kindness appear to be no obstacle. He runs a wallet-busting bijou restaurant in Hastings, hence what he's bought from you. Powers are clever at managing their quotas.' Rosie frowned. 'Enough of him. I was so sorry to hear about Karen. How hard for you all, losing a colleague. And in such dreadful circumstances.'

'Yes.' Freddy had been accepting condolences all week.

Had Karen known she was so liked by her customers?

Rosie bought two plaice fillets, all the prawns and a large hake, which Freddy cut into strips. A good haul for one street. She accepted the small change that, at Waitrose, would have been irksome but on the round had proved vital.

'...I used to see more of Karen than my friends. Terrible thing to happen when life was going her way. She'd just dropped an awful man. She said she was cashing in, whatever that meant. I did wonder if she planned to leave you guys and look for pastures new. Forget that – I'm sure she was happy there.' Rosie put her fist to her mouth in cartoon apology. 'And her boy killed her? That is hard to fathom. Although boys can lose it, if it's been them and Mum. My youngest nephew went on a coke spree when my sister fell for her accountant.' She squatted down and retied the laces on her pink hi-tops. 'Kids, eh? I decided to do the planet a favour and pass on that one.'

What was Karen cashing in? Not the fish round; it wasn't Karen's to sell. Did her brothers know Karen had planned to leave? Surely not, or Andy would have said.

'Did you know Karen?' Rosie asked.

'Yes. *No*. A bit.' Freddy struggled. Rosie had strayed beyond the usual fishmonger–customer to and fro. 'I was at school with her.' Freddy didn't offer an example of how she had known Karen. Like when she'd taken Toni to the sick bay when Karen had pushed her off a wall. Toni had said she tripped. Mags had worried that Toni's lie was as much a sin as Karen's deed.

'Hey, what if this man who Karen wanted to dump killed

233

her?' Rosie cradled her purchases, 'I simply can't believe it was Dan. Karen adored him, talked about him all the time. Ask me, he's low-hanging fruit. The police should pick on a suspect their own size. It wouldn't be the first time they've thrown their weight behind an erroneous assumption. Take the Yorkshire Ripper.'

'I don't think they are assuming anything.' Although she was cross with Toni, Freddy felt compelled to stick up for her. 'Did you tell the police?'

'I mentioned the boyfriend. The woman wrote it down, but obviously they ignored it.'

Rosie tugged her puffa jacket closer around her and at her door called back, 'I'll look out for you next week and fight off Alistair for you.'

Freddy started to say that she could do her own fighting, but Rosie's offer wasn't like Sarah's need to control her. They could fight him together.

What was Karen cashing in?

Sarah was already in the street. Leaning against her car, legs crossed, elbow cupped in a hand as if she was thinking great thoughts. In casual gear of button-down shirt, jeans and the same pink hi-tops as Rosie had worn. Casual though it was, her outfit would have matched the value of one of the pricier pre-orders.

The cool-chick pose used to work on Freddy every time. She'd melted at the sight of Sarah lounging in the Waitrose car park. But, as domestic disputes overtook, the magic dwindled. When Andy had opened Sarah's letter, it vanished altogether. Now Freddy felt a burst of white-hot fury. She'd uninstalled Sarah's tracker, so Sarah must have followed her.

'What the hell are you doing here?' She pulled over, her fury increasing when she scraped the hubs against the kerb.

Languid, Sarah pushed off the bonnet and strolled over. By the time Freddy climbed out, Sarah had lifted the hatch and, with her super-concerned face, was contemplating Freddy's wares.

'Seriously, darling? You prefer chuntering around the sticks flogging fish to working at my firm with your own office?' Sarah frowned up at the sky. 'It's going to rain.'

Freddy didn't bother with a reply. Her answer to Sarah's proposal that Freddy be the office manager for her business, mooted when they got together, was yes, she absolutely did prefer selling fish from a van. Even on a wet day with no customers.

'I did *not* give you permission to tell my brothers I'm contesting Mum's will.'

'You are contesting it. *Great*!' Sarah exclaimed. 'I'm on your side, Freddy.' A favourite line.

'Read my lips: I am *not* contesting it.' Freddy breathed heavily, her temper rising. 'I had to pretend to Andy that I authorised you to write it or he'd have got you chucked out of the profession.'

'I was acting in your best interest. I always do, babes.' Sarah was unruffled.

'I'll be the judge of that.' Freddy slid out the last pre-order. A consignment of Dover sole and prawns for a restaurant on the quay which boasted gourmet dishes of sustainably caught seafood. Newhaven had gone up since her day.

She had planned to go to the battery after she finished. Now she knew she wouldn't find Mags there, it was more of a personal pilgrimage. *Their shrine*. She would have to lose Sarah.

'How many times have I signed stuff for you – my family's birthday cards, thank you notes – and you have never complained.' Sarah's hair was immaculate. Whenever she travelled for work, she located the best hairdresser in the area in advance to ensure a daily wash and blow dry. Sarah had the knack, whatever the circumstances, of maintaining her routine. Freddy envied her. Unforeseen events – her mum's death was an extreme example – threw her into turmoil. Her own hair was salted by the sea and swept about by the wind.

'That's different and you know it. I told you to do *nothing* about the will.' Freddy slammed shut the van and stalked over to the quay. She went around to the restaurant's side door. A woman in dark glasses, a coat slung over her shoulders, answered the ring. She looked this way and that and, seeing Sarah, shrank back inside like a fugitive.

'You'll keep bringing this?' She spoke in an undertone.

'If we have what you order in that day's catch.' Freddy had answered this question from many pre-order customers. Did they expect her to be murdered too? Thinking of the A26 car, the idea chilled her.

'Karen came every week. God rest her.' The woman, 'Mrs V', according to the order, essayed a sign of the cross. She pushed a fat envelope of cash at Freddy. Freddy had stopped counting on receipt; it implied a lack of trust for clients who Andy said were prestigious. This order was worth £350, of which £50 would be Freddy's. At this rate, she'd earn more than at Waitrose in less time. All pre-order customers paid in cash; this was fortunate, given the many digital dead spots – Lewes town centre, Piddinghoe church, Newhaven Fort – on the round, where a card wouldn't work.

'Like I said, if we have what you want.' Freddy slipped the money into her leather bumbag. Another customer who missed Karen. Who'd have thought?

'It's dodgy selling to strangers in their houses,' Sarah said as they walked back along the quay to the van. 'I doubt your brothers keep a check on you. And you won't let me track your phone.' She paused to show nothing escaped her. 'We could get them on employment rights, bet you're on zero hours.'

'Leave it.' If Sarah got a toehold into the fishery's working conditions, she'd be launching a class action. 'There's a list of pre-order addresses in the office and, anyway, I don't go into people's homes.' Freddy took the book with Karen's orders off the dashboard. Printed sheets listing the daily orders were interleaved between the pages. Karen drew a line through each completed order and added in the price – £100, £150, one was £2,000 – beside each item. In the last week of her life Karen had sold over three grands' worth of pre-orders. Andy assembled the orders for Freddy. That morning he'd let slip that Karen used to do it. Freddy would offer to take over. It might thaw relations. Since Sarah's letter, Andy had been Mr Frosty.

'It's not only fake utility workers and roofers duping old people. As I'm always having to tell some judge or other. What about those external workers who are victims of the resident of a house?'

'What do you mean?' Freddy berated herself. She'd been sucked into one of Sarah's doom scenarios. When they first fell in love, Freddy had loved hearing the stories of

Sarah's clients – dodgy roofers and plasterers, bank robbers, fraudsters and gangsters. Sarah was the brave hero, there for those who, for whatever reason, had strayed off the legal beaten track.

'...suppose an elderly woman wants you to change a light bulb?'

'I'd refuse.' Freddy was prompt.

'You would not.' Sarah was in her stride. 'You'd have to agree. Your Catholic guilt would kick in. It would spread through the neighbourhood how the fishmonger left a pensioner in distress. You'd tell yourself it might encourage her to buy more fish. So, you climb onto the chair she's got ready and ask for the bulb. *Silence*. She must be hard of hearing. You ask again, louder. Still silence. You look down and there's her psychopathic son grinning at you. In his hand is not a lightbulb but a carving knife.' Sarah's eyes blazed.

'I'd escape.' Freddy pictured Alistair with the knife. And no Rosie to help her.

'Have you noticed that, whenever we think of being in a dangerous situation – a terrorist with a gun, a chase through tunnels – we always escape? We can't imagine our own deaths.' Sarah paced in front of the van as if laying out her strategy to an obdurate client. She catastrophised everyday life to the proportions her clients experienced.

'I don't imagine those situations.' Although Freddy had heard the grind of the engine, bramble thorns cutting into her flesh, all week. In the reruns she always escaped and the driver died a painful death.

'The knife-wielding man locks you in the cellar, where, later, he'll wall you up. His sweet old ma hobbles to the van and chooses the fish of her fancy. Mr Knife relieves you of your cash.'

'What about my van?' Freddy felt the damp of the dark cellar against her back, a sick fear preventing her from thinking straight.

'He drives it to wasteland; he'll be familiar with likely sites.' In full throttle, Sarah faced Freddy, the open van door between them. 'Come on, Freddy, who'd report you missing? Not your brothers. If you disappear, so does your inheritance claim. I don't trust that Andrew. Greed emanated from that man.'

'When did you see Andy?' *Sarah had been to the fishery.* 'That man, as you call him, is my brother and what you smelled on him was devastation. He'd never for a minute think I'd do that to him. And he was right, I wouldn't.'

'He was quite rude,' Sarah remarked airily. 'I bumped into him this morning in the car park. Seems he lives opposite my hotel. I introduced myself.'

'I was mending bridges with him. You've blown it.' Freddy didn't need to ask Sarah how she knew it had been Andy. Sarah always found things out. 'When we were kids Andy was my best friend.'

'Oh, I thought that was Mags.' Sarah was nasty. 'Those bridges were because you toed the line. Andy's a cold fish.' She looked pleased at the pun.

Freddy lost her temper. '*Jesus*, Sarah. You have crossed a line. If I messed with your brother, you'd kill me.'

'Mess with him any time you like, he's a pain.' Sarah checked her hair in the van's wing mirror.

'I wouldn't meddle with your affairs, that's the point.' Freddy saw red. She locked the van and plunged off down

Fort Road. She reached the beach and, her boots sinking into shingle, made for the cliffs. Like an alchemist, she had transmuted love for Sarah into molten hate.

'This place is even more depressing in the day.' Sarah considered a sign for hang-gliders. '"Do not use or land on grass slumps below cliffs as this is a wildlife sensitive area." *Slumps* – sums it up, doesn't it? Concrete and old fences. Slit my throat if I end up here.'

Freddy had never considered the beaches where she had roamed as a child and teenager as depressing. Beneath the cliffs, shingle gave way to the grassy slumps with sea campion, golden samphire and yellow-horned poppies in the lee of lumps of fallen chalk. Today, clumps of thrift flowered pink against the browns and greens. It was paradise. *If only Mags was here.*

'Wow, creepy.' Sarah was peering through the grille across the entrance to the battery. 'Was it a prison?'

In their arguments it was Freddy who stormed out without the door key or confined herself to the attic without supper, like some heroine of a Victorian novel. Now she'd done what she'd intended to avoid. She'd brought Sarah to the lunette battery. She felt a jolt of guilt. She had failed Mags. She had failed Andy. Inwardly, she said a Hail Mary. Perhaps she should go and see Father Pete.

On autopilot, Freddy reeled off the battery's history as if her school project had been yesterday. '...rendered redundant when that pier was built to protect the harbour from the easterly drift of silt and storms. The pier is in the line of fire. The battery isn't used now.' As she said this Freddy noticed that the padlock looked new, silver against the rusting iron gate.

Wind gusted through the grille, a high humming that Mags used to call the mermaid choir. On the horizon the ferry was heading for France. Freddy felt sadness wash over her, as if the ferry had abandoned her.

'A perfect place to dump a body.' Aside from gangsters and thieves, Sarah defended rapists and murderers. Evil was her business. Freddy would lie, head in Sarah's lap, picnicking in a buttercup meadow, and Sarah would spot loose earth from a shallow grave beneath a willow tree. A lost glove on a post was a murder clue. A rope from a branch was not the remains of a swing, but a murderer's noose. The lunette battery would be a gift.

'...by the time it's discovered the incriminating evidence has degraded. *Alakazam*, you have the perfect murder.'

'There'd be a smell.' Freddy wanted to yell her head off at Sarah. Become a whirling dervish at one with the elements.

A lone angler fished from the end of the pier. Miles out, stick figures against the slate-grey sea flecked with foam; the sails of the Rampion windfarm would be turning fast. No actual rampions on the beach, battered by the waves and the gales, the shore was fringed with sea kale and discarded twine. Freddy balanced on a gun turret plate, an iron dais rusted to ochre. Like it or not, she belonged here.

'Any smell would be attributed to the carcass of a seagull or dead fish.' Sarah was channelling Hitchcock.

'*No one's dead.*' Freddy scrabbled up a pebble and hurled it at the waves; it fell far short. 'Get the *hell* out of my life.' Her shout echoed in the battery. The wind whistled. *The Mermaids' song.* 'Stop *stalking* me or, so help me God, I'll tell the police about the letter.'

'I am not stalking you.' Sarah was lilting, ever comforting. 'I saw your van on the ring-road, Power Fisheries, hard to miss.' She was trying for humour. Freddy was long past making up. 'I got your messages, OK? I listened. I'm going home. *Our* home. If you want it.'

'*I love you, Sarah, let's go home.*' The words opened up a future. Freddy's heart was flinty and grey. Her lips sealed.

Sarah walked away. Her shoes crunched on the shale. Freddy watched the silver Alfa – sleek and beautiful like Sarah herself – glide soundlessly away.

Freddy was alone. She was, as Father Pete said, free to follow her dreams. Never again need she tangle with Sarah over forgetting to fix her toothbrush onto the electric holder after cleaning her teeth, misfiling cutlery or putting out the wrong recycling bin.

'Great place to dump a body,' Sarah had said.

'Mags!' Freddy yelled, her voice feeble in the wind. She tugged at the padlock. The reek of decay from inside the dark chamber was seaweed and stagnant seawater. A dead seagull. That was all.

Hands plunged disconsolately in her yellow slicker, Freddy felt far from free. She pulled out Mags's *Revelations of Divine Love* from her coat. She could do with a revelation. The little volume was Freddy's proof that Mags had come there. Did she come to tell Freddy that she was going away? Did she realise too late that she'd dropped Mother Julian?

Freddy should tell Toni about Mags's text. She couldn't bear to see Toni's I-told-you-so look. Except Toni wasn't like that. She had never needed to be right.

If Mags had known she'd dropped Julian, she would have

come back for it. Freddy looked again at Mags's message.

I'm walking on a pilgrimage. Leave me alone.

Didn't you *go* on a pilgrimage? The walking was a given, surely. Freddy tried to take refuge in Toni's refusal to start a missing-person enquiry. Toni was a CID detective, the expert. Mags had only been missing for six days, including this one. The text proved she wasn't missing. Mags would be avoiding her. She'd called Sarah a stalker, but maybe that was Freddy. Stalkers refused to believe the evidence of their own eyes. If she told Toni about the text, she'd tell Freddy not to worry.

Mags would never have gone on a pilgrimage without Mother Julian, would she? And she wouldn't have rung in sick to the library, effectively stealing time. That was a sin.

The lighthouse at the end of the pier winked, the lamp brighter now that darkness was falling. The lunette battery had always been a happy place. It wasn't tonight.

33

TONI

'He never asked me.' Ricky drove the cutter wheel across his pizza with such force Toni thought he'd crack the plate. 'I'm a partner.'

'He's the CEO.' Toni was pissed off to find out from Ricky that Freddy was staying in Newhaven. She hadn't seen her since refusing to instigate a search for Mags when she had turned up at the pub four days ago.

Toni needed to explain. Someone was reported missing nearly every minute. Police resources were tight so priority went to children, the largest demographic of the missing. Mags didn't fit key categories – not a domestic violence victim or mentally ill or suffering from dementia. Ricky said Mags was on a pilgrimage. She'd since been to the library and found that Mags had told them she was sick. However justified she had been in turning down Freddy's request, Toni felt bad. Freddy was upset and, as she'd split with her partner, she had no one there for her.

'Are you listening?' Ricky was asking.

'What? Yes.'

'What did I say?'

'Christ, Ricky. Lighten up. This is meant to be a nice night out. Recently, with all the extra fishing, you've been a nightmare.' Toni pecked at her La Reine. 'At least you are a partner. Freddy is reduced to begging for a tinpot job from Andy.'

It's a good job.' Ricky swigged his Peroni and rummaged a hand through his thick black curls. His saving grace was his god-like looks. And that he was nice.

'Seriously, about the boat, you said you're ahead for this year. Can you slacken off?'

'There's always costs.' Ricky got the waiter's attention and ordered more drinks. 'Andy should have asked me about Freddy.'

'You'd have said no.'

'I might not have.' He carved out a slab of pizza, folded it onto his fork and crammed it in his mouth. 'She's my sister too.'

'What, so you're okay about Freddy coming back?' That would make things a lot easier.

'Not okay exactly. Just that I'd have liked a say. Andy does what he likes.'

'So do you,' Toni said under her breath

Against her advice, Ricky had taken out a hefty loan to buy a twelve-metre trawler in which he fished on the Channel several days a week. Power Fisheries used independent fishermen, mixing up suppliers according to cash flow and customer orders. Since Ricky was a boy, he'd been fascinated by the sea, like his sister. But while Freddy learnt to dive and explore the depths almost as soon as she could walk, Ricky had wanted to stay above the water.

When Ricky and Toni got together Ricky confided his ambition. Toni encouraged him to live the dream, to be himself. Andy had stipulated that Ricky carry the risk. He had agreed that the company would guarantee to buy his stock. At first it had gone well. Toni had never seen Ricky so happy. But over the last weeks, that had changed. Absorbed in various investigations, Toni had taken a while to see that Ricky was discontented and short-tempered pretty much all of the time. She put out a hand. 'Your mum being ill and then going so quickly, it's going to take time.'

'My sister bogged off years ago, chucking up her chance to be in the firm. She broke Dad's heart. It killed him. As soon as Mum passed, back comes Freddy, wanting her share. Christ knows how you give her the time of day.' He drowned the last segment of pizza in chilli oil. 'You should never have texted her.'

'That was Mags. Anyway, Freddy was my friend. Is. And like you say, she's your sister – you should talk to her. Life is too short.' Especially for Daniel Tyler and, perhaps, Daisy Webb. Thinking this, Toni put down her fork. She bit her tongue to stop herself telling Ricky the truth. It was Freddy's secret, not hers. The night she left, Freddy had spent the night at Toni's, a large house overlooking the sea on the edge of town. With sandwiches made by Toni's mum, who gave her a ten-pound note from her purse, the eighteen-year-old Freddy had set off into the blue. As she'd promised her pig of a father, Freddy had never contacted Andy and Ricky and, until three weeks ago, had never returned.

'It wouldn't help.' Ricky looked glum. Their date night was sinking fast.

There was a terrible crash, followed by clapping and cheering from first the kids at the table then others in the restaurant. Their waiter, a young woman no older than Daniel Tyler, stared bewildered at a broken plate and a pizza crust at her feet. The manager, an older woman, zoomed in with a long-handled dustpan and brush and swept up the pieces.

'Why do people cheer when that happens?' said Toni. 'She might have the breakage docked from her wages.'

'We did it at school. One back on the teachers.' Ricky had joined in the clapping.

'You have to be kidding. Mother Goose would have had us in solitary. Anyway, this isn't school.'

'Solitary – isn't that what nuns do anyway?' Ricky grinned. The broken plate had upped his mood.

'We were told purgatory was worse than Hell. Your soul is forgotten or something. Hell sounded more fun to me.'

'You dare sit there having a laugh with your boyfriend, after what you've done!' One of the group who had smashed the plate broke away as the others stepped out into the street.

What first occurred to Toni was that the girl was stunning. Short jet-black hair curled and bouffant, eyeliner sweeping from the outer corner of her eyes. A short dress with a wide twirly skirt, like she'd stepped from a Forties advert promoting something wholesome and fragrant. What occurred next was that the girl looked like Karen Munday.

'Sorry?' Toni dabbed her lips with her napkin.

'You should be shot for saying Dan was a murderer!' she screamed. Ever the detective, Toni noticed lipstick on a front tooth.

'*Hey.* Cool it.' Ricky shoved back his chair, catching the tablecloth. The glasses clinked.

'I've got this,' Toni snapped at him.

'Oh, what, you arresting me for no reason, like you did Dan?' A good few centimetres shorter than Ricky, the girl didn't flinch. '*You're* not a copper, so piss off out of it.'

'Time to leave,' Toni didn't bother to point out that she hadn't arrested Dan. He'd died in the crash. This girl wasn't bothered with facts.

'You don't get to order me around.' Doris Day with her hands on her hips.

'Can I help?' It was the manager.

'This young woman is leaving.' Toni didn't take her eyes off Whip Crack-Away.

The girl snatched up the water jug from the table and hurled the contents over Toni, drenching her. Ice cubes dropped onto her lap and skittered over the tiled floor. Ricky grabbed the girl and shoved her arm up into a half-nelson.

'Call the police.'

'I *am* the police. Let her go, Rick.' Toni mopped herself with a napkin. To Doris Day, 'What's your name?'

The girl made a snarling noise, but the fight had gone out of her as the reality of assailing a police-officer sank in.

'Jade.'

'Jade what?'

'Munday.'

Shit. Toni should have known that in a town this size the striking resemblance to Karen would not be coincidental. 'So, you knew Daniel?'

'He's my cousin. He is innocent. He'd never hurt Aunty Kaz.'

Involuntarily, Toni ran her finger over the raised skin on the back of her hand where, long ago, *Aunty Kaz* had stubbed out her cigarette.

'Jade, listen. It's terrible how your family have lost two relatives in this way. But you hunting for someone to blame won't bring your Aunty Kaz or Dan back.' Toni kicked an ice cube. 'I'd suggest you go home. Right now, life's shit, so this time I won't arrest you for assaulting a police officer.'

'Stupid bitch! You let her off lightly,' Ricky said when Jade had gone. He stroked back Toni's sodden fringe and kissed her forehead. Toni longed to sink into him.

'She's the tip of the iceberg. I've had anonymous notes at the station. Malcolm gets off – he's a bloke. Trolls hate that a woman was in charge. Others think it inconceivable that a blond cutie like Daniel could kill his mum. I'm a witch who should burn in Hell. Admit it, Rick, you agree.'

'That you're a witch?' Ricky winked. He gave Toni a wad of napkins from the dispenser. 'I do not agree. You did a good job, Inspector Kemp.'

Toni didn't say that one of the notes had accused her of using a dead boy to bump up her solve rate. In the dead of night, Toni believed she had done that too.

There was a light on in Mags's flat.

'Rick, I just want to drop in on Mags. Make sure she's OK; she called into work sick.' Ricky's arm through hers, Toni gave it an encouraging squeeze. 'I haven't seen her since Reenie's funeral.'

Since Freddy had confronted her in the pub, Toni could

not forget how worried she had looked. On the rebound from a relationship with this Sarah, did Freddy hope that Mags would forsake her faith, come out as a lesbian and live with her happily ever after? If so, Freddy was barking up the wrong everything.

Surely nothing sinister could have happened to Mags. She led a comparatively regular life, moving between her flat, the library and church, and had mentioned going to Lourdes but, to Toni's shame, she rarely gave attention to Mags's religious goings-on.

Yet Toni couldn't get out of her mind that when she'd seen Mags coming out of the church last week she had been agitated. She had said she had to tell Freddy something. She had *not* been avoiding her. She had said she was going to see her. What had happened to change her mind?

'Mags was there for Mum. It's payback time.' Ricky's words were clumsy, but the sentiment was there. He pressed the buzzer to Mags's flat. They waited in silence.

Toni had doubts swilling around in her head. Doubts about Mags, doubts about the Munday murder. Jade Munday had struck a chord. If they saw Mags, it was one doubt she could allay.

A man came up the path to the flats. They stood aside for him to enter. With a nod to security, the man didn't hold the door for them, but didn't look behind to check it had shut so missed the bit where Ricky wedged his foot in the gap. They heard a door bang on a flight above.

'What floor?'

Toni had been to Mags's flat twice – to borrow a novel by Graham Greene when she'd flirted with joining a book group – and the other day. Now, rattled by Jade Munday, she went blank. She usually met Mags at a curry place on the high street.

'Second on the right, I think.'

Bounding up the stairs, Ricky rapped his fist on the door. Toni winced. If someone banged on her door at ten at night, she'd think twice before answering it, and she was a police officer. The door had no spyhole.

Toni put her ear to the door and called softly, 'Mags, it's Toni. Me and Ricky. To see how you are.' She felt the full force of her mistake. Mags would hate uninvited callers.

'Looks like she's in bed, Tone. Sleeping off her bug, maybe.'

'Sshhh, then.' Toni was about to drag Ricky away when he tilted the letter box and, crouching, peered through.

'There's mail on the carpet. Mags, you there?' he called.

'Don't. You'll scare her,' Toni said.

'Looks to me like she's out. Andy did say she was walking on a pilgrimage.'

'Now he tells me.' Toni gave Ricky a biff on the head.

'You said Mags wasn't well. I imagined that you'd know better than Andy.' Ricky looked aggrieved.

'That woman at the library said she'd heard that Mags rang in sick, but didn't know who took the message. Thinks it's some bloke called Edward who's no longer working there. She rang him, but he's "disaffected" as she put it, so isn't answering.' Toni hadn't pushed it; at least she knew Mags was not missing. Something to tell Freddy, if Freddy would speak to her. 'If she's on a pilgrimage, that explains it.'

'C'mon, babes. Bed for us, I've been awake about twenty-four hours.' Ricky gave a vast yawn and shrugged up the collar of his fishing jacket.

Outside on the forecourt, Toni looked up at Mags's window. Although it would have allayed her doubts, Toni dreaded to see Mags there and know that, as well as avoiding Freddy, Mags was avoiding her too.

34

FREDDY

There was no sign of Andy when Freddy returned the van to the fishery. Ricky was out on the boat. Andy hadn't asked about Sarah. Had he guessed their true relationship? She should tell him. He'd support her over a vengeful ex. But Sarah wasn't out for revenge, she was on Freddy's side. With the bit between her teeth, Sarah would work at loopholes and tease out obscure clauses to win her the fishery. But for Freddy, winning would be losing. She would lose her family for ever. Pray God Sarah would drive to Liverpool and get on with her own life. Freddy felt a twinge of guilt. Sarah was only doing what she thought was best.

The unsold fish lay reproachfully on thawing ice in the van. The round, like any retail outlet, was weather dependent. It had rained all morning, with more forecast for tomorrow. People wouldn't pop out to buy a fishcake, only to get soaked. Freddy suspected her sales so far were a vote of sympathy. They'd dwindle when Karen's murder was out of the news. Brought up to be the best, even in the short time Freddy planned to run the round she'd wanted to exceed targets. It was pitiful to compete with a dead woman.

Freddy parked at the back of the compound by the rows of shipping containers in which were stored discarded fishing gear such as kits – boxes for fish – and spare machinery parts for the descaler and the freezer tunnel. One was marked 'Bait Motel' – Ricky's sense of humour, Andy had said. Freddy smiled now. It was hers too. Freddy had not reminded him how their dad would have called the rusting containers a shanty town. Were Fred alive now, he would not have collected redundant nets for recycling. *Not my problem, I've got mouths to feed.* Her dad had boasted of a 'tight ship'. Freddy frowned. Since David Bromyard had claimed she'd been on his trawler with her dad, she'd had flash images of a deck, red life-rings, a giant arm dipping out from the side into the sea. *She's a brave little lass, Fred.* A memory? No, auto-suggestion. She'd been on a trawler more recently. Freddy wanted to fish from a trawler. She had the introductory marine fishing qualifications. Her thirty-eighth-birthday present from Sarah was a three-week course in Oban in Scotland. Sarah had visited at weekends, grousing when Freddy was too deep in commercial fishing manuals to be grateful to Sarah for her present or her presence. More likely, Bromyard had been sucking up to her to reach Andy. All Freddy's life, people had cosied up to the Powers, for jobs, cheaper fish.

The van's freezer only functioned with the generator running so no stock could be kept in it overnight. Holding back a bass fillet for her dinner, Freddy laid the remaining fish into polystyrene boxes. She'd had a run on smoked haddock. Cullen skink was popular everywhere. She should note who bought what from which street. Yesterday, in a cul de sac near Lewes town centre, three chatty neighbours convinced each other to buy a total of eight plaice fillets. Would they all want plaice next week? Would they want anything from Freddy at all? Like small animals, while humans were creatures of habit, they liked a change. Freddy would need at least a month to understand buying trends. She wasn't leaving until Mags came back from where she had gone on her pilgrimage.

With a long-handled scraper, Freddy raked melting ice out of the van onto the concrete. She'd forgotten to put on the pair of wellies that Andy had lent her. Her trainers were soon soaked.

Freddy had believed she was telling the truth when she'd assured Andy – and Sarah – she didn't want a share in the fishery. Yet, once, it had been all she'd ever wanted. Sarah got frustrated when, maudlin over a bottle of wine, Freddy maundered on about how she'd have bought a trawler – a fleet – managed the whole process. Sarah pointed out how Freddy's plans featured Freddy as boss-lady with her brothers in second place. God had heard and tipped the scales.

Washed-out light slanting from the freezer room illumi-nated a skip filled with ghost fishing gear – the equipment retrieved by fisherman from the sea. Not only a philanthropic act, stray gear was a hazard; it could sink a trawler. Freddy lugged the boxes inside.

Freddy felt pride in Andy for spearheading a local recycling scheme. He'd put it on his kids, but she knew him. Andy only did what he wanted. Andy had the job she'd wanted. Ricky and Andy had both stepped out from Frederick Power's shadow, but unlike Freddy they hadn't had to relinquish their dreams.

Freddy went ice cold. Not from being in the freezer room. As when she'd seen the dent on Ricky's car, she had a presentiment of evil. Would Ricky kill to keep his dream alive?

Quickly, she stacked the boxes in a corner and laid the sign saying 'Karen's Round' on top. She didn't feel inclined to change it.

If Freddy told the boys what their dad had said, would they, as Toni predicted, forgive her? Her brothers were nicer men than their father. No way had Ricky tried to run her down.

Freddy slammed shut the freezer door and bolted it. She'd been walking back to her mother's house each night – her own pilgrimage – but rattled by her train of thought, wanted only to get away.

The tyres splashed in meltwater as she reversed out from the containers. A light burned in Andy's window. He was at his computer. He'd told her he handled orders from restaurants and wholesalers. He handled everything. It was ten to eight: he should go home. The fishery was only quiet between six in the evening and three o'clock the following morning, when packers and processers would arrive to handle the catches of the day.

If she stopped by, Andy would ask her about sales and Freddy would have to admit they were average. She drove out of the fishery.

★

256

Freddy leaned on Mags's buzzer.

No answer. She stepped back and craned her head up at the window of what Toni had told her was Mags's flat. She could see the ceiling of one room. A simple lampshade. Other windows in the block reflected fluffy clouds in the evening sky, suggesting that, as Toni had said, the light was on.

Reluctantly, Freddy gave up. She drove to her mother's with a dull sense of foreboding. When ever would the Mermaids be together again?

It might be spring, but it was colder in Reenie's house than outside. Freddy put a match to the fire she'd laid that morning and switched on the lava lamps. Sarah would have found the murky underwater light in the room depressing, but for Freddy it was bliss. As she set about feeding the other inhabitants – Roddy the degu, Karen's hamster Brad and the fish – she felt a semblance of relaxation.

A red, speckly guppy was nosing around Flounder as if to encourage a response from him. Roddy had probably been working at the bars all day – he struck her as neurotic. It wasn't fair to blame him for being owned by David Bromyard; besides, he belonged to Mrs Bromyard. Nor was it fair to blame David Bromyard for having been friends with her father. Outside the house Fred Power could be charming, full of jokes and generous. Only Fred's family saw his dark side. The reason that Freddy wouldn't let Roddy out of his cage was that, as Toni had said, degus took a lifetime to recapture.

Freddy had bought a portion of chips in town. She took it through to the kitchen, got the bass out of her bag and began preparing her supper.

She dropped butter into a frying pan and, when it had melted, doused the white side of the fish in the golden pool. She turned it skin side down in the sizzling pan. Her mum used to have an Aga; always on, it had kept the cottage warm. Somewhere along the line it had been swapped for an induction hob, probably Andy's doing. Freddy quartered a lemon, tipped the chips out onto a plate and scattered vinegar over them. The brown sort, not one of the wine varieties Sarah insisted on. And without Sarah there to object, Freddy scattered a liberal pinch of salt. She slid the bass onto the plate.

Flames had engulfed the logs. Freddy tossed in another and, laying her plate on Andy's fish table, settled to watch *The Little Mermaid*. The lava lamps' blue and green glow, mingled with the muted aquarium light, washed over her. Evening light filtered through the coloured plastic. The shells patterning the carpet, their turreted whorls and spires tinted fawn, orange and purple brown, became the sea bed. She was in King Triton's kingdom, away from the struggles of the human world. Freddy ate her fish and chips, hungry for the first time since her mum died.

Aged twelve, Freddy used to watch the film with Mags and Toni, scoffing sweets and guzzling squash and Coke. It had been Mags's idea, one afternoon as she and Mags had paraded arm in arm along the shore, to call themselves the Mermaids. In their later teens, the Disney movie became a backdrop for less innocent pastimes. Coke was mixed with Jack Daniel's, the soundtrack drowned by innuendos and hysterical giggles over their revised narrative, in which Ariel got off with the prince in the boat – Toni's idea – or Ariel entered a mermaid's nunnery – this from Mags. Freddy didn't offer her fantasy. It featured herself in the boat with Ariel, comforting her because the poor dear prince had drowned in a shipwreck. The princess soon stopped being sad.

All evening Freddy still expected Sarah to turn up, but by eleven, when she thought she was safe, there came the knock. She paused the film and crept into the hall.

'Freddy. *Me.*' Toni.

Freddy flung open the door.

'I'm worried about Mags.' Toni strode in. 'Me and Rick went to her flat. No sign. That light could have been on for security, but Ricky saw post on the mat. He says she's on a pilgrimage, but I checked with the library and they say she's sick.' She glanced at the television. Freddy saw her take in the film.

Freddy felt cold, although flames crackled in the fire. 'I had this text four days ago. I was going to tell you, but...' They both knew why she hadn't told Toni.

'She's *walking* on a pilgrimage? Funny way to put it – do they do them on bikes?'

'I don't think so. Yes, I thought that too,' Freddie blurted out. 'I know it's ridiculous, but could she be trapped in the battery? Maybe she tripped and got knocked out? That night when she was meant to meet me. It's where I found Julian.'

'*Whoa*, slow down. If she was trapped, why send a text saying she's on a bloody pilgrimage?' Toni's gaze was fixed on the screen, where Ariel was combing her hair with a fork at the prince's supper table. 'So, drama over then, that's a relief.' Toni didn't look relieved.

'Mags would never go on a pilgrimage without Julian's *Revelations*,' Freddy insisted.

'OK.' Toni zipped up her anorak. 'There's one way to find out.'

They were going to the lunette battery. Not a police search, Toni reiterated; it was unofficial. There was no reason to think Mags was in danger. Freddy clung to those words.

'If Mags has gone to Lourdes, she'd have taken the *Revelations of Divine Love*,' Freddy said again. She was hunched on the heated seat in Toni's Jeep, a tank of a thing with tyres more suited to the desert than to Newhaven's streets. A lavender air freshener in the shape of a police officer's helmet swung like a thurible from the rear-view mirror.

Freddy found herself longing to be safe in the subterranean light of her mum's front room. She was sick with dread about what they might find at the battery.

'This calls for chocolate!' Toni braked outside the Co-op. 'I've given up smoking.'

'I didn't know you did smoke.' At the convent Toni had been more passionate about the perils of cigarettes than the Trinity. Her campaign had started after her dad – a chain-smoker – was murdered.

'I don't.' Toni went off into the shop.

Freddy glanced around the Jeep. It smelled of leather and lavender. Solid and tangible. She hadn't expected Toni to take her seriously. It made everything real. Something had happened to Mags. *Something awful.*

'Bet you still like them!' Toni dropped three Creme Eggs into Freddy's lap. 'Old stock left over from Easter, but they'll be fine.'

Freddy's mind worked fast. At school Toni hadn't only been a militant anti-smoker. 'Please say you didn't nick them.' She tensed, as if the clutch of eggs were hand-grenades.

'I didn't nick them,' Toni parroted.

'*Christ*, Toni, you'll be chucked out of the police if you're caught.' Freddy now knew a lawyer *and* a copper who broke the law, easy as you like.

'Have I *ever* been caught?' Toni's pride was palpable.

'Take them back.' Freddy thrust them at Toni. 'Say you're on a diet, you bought them in a moment of weakness.'

'Du-uh. That *is* how to be caught.' Toni was cheery.

'Stealing is a sin. For God's sake, *think*! Why did Jesus die?' Freddy had appealed to precisely the wrong source.

'I don't know, why *did* Jesus die?' Toni was the straight guy. 'Not from too much chocolate. Come *on*, Freddy, this is a crisis. Think of Sister Agnes.'

Sister Agnes had had a soft spot for Toni. She'd slip her Twix bars in breaks and award her commendations, even when she forgot to tidy the prayer books. The Kemp family's conversion to Catholicism had been pragmatic, but while Amy Kemp had got stuck in, Toni remained sceptical. Yet she had a strong notion of crime and punishment. She had once told Freddy she feared her piss-takes of the Hail Mary and Our Father had caused her dad's murder. It hadn't surprised Freddy when she'd joined the police.

'Then I'll go.' Freddy was out of the Jeep and in the Co-op before Toni could argue. The cashier, a pimply kid with product-laden hair, eyed her like he knew why she was there.

Nonetheless, she felt terrible about the Creme Eggs. However she had come by them, like Sister Agnes, Toni had meant them as a present. Unlike Sarah, who always got Freddy things she thought she should have: a posh briefcase, a fountain pen – stuff Freddy had no use for – Toni had remembered what Freddy liked. She *knew* Freddy.

The first aisle was tins of pulses, baked beans, soups. Fruit and veg were on the left.

She found the Creme Eggs jumbled in a bin right in the sightline of the cashier. It would be as hard to surreptitiously return the stolen goods as to steal them. Affecting interest in the cut-price Lindt rabbits, Freddy was aware of the eggs softening in her sweaty hand. Panicked, she chucked them onto the bin and trotted to the exit. She had cleared the trolleys when a siren blasted. A light over the door flashed.

'Stop. Hands above your head.' *Sweet Jesus.*

'I haven't stolen—'

'I've pressed the panic button, the police are coming,' the boy at the till informed her.

'Please, there's no need,' Freddy stammered.

'They will arrest you,' he told her.

A knock on the glass door. Toni was gesticulating at the cashier.

'We're closed!' he shouted.

'She's the police.' Freddy lowered her arms.

The door swished open.

'What's occurring?' *Whack.* Toni slammed her badge on the counter.

'You took your ti—' Toni's warning glance silenced Freddy.

The cashier explained that he'd apprehended a shoplifter.

'Please would you empty your pockets, madam?' Toni asked Freddy.

'Yes, officer.' Freddy fought a rush of wild laughter.

'Ho hum.' Toni scrutinised the scrunched tissues, a receipt for milk and bread (from the Co-op) and coins laid out by the scratch-card dispenser. 'It seems you were mistaken, sir.' Her smile rivalled that of the Madonna. 'We can let this lady go on her way.'

CCTV. Freddy cast about. The camera was focused on the confectionery section. Toni had known that she would not be seen when she took the eggs from the bargain bin.

'She never bought anything,' the man complained.

'That is disappointing, but not a crime,' Toni said.

'You were here before.' The boy had recognised Toni. Freddy felt faint.

'I bought chocolate.' Toni always paid for something.

'Police.' A tall thin man stalked past the trolleys into the shop. He saw Toni and stopped. 'Guv, what are you doing here?'

His pudding-bowl haircut was vaguely comic, but Freddy instinctively knew not to underestimate him.

'I was passing.' Toni was smooth. 'You?'

'Me too. Heard it called in.' He regarded Freddy. She smiled. He didn't smile back.

Out in the street, Toni was hearty. 'Mal, this is Freddy Power. We were at the convent back in the day – she's Ricky's sister. The assistant had her for a crim!' She put on a severe face. 'Detective Sergeant Malcolm Lane to you, Freddy.'

'Actually, I really need to talk to you in private, boss,' Malcolm Lane said.

'Sure.' Toni pulled an odd face at Freddy. 'Catch you soon, yeah?'

Freddy was crushed. Had Toni been humouring her about Mags all along?

35

TONI

'Guv, the Munday murder.' Malcolm wandered over to Toni's Jeep. 'Could we have made a mistake?'

'Don't you start.' If Malcolm looked inside, he'd see she wasn't carrying her police radio and couldn't have picked up the call. 'No, we couldn't have.' Toni worried Freddy hadn't got her hint that their search was only delayed. She hadn't wanted Malcolm to realise she and Freddy were together before he arrived or he'd sniff a rat around the shop-lifting debacle.

'What if Mrs Haskins was right and there was a man?' Malcolm ignored her.

'Then I'm a llama.' Pulling her hands down her face, Toni paced away from the Jeep. The night was going from fairly bad to very bad. Since they'd wrapped up the paperwork, Toni had shut the hatch on her niggle of doubt. *Was the killer of Karen Munday still out there?*

'Her sister, Mo, asked to see me. She said Karen *was* seeing someone. Mo thinks he might have been married.

She even wondered if it might be a woman because, quote, "Karen had a weird streak."'

'It doesn't mean he *or* she murdered Karen.' Toni took a Creme Egg out of her pocket. It had got warm; the foil came off in flecks. 'What made Mo think that?'

'Karen was wearing expensive jewellery, a fancy watch and she'd recently bought two Alexas – that one we found in Daniel's room, and she gave one to Mo. She made decent money on the round, but as we said, not enough for luxuries. Her bank account was healthy but not heaving. She had nothing outstanding on her Visa card. Where was this cash coming from? When Mo questioned her about the bloke, Karen told her to mind her own. Mo was sure that if the bloke was single, Karen wouldn't have kept it quiet.'

'And Mo didn't think to say this in her statement?' Toni bit into the top of the egg. She liked to lick a hole in the chocolate and hook out the creme with her tongue, accompanied with a gin and tonic over Netflix. She disliked cramming it down on a pavement, but needs must.

'Claims she forgot. My guess is she's not happy with us saying her nephew murdered her sister and wants to reel us back. But didn't Andrew Power also say she had a bloke?'

'That was conjecture.' *Yes, he had.* Toni barked, 'It's not enough for a case review. If I tell this to Worricker, he'll call us clowns. I'll be on points duty and you'll… never mind.' Malcolm would have her job.

'Mo said she popped in on Karen after work one night and was sure someone was, as she put it, "skulking" in the kitchen. Daniel nearly gave him away, but Karen shot him a death stare. When Mo asked Daniel about it later, he acted dumb. Mo said Karen had got to him. She said Daniel seemed scared.'

'The kitchen's off the front room. How hard would it have been for Mo to take a look for herself?'

'I got the impression she was scared too.'

'That figures.' At the convent Mo Munday had been in Amy's year and, unlike Karen, a bit of a mouse. 'OK, you and me will pay another call on Mrs Haskins and ruin another crappy TV show for her.' Toni got in the Jeep. She tossed the Creme Egg wrapping out of the window. This is between you and me for now, okay?'

'Yes, boss.' Malcolm picked up the wrapper.

Toni drove into the town centre, parked and shut off the engine. She rested her head on the steering wheel and groaned.

Had they slapped a posthumous murder charge on an innocent minor?

The files for Karen Munday's murder were on Malcolm's desk, ready to be filed in the registry. With the practised fingers of a detective, Toni riffled through the top file until she found Karen's house key, with a pink heart keyring, bagged and recorded.

After she left Malcolm, still standing outside the Co-op, Toni had intended to go and see Freddy and head for the battery with her. But what Mo Munday had told Malcolm had brought her own doubts to the surface. She had to face them.

She left the Jeep around the corner from Karen's house.

As she unlocked Karen's door, Toni expected Mrs Haskins's curtains to twitch, but all was dark and still.

She let herself in, kicking aside the junk mail that had piled up since Forensics had finished. The house was tomb silent. The unfinished box of Maltesers was a possible gift from Karen's killer. It had yielded no fingerprints, no DNA. The crime scene cleaners were due. All trace of Karen Munday's life with her son would be deep-cleaned away. The house would be sold. New people would live there.

The room smelled of forensic chemicals. And something else. The smell of abandonment. Of life extinct. Toni ventured up the stairs. She paused on the landing, outside the toilet where Karen had died.

The bedding, including the mattress, had been taken away. Dust furred the slats of the bed frame.

Toni had come back to the crime scene in search of anything they had missed. Any sign of the man Mo Munday claimed existed. She had to banish her doubts or it would eat away at her. Karen was not a friend. She had been an enemy. But Toni was a detective; her duty was to the victim. She would do right by Karen. Toni had come to Karen Munday's house to make peace. Only Karen could whisper from the walls who had extinguished her life.

Tell me.

Toni felt confusion mixed with sadness as she explored Karen's home, noting magazines emblazoned with Kardashians, a huge make-up case with lipsticks of every colour in the bedroom, Karen's pink teddy on a chair. She had never told the others her fantasies that Karen would die and never come back to the convent.

When Toni got to Daniel's bedroom, unlike the last time,

when she had been looking only for clues, she thought her heart might break. The pictures of boats; Ricky holding an oversize fish. A section of trawling net with floats attached was draped from the ceiling. An orange buoy like a baby space-hopper crushed a length of Scalextric. Daniel had abandoned his boyhood. He would never become a man. Toni felt Ricky's pain. Everything in the room spoke of the boy's passion. The sea. Toni wouldn't give Ricky a child of his own. Ricky had lost the only son he'd have.

Was it only that she couldn't accept that a boy could strangle his mother? Was that why she was gnawing at the case like a dog at a bone?

Tell me.

Toni heard a noise. She crept onto the landing and looked down the stairs. Someone was manipulating the door lock. Toni had slipped the snib up to prevent anyone opening it. A habit gained from examining crime scenes on her own. You never knew who might turn up. She was congratulating herself on taking the precaution when she heard the door open. The snib must have dropped. Whoever it was downstairs was practised at breaking and entering. *They had entered.*

There was nowhere to hide. Karen's wardrobe had been emptied, but she'd be a sitting duck if the intruder looked inside. There was no attic or basement.

She retreated to Daniel's bedroom. The nut on the window latch had been sealed with layers of gloss paint, it wouldn't turn. She heard brushing as the door was pushed over the junk mail. Her finger and thumb damp with sweat, she couldn't grip the nut. Someone was moving about in the kitchen.

They were looking for something. Karen's man? She

should ring Malcolm, get backup. Toni patted herself down. Her phone was in the Jeep. *Idiot.*

The man – now she was sure it was The Man – was searching for something, something he'd missed, that would give him away. Toni did a mental inventory of the downstairs rooms: the television, a table, a carved wooden giraffe, a photo of Karen and Daniel. None would give the killer away.

A burglar. The whole of Newhaven knew the house was empty. Toni smacked her forehead. She was a police officer – why the hell was she hiding up there?

Missing the days when she'd carried a truncheon on the beat, Toni switched on her torch and looked for something that would do as a weapon. A leather belt lay like a snake on the carpet by the buoy. A smack with that might cause surprise but, if it went wrong, he could strangle her with it.

She heaved up the buoy. It was heavier than she'd expected. She got a grip and lugged it out of the room and, holding it in front of her, struggled down the stairs. Its unwieldiness would play in her favour.

The living room was empty.

Covering the front door, Toni inched towards the arch to Karen's galley kitchen. *Had he left the house?* She'd have heard. *She should have got backup.* She didn't have her radio. Toni had always despised those lone-ranger cops who believed themselves too clever to need the team. She needed Malcolm to walk in.

A footstep. The intruder had been in the backyard. Toni positioned the buoy. She'd run at him and knock him flying.

'Police. *Freeze.*'

A shadow fell across the couch. A tall man filled the archway.

'Good Lord, guv, can I give you a hand with that thing?' Malcolm asked.

'There's no way we'd have missed it,' Toni said again.

Sealed in an evidence bag, the leather belt lay on the table between Toni and Malcolm.

'Which means someone left it in Karen's house after we swept it. I went there to look for anything we might have missed, but I didn't anticipate finding planted evidence. It doesn't stack up. It's a dodgy strategy – it narrows the field and provides a direct line from framed to framer.' Malcolm poured sugar into his coffee and tutted.

'What?'

'I forgot, me and Lizzie are on a sugar-free month.'

'Don't stir your coffee,' Toni rubbed her eyes. She was a dead woman walking. Or slumped in a chair. 'No one had broken in. They had a key. That narrows it down to Mo. There's a cousin, I met her, Jade, earlier this evening. Yesterday.' Ricky hadn't missed her in bed or he'd have texted. At least she could say it was work and not that she was with Freddy.

They were at the McDonald's in the retail park off the ring-road. Through the glass she could see the old Parker Pen factory. Next door was what had been Cash-Bases, where she'd had a holiday job one summer, making the cash trays for tills. The restaurant was empty but for four girls huddled over the debris of a meal, faces in their phones, and a middle-aged man in an anorak at a table near the teenagers munching his way through a box of twenty chicken McNuggets. While the detectives had been there, as if it was television, he hadn't taken his eyes off the girls. Toni was limbering up for a caution.

'If this belt was left after we finished up, either it was by accident or to incriminate someone other than Daniel.' Toni unwrapped her cheeseburger. 'Stupid move, as you say. Someone's taking the piss.'

'The case is closed. There's no need to skew the evidence.' Malcolm stirred his coffee.

'Difficult to leave a belt by accident, unless they changed their trousers and forgot to transfer it.' Toni pulled a face.

'Could be Mo Munday's.' Malcolm ate one of Toni's chips. This was typical. He'd said he'd had supper so didn't want food. She'd had supper too. Toni pushed the carton towards him.

'She's an even less likely killer than her nephew.'

'Until tonight we had him for it.' Toni squirted a dollop of ketchup on her cheeseburger. 'Actually, the belt looks like one Ricky has. That fish motif is on a belt I got him for his birthday.'

'You're never saying it's Ricky?' Malcolm watched the man watching the girls.

'No.' Toni heard her hesitation. 'Definitely not.'

'We'll get it examined. See what it throws up.' Malcolm was tucking into the chips.

'We need to find this man who Mo Munday believes Karen was dating.' Toni snapped a string of cheese stretching from her mouth to the burger and licked her fingers.

'Mo said Daniel looked frightened. That rules Ricky out,' Malcolm said. 'He can't have been scared of him.'

'You said Mo thought this man was in the kitchen one time she was round. If that's true, Daniel already knew about him. It sticks a pin in Daniel seeing him with Karen and going nuts. We know they didn't have sex in the house, there was no semen in the mattress.' She put down the cheeseburger. 'If he exists and he's innocent, where is he?'

'Justice and truth are nothing in the face of putting your marriage on the line. If he isn't the killer, he'll think there's no point.' Malcolm finished the chips. 'Or he is the killer.'

They sat in silence. Keeping a bead on Mr Chicken Nuggets, Toni resumed eating her burger. After a minute she said, 'Why are you off sugar?'

'It's a killer. Worse than carbs. And to lose weight.' Malcolm looked sheepish.

'Christ, Mal, if you lose any more weight, you'll be the thin blue line.'

'Were you at the Munday house because I said we might have the wrong killer?

'Yes,' she admitted.

'You have doubts too?'

'Yes.' Not true. Toni was now certain Daniel Tyler had not murdered his mother. 'We'll visit Mrs Haskins in the morning, see if she's dredged up any detail about this man she saw. Now we have homes to go to.'

Toni rapped on the creep's table and flipped out her badge. 'Time to go, mate. If you stay a minute longer, then myself and my colleague will escort you to the station for a wee chat. About underage sex.'

Toni was set for accusations of police harassment and wrongful arrest but, shoving aside the box – the nuggets eaten – the man tripped over himself scuttling from the restaurant. The girls, thumbs busy on screens, paid no attention. She made a mental note to tell Uniform to keep an eye out.

Toni was driving back to Ricky's flat at the top of Gibbon Road when she remembered Mags. *Shit.* She didn't seriously think Mags was in trouble, but she'd wanted to help Freddy. She texted, *On my way to pick you up.*

36

FREDDY

I'm at the battery.

Freddy hadn't expected Toni to come back. Like Ricky and Andy, Toni seemed to believe Mags had gone to Lourdes or Walsingham. But Toni had come back. She had always been there for her. Right from when Freddy turned up on the doorstep of Toni's family home after her dad had chucked her out. *A freak of nature.*

She had been sitting by the fire in what the Kemps called a drawing room. Toni's mum had given her a bowl of stew with thick brown bread that she'd made herself.

A steaming mug of cocoa had followed, along with tissues for Freddy's tears. Toni's sister, Amy, had played music on the piano, Clara Schumann, she'd said. Toni had said it wouldn't help. It had. They had invited her to live with them. Two Mermaids in one house, Toni whispered. But Freddy had been forbidden to stay in the same town as her family. And she couldn't bear to see Mags. She had to get away.

Out in the darkness, waves boomed against the pier.

275

The lights of Brighton along the coast tinted clouds with faint orange light. Although Freddy had grown up by the sea, she marvelled at how it was still there at night with no one watching. Humanity was nothing against the might of nature. Behind her the lunette battery emanated silence.

Headlights strobed over the beach and Freddy caught a glimpse of the English Channel, a vast, swirling cauldron of black. She started towards the vehicle then stopped. It might not be Toni. She retreated into the entrance of the battery.

The crunch of shingle. The torchlight missed her. She shrank further, the grille pressed into her back. She felt dank emptiness behind her. Imagined the passageways leading to—

'Freddy?' Toni hissed.

'Thank *God*.' Freddy expelled air.

'I had to stop Malcolm from taking you into custody for further questioning.'

'Ha flipping *ha*. Don't expect thanks. *God*, Toni, I can't believe you're still nicking stuff. It's not like you need the money.' Freddy's fuse was too short to mention.

'It's not about money.' Toni was gruff.

'What *is* it about? You're risking your career for chocolate.' Freddy had never faced Toni about her thieving. *Great timing.*

'I'm risking my career being here,' Toni said. 'Since Daniel Tyler's crash, we have had a patrol on the beach. All it takes is for the guys to drive along and see us. I can pull the wool over a cashier's eyes at the supermarket, but the average copper will see through me at a shot. Let's do this.' She shoved the torch at Freddy. 'Point it there.'

Freddy shone light on the padlock.

'Hold that.' Toni passed her something heavy. A sledge-hammer.

She adjusted the aim of the torch. Toni was spraying an aerosol at the padlock.

'Is that oil?' No point in easing a lock only to smash it with a hammer.

'Cold air,' Toni muttered.

'Isn't there enough of that?' Freddy shivered.

'For metal to freeze it must be at least thirteen below.' Toni tilted the aerosol to better get her target.

'Clever what you learn in the police.' Freddy felt a burst of fondness for her mate. Even as her face was going numb.

'I read it on the internet.' Toni stuffed the can in her anorak. She grabbed the sledgehammer off Freddy, raised it up, then brought it down on the padlock. The clang reverberated in the vault. *Once. Twice.* Anxiously, Freddy scoured the beach for any sign of the police patrol. She did not want Toni to get in trouble.

Toni pounded away with impressive precision. At last the shackle sheared off from the body of the padlock. She dumped the hammer and pushed on the grille.

It squeaked and whined. Had it never been opened? Freddy wanted to be wrong. She prayed to God. With every bit of her. *Please make me wrong. Make Mags be at Lourdes.*

'I'll go first. I'll need to seal it, if it's a ...' Toni didn't need to say 'crime scene'.

'Are you sure?'

'I'm a police officer. Where normal people run away from danger, we run towards it. Keep behind.' Toni was trying to make Freddy feel better. Nothing would do that.

A passage ran the length of the battery in each direction. From her history project, Toni knew that the patches of solidity in the darkness were doorways to the gun cells. From somewhere was a regular drip of liquid. The silence was sepulchral. They moved deeper into the cliff. Freddy could no longer hear the sea. Although they were beyond the reach of the tide and the rain, the walls were coated with brown-reddish slime.

Freddy felt sick to the core at what they might find. Had Mags fallen and was hurt? If they shouted, no one would hear. Had Mags shouted until she became too feeble? Karen had been murdered by her son. Murder was a way to die. *Had someone murdered Mags?* As if a voice whispered to her, Freddy knew she would not see Mags again. Breathing in the fetid air, she put her hands to her face. She was in hell.

37

TONI

'Nothing here.' Toni smelled Freddy's fear. Toni had been frightened of finding Mags, but she could at least retreat into detective mode. She'd worn gloves to smash the padlock and explore the battery. Not for cover, but to keep the scene clean. Mags wasn't in the battery but, call it a hunch, Toni didn't think she had fled Newhaven to get away from Freddy and seek solace at some shrine. Mags might not have told Freddy, but she would have told the library the truth. Toni had never known Mags be ill or to lie. *Apart from the big one.*

'What's that?'

'What?' Toni was instantly alert. In this tomb they wouldn't hear the patrol.

'Here.' Freddy's voice was muffled in the musty dark.

Toni found Freddy in one of the gun cells. She was aiming her phone torch at the ground.

'Down there. I saw something.'

'We should go, Freds.' Toni was getting a nasty feeling. She squatted down and, her own torch held at her shoulder, spotlit a puddle of revolting liquid, which, were the place accessible to the public, she'd assume was piss. Freddy peered down. A cluster of silver glinted in the light.

'It's Mags's crucifix,' Freddy breathed.

'You can't know that.' But Toni knew it too.

'It is.'

Toni shone her torch down.

'The chain could have broken and it got blown in.' Freddy was unnaturally bright. 'It needn't mean… it means *nothing*.'

'No way was it blown in. The way it's bundled up like that looks deliberate. It would never have fallen like that.' With a deft flick, Toni took a photograph with her phone then lifted the crucifix up and held it to her torch. Four letters were engraved in the silver: *MPTM*.

Margaret Pauline Theresa McKee.

Toni lowered the crucifix and chain into an evidence bag. She touched Freddy's arm.

'I'm calling it in.'

38

FREDDY

Two minutes past midnight. A police helicopter clattered over the cliffs, the searchlight creating shadows, as if the shingle itself was shifting. Miles off shore, the lights of the Rampion Windfarm winked red in the darkness.

'They've found a dead body, it's been in there for years.'

'I heard it was some woman?'

'That teenager who stabbed his mum was a serial killer.'

The senseless chatter of onlookers. Bad news, true or false, travelled fast. A police constable had sent Freddy behind the cordon, where she was jostled by the gathering crowd, drinkers from the Hope and Facebook followers. Phones like the flames of votive candles, the light making ghouls of them, they texted their friends.

Mags was none of their business. *Yes, she is,* they chorused. *She is public property.* Before Freddy got banished behind the 'Do Not Cross' line, she'd heard Toni tell DS Malcolm Lane to organise a six a.m. press conference. Soon Mags would be headlines and trending on Twitter.

Freddy was sure she and Toni hadn't searched the battery

properly before Toni radioed for help. They had done a cursory check of the gun cells. Freddy crossed herself and prayed that Mags was at Lourdes and unaware of all this fuss in her name.

'Could you come with me, please, madam?' The PC who'd warned Freddy to keep back or she could contaminate the crime scene was holding up the tape. Numbly, she dipped beneath it. Freddy tripped and stumbled over the beach to officers clustered around an unmarked car.

'Freddy, we're going to need your ex's details.' It was Toni, notebook out, detective's face on.

'Ex?' Freddy could only think of Mags.

'Her name is Sarah, wasn't it, Freds?' Toni prompted with the ghost of a smile. *Freds.* Toni was being super kind. Like when Freddy had come to the Kemps' house after her dad chucked her out.

'Sarah Wood.' Freddy recited the number and address. 'Why do you want her? Sarah never met Mags.' *Sarah had been on the beach that night.*

'That's great for now.' This from DS Lane. Toni was walking off towards the battery.

'Why do you want Sarah?' Freddy's voice was feeble; it was whipped away in the wind.

A murmur had gone up from the crowd. One of the guarding officers was undoing the tape. People retreated to make way for a vehicle. Flashes, the stutter of fake shutters on phones held high. A van stopped five metres from the battery. White suits. Forensics. Freddy gasped, 'Is it Mags?'

'Sarah was in this vicinity. We have to talk to all potential witnesses. To eliminate her from our enquiries,' DS Lane said.

'Have you found Mags?' Freddy persisted.

'Frederica, please would you come with me.' Lane ignored her. 'We need to ask you a few questions.'

'Like I said, it's routine, Freddy.' Toni was back.

Actually, Toni hadn't said it was routine. Nothing would be routine again.

Across the lonely stretch of beach came the looming moan of the foghorn. Rolling fog made the air bitterly cold and damp. Freddy could no longer see the ridge of shingle or the sea beyond.

39

TONI

'A Sarah Wood is in reception,' Sheena said. Toni took off her headphones.

'Are you sure?' Anxious he might be hard on her, Toni had planned to listen in on Malcolm's interview with Freddy. 'She's coming from Liverpool.'

'Lewes.' Sheena didn't quite manage to hide her delight at wrong-footing Toni. 'She's staying at the Premier Inn. Seems that, contrary to what your friend Frederica told you, Sarah Wood never left Sussex.'

'Show her into room three. Offer water, no tea or coffee. Let her sweat. Then get on with reading those diaries.' A search of Mags's flat had thrown up a stack of diaries under her bed. It made Toni queasy for Sheena to read them, but Toni and Malcolm had enough to do.

Toni had brought in the Homicide Assessment Team. The HAT detectives – from Brighton – had assessed the murder environment and, as Toni knew they would, referred it to the murder squad. Aka Malcolm and Toni. Mags had been missing for a week. Her crucifix, the copy of Julian and the fact that she'd called in sick – although no one had actually spoken to her – told the police that Mags had not gone away of her own accord. They had traced the message that she'd sent Freddy to near the battery. Toni hadn't told Freddy they were not looking for a missing person. This was a murder investigation. Toni could hardly believe it herself. The chances Mags was alive after a week were bad.

'Sergeant Lane found this. He said you might want it. ' Sheena handed Toni an evidence bag. Toni looked through the plastic.

'I do. Tell him thanks.' She was going to enjoy her interview with Sarah Wood.

'And he said he's organised the press conference for six p.m.' Sheena would have perceived Worricker granting the SIO role to Malcolm as demotion for Toni. It was not. To avoid compromising the investigation if it got to court and to provide resilience, Toni would deputise for Malcolm. With a budget barely enough to police a duck pond, and as one of the few highly experienced SIOs in the county, Worricker had said that ACC couldn't afford to take Toni off the case. He'd told Toni she'd have to swallow down her connection to the potential victim and treat it like any other murder. *Any other murder. What was that?* This was Mal's first homicide. He'd nearly had a heart attack when she told him he was the lead.

'A reminder.' Toni told Sheena. 'No mention of the crucifix – call it jewellery. Or the Julian book – that will sound weird to the average punter. We have to grab the public's attention and get them on board.' She sighed inwardly. A single female churchgoing librarian was not sexy. The team would have to push to stoke the media's interest. Lines like 'this is the worst case of murder that in twenty years I've…' would not play out. Especially without a body. It wasn't a mother strangled by her crazed son. *Wild West Britain is open for business* had been one headline for the Munday case. The team needed all the help they could get.

Toni gathered up her notebook and Mags's hastily compiled file. Slim, it included Sarah Wood's details, scene photos, a picture of the crucifix and a shot of a stain in the last gun cell, which Toni needed with every fibre of her being not to be blood.

'There's the possibility that Margaret McKee will turn out to be on a pilgrimage. Check out likely sites. Lourdes, Rome, Walsingham.' Toni mustered up a few places where Catholics trotted off to for devout worship. Mags had been to Lourdes before – would she go back?

'What is this about?' Sarah Wood demanded when Toni backed open the door and laid her papers on the table. Toni switched on the recording machines and reeled off the usual stuff. She informed Wood they were being filmed for the sake of both parties.

'Bullshit. It's to cover your arses,' snapped the defence lawyer.

'Thank you for coming so promptly, Ms Wood.' Toni showed a pleasant demeanour while she struggled to put warm, chatty, tempestuous Freddy in a relationship with the ice-queen in Armani. 'I understand you are in Lewes and not at your home in Liverpool.' Fingers steepled, Toni rested her elbows on the table. *Open, inviting, encouraging.* Pointless, a defence lawyer, Wood knew every trick in the book; Toni had to box very clever.

'Yes.' Wood hesitated long enough for Toni to expect 'no

DEATH OF A MERMAID

comment'. 'Do I need a lawyer?' Wood's Liverpool accent had been ironed out by a private education or good effort.

'You are best placed to decide that.' For the camera, Toni gave the semblance of a smile. 'Why are you here?'

'I'm visiting someone. Not that I need to tell you.'

'This is a murder investigation.' Toni noted that Wood showed no surprise that they presumed Mags was dead. 'You will be well aware that we need the name and address of this person. Is there a reason why you would withhold the information?'

'Frederica Power is my lover. We live together.' Wood was daring Toni to blink. But Toni's quelled intake of breath was because Wood had called Freddy her lover. Freddy had said they'd split up. Why lie?

'Freddy has been here for her mother's funeral. She's staying in Newhaven. I don't know the address. Her family own a fishery; it should be easy enough to find her.' Wood was playing her. She knew the damn address. Freddy said she'd been there. She was a cool customer. Cool enough to kill?

'What were you doing on the evening of Saturday the eleventh of May?' Toni's stomach clenched.

'No idea.' Sarah cradled an eye-wateringly expensive handbag on her lap.

'You don't recall what you were doing last Saturday night.' Toni spoke to the tape as a less than subtle reminder that Wood was on record. 'A week ago.'

'I forgot the date. I was on my way here. Freddy wanted me with her.' Wood must be confident Freddy would back her up. Toni had a nasty feeling that Wood might be right. Freddy was loyal. Toni wished she could tell Freddy she must be completely honest. Unlike Mags, who believed she did everything in the face of God, Freddy had saved Toni's bacon more than once by lying to the nuns.

'Where did you meet Frederica?' Freddy had said she'd been shocked when Wood turned up at the battery. Sheena would check Freddy's phone records to confirm. Unless her pillow-talking lawyer got to her, Freddy would be cooperative. Malcolm would get the truth out of Freddy. *That was what Toni was afraid of.*

'I went to her mother's house. Before you try to trip me up, I found it on the electoral roll, but I don't have the address off pat. You'll find it on my satnav if you get a warrant for my car.' All in a day's work for a defence lawyer's investigator. 'It will on be my phone, which, sadly, I've left in the hotel.'

'You left your phone at the hotel?' Toni was working up a healthy dislike for Ms Wood.

'Come on, I'm sure you can do better.' Wood was playing her like a harpsichord. 'Weren't you at that ghastly convent with Freddy? Didn't you girls have to have top-notch brains to get in? Or at least have got God.' Wood gave a death smile. 'For the tape, when I got the call from your colleague to come into the station, I rushed out, leaving my phone on the dressing table thingy.' Toni would bet a month's salary that Wood had her phone in her lovely handbag. She knew Toni could only search it if she arrested her.

'You are Frederica's *partner*, yet you had to look up her mum's address?'

'Freddy didn't get on with her family. You must know that bigoted git of a pater chucked her out. Because she was a lesbian.' That challenge again.

Lesbian shezbian. Toni wouldn't be caught out that way.

'You also must know what happened next,' Wood was goading.

This time Toni gave the briefest assent. She felt mild annoyance that, while Freddy had told Wood about that time, Toni was bound by a promise she'd made to Freddy not to tell Ricky.

'You met Freddy at her mother's house?' This was not what happened, but she hoped to lead Wood down a path.

'Yes.' Wood was dismissive. 'I expected Freddy to return to our home with me, but she's been roped in to care for her mother's animals. Some holiday scheme for pets. Freddy's a walkover.' *Not very nice.*

'What time did you get there?' The woman was lying her head off. Toni helped her along.

'About eight?' Wood rolled her eyes. 'I don't count minutes when I'm off the clock.'

'You met Frederica Power at her mother's house?' Toni hadn't yet got background, but knew Wood had kept a bunch of bank robbers out of prison on a technicality. They were never going to be besties.

'Yes, *ma*-yam.' Bronx now.

'Strange.' Toni raised her racket to deliver an ace. 'Can you explain why we found your railcard on the ground outside the lunette battery?' She had the satisfaction of seeing Wood quell surprise.

'I must have dropped it.'

In addition, we have a witness who places you on the beach by the lunette battery in Newhaven at that time. Could you explain this discrepancy?'

'Am I a suspect for something, Sergeant?' Only a detective

could have spotted that Wood was rattled. She looked desperate to snatch the card.

'Detective Inspector. *For the tape*,' Toni said. 'You may be a key witness to a murder. Did you or did you not go to the lunette battery that night?'

'As you'll know from your *witness*, I was there briefly. I met Freddy there and I must have lost my card then.' Wood had regained her poise. 'We spent the rest of the evening at her mother's little house.'

'While you were there, did you see anyone at, or around, the lunette battery?'

Wood faked a yawn and Toni was irritated to catch it. 'Only Freddy, who, I am guessing, is your witness. If you've talked to her, I should have been there.' Now Wood looked properly cross. 'I'm her lawyer.'

'Did Frederica tell you why she was at the battery?' Toni ignored this.

'Why should she?' Answering a question with a question. Wood was swaying on her tight-rope. It was obvious Freddy had not told her.

'You weren't inquisitive, or even concerned, to find her on a beach at night alone?'

'Freddy hasn't been herself since she heard her mother was ill and then died. Bear in mind, Detective *Inspector* Kemp, this is a woman who was not informed, either by family or supposed friends, that her mother had cancer.' Snatching an advantage after an unforced error, Wood drilled Toni with a stare. Still feeling shit for not telling Freddy about Reenie, Toni would not be chastised by Sarah Wood.

'Have you heard of a Margaret McKee?'

'I… I may have heard the name. I hear a lot of names in my work.'

'What about Mags?' Toni cooed.

'I think that was the name of who Freddy was meeting.' Wood was improvising.

'You and Freddy have discussed Mags?'

'Hardly at all. She wasn't important. To either of us.'

'But you knew Mags's full name is Margaret McKee?'

'If you say so.'

'You said Freddy told you that her father threw her out for being gay.'

'Of course. We share everything. I didn't realise Margaret McKee was *that* girl.' Sarah looked askance. 'The one who dumped her high and dry. She lost her home, her livelihood and now her inheritance.'

'How did you know Frederica would be at the lunette battery?' Toni resisted tipping the beaker of untouched water over Wood's head. Keeping her powder dry, she tried for nice cop laced with ill-disguised admiration for Wood's intuition.

'I looked on my phone.'

'You rang Frederica?' Despite her grim mood, Toni was close to enjoying herself.

'I used Find my iPhone.' Wood was discombobulated now.

'Do you mean that you were tracking your partner?' Toni scribbled *Stalker* and shifted her notebook to give Wood a chance to show off her upside-down reading.

'Not like that.' Wood scowled at the page. 'For safe-guarding. She's my partner.'

'Did Frederica know that you tracked her?'

'Of course.' *Freddy had not known.* She'd told Toni that she'd since deregistered her phone so that Sarah Wood couldn't find her. Had Wood spotted this? Whatever, Freddy had told Sarah their relationship was over, but Woods had ignored her.

'How long were you at the lunette battery before you saw Freddy?'

'Minutes. I didn't see the McKee woman.'

Toni shuffled the file. The next bit was theatre; she had no evidence. 'Ms Woods, in your capacity as a solicitor, you sent letters to Freddy's brothers purporting to be on her behalf. Please tell me the contents of these letters?'

'I don't play games, Inspector.' Sarah kept her gaze on Toni. Buddha calm. 'Sorry, Detective Inspector.'

'Please answer the question.' *Damn.* Toni had dared hope that Wood would collapse under the weight of likely exculpation from the legal profession. Instead, she appeared boosted. Her eyes on the file, she'd have noted Toni didn't have the letters.

'What has this to do with why I am here?' Wood was icily benign. 'Did Mags McKee have something to do with Reenie Power's will?'

'We're looking at Mag— Margaret's disappearance from all angles.' Toni felt an uprush of emotion. *Compartmentalise.* 'As I understand it, Frederica Power knew nothing of the letters and they contravened her actual intentions. Can you confirm that?'

'Detective Inspector Kemp, I don't see how this tranche of questions has a bearing on the disappearance of Margaret McKee. As you well know, my professional relationship with Frederica Power is bound by client confidentiality. Unless

I'm under arrest, I would like to leave.' Wood gathered up her handbag.

'That's it for now, thank you.' Toni shut her notebook, gave the time and date, and ended the interview. For a woman used to clients who routinely sank their enemies on the bottom of the Mersey, her questions must have been a stroll on the prom.

'Freddy's not short of friends.' Toni put out her hand, ready for Wood to ignore it, but Wood was too good for petty negligence. 'We may need to talk again.'

'I'm at the Premier Inn in Lewes until Freddy's finished her business. I'm sure you would rather I remained in the area.' Sarah Wood let go of Toni's hand.

Toni watched Wood walk, with more grace than Toni could have achieved in four-inch heels, to a silver Alfa Romeo that would have had Ricky prostrate with envy. Wood had been clever. The letters were her word against Freddy's and she was confident that Freddy would confirm it. Wood's crime was that she was one possessive girlfriend. Mags and Freddy's passion was over twenty years ago, but she'd practically spat Mags's name: *this Margaret McKee*. Toni couldn't get aerated by women Ricky dated even five years ago. They belonged in his past.

Mags did not belong in Freddy's past. Freddy wasn't over her. Sarah Wood, intuitive enough to see through walls, must have seen it. How happy had Wood been that Freddy was meeting Mags at the battery?

40

MAGS

Random holes let in drifts of light. The only sense Mags had of when day became night. After dark the holes all but vanished. Gradually, she made them out, like far-off stars in the sky. She had lost count of the number of days it had been since that nasty sack had been pulled over her head. She was bundled into a car. Sick with fear, she had tried to note detail. The seats were leather. A satnav said they were on Fort Road until the driver turned it off. She had shuddered with terror. The lunette battery had been hell, but it had been familiar.

Where was she? What day was it? She was disoriented by terror. She had a percussive pain in her head. She must have passed out because she was no longer at the battery. She imagined she'd heard Freddy's voice far off, as if under water. Flounder was in there too. At moments the anguished panic at what had happened to her and what was to come overwhelmed her. Otherwise, Mags was numb.

On the first day – or night – Mags had woken, a headache raging – and automatically moved to get painkillers from the bathroom. She hit a wall. A cymbal clang that vibrated through her skull. She had felt sick and crumpled down. She wasn't in her bed. Pulling up a coarse cover, she curled up. She must have passed out because when she next opened her eyes there was enough light seeping through the holes to make out her surroundings. Her cell was a metal container. The mattress, a single unyielding futon that smelled fusty and damp. She was under a tarpaulin. The pillow was one of those memory ones and was brand new, she'd found a price ticket from John Lewis on the floor. Trembling with fright and the cold, Mags puzzled that she had a flimsy plastic bucket for a lavatory but had been provided with a fancy pillow that would adapt itself to her comfort. She tried to think like Toni. Did this mean she was going to be kept there a while? If she was a hostage, she might be released. *What was she worth?*

Had they found the crucifix? *Have you?* she asked Toni in her head. If the police had drawn the conclusion that she hadn't accidentally left it there – Freddy and Toni would know she never took it off – were they searching for her?

She fought the horror; it made her useless. She tried to think like a detective. If she were Toni, she would notice the paint-flaked metal walls. She would deduce that those stains beneath the holes were where rain had got in. This meant the container was somewhere outside. Mags walked herself pedantically through each observation. She'd resisted the bucket until bodily need eroded inhibition.

From inside the container she couldn't make out sounds. She guessed it was on wasteland. It wasn't in a street or a garden. There was no one nearby.

Out of nowhere, Mags felt fury. She let rip. She kicked at

the door. She screamed at the top of her voice. Subsiding, she heard the incessant drumbeat of her blood in her ears. It didn't bring her warder running. From the quiet, there was a hushing whisper, a dull hum that could be traffic. She had bruised her knuckles pummelling the walls and, from the pain shooting through her foot, had broken one of her big toes.

Edward! Let me out.

There was no way to escape. Even if she had a metal cutter, there were no edges to cut. From the noise when the door was opened, Mags guessed it was secured with a bar. Mags had never suffered from claustrophobia. Fear had changed that.

If she were to escape, the only chance would be when her kidnapper brought the cheese sandwich and water. Mags scoured her brain for anything Toni would suggest. Toni had gone quiet.

41

FREDDY

'How long have you known Mags McKee?' DS Lane had informed Freddy that, because of her connection to Detective Inspector Kemp, he was leading the investigation.

'Twenty-nine years. Since we were eleven.' A milky scum had formed on the tea. When the constable had offered it, Freddy thought it would look uncooperative to refuse. 'I haven't seen her for a long time.' Facts only; don't blather. She raised the cup to her lips and put it down again. She wouldn't be able to swallow.

'Did you arranged to meet Margaret McKee at the lunette battery?' DS Lane knew she had. Freddy had heard Toni telling him before she'd got sent beyond the cordon. 'Frederica?'

'Sorry. Yes. It was Mags's idea to meet where we used...' Freddy gulped down tea to hide her embarrassment. *Mags*. She wouldn't tell Lane the truth about Mags without asking her first.

'When Mags didn't come to the battery, what did you do?' Lane wrote something in his notebook which Freddy couldn't see. *Suspect shoplifted from Co-op.*

'I wandered about a bit.' Freddy tried to appear innocent. *She was innocent.* 'I went down to the shore in case Mags was there. I was late. I hadn't seen her on the road, which is the best route.'

'She wasn't by the sea?'

Obviously not. Freddy shook her head.

'For the tape, Ms Power has shaken her head.' He was severe.

'She wasn't there,' Freddy informed the machine. 'I haven't seen Mags since we made the arrangement to meet. At my mum's burial. In the cemetery.'

'What did you do then?' Lane was scrutinising his notes. Shouldn't he be examining her every expression?

'I thought I saw her. I ran back up from the beach, but when I reached the battery, it was my… it was Sarah Wood.' Freddy felt herself flush at the memory of the joy dashed, as if against the cliff.

'Sarah Wood.' Lane was looking at her now. 'We have her down as your partner.'

'She's *not* my partner,' Freddy retorted. 'We split up. On the day I came to Sussex.'

'Was that a mutual decision?'

'No. I texted her.' She felt sudden shame. What would he think of her?

'Was Ms Wood happy with this outcome?' If Lane disapproved of digital dumping, he gave nothing away.

'Sarah wants us to get back together. It's why she came to Newhaven and why she met me at the beach.' Impatient for him to get out there and find Mags, Freddy had the urge to tell him where to shove it, but the shoplifting had put her on the back foot.

'How did Ms Wood know you'd be there?' Lane shuffled papers as if he didn't care about the answer. *That old chestnut.*

'She tracked me on her phone.' She flung him a nugget.

'How long had Wood been there?'

'I don't know.' Freddy frowned. How long had Sarah been there? 'I was only down at the beach a few minutes.' She felt disappointed that he hadn't pursued the tracking. She was angry Sarah had followed her to the battery. Was that why Mags had left? After a week, this felt less likely.

'Is it possible Sarah had been watching you without you knowing? She tracked you there using her phone.'

'It is possible. But unlikely. Sarah likes to face you with things.' Freddy felt misery at the mess she had dragged back with her to Newhaven. To Mags.

'Could Sarah Wood have been coming *out* of the battery when you saw her? Rather than, as you supposed, going in.' Lane laid down his pen.

'There's a gate over the entrance. It's padlocked.' That had never occurred to her.

'Did you know this already or did you only notice it was locked while waiting for your friend?'

'Yes.'

'Which?'

Had she seen it? Or was it when she had gone back later, when she found Julian's book on the beach?

Freddy was suddenly certain that on the night Mags disappeared the grille had been closed. *With no padlock.* 'I'm afraid I don't remember.' Had Sarah been in there with Mags? A mad idea. *Why had she lied?*

'Could she have been hiding in the battery? Could Sarah

299

have glimpsed you through one of the gun-holes on the shore?' Lane scoured her face.

'I doubt it. Why would Sarah hide?' Freddy had a falling sensation. The police hadn't found a body in the battery. Toni would have said. *Wouldn't she?*

...by the time it's discovered the incriminating evidence has degraded. Alakazam, you have the perfect murder...

Freddie's face felt on fire.

'Would you call Sarah Wood the jealous type?' Lane pounced.

'No *way*.' Freddie heard the false ring in the emphasis.

'Sarah was tracking your phone. She knew where to find you. Is she possessive as a rule? She could, for instance, have called and asked you where you were.'

'Sarah gets insecure. No more than anyone.' Freddy fumbled for the truth. They would get hold of their phone records so would know this was rubbish. *Sarah called and texted about thirty times a day.* Freddy suspected that DS Lane didn't get insecure. He had a ring on his wedding finger so there was someone to be jealous of. How could she explain that, beneath the hard as nails exterior, Sarah was a lamb?

Freddy wished herself on the other side of the desk. As Toni's deputy. She'd help her sniff out clues and corner killers. She'd go home to someone she loved. Not Sarah. *Mags.* Freddy blurted, 'Sarah's not violent, she'd never hurt anyone.' In her effort to make it up to Sarah for not loving her, Freddy overegged it. Her nose was itchy, but if she scratched it Lane would see it as a sign of lying.

'Can you vouch for Ms Wood's whereabouts *before* your meeting at the battery?' Lane leaned in.

'We didn't *meet* there. I was meeting Mags.'

'It's possible, isn't it, that Sarah arrived first. Found Margaret McKee waiting for you and mistakenly thought Margaret was a rival. She flew into a jealous rage, attacked Margaret and dragged her unconscious into the battery. When you arrived, Sarah stayed hidden inside a gun cell. When you were out of sight, she left the battery and met you coming up the ridge.'

'That's not what happened.' Freddy scratched her nose. 'She can't have hurt Mags. No one could. She's too lovely for anyone to hate her. Mags is a special—' Freddy started to weep, her shoulders shaking. She wouldn't call Mags Margaret, it made her a stranger. Mags was a stranger.

Malcolm Lane pushed a box of tissues across the table to her.

Could Sarah have attacked her? The idea was ludicrous. Freddy choked on her tears.

'We'll leave it for now, Frederica.' Scraping back his chair, Detective Sergeant Lane rose. He held the door open for Freddy.

Freddy had expected to spend all night and the following day in the interview room. Until the moment that she owned up to a crime she couldn't name.

'One more question.'

Did you steal those Creme Eggs? Freddy blew her nose.

'When did you and Sarah Wood decide to contest your mother's will?'

42

TONI

'We don't know Margaret McKee has been murdered.' Malcolm handed Toni the coffee machine's wrong answer to a latte. At four in the morning the police canteen was closed. Hot and caffeinated, it would do.

'She's been missing over a week. We have two pieces of crucial evidence. The crucifix and the Julian of Norwich book. Items that Mags would not have left behind. The links on the crucifix were intact. It suggests that Mags took it off deliberately. Was she sending us a message and we got it too late?' Toni stirred sugar into her coffee so ferociously flecks of foam flew across the table. 'Unless she's being kept somewhere, it's unlikely Mags is alive.'

'I'm sorry, Toni.' Malcolm rarely called her by her first name.

'Thanks, Mal.' Tears threatened. *Compartmentalise.* 'Sarah Wood lied about the letters, she lied about going to the battery. She showed no compassion or concern that Freddy's ex might have been murdered. Crucially, she showed no surprise that we're treating this as murder.'

'Frederica confirmed that she requested Sarah Wood to write those letters. You think she lied?' Malcolm took a pull from his cyclist's water bottle.

'I *knew* she'd do that. It's not a lie. She's protecting Wood.'

'That figures. Frederica said she was OK that Wood tracked her phone. I'd be filing divorce papers.'

Toni couldn't match up the forthright, confident girl who always volunteered to read in class with the desolate-faced woman in Sarah Wood's car, staring out as if she'd been drugged. How far would Freddy go to cover for Sarah? Toni felt furious with Freddy and protective at the same time. She barked at Malcolm, 'For God's sake, stop calling Freddy Frederica.'

'Are you really OK with being my deputy?' Malcolm talked to the water bottle.

'I told Worricker I was and I am. You have to feel OK with me as your deputy or they'll helicopter in someone else.'

'I'd rather it was you breathing down my neck.' Malcolm whistled.

'Worricker is breathing down *both* our necks. He wants a review every day. Success breeds expectation. He said we got the Munday case wrapped up double quick and he wants an encore.' Toni gave a wry laugh. 'If he only knew how that case is rapidly unwrapping. One of the Mermaids is dead, another is missing.' When she had explained about the Mermaids to Malcolm he had nodded as if he'd once been a Mermaid himself.

'Could the two be connected?' Malcolm traced his scar with a finger. 'Could Margaret have killed Karen?'

'Worricker says not. And frankly, I'm not convinced.

Mags has nothing to gain from Karen's death. She does gain by avoiding Freddy.' Despite her worst fears, she stuck to the present tense.

'Could Frederica be involved?'

'*Crap!*' Toni shouted. 'Listen, Mal, Freddy came to me last Monday – you saw her, at the Tarring Neville piss-up. She asked me to open a missing person's file on Mags. Why do that if Freddy knew who killed her?' *What better way to misdirect Toni from a murder?* Seeing Malcolm resist saying this, Toni said, 'If, like you think, Sarah Wood murdered Mags in a possessive fit, I truly believe that Freddy would hand her to us on a plate.'

'I think she's hiding something.' Malcolm drank from his bottle. 'I asked Freddy if there was a lock on the battery gate. She claimed not to remember. 'Fraid I didn't believe her.' This time he looked at Toni.

'More likely Freddy's convinced Wood is innocent. Maybe she's worried Wood had a bit of a nose about the battery. Gotta say my money's on Wood.' Toni swilled the latte. 'The padlock I broke to get into the battery looked new.' Never mind the case, life was unwrapping. Something had to feel familiar.

'Shall I get Sheena onto the council about it?' Malcolm said.

'This is your gig. Freddy was at the scene, that makes her at least a person of interest.' Toni went to tie her hair back, forgetting she'd had it cut shorter. 'But, here's where me knowing Freddy is a perk. Freddy would be too squeamish to handle body disposal. I remember one time when we were kids, she went white when their cat devoured one of the gerbil guests. It was Andy who opened the cage. Ask me, it was deliberate. Andy was probably tired of being the one dangling from a fish hook. Freddy took the blame because she knew Fred Power would give Andy hell. The worst Fred did to Freddy was make her break the news to the owner that their pet got murdered on his holidays.' Unknown to Fred Power, Toni had stepped in. It was her first death knock.

'She's a fishmonger – she guts and fillets for a living,' Malcolm said.

'It's not the same as killing the love of your life.' Toni bit her lip. She should not have shared Freddy's secret. She tapped her notebook with her pencil. 'So anyway—'

'Wait. Freder— Freddy – didn't tell me that.' Malcolm was flicking through his own notebook.

'Probably didn't think it relevant.' *Damn.* Even Ricky didn't know.

'You don't think so?'

'Yes, of course it's relevant. But please, Mal, tread carefully.' Toni scrubbed at her hair. 'In the last year at school, Freddy and Mags were together, OK? It was super hush-hush. Even when Freddy told her parents – she is actually a rabidly honest soul – she kept Mags out of it.' Toni paused. Freddy had always tried to keep people safe. The Mermaids had done that for each other. 'Freddy's dad went mad. Called her cruel names – filthy dyke, freak of nature, worse. He slung some clothes randomly in a Sainsbury's bag, tossed her a couple of twenties and told her never to darken his door again. Fancied himself as keeper of morals. As you know, he disinherited her. Reenie followed his wishes, which surprises me, as she wasn't evil like him. He told Freddy that if she told the boys or anyone round here, about her "problem", she'd burn in hell. Freddy kept her word. I was gobsmacked Reenie didn't change the will. Freddy was her favourite.'

'You haven't been tempted to tell Ricky?' Malcolm's cheeks tinged pink as he caught himself asking his boss a personal question. Toni rescued him.

'I'm gagging, but I can't without Freddy's say-so. She won't let me. It honestly wouldn't bother Ricky or Andy. Andy reckons his nine-year-old son is gay. OK, so with Andy it's because the lad likes pink and does dancing on a Saturday morning, but you get the point. Fred Power was a shit. It's a miracle his kids turned out so well.'

'Terrible to disown your child,' Malcolm said.

'It *was* terrible.' Toni shivered at the image of Freddy on their doorstep clutching a bulging plastic bag.

'I wonder why Freddy's dad kicked off.' Malcolm screwed back the top of his water bottle.

'Yeah, well…' Freddy wasn't the only one with a secret. It wouldn't be Malcolm who heard it first. 'Let's just say, Fred Power was evil.'

43

MAGS

Mags had found the fishing hook in a groove on the container floor, not that in the darkness she had seen what it was. Lying awake, restless fingers spidering behind the mattress, she'd felt something sharp. She'd imagined a wasp that had got through one of the holes and was sleeping with her. She welcomed any company. But her finger tasted of blood. More carefully, getting onto her knees, Mags had dislodged it.

When at last the morning came, Mags held the metal object to the hole nearest to her and examined her find. She hated the idea of a fishing hook. A barb ripped into the fish's mouth or, worse, was swallowed and shredded its insides. The phrase 'to swallow something hook, line and sinker' expressed gullibility. But fish knew nothing about trust or lies. Was she a fish on the end of a hook? Had someone fooled her, hook, line and sinker?

She had sometimes gone with Toni and Freddie to fish off Newhaven pier. One of Toni's rebellions against the nuns at Our Lady. Mags knew Toni had fished with her dad and, not believing in an afterlife, it was in the activities they had shared that she hoped to find him. Freddy had grown up filleting fish. It confused Mags, huddled with a book on a camp stool by the pier wall, that although she found fishing itself so brutal, the sight of Freddy reeling in her fishing rod was very attractive. Her hair blown back by the wind, slicker tied around her waist, her forearms strong as she battled with the rod. It gave Mags an ache that she didn't want to understand.

This hook was large. It couldn't be for the kind of fish Toni and Freddy had tried to catch. Mags manoeuvred it through the hole then levered it back, tugging at the edges. The container was ribbed, sturdy; it would be difficult to damage. That was the point, it had to swing out of a ship's hold on the end of a crane or survive a building site. But the metal between the ribbing was thinner and it gave as she dragged on it with the hook. The container thrummed with each tug. Mags held her breath. When she'd shouted earlier no one had come, but it didn't mean her captor wasn't nearby.

Mags worked at the hole for what could have been hours or minutes, her feet jammed against the wall to steady her grip. The hook, perhaps for catching a shark or a whale, was stronger than the container and held its shape.

She had increased the five-pence-piece-sized opening to the size of a two-pound coin. Mags slumped, weary and frightened, on the futon. It would take days to peel back enough metal to escape through the hole and she might not have that time. Then it struck her. She could only work on the metal between the ribs. At best an oblong. It was far too narrow to squeeze through. All she had done was pass the time.

She fitted two fingers through the hole. Immediately, she heard sounds, as if her fingers were an aerial. Wind hustled the walls of her container. *The humming of the mermaid choir.* Cold air whipped her fingers. While her fingers were on the other side of the wall, a small part of her was free.

Fearful that he would come soon, Mags concealed the hook beneath the futon. The barb tore the fabric. Who was doing this?

Mags had dropped Edward. Her ex-assistant would easily disguise his voice on some app; he'd done silly voices at work. But he wasn't up to furnishing a container and keeping her prisoner and he'd have had to tell her why she was locked up before now.

The only person with reason for revenge was Freddy. *Please, not Freddy.* It was more likely a stranger. A psychopath.

Mother Julian had spent much of her life alone. Mags had once dreamt of a similar life; she longed to live in communion with God. She shut her eyes and spoke Julian's words.

"'If there is anywhere on earth a lover of God who is always kept safe, I know nothing of it, for it was not shown to me.'"

Was this a place in which Mags could be safe? Was she too bound up with fear to see? She shut her eyes and prayed, her fingers taking each bead of her rosary.

Ave Maria, gratia plena
Dominus tecum...

Time passed. *Decades.* Mags's lips moved silently. Her

voice mingled with the Mermaids'. Toni, as always, a beat behind. Freddy's arm was around her.

Freddy. I love you.

Her mind cleared. She knew who had imprisoned her. And she knew why.

The container door shrieked back. This time Mags did not put the bag over her head. She clutched the fishhook and plunged at the figure silhouetted against the sky.

44

FREDDY

'You shouldn't be here,' Freddy told Sarah. 'The police already suspect us...' She couldn't finish the sentence.

'Chill, babes, I've got this. The police have nothing on me or you.' Sarah pulled the Alfa Romeo into the street and stopped outside what she'd taken to calling the Power House. 'Where would I go?'

'Liverpool?'

'I couldn't leave you with your brothers, and now this woman disappearing. Besides, I told your mate Toni I'd stay in Sussex.'

'Quick, *inside*.' Checking up and down the street, itself a sign of guilt if the police were watching the house, Freddy hustled Sarah into the lounge. There was a hole in the cage by the fish tank. '*Nooo*.' She spun about.

'What did I just say? They have no evidence. It was bluff.' Sarah grabbed her.

Freddy wrestled free and wailed, 'Roddy's escaped.'

'Who's Roddy?' Sarah asked. 'Is he a suspect?'

Freddy pulled out her phone. She dropped to the carpet

and peeped under the couch. Nothing, not even dust and fluff. *'Jesus, Mary and Joseph.* Devious little blighter, he could be anywhere.'

'Roddy's a *guest.*' Sarah laughed. 'Wow, he bit through bars. What is he – a rat?'

'A degu.'

'Is that a rude word?'

'Degus are small, not unlike a rat actually, if, arguably, prettier.' Freddy pulled out the television. She flapped back the curtains, noticing the hems she had helped her mum sew one rainy afternoon. She lifted the bucket of logs, spilling two on the shell-patterned carpet. 'They're supposed to be sociable and love a cuddle. Roddy is stand-offish and irritable. He can shoot out of his cage and run like the wind.' David Bromyard or his wife had written 'runs like the wind' on the instructions.

'You've obviously lost Roddy before.' Sarah raised an eyebrow.

'It's in his instructions.'

'Instructions?' Sarah was peering under the sideboard.

'Clients fill in an information sheet – diet, feeding habits, vet number. They sign a permission form in case the animal has to be put to sleep or needs urgent surgery.'

'Your mum sounds like a sharp woman. She could have been landed with hefty vet bills or sued for feeding chocolate to a chinchilla.' Sarah crooned, 'Roddy. Come and get your beetroot.'

Freddy was consumed with misery. Mags had disappeared, Reenie was dead. Mags and her mum would have taken a lost pet in their stride. Toni too. Freddy had admired Mags's ability to sort stuff – she sorted Karen Munday – as if, with

God on her side, Mags could handle anything. Not that Mags had seen it that way. If Mags were here, Sarah and Freddy would not be suspects in a murder case. *Murder.* Freddy couldn't bear it. The world had turned upside down. If Mags were here, it would mean she was alive.

'Roddy's owner is due to collect him this morning. I *have* to find him.' Freddy should move the search into the kitchen. But if Roddy was in there, amidst cupboards with gaps, the pots and pans, she'd never find him.

'Game on.' Sarah began pulling cushions off the chair and the couch. Used to pulling apart police cases, this was her territory. 'Seems rather a pointless pet. William Morris said things should be useful or beautiful. Sorry, Rodders, you're not ticking either box.'

'Roddy is sweet.' Freddy felt the need to defend the missing rodent, although, thanks to her unease with his owner, she'd given him scant attention. 'Mrs Bromyard's had him six years.' The idea of her dad going out on Bromyard's trawler still needled at her. Even if he had lied about being seasick, he'd never have submitted to obeying a captain. But why would Bromyard lie? She flopped down on the couch.

'Some people hate to be touched or to touch. The sort to have an alligator in the bath. Maybe Mrs B's a cold fish. Pardon the pun.' Sarah said this whenever she used a marine metaphor. 'Rod-*eee*.' She crawled along the skirting board and reached the television. 'Hey, I've found him. He is sweet. He's washing his face with his paws. Get a ruler, or a stick or something.'

'I looked there.' Freddy was listless.

'I'll oust him. Come on, Mr Roddy, playtime's over.'

'Wait, lure him with a treat.' Freddy passed Sarah another beetroot bite from inside Roddy's cage.

Sarah closed off one end of the alley between the television cabinet and the wall and propped the cassette cover for *The Little Mermaid* at the other. 'Line up another cage or we'll go through this all again.' She lowered the treat towards the degu. 'Roderick, I advise that you settle. This is the best offer you'll get.'

Roddy preened his whiskers, apparently unimpressed by the beetroot. No one moved.

The mantelpiece clock ticked. Neither woman spoke. As if eager Darwinians, they observed Roddy nibble at his flank then, like an aproned Beatrix Potter character, stand on his hind legs, front paws together as if about to offer a cup of tea.

'He's rather endearing,' Sarah whispered. 'I'd like him as a pet.'

'Not if he spent his time behind the furniture, you wouldn't,' Freddy said. 'We could be here all day.'

'Who's a pretty boy?' Sarah warbled. Freddy recalled the funny, playful Sarah from the early days. Before Sarah had wanted more from Freddy than Freddy could give: marriage, children and to be the only woman Freddy had ever loved.

'Don't grab him by his tail.' Freddy was reading Roddy's instructions. 'They come off and don't grow back. Christ, I'd forgotten that.'

'Poor chap.' Sarah inched the *Little Mermaid* cover closer to Roddy.

Quick as a flash, he sped towards the other end.

'I knew he'd do that.' Freddy was dancing back and forth

like a goalkeeper waiting for a penalty. As if, should Roddy get out of the alley, she could anticipate which way he'd go.

'So did I.' Sarah was calm as, Roddy nestling in her cupped hands, she got to her feet. 'Are you named after Rod Stewart?' she asked him. Roddy sat upright in her palm as if perched on a lily leaf. He ducked forward and pushed his face against Sarah's chin. She cried out with delight, 'He *kissed* me.'

'Don't let him go.' As Roddy gnawed at the beetroot bite, Freddy suspected the kiss was cupboard love, but it was reward enough for Sarah. She grabbed Roddy's carrier. 'Stick him in there – he's going soon anyway. I'm not risking him wrecking another cage.'

'He likes it with me.' Sarah sat down on the couch.

God save us. Freddy put the carrier next to Sarah. She took her mum's chair by the fish tank. Half an hour until David Bromyard was due. She needed to get Sarah to leave. She pressed her face to the aquarium glass. A gold gourami flittered around the prince and princess. The figures who would never kiss held for ever at each end of the boat. Freddy remembered the first time she had wanted to kiss Mags. They'd been in the living room, side by side on the couch, the warmth of Mags's thigh against her own through her jeans. At fourteen, she hadn't kissed anyone, unless you counted Tony Stokes, a fisherman's son who she'd snogged behind the fishery, which Freddy did not. Her whole body had thrilled at the idea of being in the boat with Mags, of pulling her towards her and feeling her mouth against hers.

'Was she the love of your life?' Sarah was watching her.

'Who?' Freddy felt the ground give way. The shell pattern

was all around her, the bubbling of the oxygen pump deafening.

'Margaret McKee.' Sarah stroked Roddy's head with a forefinger. '*Mags.*'

In the beginning, when Sarah and she were in love, they'd done that thing of swapping stories of past escapades, revelling in the rerun of traumas that led them to the heady present. Beyond Sarah saying Mags was mad to let Freddy get away, after Freddy had told her the story of Mags Sarah had never referred to her again.

'Yes. She was,' Freddy said.

'Is that why you're here?' Sarah brought Roddy up to her face and rested her cheek against his whiskers.

'I came because of my mum.'

'That's an answer to a different question. Your mother is dead.'

The fish tank bubbled. From far off came the hoot of the Newhaven ferry coming into port. Although it was the morning, Freddy wanted to light a fire. The damp that lay in wait within the empty house had chilled the room.

'I need to know she's safe. It's not like Mags to disappear like this.'

'How do you know what she's like? You haven't seen her for twenty years.' Sarah gave the degu a parting kiss and lowered him into his carrier. She moved it around so that the door was facing away from her, as if she couldn't bear to look at him. 'Or have you?'

The unexpected question was like a mallet blow. Freddy rubbed the side of her head, as if she'd had been hit. 'I've seen Mags since I got here. At my mum's burial. She suggested meeting, but well...' Freddy couldn't finish.

In the blinding sunshine, close together, surrounded by gravestones. The exchange had been over before it began. She had gone over every word each had uttered, scrutinising them for nuance and hope. Now she relived the crushing disappointment when the woman by the lunette battery was Sarah and not Mags.

'How did you find out about your mum? When I bumped into your brother in the car park, he said he hadn't texted you.' From Sarah's expression, Freddy could see that she already knew the answer.

'Mags must have got my number off Toni. When I last saw her, I didn't own a mobile phone. Nor did she. Sarah, don't do this.'

'Sounds like she wanted to try again.'

'I doubt it.' Freddy hadn't dared consider this. She felt herself flush.

'Why do you think she wanted to see you then?'

'Probably to tell me about my mum, her last days or something. Maybe she hated how things were left and wanted closure. To make peace with God.' Freddy was furious at the coil of possibility burning in her stomach. Had Mags been working up to telling Freddy she loved her?

'If this Mags did want to start again with you, would you agree?'

The hesitation was too long.

Sarah got up. She paused by the carrier, touching it. 'What was it that Princess Diana said about there being three in the relationship?'

'Marriage.'

'What?'

'Diana's actual word was "marriage".' Freddy could have

kicked herself for bringing up the idea of getting married. Although she hadn't mentioned it for a while, Freddy knew marriage was what Sarah wanted. *The long haul.* Freddy blurted out, 'Mags is missing.'

'The police think she's dead.'

'I know.' Freddy saw a flicker of shame in Sarah's face. While Sarah could never resist a barb, she always regretted it. Sarah was hurt. In retreat, she fired at Freddy from her cover.

'When you arrived that night' – the words came out of nowhere – 'did you see her?'

'See who?' Sarah was by the door.

'Mags. Was she at the battery when you got there? Did you say something to her or—' Freddy fumbled in a mental fog.

Another long silence.

'You. Make. Me. Sick.' Sarah's voice cracked. 'Tell me, *Frederica*. What have the last two years been about that you could ask me that?'

'I don't think...' The hours since DS Lane questioned Freddy had been agonising. She was in a nightmare from which she couldn't wake. She wished herself on a rock beneath the waves.

'I've come for Roddy. I'm sorry I'm here so late. I've just got on shore. My wife would have come, but it's her Weight Watchers night.' Mr Bromyard pulled a face.

'No problem.' Freddy tried to smile, but her face felt Botox stiff. The questions she wanted to ask Bromyard swarmed in her head. *Why did my dad take me out on your boat? What were you whispering about in the fishery?* But something was stopping her from speaking.

'Roddy's fine with the wife, comes when she calls, does circus acts. With me he's a little tyke. I had a nasty nip off him and he's a tinker for escaping. Did he behave?'

'He was perfect, Mr Bromyard.' Owners of pets with teeth or wings rarely welcomed a truthful response. Freddy placed the carrier on the couch. Bromyard was counting out notes from a wad of money. Like her dad, it seemed he carried big amounts of cash on him.

'Call me David.' David Bromyard scratched his five o'clock shadow with a rasping sound. Something glinted in the greenish subterranean light.

'My dad had a ring like that.' Freddy pointed at his hand. 'My brother Andy wears it.' She was compensating for her diffidence by being extra nice.

'I know.' David Bromyard fiddled with the ring. Had Andy given it to Bromyard? Or more like, sold it. 'If I'd had a say, I'd have wanted you to have his ring.' He made a strange noise, between a laugh and choking. His face was slick with perspiration. The hand with the ring was shaking. He was ill.

'Why have you got the same ring? Dad said he had it specially made.' Something bad was about to happen. Sarah was on her way to Liverpool. Toni was tied up with finding Mags. Andy had been wearing the ring the last time she'd seen him. Did Andy owe Bromyard money? Who could Freddy call?

'I always had a soft spot for you. Lovely little thing, you were, not scared of anything.' Bromyard bit his bottom lip. 'It wasn't fair how it went. You couldn't help being keen on... girls and that.'

'What do you mean?' Freddy knew what he meant. Bromyard had found out she was gay. She didn't care who knew, but who had told him? *Fred.*

'Your dad came to see me after he made you go. He told me everything. I said it was wrong of him. How could he do that to you? What with him, with me. It wasn't kind.'

'You obviously didn't know my father. He didn't do kind.' Freddy was getting angry now. 'My dad believed the only kind of love was in the Bible. He was a good Catholic boy.' How dare this stranger tell her what to think about her own father?

'Fred was good, really. He kept his best side hidden. I'm glad he isn't around for this Munday business – it would have broken his heart.' David Bromyard held up the hand with the ring on what would have been the wedding finger, were it on his left hand. He licked his lips. Freddy had never seen someone look so terrified. 'Fred gave me this. One for him,' he stammered. 'One for me. It was the nearest thing.'

'Why did Dad give you a ring?' Freddy heard whistling in her ears. All the presents her dad had given her were fishing related. He gave Reenie household stuff, a washing machine, vacuum cleaner, iron, gifts designed to service his own life.

The ticking clock merged with her heartbeat. A sonar signal for evidence of a wreckage. Of drowned souls. Lives lost. *Lost lives.*

'Fred and me, we were… together. I loved him.' David Bromyard spoke with gigantic effort.

'Together? Dad didn't have friends.' When she'd told

Sarah that, Sarah had called her dad a sociopath. The air was like sheet steel, convex, concave.

'Like you and Margaret McKee.' Bromyard was tomato red. 'Fred said he loved me. He said it just the once. After he threw you out. I said he was wrong. Why couldn't he tell you about us? He loved you, he wasn't so good with Andy. He'd ask me what presents you'd like, he said I was clever, like you. I suggested books about the sea. Malcolm Saville, Little Tim stories.'

'*That's not true.*' Freddy thrust the carrier at Bromyard. 'This is *shit*.' She fumbled with the door. 'Go. *Now*.'

'...Fred wouldn't tell you kids. We fell out over it. I'd come back from sea and he was waiting on the dock.' The choking sound again. 'Freddy, your dad liked it with blokes. I wasn't the first. I think I was the last.'

'My dad's not here to defend himself. Those rings are two a penny. His ring belonged to my grandfather. Andy will leave it to his son.' Freddy made it up as she went along. She shouted, 'Take Roddy home to your *wife*.'

'I hated the hole-and-corner thing, slinking in darkness, and Fred felt disgusted after.' Bromyard was crying. Obscurely, through dismay, Freddy wondered if Bromyard was the first man she'd seen cry. The boys had been stiff upper lip at her mum's funeral.

Her dad had cried when she told him about Mags.

'...in this industry you've got to be a real man. Fred and me were real. If we'd come out, that was our livelihoods sunk. We'd have been drummed out. We had to keep it quiet. I still do. Apart from stuff on those apps sometimes, I'm with my wife. I loved Fred.' Bromyard spoke between sobs.

'This is such crap. My dad was the personification of

homophobia.' Freddy wouldn't normally think of taking on a man of Bromyard's build who, although about seventy, could go a few rounds in the ring. Thrilling with fury, she could smash his face in. *Shut. Him. Up.*

'My mum is barely in her grave. Dad loved *her*. She loved him.' Had Reenie loved Fred? '*Go.*'

Freddy slammed the door on Bromyard. She was unaware of getting a glass of Jack Daniel's and slugging it. Her phone rang.

'Freddy.' Toni's voice sounded muffled, as if she had a cold.

'Toni.' Freddy poured out another drink.

'We've had a DNA match. The crucifix you found at the battery does belong to Mags.' Toni cleared her throat. 'We found minute traces of her blood in the links.'

'Blood?' Freddy said the word as if it was new to her.

'We're holding a press conference in a few minutes. I wanted to tell you. We're announcing' – Toni cleared her throat again and, as if reading the announcement, continued: 'Mags was attacked at the battery, she was rendered unconscious and taken to a different location where a person or persons unknown murdered her.'

45

FREDDY

The fishery was shrouded in darkness. Freddy opened the gate and the car park became awash with pale white light. She waited. If any fishery staff were in, she would say she was checking on tomorrow's pre-orders. That was true. Whatever, Freddy was the sister of the proprietors, she didn't have to explain herself.

Andy and Ricky were on the trawler. Andy had said he liked to keep his hand in. Now of course, with Daniel dead, Ricky didn't have a mate. Despite him being unpleasant to her, Freddy did feel for him. He'd lost not only his mum, as she had, but his young apprentice.

Beyond the railway bridge, waves pounded the shore, punctuated by an insidious hiss as water pulled back. The gale was strengthening.

It was something that Bromyard said. The remark rose to the surface of her exhausted brain. Something about being glad Fred wasn't around for the Munday business. She'd assumed he meant Karen's murder. Then she remembered the numbers written in Karen's order books. Numbers that didn't tally with the pre-order totals. The anxiety of some of the pre-order customers, their furtiveness.

Had Karen Munday been operating a scam? If so, how did David Bromyard know about it?

Freddy decided to start with Andy's office. She plugged in the numbers on the keypad and got a red light. The lock stayed locked.

As kids, she and Andy had been alike; two peas in a pod, her mum said. Freddy knew how Andy's mind worked, what he liked, what he hated. He'd loved football, although he was rubbish at it. Freddy taught him to fish. He'd done better than her but their dad only praised Freddy's once-in-a-blue-moon catch. A skilful artist, Andy had once drawn the structure of a fish for Freddy's homework. She got the top mark. But she couldn't guess the code for his office. She didn't know what mattered to Andy now.

Freddy had no idea of his children's birthdays. Her nephews and niece had greeted her shyly at the funeral. They had grown up without knowing their aunt.

Andy had said Kirsty had the same birthday as Mags.

Freddy didn't need to trawl her mind for Mags's birthday. The first of May 1979. Sister Agnes had said she was *Mary's girl*. Freddy prodded the buttons. One, five, seven, nine. The red light.

Freddy had put Mags's birthday. Kirsty was a year younger. She tried again, swapping the seven for an eight and the nine for a zero. She got the red light. She reversed the month and day; the American way would be very Andy. The red light taunted her.

If it was one of Andy's kids, Freddy had no hope. Andy wouldn't have favourites. He had experienced the damage preferential treatment did to the other siblings. In the face of their dad's criticism, he'd developed a hard shell. Even before she left Newhaven, he'd got colder. Less reachable. He'd learnt to look out for himself.

Andy had loved football. The only date she knew was when England won the World Cup. Freddy stood close to the gutting room door as a gust of wind harassed her. Andy had had a poster of the winning team on his bedroom wall. She could have told a quiz master that the captain was called Bobby Moore; his curly hair was lighter than Andy's had been.

Sarah said, walk away from a problem, turn your back, then the answer will come. At the start of their relationship, Freddy had won a game of Trivial Pursuit using this method. Resistant to Sarah even now, Freddy nevertheless walked away from the containers. The car park was dark again. By the faint light of the moon, she made out one delivery lorry and her fish van.

The area flooded with light. Freddy had strayed within the arc of the sensor. Ricky's car shone as if recently polished. Again, Freddy found it hard to equate her baby brother with the expensive Mazda, with any car.

She looked at the dented bumper. A scrape ran right along the paintwork. Gingerly, she touched it. Grit. Her mind raced. The grit suggested Ricky had come up against a kerb or a stone, not another car.

Headlights powering towards her, the grind of metal on stone. The purr of the accelerator. Silence.

Ricky could have done the damage in the car park, anywhere.

1966. Out of a miasma of doubt, fear and misery, Freddy

plucked the answer. She jogged back to Andy's office and, pulse going ten to the dozen, keyed in the numbers. She was rewarded by a green light: the door opened.

When she turned on Andy's computer Freddy was faced with a password request. Despite the numbing chill in the room, she pricked with heat. Without expectation of success, she tried 1966 again. She sent up a silent prayer that her brother put ease of access before security.

He'd always been a trusting boy. Sarah, who had defended more than one teenaged hacker, would have had a fit.

Freddy opened the sales processing software and scrolled to the last week's orders. It was fiddly. She had to compare the nightly catches purchased from the various trawlers, including Ricky's, with the orders delivered locally by her and in the vans around the country. Power's delivered as far as Grimsby, which, given it was itself a fishing port, was mad. She found none of the orders that she sold on the fish van. She searched all the files but found no trace of them. Freddy recalled Sarah's query about the lack of a paper trail. The uneasy feeling grew. She had told Sarah the orders were handled in the office, but she had no idea if that was true. Nothing referred to the thousands of pounds she had taken in the few days she'd done the round.

An idea began to form. She had few 'walk-in' customers. Most of the sales she had been making in the short time she'd been on the round were pre-orders. It was a glorified delivery van. Had Karen Munday been selling fish purchased outside quotas behind Ricky and Andy's back? It would explain the hefty discount the customers were getting.

The only way landed fish would not be registered on the system was if it was never officially landed. Freddy grabbed some paper from the printer and the recycled fishing gear pen. She sketched out a diagram of how it would work. A trawler – it would be several, but keep it simple – took in a catch beyond the allotted allowance for a specific species. She drew a picture of a fish next to the boat and labelled it 'Skate'. Some or all of the crew would be in on it. They would stow the illegal catch in a secret hold in the trawler. Freddy added a square to the boat with a cross. The legitimate haul would be unloaded at the harbour and registered by the inspectors. An arrow indicated this. The catch was sold to Power's. She added a signpost saying 'Harbour' and a rectangle for the fishery. The trawler was berthed and the crew went home. What happened to the secret catch? Freddy sucked on the pen.

It would be unloaded at a different time and somewhere further up the coast to avoid attention. Or someone was paid *not* to see. Freddy drew a stick figure with a line from the harbour. Where was it stored? That was the easy bit; for the short amount of time the stash would be stored, it could be a lock-up. Freddy drew a cube and fussed over making it three-dimensional with an arrow pointing from the trawler. *A shipping container.*

For the scam to work, there must be customers willing to take top quality fish at knock-down prices, no questions asked. Rosie had said Alistair, the would-be councillor, ran a restaurant in Hastings. His margins would be vulnerable to price. Better to pay less for the fish in the first place. Obviously, he'd have to hide the illicit stock from inspectors his end. A chest freezer in his home would sort that. Freddy added in the end-customer. Alistair would bring in quantities daily and infiltrate them into the recorded supply.

The scam was low risk with high dividends.

Freddy knew from Sarah that crimes operated best with as few involved as possible who might blab to the police or make an error. Karen would have ruled with an iron rod. She was creaming off a fat profit. In one day, Freddy had delivered twenty pre-orders worth five thousand pounds. Karen could pay the fishermen a decent whack, give a discount to the restaurants and still have plenty for herself. Everyone would have a reason to toe the line.

Freddy sat back in Andy's chair. Her diagram only worked if the fishery was involved. She knew it was; she had been processing the pre-orders. It was Ricky's job to take the phone messages and make up the orders. Since Freddy had taken over the round, Andy had done it to avoid her and Ricky crossing paths. Did they both know?

Ricky had to be one of the fishermen supplying the secret catches. Even though it was inconceivable he would risk losing the business their father and grandfather had built up, inconceivable wasn't the same as impossible. Ricky had been against her working at the fishery. He didn't want her discovering exactly what she had discovered. Even as a kid, Ricky had wanted a trawler. Had he got it at any cost?

Was Andy involved? *No.* Andy would not have offered Freddy the fish round. One morning, when Ricky was at sea, Andy had had to text him to find where the pre-orders were kept. He'd had no idea. Where did he think the pre-orders came from?

Andy had still been at the office late the night when someone – Ricky? – had nearly mown Freddy down. Did he suspect it was deliberate? Was that why he'd asked her to work with him? She'd assumed he was pleased to have his old ally back. Then Sarah sent that letter and his trust in Freddy blew up in his face. She would be Andy's ally again.

Did Toni know?

Toni was still shoplifting. She'd spent years in the Met. Was she a bent copper? Freddy couldn't bring herself to add the police to her diagram. Sarah talked about officers compromised by greed who were in her clients' pockets. Of evidence lost, papers mislaid and the memories of key witnesses failing before they got to court. Not because the villains got to them, but after they'd had a visit from the police. Was Toni – a detective inspector – helping Ricky and Karen Munday run an illegal fishing business? A business that, from an early age, Freddy's dad had told her was very bad.

It was illegal.

The Munday business that David Bromyard had been grateful Fred Power hadn't lived to see.

The sums Freddy had taken over the last days, if usual, would go a long way towards a new car and the expensive clothes Toni had seen in Karen's bedroom. And Ricky's Mazda. Freddy's van could not be the only channel for selling on the black fish.

Freddy had been surprised at how upset Toni seemed by Karen's death. She had put it down to Toni being a good person; she could forgive and move on. What if it was the business that they'd operated together which Toni missed? She shook her head. *No way* had Toni been involved in something illegal with Karen Munday. With anyone.

Freddy circled the office. She stopped by the desk that Ricky used when he was there. The drawers were locked. She scoured around it. Something was behind the monitor.

She pulled it out. It was a file of green cardboard. The letters 'GL' were on the front. She flipped it open.

GL was *Gold Light*. Freddy was staring at the list of pre-order customers.

Outside, the security light was triggered. Freddy switched off the light and crept to the window. She became aware that the wind was battering the Portakabin, like a ship in a storm. It was half past two. *Christ*. Staff would be arriving to meet the catch. *Ricky and Andy would have landed.*

Freddy fumbled as she tried to shut down the computer and clicked restart. She reached round the back of the machine and turned it off. When Andy fired it up in the morning, a message would pop up saying it hadn't been properly turned off. She doubted he'd give it a second thought.

She heard the scrape of a shoe outside the door. Hot now, despite the artic temperature, Freddy cast about the office, but she knew already that there was nowhere to hide. A shadow filled the frosted door panel. She heard the click of the code. *One. Nine. Six. Six.* Her mind whirred. *What would she say?* She retreated to the filing cabinet, as if she could slip between the tiny gap behind.

'*We'll talk tomorrow.*' Ricky raised his voice above the roar of the wind. Freddy strained to hear who he was talking to. Silence. She prayed that Andy wasn't with him. Since Sarah's letter, Andy's trust in her was wafer thin.

Freddy had been reckless – *stupid* – to come to the fishery. Ricky would jump to the conclusion that she was scoping out the company's worth, that she did intend to contest the will. He would fear she was on to him. *He must not find her there.*

The shadow had gone. Freddy tiptoed to the door and put her face to the glass.

The memory of hiding behind a stack of crates with Andy in the fishery reeled like a film in her head. Other kids would have played hide and seek for fun. Whenever she and her brother hid from their dad, they were terrified. It was not a game.

Freddy felt it now. *Worse*. Ricky knew she was hiding there. The car park light went out. A ruse to make her think he had gone.

In the dizzying blackness, Freddy stumbled for the door. A tiny light made her freeze. It was the luminous face of her watch. She was losing it. She found the door and, breath held, eased it open. The handle was snatched away. She was smashed against the wall.

An eerie cry funnelled along the criss-cross of alleyways between the shipping containers. The wind howled. From the containers came a thump as wind battered the metal.

Cold air whipped her face. Shadows flitted across the Bait Motel. *Shadows of what?* There were no trees, no bushes. Freddy edged along the prefab wall to the corner by the kitchen.

Off to her left, the factory door was closed, the pink glow of the fly-killer lamp showing in the windows. The high galvanised fence, the spikes like spears, was unscalable; the only way out was through the gates. It would activate the light.

A bang. Another bang. Freddy stayed still. She traced the sound. It was Andy's office. She hadn't shut the door properly. It was hitting the outside wall of the descaling room. Freddy waited. Would it bring Ricky out of cover?

She let it bang ten more times, then risked Ricky seeing her. For every step, she was hurled back by a fierce gust. The door was closed. The banging came from the containers. Something had blown loose in the gale.

When she reached the corner of the prefab, Ricky's Mazda had gone.

The humming of the wind froze her blood. It was too harsh, too frenetic, to be a Mermaids' song. It came from hell. In a lull between gusts, from the scrub on the other side of the railway line, Freddy heard a herring gull's answering lament.

A clang.

Another bang. Not the wind. Walk away from a problem and the answer presents itself. The illegally caught fish were stored in the containers. Ricky had moved his car so she'd assume he had gone. Any minute he would come down one of the alleyways between the containers.

Toni had said a police officer ran towards danger, not away from it. Freddy slipped along the gap between the first line of containers. Deep in shadow, the dark was substantial. She groped and snatched at it. She stumbled against a metal wall. The sound was dull, but it seemed to Freddy that the vibration rang on and on. It gave her away. She hived off a side alley and waited. The gap was too tight to crouch.

'Freddy.' A bright light.

'Who's that?' Freddy shielded her eyes too late. The light burnt onto her retina, rendering her blind.

'It's OK, it's me.' Her brother gripped her arm. 'What the hell are you doing?'

46

MAGS

Mags had only surprise and the fish hook on her side. Her ankles bound, she lunged at him and slammed the hook into his body. She aimed for his crotch, the pain would give her more time, but she'd underestimated how fear messes with your brain and, flailing, she shoved it in his stomach. She felt the yielding of flesh, so much easier than the metal of the container. She pulled out the hook. The barb ripped his flesh. 'God forgive me,' Mags said as she went for a second try. Her head was a jangle of voices. *Have... mercy... O lord... Christ have mercy... my most grievous fault, pray for me... Oh God, to whom every heart is open, every desire known...*

She shoved past him and, rolling and pushing, plunged down a corridor of shipping containers.

Mags knew where she was.

The wind was raging. It was what she'd heard from her metal prison. Now she caught his groaning. Soon he would recover enough to come after her. She slipped and kicked against one of the containers.

Clang.

The sound would give her away. Moving like a worm, pushing and curling her back, Mags rolled into a gap between containers. At the end, her way was stopped by a high fence. The old fence had been chain-link, and possible to climb. Beyond, Mags saw the top of the lighthouse. She smelled the sea. She reached her arms through the bars. *More of her was free.*

It was pitch black behind her. He would have a torch so had only to look along each of the gaps between the containers, working his way down the alley, until he found her. He knew she couldn't get far. Mags lay flat so that, even with his torch, he might miss her.

She was freezing. Her teeth chattered with mortal fear. Her body was toxic with the adrenalin that had flooded her veins over the last days. Her face was hard up against one of the bars, her neck cricked. Mags tried to ease backwards and grazed her nose on the side of a strut. A hysterically silly injury. The stinging made her reel. Her mind began to work. The edge of the strut was sharp. *Like a knife.* Mags shifted onto an elbow and thrust her hands into the gap between the struts. It flayed her skin but determination was an anaesthetic. She ran the plastic cable up and down the strut. In seconds, it snapped. Mags was euphoric. It took only slightly more time to free her ankles.

Mags scrambled up. The stiffness was excruciating. She staggered. She could remain where she was. Lying flat, looking up at the stars. It felt good. *Not that good.* Mags had no choice. She would run for it.

That was her mistake.

47

FREDDY

When Andy had found her at the fishery in the small hours of the morning, Freddy had gabbled an excuse about wanting to see the boats come in, and arriving too early. She could tell from his face he didn't believe her, but nevertheless he'd given her a lift back to their mum's, even coming in and helping to feed the pets. By the time he left, she was pretty sure she'd won back his trust. Now, as she prepared to go out on the morning fish round, she risked losing it by sharing her suspicions that Ricky had tried to run her down after she left the pub in Tarring Neville.

'Freddy, you're off beam, mate. This is Ricky you're talking about,' Andy said. He'd come in early and helped her with the pre-orders. Ricky was down at the harbour sorting his boat. *Stashing his illegal haul.*

'It does seem mad.' Freddy couldn't reconcile the toddler who'd joyfully romped in his bouncer suspended from a doorway with a cold-blooded killer who could murder his sister. Fred had changed Ricky's nappies. She'd dandled him on her lap, rocking him to sleep to *The Little Mermaid.* 'It makes no sense to me either. Ricky's car was there when I left here the other night. The bonnet was warm. He'd been in it. I'm sure he heard our conversation.' Freddy took a breath. 'And I think he was there the night you found me.' She hesitated. She should tell Andy she believed Ricky was dealing in black fish. That he stowed it in one of the disused shipping containers and sold it on. *She was selling it.* Andy was having trouble believing Ricky had tried to kill her. One thing at a time.

'Ricky could have been earwigging, that I can get, he thinks I cut him out of stuff. I have to make snap decisions and he's often incommunicado on that boat.' Andy shook his head. 'But seriously, our baby bro? I saw that dent – I keep meaning to ask him about it. It's weird he hasn't whinged – he must have noticed it.' He laughed. 'If I rest a finger on his precious motor, Ricky goes mental.'

'He won't want to draw it to your attention.' Freddy mechanically assembled the fish on the ice. Once, she'd have loved the fish round. But, sickened over Mags and now sure the round was the cog in a fishing scam, it was a terrible chore. 'Ricky wants me dead.' The words made her heart stop. *Her brother wanted her dead.*

'Steady on! OK, he's upset about you leaving us with Dad. That you thought yourself a cut above. I've said, you were young. You wanted more. Truth is, I didn't get it. It was like you dumped us.' Andy scuffed his shoes about on the concrete. Freddy noticed the blocked heel that compensated for his limp. Not obvious unless you were looking. 'Thing is, you know Ricky was close to him. He didn't see half what you and I did. Then you sent that solicitor's letter.'

'I thought we'd got past that.' She made the decision to trust Andy. 'Thing is, Sarah sent those letters without asking me. I had no idea. If you report her, it will destroy her career. She did it for me. She – she's my partner.' Standing outside the fishery, the salty smell of the sea on the wind her life, Freddy felt herself flush. 'She was. We've split up.'

The air was cold. The sky bright blue as if from a holiday brochure. In the crisp sunlight, the rusting containers gleamed off-white. A crane on a building site in the centre of Newhaven swung a load of bricks slowly round.

At last Andy spoke. 'Wow. That must have been a shock, her doing that.' He believed her. 'All the same, it's one hell of a thing that Ricky would run you down.' He had made no comment that her partner was a woman.

'He always had a temper.' Freddy had a vision of Ricky smashing a bottle against the fish tank when he was five. Thankfully, it was plastic.

'He's not a murderer.'

'You said that about Daniel Tyler, yet he killed Karen,' Freddy reminded him.

'That's different.' Andy said. 'And I didn't say that. It was Ricky who thought the kid was a saint.'

'I swear it was deliberate. It wasn't a drunk driver. The car drove straight at me, then had no trouble turning. He wasn't pissed.'

'I can't take it on. What with Mum.' Andy looked close to tears. 'Ricky's been a pain lately. Angry, loses it for no reason. I wondered if he and Toni had issues.'

Toni hadn't said anything, but maybe she wouldn't tell Freddy. This made her sad. Toni had once told her everything. Toni had said she should tell the boys. 'Andy, about me leaving.'

'Let's not go there. It's done and dusted.' He pinched his eyes.

'Dad made me promise to say nothing. I had to swear on the Bible. He said he'd hurt you if I did.'

'So, don't.' Andy grabbed a length of towel from a roll on the shelf above the fish van counter and blew his nose.

'I didn't just up and go like he said. I told him I was in love with a woman. He went mad. I thought he'd kill me. He got me by the hair. Mum couldn't stop him. When he ran upstairs, I hoped it was over. But he came back with a few of my things shoved in a bag. He told me I was a freak, a disgrace. Horrible things. He *had* no daughter. He told me to leave Newhaven and never tell you or Ricky why.'

'He kicked you out because you were gay? *No way.*' Andy's reaction was exactly what Toni had said it would be.

'He said it wasn't even a half-life. I would burn in hell. That man, David Bromyard, who claims to be his friend, said he'd told Fred Power that was cruel. For what it was worth. He tried to make me say who the woman was that I was in love with. I wouldn't.'

'Bromyard was his friend. Stupid git.' Andy curled a lip. 'Then again, Dad could fool people.'

They stopped talking as a delivery driver walked past. He greeted them with the tip of his baseball cap and tossed a lighted cigarette into a puddle of meltwater.

'It wasn't a reason to leave for good. I didn't need you protecting me. I can stand on my own two feet.'

'I couldn't risk him hurting you.'

'He did anyway, but you weren't there. We could have got the police involved. I said that enough times to Mum. She wouldn't have it. *Jesus*, if he hadn't dropped dead, I swear I'd have killed that bastard with my bare hands.' For a moment Andy looked like he meant it.

'I had to go,' Freddy said. Andy didn't care about who she slept with. He was angry with her for abandoning him. 'I should have found a way to get in touch. These days, with mobile phones...'

'We had phones then.'

'You didn't.'

'I did, actually. To show off to Kirsty. It can't all have been because you were with Mags.' Andy began tearing the square of towel into strips. 'What about Mum? Was she there? Did she know?'

'Mags?' Freddy went cold. 'How did you know?'

'Obvious. It had to be one of your Mermaids. It wasn't Toni, so who else?'

'Yes, it was Mags.' Freddy couldn't look at him as tears threatened. Andy's response brought it properly home. 'Please don't say anything to her. She'd be upset that you know. She's moved on.'

'Chance would be a fine thing. If she's not walking on this flipping pilgrimage like you said, it seems she's vanished.' Andy went quiet. 'It's all gone to shit, hasn't it, sis?'

'Yes.' Although it was her that had alerted Toni in the first place, Freddy couldn't let herself believe that Mags was dead. She clung to a sliver of hope.

'You said Mum was there.' Andy looked like he was thinking what Freddy was thinking. To keep the peace, Reenie Power had hung Freddy out to dry. Her mum had been there and she had done nothing. *She had not changed her will*.

'Tell Ricky, then he'll stop being Mr Nasty,' Andy said.

'It won't change things. I don't think he tried to knock me down because of that.' Freddy couldn't tell Andy about the black fish. When she'd gone into Andy's office that morning, the green file with the list of pre-orders was no longer behind Ricky's computer. She needed to bring Andy proof.

'He would totally get it. He's open-minded,' Andy protested. 'You know what? This whole thing has got out of hand. I've got a suggestion. *Two* suggestions. Let's go to Mass, all of us. We'll light a candle for Mum together. And later – now don't shoot me down until you've heard me out – you and me help Ricky crew the trawler, and we'll *all* go fishing. The Power dynasty riding the waves, yeah? Please, Freds.' His eyes glittered with excitement.

'Ricky would never agree.' Freddy reeled at the idea.

'You said you have the marine qualifications. So have I. I'm the boss. Ricky will agree.'

'Okay. I'll come to Mass.' The church was the only place she would find Mags. Alive or...

'One thing, Freddy.' Arms folded, his face rigid, expressionless. 'Mags shouldn't have turned you down. Keeping that secret, it's a sin.'

In his clumsy way, Andy had stuck up for her. Toni had been sure that Andy wouldn't care about her being gay. But Freddy knew that, while the solicitor's letter had been a blip, Andy would never forgive her for leaving. She gave a sigh as she reached the ring-road and made for Bishopstone, one of the outlying villages, where, thankfully, there were no pre-orders so she wouldn't be knowingly illegally trading fish.

She would never forgive herself. Her love for Mags had destroyed lives. Yet guilty though she felt, Freddy knew it had been right.

48

TONI

'You can't see her.' Josie Webb stopped Toni and Malcolm by the nurses' station, where they were squirting foam cleanser onto their hands from a wall dispenser.

'Josie, we'll have to ask you to lower your voice,' a nurse said. He turned to Toni and Malcolm. 'You have five minutes.'

'Tell them to *go*. Leave us alone.' Mrs Webb's voice was louder. 'You have your killer. That little bugger murdered his mother and he's made my little girl a paraplegic. The only reason I wish he'd lived is so I could strangle him.'

'Have you told Daisy?' Toni was horrified. She'd assumed Daisy was turning a corner back to full recovery.

'Yes.' Josie swayed as if on a boat. Toni caught her by the shoulders and held her. Josie sobbed into her neck. 'She blames me.'

Toni stroked Josie's hair.

'She says I fooled her. Everyone knew, and I let her think it was a bang on the head.' Josie was trembling. 'We were holding off until Daisy was strong enough. I'm sorry, you've had a wasted journey. She's won't talk, not even to Annette, her favourite nurse.'

'Daisy's lashing out – mums are always the first in line.'

Toni had shouted at her mum. *Why didn't you stop him killing Dad?*

'I must be strong for Daisy.' Josie pulled away and brushed her sleeves, trying to reclaim her brisk efficiency. Toni recalled Josie's dignified eloquence to camera: *'If you have information about this incident, please tell the police. No one should go through the pain that we are suffering.'* It was pure gold.

'Mum, let them in,' a feeble voice called from the room. 'I asked them here.'

Toni the detective snapped back into action.

'We got a message that you remembered something Daniel said in the car?' Swiping up a bundle of wool stuck with a crochet needle, Toni slid into the bedside chair.

'It's like a wall with Danny on the other side.' Daisy shut her eyes. Tears oozed from under the lids. Toni reminded herself that Daniel Munday had been Daisy's boyfriend. Or was Daisy crying for herself?

'What was Danny saying?' Malcolm used 'Danny' to reignite the familiar for Daisy. Malcolm had a knack with young people; he had one at home.

Josie Webb began pacing the room, out of Daisy's eyeline. Her life, like Daisy's, had been bombed to smithereens.

'He said about a man being there, that he never guessed,' Daisy said.

'He never guessed he was there?'

'He never guessed what was happening.'

'Do you mean Danny discovered his mum had a

boyfriend?' Toni dimly saw that the ball of wool was a crocheted exotic fruit.

'I don't know, he was shouting. I got scared.'

'The man was shouting?' The man Mo Munday said her sister was seeing in secret. *Daniel had recognised him.* That narrowed the field.

'Dan.'

'He had no right to scare you.' Josie stopped by the bed.

'Do you mean Dan was shouting in the car? While he was driving?' Toni said. Something was off key.

'"He called me his friend."'

'*Your* friend?' Toni echoed.

Daisy rounded on Toni. 'No! It's what Danny said to me about the man. "He called me his friend." He was stupid, I said so. Blokes like that, they don't have friends.'

'Did you see this man?' *Ricky was Daniel's friend.* Toni dreaded Daisy's answer. *Mags is walking on a pilgrimage.* Ricky had used the same phrase as in the text Freddy had got from Mags's phone.

'He said he'd kill me if I said I'd seen him at the house.'

Heads snapped around.

'You were at Daniel's house?' Toni scrunched the wool fruit. 'Was Karen – Daniel's mum – was she alive when you were there?'

'Dan didn't kill her, if that's what you're saying. That man will have done it.'

'Wait, was the man here?' Toni caught up with Daisy.

'I just said,' Daisy said.

'Darling, tell the police. You can trust them,' Josie whispered.

Toni had seen no need to put an officer outside the room.

She shot a look at Malcolm. He nodded and was out of the door. *CCTV, description of every bloody visitor, find this man.*

'I can't trust any of you.' Feeble, Daisy pawed at her mother's hands, clinging onto them as if she might slide off the bed. She pushed out the words between sobs. 'He's got a fish. On his wrist. On the inside. If I tell you, he said I'd end up like Karen.'

'With *me*!' Toni yelled to Malcolm, who was at the nurses' station. Without waiting for the lift, she crashed through doors to the stairs.

'Do you know who this man is?' Malcolm caught up with Toni by the car.

Toni leaned out and slapped the blue light onto the Jeep's roof.

'I do.'

49

FREDDY

Freddy dipped her finger in the font by the church door and, dabbing her forehead, made the sign of the cross. She took an Order of Mass from a pile on a table. Her family had an unofficial pew near the front on the left of the aisle, but, with the hint of a bob to the altar, Freddy sat further back on the opposite side. She couldn't see Andy and Ricky. Even if she'd not been working on Mags's case, Toni wouldn't come to Mass. Her brush with God had been brief.

The church was filling. Little children were at the back, their prattle and fuss over the tattered books and toys attracting annoyed glances from some worshippers, indulgent nods from most. Freddy knew that there was no question of one parent babysitting at home. A cradle Catholic meant exactly that. Every Sunday, Freddy had been one of those kids, she and Andy trying to quell Ricky's cries and gurgles. The memory hurt. Ricky had been a lovely baby.

Freddy loved the pageantry and ceremony of principal celebrations – Christmas, Lent, Holy Week. In their teen-aged years, Mags had put her forward for readings. Freddy would have liked to be Christ in the crucifixion of Jesus on Good Fridays; it struck her as dramatic. But it was a man's part. She'd settled for narrator. She always got stern looks from Mags for being late with the responses. Unless Freddy had a role, she tended to be distracted. Today she was beyond distraction. Freddy felt dead inside. *Where was Mags?*

Ricky would hate Andy's idea of them crewing the boat. Reenie Power's will had suited him. Never good at sharing, Ricky would fight Freddy for any part of the business. That night on the road, he'd pointed his car at her and stamped on the pedal. Ricky would never forgive her for leaving either.

Andy didn't know about Gold Light; that for Ricky everything was at stake. *Ricky must have killed Karen. Did that mean he killed Mags too?* Freddy gripped her missal as she let herself recognise this. The police had interviewed Ricky. They let him go. Did Karen threaten him that she'd tell Andy – *or Toni?* – about the scam? Daniel Tyler had come home that night, found his mother dead and Ricky there. He'd rushed out, picked up his girlfriend and lost control of the car on the beach. Or crazed out of his mind by what he had seen – Ricky was his mentor, his role model – had Daniel deliberately driven into the concrete block?

Was Ricky having a relationship with Karen? Was he the man that her customer, Rosie, had said Karen had dumped? Freddy shied from the questions, unconsciously dipping her head. Ricky had fooled Andy, but he'd know he couldn't fool her. *Had he not fooled Mags either?*

Freddy caught sight of DS Lane in a back pew. *Was he here for Mags?* From the way he was sitting, forward with his eyes darting around the congregation, Freddy doubted he was a Catholic. He saw her and nodded. Catholicism welcomed all comers, believers or not. Freddy did not welcome a police detective. Had he followed her? Did Toni know what her *boyfriend* was doing? More questions.

Freddy shifted in the pew. There were too many people to ask to move and leaving would arouse Lane's suspicion. How dare he waste police time trailing her while whoever had got Mags remained free? *Had Ricky got Mags? Had anyone got Mags?* Subsiding in her seat, Freddy stared at the crucifix. Jesus's suffering was her suffering.

Father Pete was greeting the congregation.

'...and the communion of the Holy Spirit be with you all.'

'And with your spirit,' Freddy hurriedly responded. She might be lapsed, but she didn't need an Order of Mass nor the hymnals in the pew shelf. Catholicism was in her marrow. Clutching her missal (rarely opened, still it went with her everywhere), she knew every word.

Absorbed by the ritual, she made the responses and sang the hymn. The organ's solemn notes wrapped around her. She snapped to when Andy approached the altar. He was doing the reading. Freddy felt pleased; in the past, Andy's dyslexia had barred him from taking part.

She knelt for the liturgy of the Eucharist. Father Pete's words washed over her.

Blessed are you, Lord God of all creation,
For through your goodness we have received
the bread we offer you:
fruit of the earth and work of human hands,
it will become for us the bread of life.

Right on time, Freddy joined in the response, 'Blessed be God for ever.'

Freddy had not intended to receive a blessing but found herself lining up with other worshippers. When Father Pete's finger touched her forehead and he looked into her eyes, she feared she'd fall at his feet. Freddy forgot to cross her arms over her chest, as the lapsed Catholic she was, and took the host. Glancing back, the wafer melting on her tongue, Freddy saw Andy in line halfway up the aisle, Ricky behind him. Andy winked at her. Ricky looked through her. Did God see Ricky for what he was? *God forgave sins.*

'The Mass has ended, go in peace.'

'Thank you for coming.' Andy indicated a bench by the statue of Mary in the church garden.

'I was coming anyway.' Freddy was ungracious.

'I told Ricky why you left the fishery.' Andy hustled their younger brother forward.

'Being gay is no big deal. You should have told Dad that.' Ricky squared his shoulders. 'Instead you went and left us to handle him. And you never came to see Mum.'

'I could count on one finger the times he laid a hand on you,' Freddy said. 'Believe it or not, it was no fun being his favourite.' Her temper rising, Freddy made a decision. She would crew Ricky's boat with Andy. Forget kissing and making up, she'd search the boat, find the secret hold and show the illegal haul to Andy. It would be enough to convince him. Freddy couldn't tell Toni, because it was possible – *and unbearable* – that Toni already knew. She'd persuade Andy that they had to report Ricky to Malcolm Lane.

'And you want her in?' Ricky grimaced at the sky, as if at God. 'She's not coming on my boat.'

'Guys, remember where we are,' Andy hissed. 'And it's not your boat until you pay me off.'

'What do you guys know about David Bromyard?' Freddy blurted out.

'He's one of our suppliers,' Andy said. 'I told you he was Dad's friend.'

'What about him?' Ricky looked worried.

The Munday business. Bromyard must know about the scam. He was a supplier.

'Bromyard implied they were more than friends.' Her mouth was as dry as leather. She didn't want to have this conversation. Now was not the time to mention Bromyard's ring.

'What's that supposed to mean?' Ricky leaned in.

'Listen, guys. We're going fishing tonight. A reunion. Mate, this is *not* up for discussion.' Andy glared at Ricky. 'We'll crack open beers and toast Mum. Eight o'clock at the harbour. Freddy, I'll lend you the gear.'

Shrugging like he didn't give a toss, Ricky mooched out of the garden. Freddy knew Ricky well enough of old. He was very angry.

'That went well.' She got up from the bench.

'Leave it to me.' Andy seemed calm. 'I'm going to suggest you come in with us. Don't say anything now. Think about it. It should be all of us. We'd rake it in.' He went to the path at the side of the church, then stopped. 'What's all this about Bromyard? You keep bringing him up.'

'Oh, nothing. His wife's pet was at the hotel, that's all.' Freddy flapped a hand.

After Andy had gone, Freddy sat on the plinth at the foot of the statue of Mary – *after whom Mags was named* – and closed her eyes in prayer.

50

FREDDY

Seagulls wheeled above. The lighthouse was a dot then it vanished. The trawler kept a steady eight knots out into the Channel. To the west, lighter grey in the gathering dark was all that remained of what, hours earlier, as they had prepared the trawler, had been what Andy declared a glorious sunset. A distant inferno, more like, Freddy had thought.

Now black clouds bunched on the horizon. A storm was forecast.

Freddy was there not to catch fish but to trap Ricky.

While they'd stowed boxes in the hold and the boys checked the fishing gear, the fishing scam hung, like a dead albatross, from the radar mast.

Leaning over the rail at the prow as the *Teresa-Mary* ploughed through the waves, Freddy breathed in cold, salty air tinged with diesel and gutted fish. When she'd done the marine courses in Aberdeen, she had recalled her childhood. Believing she'd never been on a trawler before, it had made no sense. Now it did. She was transported back to being three years old, when she had gone on David Bromyard's boat with her dad.

Bromyard had told the truth about her dad.

In a sense, she had known it all along. She felt sick. Not because he was gay, but because he'd made her mum's life a misery and denied his children happiness, all to keep it quiet. He was both a homophobe and a hypocrite. Bromyard had been trying to tell her that her father had punished her for what he was himself. It was Bromyard who had suggested her dad buy her the *Seaside Book*. Bromyard had been in the background, trying – as Freddy had for Andy – to keep Fred Power's temper at bay.

Her face wet with spray, Freddy let herself imagine that the trip was exactly what Andy wanted it to be. Reenie's three children would be friends again. They would work together, Andy in the fishery, Ricky on his boat and her on the fish round. Toni was as honest as the day was long. Freddy wouldn't need Mags to be in love with her, if she only knew she was all right.

Ricky had told them he'd chosen a fishing area that was flat, comprised of shingle, away from the windfarm and larger vessels. There were no wrecks or hangers, which she knew were lost anchors.

Freddy's fantasy of an ordinary fishing trip evaporated as a wave slapped the prow. The albatross swung above her. A body dangling lifeless from a gallows. *Murder.*

Blinking back tears, Freddy let herself feel what the police believed. Mags was dead.

She pushed off the rail and, making her way across the deck, craned her head up at the wheelhouse. Ricky was crouched at the boat's controls. Andy was behind him. In the cabin light, Freddy couldn't tell if they could see her. Ricky had barely acknowledged her. Had he guessed that she knew?

Freddy suddenly considered that coming on the trawler had been a mistake. Andy couldn't watch her all the time. He didn't believe he had to protect her from Ricky. The confidence she'd felt in the church garden that morning dwindled with the last of the daylight.

Freddy needed to get Andy on his own soon.

They were a good thirteen miles out to sea. The storm was building. Freddy zigzagged along the deck with the roll of the boat.

Life on a trawler was not romantic. The work of gutting fish, slicing off heads, tossing away their insides, demanded a strong constitution. Incipient danger from vicious weather, treacherous currents and a trawler's precarious stability left little margin for error.

She clambered down the stairs from the aft deck to the galley. She had to hope that Andy talking to Ricky was deflecting him from seeing she had left the prow.

While, above the deck, the winches, gantries, drums and derricks were brutally utilitarian, the galley was a Victorian explorer's lair. Wood-panelled walls with lipped shelves to prevent bottles and containers – Branston pickle, salt, HP sauce, mayo, waterproof canisters of tea and coffee, a pocket torch – from slipping off as the trawler heaved. A flat-screen TV on the wall was angled at cushioned benches around a polished oak table. The *Teresa-Mary* was a six-berth vessel, but Ricky had converted three of these into compartments for tools, life jackets, spare slickers. Through portholes, the sky and sea were opaque black. Freddy realised with a jolt that she had stayed the night on Bromyard's boat. Tucked up with her teddy, she'd looked at the night through the circular window.

King Triton was David Bromyard, not her father.

She regarded the cabin that was Ricky's home from home. Toni had said that if he had his way, Ricky would live on his boat. She got seasick so only went on board when the trawler was in the harbour. Had she paid little attention to Ricky's work? Freddy prayed that this was true.

She crept to the other end, where there were steps that she knew led directly up into the wheelhouse. Ricky could go below without getting wet or letting in water. To the left of these was the fish hold and a net store. Checking behind her, Freddy wrenched up the handle and hauled open the thick door to the hold.

Icy air hit her lungs. The insulated hold was like a vast cathedral. The floor was covered with what she estimated was at least a metre of crushed ice. Freddy knew from Ricky's log book that the boat's fuel bunkers were full and the trawler was carrying over a tonne of ice. *Was it all in here?* The trip was for one night – the plan was to catch a haul of Dover and lemon sole, and plaice. Most of Ricky's trips were a minimum of three nights. Daniel Tyler had been his only crew. Had Tyler known what Ricky was doing? It was possible he had not. Ricky could have got him filling another hold without explaining why he was doing it. But Freddy doubted this. Daniel must have found out and murdered Karen for threatening to betray him to Ricky.

There was no porthole on the starboard side of the hold. Not unusual, although many boat designers respected symmetry. Her pulse racing, Freddy gripped a safety rail and, keeping to the narrow ledge around the ice, made her way to the other side. She tapped the metal. The hollow prang told her nothing. The wall was too thick to indicate what was – or wasn't – behind it.

She leaned out, clinging fast to the rail, and made sense of the hold. The net was released down from the hatch in the ceiling. The catch landed on the ice. Daniel would have the job of collecting it up and sorting and grading. She moved along to a narrow metal plate – the platform from which they gathered up the catch – a grooved shape was outlined on the starboard side wall. It was a door. She had assumed that one side was the trawler's hull. Why have a door there?

Freddy tried to fit her fingers into the groove. It was too narrow. A plastic seal ran along the bottom and top. She tried pushing, but it was solid. She tightroped along the ledge back to the entrance to the fish hold and returned to the galley. Now it was obvious. The door to the fish hold was off centre. It wasn't immediately noticeable because the stairs were dead centre, with compartments either side. The symmetry misdirected the eye.

The difference between the wall of the fish hold and the side of the hull was about two metres. Freddy swept her hands down the compartments. She was rewarded. Had she not been looking, she would have missed the inset ring. She pulled. The compartments swung out, blocking the way to the stairs. Freddy stared at what she had hoped against hope not to find.

The secret hold where Ricky hid the black fish.

The hold tapered at the prow end. It was as high as the main hold, reaching right to the deck, rising several metres. Space enough to store a quantity of fish worth thousands of pounds. Ricky, and Karen, when she was alive, were minting it.

There was no ice. Freddy was stunned with disappointment. Ricky did not plan to store fish in the secret hold on this trip. With Andy and Freddy on the trawler, he must be playing it safe. He might have been able to fob Daniel off with a story, but not Andy. The existence of the secret hold was not sufficient proof for Andy. Ricky could say it was the overflow store if a haul was particularly good.

Freddy slumped on the bottom step below the wheelhouse. The odour of stale blood filled her nostrils. *Ricky murdered Karen because she was blackmailing him for a bigger cut.* That had to be it. And then what? Had Daniel found his mum dead and his boss standing over her and driven off into the night? Freddy's head felt it would explode as the narrative rushed in unbidden. Her brother was a murderer.

Insidious fear crept up Freddy's spine. *Toni must know about Ricky.* That would explain why she hadn't phoned in the last few years. She had been keeping her distance since Freddy had been there. Toni hadn't told Freddy that her mum was dying. She had been quick to decide that Daniel Tyler killed Karen Munday. She knew about the illegal fishing. Ricky had always been tempestuous, acting on the spur of the moment, compounding his mistakes because he couldn't be wrong, whether it was playing a board game at Christmas, or breaking a toy and blaming her or Andy. He had murdered Karen in the heat of the moment and now he was in a different league.

Toni had put the blame on Daniel, interviewed Ricky for form's sake and closed the case. It closed the circle of the diagram that Freddy had begun to sketch out. Ricky landed fish over his quota. Karen sold it on and the blind eye of the law was turned by DI Kemp, the cop who shoplifted and got away with it.

Freddy was paralysed by a mixture of fear and a terrible sense of treachery. She rubbed at her eyes with the heel of her palms. She felt confused and purposeless.

After a few minutes, she mustered herself. She must get Andy on his own. She would convince him. The boat heeled. She fell against the compartments. A roll of gaffer tape slid across the floor of the secret hold.

There was something at the prow end. Freddy felt in her oilskins for her torch and switched it on. Now she saw that the walls of the secret hold were scuffed with black marks. She bent and touched one. Rubber. As if someone had kicked the walls. She ventured towards the shape at the end; her mouth dry, she licked her lips.

A tarp was wedged in the tapered end. Gingerly, Freddy lifted an edge and tugged it out from the prow. She whimpered in a dread anticipation of what lay beneath. Something fell from a fold in the tarp. Freddy lurched with the boat and nearly crushed it with her boot.

A rosary necklace. The chain of delicate silver, the beads a translucent blue. It was identical to Freddy's. Hers was in her handbag, which she'd left in Andy's office.

The rosary belonged to Mags. Freddy tore at the tarp, flapped it, heaved it and smacked at it, as if it could yield the answer. She had wanted proof that Ricky was fishing illegally. Instead she had Mags's rosary. Freddy crumpled to the floor. The rosary was proof that Mags had been in the secret hold.

The trawler tilted violently. At the other end of the hold,

the door slammed shut. Freddy skidded on the metal floor as she plunged towards it. The rosary dangling from her hand, she turned the handle. The door was stuck fast. She pushed. The metal didn't yield. Freddy heard someone on the steps.

'Andy.' Her voice echoed in the metal-clad hold.

Whoever was on the steps was going up to the wheelhouse, not coming down. Over the wind and crashing waves and way above on deck, Andy wouldn't hear her.

Freddy smashed her shoulder against the door. Reality dawned. The door had not shut with the roll of the boat. *Ricky had locked her in.*

Freddy sank to the floor, her back against the hull. She wanted to close down. To be nowhere. To give up.

After a minute she forced herself to piece together the story of what had happened to Mags. It was like putting one foot in front of the other on a high wire.

Mags had gone to confession, and afterwards told Toni she must tell Freddy something important. When she nursed Reenie, Mags could have overheard Ricky talking to someone about the scam. Mags would have confronted him. Ricky couldn't risk Mags telling Freddy. He'd know Freddy would guess that Ricky – her baby brother – had also killed Karen. Ricky had attacked Mags. He'd hidden her in the battery. Mags was there when Freddy and Sarah were outside. Mags had deliberately left her crucifix and Julian for Freddy to find. Malcolm Lane had told the media Mags had not been killed there. Freddy pulled at her hair. *Jesus.* If she'd tried to get into the battery, Mags would still be alive. Was the rosary another clue from Mags?

Freddy forced her brain to work. Something caused

359

Mags's kidnapper to think Mags would be discovered, so he moved her. That something must have been when Freddy asked Toni to help her break into the lunette battery. Freddy heaved with dry sobs.

Part of her couldn't believe it. Toni was a Mermaid, and she had offered to help her. Freddy found she couldn't finish the story.

'What are you playing at, bringing Freddy on board?'

'Listen, mate, I told you, I'll sort Freddy. At some point, she'll face facts and give up waiting for Mags McKee to come back from her pilgrimage. She'll go back to her lawyer girlfriend. Be nice to her, OK? You have no reason not to be, now you know what Dad did to Freddy, that she didn't just dump us.'

'Mags is dead.' Ricky wasn't listening. He adjusted one of the many dials on the dashboard in the wheelhouse. Andy was standing behind him.

'Or she's worshipping at some Italian shrine. Will you leave Mags out of this? What's the matter with you?'

'Toni says Mags is dead.' Ricky hiccoughed, as if sickened by his words. 'I'm telling you, Freddy will want her share.'

'We've been here before, Ricky. Bail out, you lose the boat. That was the deal. Typical of you. Even as a kid you always wanted it both ways.' Andy was leaning against the door of the wheelhouse.

'You said it was a victimless crime,' Ricky choked. 'A few

extra fish, you said. These trips are killing me.'

They had reached the fishing grounds. The boat was anchored. The sea was rough, a heavy swell causing the trawler to rock wildly. Rain spattered the windows of the wheelhouse. Drops glistened against the black of the night.

Freddy had been on deck since the trawler left Newhaven, but while the brothers were arguing she had gone below.

'And when Freddy finds out Mags is dead?' Ricky was puce.

'You seem convinced she's dead.' Andy properly looked at his brother.

'Why do you think Toni's running a murder investigation?' Ricky snarled.

'All right, matey, keep your hair on!' Andy opened the wheelhouse door and slid across the hatch bolt.

'What are you doing?' Ricky demanded. 'This is my trawler – do nothing without my say-so. There is one God in the sky and one captain of this boat. You will both do as I say.' Ricky seethed on the edge of his chair, feet wedged behind, knees forward.

'Toys in the pram, bro.' Andy grinned. 'Just getting some air.'

'This weather is bad. I said we shouldn't launch.'

'You go out in worse than this. There are targets to meet, aren't you always saying?' Andy went to the window on the port side and, peered out. 'Toni could be wrong about Mags. Plus, isn't her dep running the show?'

'I'm deploying the nets. Then it's all hands.' Ricky pulled on a lever. The boat shook. Near the aft, one of the derricks tilted off the gantry. A metal arm with the beam suspended from it swung out over the side. A net shot free and vanished in the boiling swell. Ricky leaned over the dash and, repeating the manoeuvre, shot the starboard net. He muttered lugubriously, 'This storm is getting worse.'

'Yes, you said.' Andy clamped a hand on the back of Ricky's neck. 'Listen, Richard, we're going to invite Freddy in. We owe her. She lost her share of the business when she came out to Dad. Mad mare, but you've got to admire her guts. He put her in free fall. I never once stood up to Dad, and nor did you.'

'What happens when Freddy wants more than her share? People do that.' Ricky swivelled in his chair to face Andy.

'She won't. I don't want to be horrible, but I'm your big brother, aren't I?' Andy gave Ricky a matey slap on the shoulder. 'We're doing it my way, OK?'

'How do you know she won't get greedy?' Breathing hard, Ricky got up, legs apart, staring at his boots as if limbering up. He looked down to the prow, where Freddy had been. 'Where is she?'

'I'll find her.'

'I'll go. She needs to learn the drill. She can't wander off. You sort the deck and get the kits secured. That should have happened by now.'

The brothers looked out at the deck, where the plastic crates were sliding back and forth amidst coils of rope with the roll of the boat. A thin moonlight shone on the boards, slick with water sluicing in through the freeing holes.

Andy struggled down the ladder and prepared for the first catch. He lined up the boxes and set about getting the deck shipshape, stowing away twine and loose buoys for when the catch was landed. Seawater lashed his slicker, buffeting him as he worked. All around was pitch black. There were no stars. A fuzzy aurora haloed the deck lamps.

Andy heard ringing. Faint. It came from the wheelhouse. Annoyed, he climbed the ladder and went inside.

Ricky's phone lay beside the control panel. Andy saw Toni's name on the screen. He stopped as he reached it. Seconds later a text came in.

Call me. I know who killed M. Come back. Txx

Andy pocketed the phone and clattered down the wheelhouse ladder to the deck.

He struggled across the whaleback towards the hatch to the net hold. He was nearly blown off his feet as a gust hit him broadside. A discordant commotion filled the air. High waves smashed against the hull and surged over the rail; the deck was awash. Andy's oilskins were slick with water. The trawler, substantial in the harbour, was a toy tossed mercilessly by the elements. The sky and the sea were a wall of black.

Another wave crashed over the side and the boat listed, the angle acute. Andy was flung against the guard rail, hanging over it, a metre from the curdling mass below. A list the other way and he flailed for the goalpost gantry aft of the gunwale. He caught it.

Momentarily stable, Andy raised his arm and hurled Ricky's phone into the sea.

52

TONI

'I read her diary, boss.'

'Where are you?' Toni was snappish with fear. Sheena had rung seconds after Toni texted Ricky. She assumed it was him returning her call. She was furious for not calling him before he went to sea. Their ritual, at her instigation, was due to her anxiety – which Toni kept to herself – that if they didn't speak, Ricky would drown.

'I'm in Margaret McKee's flat,' Sheena said.

'This late?' Toni tapped her Fitbit. Two minutes past midnight. 'We already searched it.' Sheena's work ethic was all about brown-nosing Malcolm and back-footing Toni. Forget sisterhood.

Detectives were pulling apart the fishery office. Toni had emphasised they must search all the desks. *Yes, of course Ricky's.* She'd got the warrant when the CCTV came up with Daisy's visitor. The man with the fish tattoo.

The sniffer dog was being released from the cage in the dog patrol van. 'I can't talk now, Sheena.' The handler was giving the dog the shirt they'd taken from Mags's washing basket. Twenty years of policing hadn't prepared Toni for this.

'There was this weird phrase in Margaret's diary,' Sheena carried on.

'What phrase?' Even though someone had to do it, Toni resented Sheena reading Mags's private journal. It felt like the byword in violation.

'"R's intention in Mary",' Sheena recited.

'It will be religious, Mags is devout.' Against the odds, Toni stuck to a sliver of hope that her friend was alive. 'Sheena, we need you down at Power Fisheries.'

Malcolm was gesticulating. Toni made a winding-up sign to him.

'...I googled loads of stuff on Mary,' Sheena was saying. 'It means you offer an intention to Mary that you'd like to have prayed for. Or something like that. Anyway, the clue is Mary...'

Toni reached Malcolm. The sniffer dog had caught a scent. They followed a snakes and ladders route between a maze of shipping containers. Once the dog ducked down a side alley up to the fence then doubled back. The containers weren't there when she and Freddy used to hang about the fishery.

'...she meant this statue in her front room.'

'What statue?' Toni was out of breath, although she was fit enough for the mild pace. She felt her heart would burst. She wanted to run in the other direction.

The dog stopped at a container hard by the fence. Through the link fence was an abandoned junkyard. Beyond was a tract of scrubland cut in half by the railway line. With only the beach after that, the fishery, on the edge of the industrial estate, was a lonely place. A good place to hold someone prisoner. Out here, drowned by the sound of the waves and the railway, who would hear a person – *Mags* – scream? The sniffer dog was pawing at a container door. Toni's legs went to jelly. She felt a hand on her arm, supporting her. Malcolm.

'Guv, you still there?' Sheena's voice in her ear.

Rory, one of the uniforms, twisted a handle on the container and pulled. The door screeched across the hard standing.

'*Mags!*' Toni shoved past Rory and blundered inside. A light shone over her shoulder.

A mattress, a pillow. *A bloody tarpaulin.* The nights had been cold. A bait tub to shit in.

'*Bastard.*'

'Boss, are you OK?' Sheena shouted down the phone.

Toni had a sudden flash of memory. Mags, perched on a camping stool, feet up on the bait tub, reading to them while they fished from the sea wall.

'*...and in this he showed me a little thing, the quantity of a hazelnut, lying in the palm of my hand, it seemed, and it was as round as any ball. I looked thereupon with the eye of my understanding, and I thought, "What may this be?" And it was answered generally thus: "It is all that is made."*'

Toni had gathered that the hazelnut represented the perfection of existence or some such. She'd once choked on a nut at Christmas; her dad had dislodged it with a wallop on her back. Julian could keep her nut.

The Mermaids had had an exam on Julian's *Revelations* the following week. Only Mags was prepared. She knew every word of Julian.

The dog was nosing the mattress.

'Yes, I'm OK,' Toni told Sheena.

'...it was hidden inside a statue of Mary.'

'What was?' Toni asked dully.

'Irene Power's will. Her "intention". R is for Reenie. It's dated the first of March 2019. That's recent. It leaves everything to her daughter, Frederica. I'm wondering, could it have a bearing on Margaret's murder? If that's what happened...'

Toni crouched down by the mattress, her hand hovering.

'Yes, it could. Good work, Sheena. *Very* good work. Thanks.'

A hair straggled across the stained fabric. Toni shouted, 'Bag this.'

'This vent hole has been damaged, guv.' Malcolm was examining a tear in the metal. 'Looks as if Mags tried to escape and gave up. It would be impossible to cut through the walls.'

Mags had tried to escape. She had not been a passive prisoner. The sniffer dog had doubled back in a side alley between the containers. Mags had run for her life. The scent was lost within the perimeter of the fishery.

Out beyond the scrub, waves pummelled the shore. A force gale blew. Gusts battered the containers and thrilled between the bars of the galvanised fence, making it sing. *The Mermaids' Chorus.*

'Ma'am.' It was Darren, the PC. 'We've tracked down the Powers. Kirsty Power says not to worry, Andy and Ricky are fishing. They've taken their sister, Frederica. It's a family reunion.'

Ricky had only got his tattoo because of Andy. Andy,

Mr Golf and Rotary Club, came to regret his when it went septic. *Word from the wise, if you're going to be on the wrong side of the law, don't give yourself a distinguishing mark.*

Toni peered through the fence. The familiar dread coiled inside her. *Compartmentalise.* It didn't work. She could not put up walls against the growing panic. A storm was brewing. Ricky would be working hard out there, battling with the elements. Toni had to believe it was why he wasn't answering his phone. Her gut told her it was not.

53

FREDDY

The boat tipped. Freddy thought it must capsize. She assured herself that Ricky was a professional fisherman; he'd have submitted the trawler to a roll test. He'd never skimp on safety. *Would he?*

She felt for her phone and swore. Andy had put it in a drawer in the wheelhouse so it didn't get soaked with spray. *Stupid.* Sarah had bought her a waterproof phone on her last birthday.

Freddy shouted but, above the cacophony of the storm, her voice would be lost. Andy wouldn't hear. *Ricky knew.*

A dreadful idea occurred to her. What if Andy was involved? It was his idea to go out on the trawler. Freddy felt the air being sucked out of her lungs and she gasped for breath. Except, if Andy wanted her to leave, why offer their mum's house? He had known that, if she stayed, she'd look after the animal hotel. No, his motive was clear, he wanted a sibling reunion. Like Freddy, it would never occur to Andy that their young brother could be a murderer.

When Andy had been prepared to give airtime to her

theory that Ricky had tried to run her over on the road into Newhaven, Freddy had felt ill. Until then she'd wanted it to be paranoia. Imprisoned in a secret hold on Ricky's boat miles out in the English Channel, a storm raging, she realised it was real. Andy had said it was odd Ricky hadn't complained about the scrape to his car. Now it occurred to her to wonder why he had left it for Andy, and her, to see. Ricky must believe himself above suspicion.

Freddy clung to a handhold as the boat heeled at least forty-five degrees. Ricky was running a fishing scam operation. There was no ice in the secret hold tonight, not because he wouldn't risk her and Andy finding out, but because for him the night trip had another purpose. She had been doubtful when Andy told her Ricky had agreed to the reunion. She had not trusted Ricky. He didn't want a grand making-up session – how would that benefit him? He'd kill her and toss her overboard. He'd tell Andy it was an accident. *If Ricky hadn't killed Andy too.* Fear engulfed her. Freddy screamed. She crawled on her hands and knees crying. *This could not be true.*

Freddy no longer kidded herself that Ricky would not hurt his sister. She had abandoned him and Andy to the mercies of their father. That she had not chosen to leave would not make a difference to Ricky.

Ricky had got his dream by fishing outside his quota and dealing in black fish. He had risked everything to get the trawler and he'd do everything to keep it. His attempt to murder her on the road had failed. This time it would not. Sarah had said that whenever we imagine ourselves in a dangerous situation, we always escape. Freddy was in one now. She *would* escape.

Freddy pulled on the handle with all her might. The iron door didn't give. Was this how Mags had felt? Terrified and alone on a boat with a man who would kill her? Had she wrenched on the handle, shouted and smashed her fists on the unyielding door? Had her faith saved her? Had she, like Julian, waited to be received by God?

Had she imagined herself as Ariel, sailing into the sunset with Freddy?

Freddy knew Mags would have fought death until it won. Had the rosary slipped off her as Ricky was carrying her up onto the deck, or had she left it for someone to find?

Ricky had used the tarp to throw Mags's body into the sea.

'Andy!' He must wonder where she was and come looking for her.

Andy wouldn't come if Ricky had killed him.

A terror Freddy had never thought possible tentacled over her, cold and insidious. Poison flooded her veins. Freddy scrubbed at her hair, which was stiff with salt from the spray. She clutched Mags's rosary and tried to stay calm.

Arching her neck, she arced the torch upwards.

There was a hatch.

Freddy staggered to her feet, falling as the boat tipped again. She had forgotten the purpose of the hold. How else would the nets be emptied into it? She waved the torch wildly about.

An iron ladder was fixed to the wall. Freddy didn't let go of the grab rail. She couldn't face finding the hatch locked.

She thought of Mags. She had to try. Freddy rushed at the ladder, pushing against a greater force as the boat rocked the other way. She dragged herself up rung by rung.

She reached the top. Glancing down, the sheer drop dizzied her. It tilted and lurched with the trawler. At one point the tilt was so great that Freddy might have been on the float. The force of gravity pressed her against the ladder. Then tried to snatch her off it. She took a breath and twisted the handle. It was stuck fast. The feeling wasn't disappointment. It was grief. All encompassing, the loss of everyone and everything. Freddy's fingers loosened on the rung. She imagined falling backwards.

There was an arrow pointing clockwise. She had turned the handle the wrong way. She took both hands off the rung and grabbed the handle. The sea was on her side, the boat tipped, pushing her against the ladder. She twisted the handle.

She heaved on the hatch. It gave but didn't open. She could have cried with frustration. Something must be blocking it. Ricky was one step ahead all the time. This was new to her. It was always Andy who had caught her on the hop when they were kids, never Ricky. She pushed again. This time with the strength of the crazed, who can lift a car to save someone caught beneath it.

She heard a dull thud. A buoy and some crates had been stacked on top of the hatch. They were snatched up by the wind and slid across the nearly vertical planks.

Freddy was soaked as water from the deck streamed in, splashing down into the hold. She just grabbed at a rung as the boat heaved. She hauled herself up and out.

A wave the size of a house was suspended above her. She flung herself behind the gantry as it smashed onto the deck. The trawler plummeted into a trough and rose again. The hull shuddered.

Freddy had been focused on escaping from Ricky. She hadn't considered the other enemy, one far more formidable and unforgiving. Ricky was nothing if his boat was overwhelmed by the storm. Already he wasn't thinking straight. He'd forgotten to lock the hatch. He'd made a thing about closing all apertures when they got on board.

Freddy had only to lose her footing and she would go overboard. The tumult, black flecked with foam, was riven with currents like muscles beneath skin. Freddy had no life jacket. Another wave smacked her into one of the warp drums. If she slipped into the freezing waters, a life jacket wouldn't save her. She would die of cold within minutes.

An arm wrapped around her neck. She wriggled and ducked, but the grasp was strong. She shouted into the gale. '*Andy, help.*'

A towering wave engulfed the stern, water streaming over the net drum. Plastic boxes spun across the deck and bounced against bollards.

Freddy tried to twist around.

'*Christ's sake*, Freddy, don't fight me,' Ricky hissed.

54

TONI

Cars screeched up to the quay. Two men arrived on bicycles; one had a broken light but Toni wasn't about to arrest him. Despite her sick terror, she watched, impressed, as, at top speed, they climbed into dry-suits and wellingtons. Men ran down the slipway to the boat still doing up zips, clipping on helmets, shrugging into life jackets. Toni was desperate to go with them. She would brave seasickness to get to Freddy and Ricky. She had never believed he was a murderer. She hoped she would get the chance to look him in the eye and tell him so.

'Task heli. Potential casualties. Three.' His phone to his ear, Malcolm was sending up a police helicopter. He finished, 'Guv, we're on.'

Three fifty-six a.m. The helicopter swung out over the English Channel.

The *Teresa-Mary*'s last recorded coordinates were 50°44'.47N and 000°02'910W, 4.48 nautical miles from the coast off Burrow Head. Since then there had been no message on the VHS channel, no blip on the radar. It was as if the trawler didn't exist.

'They have to rely on sightings from other shipping.' Malcolm had been talking with the crew. 'Apparently, there's a Belgian trawler two miles from the *Teresa-Mary*'s last recorded position. And a Norwegian vessel six miles away. They're full steam ahead there now.'

Toni wolfed a softening Snickers bar that she found in her pocket. Balling the wrapping between her palms, she scoured the darkness outside the window. Lit by the helicopter's beam, the sea was black, laced with white spume. When she'd gone aboard Ricky's boat with its horrible oily smells, she had marvelled at the huge components, great lumps of metal. The engine rotor with blades the size of a person, gigantic reels for wire that paid out the nets. Ricky had called it the warp. All of it solid, indestructible. *It would be all right.*

Below, the swell, raked by the machine's searchlight, thrilled with currents and counter-currents. A giant maw which could swallow a liner, never mind Ricky's twelve-metre boat. She'd many times done her own trawling – through Google – and knew a beam trawler rolled easily. Make the slightest error shooting the nets or swinging them in or out of the water, heavy with tonnes of fish, and it was impossible to correct. It took a ridge of sand, a discarded net – called a fastener – to snag the trawler and capsize it. Accidents were waiting to happen. Every time Ricky went out, he took his life in his hands. Toni had known this day would come. *Except this time the accident would be on purpose.*

'Ricky's an experienced sailor. He's got all the

competency certificates. His boat is twelve years old, but that's not old in this industry.' Malcolm had done his homework. 'Fishermen come through the most terrible conditions. Like coppers.' He couldn't muster a smile.

'Why did they even go? Jesus, Mary and flippin' Joseph, it's one grade short of a hurricane on the Beaufort scale.' *Andy would have factored that in.* Toni buffed the window with a cuffed fist, although it made no difference. Sea visibility was down to ten metres, the wind speed was nearing a hundred. If it got worse the search crews would abort the mission. She narrowed her eyes. Below was roiling black, waves breaking on waves. 'I'm a detective, but I never saw through his charm. I took the piss out of his social climbing, the golf club and the business breakfasts, church every week. OK, I knew he was ruthless – Andy could drive down fish prices, even with Ricky – but I never guessed he was a killer.'

'How could you? Killers come in—'

'All shapes and sizes, yeah. But this isn't some bloke bottling another in the face. This is the premeditated murder of two women Andy knew.' Toni chucked the chocolate wrapper at the glass. It bounced off onto the carpet.

'Psychopaths are charming. Look at Ted Bundy.' Malcolm retrieved the wrapper. 'You did say Andy Power's father was evil.'

'See? I saw that in Fred senior. I like to think I'd have sussed Bundy too.' Toni needed to give Malcolm the facts. 'You won't know this, but Fred Power was gay.'

'Wait, didn't he chuck Freddy out of the house for being with a woman?' Malcolm got the point immediately. 'Wow. Freddy must feel *sick*.'

'Freddy doesn't know – none of them do. I found out soon after I joined Sussex. Fred Power was done for cottaging in the seventies. In those loos opposite the Co-op. The shop was a big old pub in those days. Fred drank there.'

'Well.' Malcolm puffed his cheek. 'I'm surprised that didn't close down the fishery.'

'It was hushed up. The Powers had power. Thanks to Andy, they still do. It never got to court.'

'Tediously typical, a gay-hater with issues about his sexuality. I do get why he didn't want to be out. I'd think twice in his business, ours too.' Malcolm was scouring the sea. 'You never told Ricky?'

'We'd just got together. I didn't want to lose him.' Toni winced. Telling Malcolm had temporarily taken her mind off what they were doing. The crazed yearning returned. *Make it all right.* 'Ricky never got the sharp end of Fred Power. He'd have shot the messenger. Fred Power's double standards destroyed his family. I'll tell Ricky now. And Freddy.' Cold fear fraying her senses, Toni prayed she'd get the chance.

55

FREDDY

'*Christ's sake*, Freddy, stop fighting me.'

In the light of a deck lamp Freddy caught sight of an anchor tattoo on her brother's wrist. *Ricky.*

Ricky was too strong. Perhaps feeling her subside, he let go. He steadied himself against the derrick. With her back to the engine housing, Freddy had nowhere to go. Blinded by sea spray and whipped by the wind, still she could make out that Andy wasn't in the wheelhouse.

'What have you done to Andy?' Her mouth wouldn't work properly.

Ricky hustled her down the steps into the galley. Freddy slumped on a bench, hugging herself. Out of the storm, she realised she was wet through and freezing cold.

'Put that on.' Ricky thrust a bundle at her. A life jacket. Any glimmer of possibility he didn't intend to harm her was quickly extinguished. Ricky evidently planned to make her death appear an accident. If she went overboard, even in a life jacket, if she didn't drown, she'd die of hypothermia.

Ricky took a remote control from the condiment shelf

and flicked on the TV. Freddy recognised *Diamonds Are Forever*. She rubbed her temples as it became clear. In the middle of a hurricane, Ricky must be setting up a scene of cosy domesticity. She imagined his statement to the police. '...*we had hauled in the nets and processed the catch. We were all below, chilling out with a Bond movie. I made Freddy keep on her life jacket because the weather was worsening...*'

Freddy shouted at Ricky, 'I'm not watching telly, Ricky. *Jesus*, we shouldn't be here! In this weather you need me crewing.' She struggled into the jacket, fumbling with tags and toggles, numb fingers making her clumsy. Ricky loomed over her. Freddy flinched. But he tightened the straps, securing the jacket.

'What have you done with Andy?' No point in placating him; even after twenty years, he'd be able to read her.

'I'm here.' Andy was in the doorway leading from the fish hold. Freddy felt a whoosh of relief.

'Turn that thing off, Ricky. We have to talk.' Andy nodded at the television.

'The nets need hauling in. We have a catch. You need to help.' Ricky struggled towards Andy. Andy didn't move. 'I'll bring her back to port. Unload this haul. Then I'm done. Freddy, you stay here. Keep out of the way.'

'Sit,' Andy ordered. 'Don't be stupid, little brother.'

'Ricky, I told you I have certification. I should be helping. You need us all up there. Andy, let him pass. Ricky, let me help...' Freddy began. For a moment she forgot that she'd asked Andy to be mindful of Ricky. That he was dangerous.

'Get over there.' Andy shoved Ricky onto the bench beside Freddy.

'The nets must be twisting, if they tangle—' Ricky went still. 'What is that noise?'

Above the boom of the waves and claps of thunder Freddy distinguished a bang. It reverberated in the galley.

'You've left a bloody hatch open.' Ricky tried to get up. 'Andy, reel in the starboard warp and land the net. I'll do the other net. OK, Freddy, you can help. You and me will empty the catch into the hold.' Ricky had gone into captain mode. Freddy had never seen him in charge of anything before. Whatever, his trawler came first.

'We are going to have a chat.' Andy pointed the remote at the television and turned it off. 'Too late for scruples, bro.'

The grating tone. The suppressed anger. Supreme control. *You will leave this town and never return. I can't even look at you, the sight makes me sick. You're damaged goods. A freak of nature.*

'Ricky, you will do as I say. We need this business. You can't jump ship now. Or, put it this way, that's exactly what you can do.' Andy was talking like his father.

Freddy had been touched when her childhood companion, the brother she'd protected from their dad, welcomed her home. He'd given her work, a place to stay when Ricky had wanted her gone. Now she realised it hadn't been kindness. Freddy's heart lurched in her mouth. Andy was not her friend. He was out for himself.

'Join us, Freddy.' Andy's voice thrilled with excitement. *Who was this man?* 'We can trust each other. Not like Karen. The Powers are back. We're extending Gold Light's reach along the coast. Dorset, Devon, Cornwall.'

It was Andy who hid the Gold Light file behind Ricky's

computer. He knew she'd find it and that she'd blame Ricky. It was Andy who had driven Ricky's car that night. She had refused to see the truth, and it had led her here.

'You were in Ricky's car,' Freddy said. 'The engine was warm but Ricky was at sea that night. Toni told me in the pub but I was too blinkered to see. You weren't just cross about Sarah sending you that letter. You were cross that I was still alive. You'd left me for dead in a ditch.'

The boat tilted violently towards the stern. Andy was thrown to the end of the table. Freddy jostled against Ricky on the bench.

'You said you dented the wing moving my car out of the way of the bin lorry.' Ricky struggled up. Yelling over the din. 'Stay here. I'm going to sort the gear. When we get into Newhaven, I'm calling Toni.'

'Let me spell it out for the stupid one in the family.' Andy pushed Ricky down. 'If you tell your copper girlfriend, I will inform DI Kemp's superiors about her propensity to go shopping without opening her purse.'

Freddy dragged her hands down her face. Andy knew about the shoplifting.

'You're talking out of your arse.' *Thank God.* Ricky didn't believe Andy.

'Karen Munday had her uses.' Andy was grim. 'She spotted Toni nicking sweets in the Co-op. You should thank me. Karen would have used it to take all of Gold Light. That was her plan.'

'Karen was a liar. Toni is a police officer,' Ricky spat. 'How come Karen was… Wait, you told her about Gold Light?'

'Of course not, stupid.' Andy was sneering. 'Dan found

your faked logbook for the *Teresa-Mary*. That boy was too bright, he realised the trips didn't match reality and went squealing to his mum. Karen demanded in or she'd report us. I told Daniel that you were the ringleader. Stupid kid went off the rails.' Andy sounded aggrieved, like a game had been spoiled. 'I was doing just fine. Dad would have been proud – I turned this place around.'

'Proud of you? It's me working all hours!' Ricky yelled.

'And Dad would have hated fishing illegally!' Freddy said. 'Whatever else he was, he would *not* have handled black fish. *Christ*. He vetted our suppliers with a fine-tooth comb, scouring their log books, watching them land catches to check they were on the level.'

'She was blackmailing me.' Andy ignored them both.

'Karen blackmailed you?' Freddy felt crushed. If only Karen had told the police, she'd be alive now. She recalled the hamster staying at the pets' hotel. 'Was Karen going away?'

'Daniel said Karen was going to a spa for a few days. Dan was worried she was going mad with money.' Ricky was as white as a sheet. Freddy felt sorry for him; he was up to his neck.

'She was!' Andy exclaimed. 'She was leeching me for a couple of grand a month. The bitch was bleeding me dry. It had to stop.'

'Bleeding *you* dry?' Ricky's ruddy complexion was chalk pale. 'You had me increase the catches, do longer trips and you never told me she was blackmailing you.'

'Karen would have got Toni for being a thief. I did you a favour,' Andy said.

Above them, waves crashed against the hull. The fish-hold hatch rang against the metal cladding like the clapper of a bell. Yet Freddy had a sensation of silence.

'You murdered Karen for threatening to blow the whistle on your scam.' Freddy was too outraged to be afraid.

'Well done, sis. You should be a detective. Munday would have taken over Power's. It's been in our family for generations. It's a dynasty. We could carry it on together.'

'But you had an alibi. The golf club. Kirsty said…' Freddy fumbled for the words; her mind wouldn't work.

'If Kirsty said I was there, I was there. Not my fault if she got her timings wrong.' Andy shrugged.

'Mo Munday said Karen was seeing someone. It was you,' Ricky shouted above the crash of the waves. His eyes were wild.

'Karen was the last girl I'd shag. You couldn't pay me. It was strictly business.' Andy had killed a woman, but still Freddy was shocked by his brutal language. She was in a living nightmare.

'Did you kill Daniel?' she forced herself to ask.

'He saved me the trouble. He did it all by himself. His girlfriend will keep her mouth shut.'

'Not Daisy too. Where would it have stopped?' Freddy couldn't believe she was having this conversation with her brother. She had risked her life, coming on the boat to prove to Andy that Ricky was a criminal. Instead she had discovered that Andy was a murderer.

'I didn't mean to kill Karen. I lost it. Karen taunted me. Like Dad used to. Laughing in my face how I was useless. What else was I meant to do!' Freddy saw the little boy who was jeered at by his father, belittled and hit. Her compassion was all gone. Nothing justified murder.

'Andy, you don't mean that,' Freddy heard herself say. From the look on his face, she could see Andy did mean it. She didn't know her brother.

Another wave smashed against the hull, the boat tipped. The storm was overhead. Sheets of water lashed the deck.

'You killed Karen. You as good as killed *Daniel*. He wouldn't have crashed if he hadn't been so upset.' Ricky was catching up with what Andy had done. Freddy felt idiotic relief that at least Ricky wasn't a killer.

'I didn't hear you complain when we were raking it in. You were the one who increased the mesh size of the nets, to limit the catch to plate-size fish and lose the small fry.' Andy was dragging Ricky down with him.

'Who gives a toss about the holes in the net,' Freddy blazed at her brothers. 'Two people have died so you can get rich.' She tried to see through the miasma of crimes.

'Come in with us.' Andy grabbed hold of a pipe on the galley ceiling as the vessel heeled. 'Climate change is the state's excuse to shut down the ordinary guy, wreck our livelihood. Stupid laws cooked up by Whitehall bean counters. C'mon, guys, it'll be a proper family business. Down the line we'll sell to Norway and retire before we're fifty. We *all* win.'

'You'll be caught eventually,' Freddy said.

'Not me.' Andy clung to the pipe. 'I only buy the fish. I have to trust my suppliers.' He had kept himself clean but made sure that Ricky was up to his neck.

Freddy lost her balance as the vessel tipped. She grabbed Andy's overhead pipe. Her face up close.

'Where is Mags?'

'Don't ask.' Andy lost his confident look. It was as if she'd slapped him. 'Mags meddled in business that wasn't hers. She stole Mum's will and she texted you.'

'The solicitor has Mum's will – what are you talking about?' Ricky protested.

'There was a later one. Mum wasn't herself. She needed me to sort it for her.'

'What did it say?' Freddy asked.

'She left every goddam thing to you: the house, the fishery, the lot. She told me she was righting Dad's wrong. She said she'd given Mags the will to take to the solicitor.' He swapped hands on the pipe. 'It was the meds, they messed with her head.'

'The solicitor never said,' Ricky said.

'You said that Mags hid the will?' Freddy said.

'Mags claimed she destroyed it. Said it wouldn't bring you back, it would upset the family. But I knew she was biding her time. First, she texted you. Next, she'd have given you the will.' Andy sounded sorrowful. 'I never meant anything bad to happen. A little scare to make her destroy the will, that was all. I saw her in the battery; she'd gone to meet you. I had to stop her.'

While Andy had almost boasted of killing Karen, he appeared actually upset about Mags.

'*Where is Mags?*' Freddy felt herself grow faint. She gripped the edge of the saloon table, her fingers sliding as a wave smashed into the hull.

Andy was silent. Freddy saw realisation dawn on Ricky's face.

'*No.*' Ricky barrelled into Andy, his head down like a bull. The boat heaved and, gathering momentum, the brothers hurtled into the passage. Ricky pushed Andy to the floor and dived for the stairs.

The boat listed violently to starboard. Water splashed into the galley, washing around Andy. The secret fish-hold was inches deep. There was an ear-splitting grinding, then a tremendous jolt. Freddy whacked into the table, and pain shot down her leg. She felt it as if it was a concept, distant. Automatically, she put out a hand and helped Andy to his feet. The roll of the boat flung them into an embrace. Freddy's instinct was to cling to Andy. She threw him off.

Ricky was halfway up the steps; he snatched for the handrail and stopped himself pitching backwards.

Andy's fingers slipped free of her hand. He was flung back. His head hit an iron strut. The crack of bone. He lay crumpled outside the secret hold.

Freddy clambered up after Ricky. On the deck she fastened the hatch.

'...*foul ground, it's... fastener caught net... tangled.*' Ricky's shout was whipped away by the wind as he battled up the ladder to the wheelhouse. Freddy got the gist. The starboard net had become tangled with something – discarded fishing gear, a rock – on the seabed some fifty metres below. It had whiplashed the trawler back, snapping it around. Every fisherman's dread.

Freddy's marine training in Scotland kicked in. Too much water was sluicing across the deck through the freeing ports. The boat heeling caused to the deck to be almost vertical. The trawler was tossed up on a wave and then flung down.

Freddy heard another shout. Ricky was a blurred sketch at the door of the wheelhouse. In a nanosecond pause in the clamour, Freddy heard him clearly.

'*There's nothing more I can do.*'

The engine had cut. They were drifting.

Andy lurched across the deck. His hair and face plastered with blood and seawater. He was screaming but, over the wind and waves, Freddy couldn't hear what he was saying.

The secret hold. The tarpaulin. Freddy knew what had happened to Mags.

Andy hung over the towing drum. He was fighting gravity and the elements to release the winch attached to the drum. He would try to save the thousands of pounds' worth of fish by hauling in the net.

If he raised the net, the boat would capsize.

She struggled against the gale-force wind, slipped and fell. She choked on ice-cold salty water. Coughing, Freddy was dimly aware that the rim of the trawler was close to the sea. *The boat was sinking.* She strove towards Andy, but she was too late.

She felt her way around the engine housing to the starboard side. The other derrick was topped, but there was no sign of the net. She clung to the rail as the boat listed to the other side.

Ricky had seen it. He flung himself down the wheelhouse ladder and stumbled across ropes; slamming into the loose kits and buoys, he skidded, legs scissoring.

Andy released the winch. The drum spun like a roulette wheel. Without the engine, the drum worked hydraulically. It yanked the warp like a spring-loaded tape measure. The cable thrashed, cutting into the dark water. The boat jerked starboard.

Freddy watched as a massive wave emerged from the surf. Suspended from the derrick, the net bulged with fish thrashing and wriggling as they fought to live. The net began to swing like a pendulum, the arc increasing.

The trawler tipped with the weight. Water streamed over the lip down the nearly upright deck like a waterfall. Freddy prayed. While the net remained outside the boat they had a chance, but not at that angle. Add a tonne of fish to the trawler and the balance would be compromised beyond correction. It was why Ricky had wanted her and Andy to bring up one net while he did the other. Andy would know this.

Andy swung the beam across. More water gushed across the deck. Ricky reached him and they were caught in a ghastly dance. They careered away from the drum and hit the port rail like boxers between bouts. Ricky pushed off. He was making for the aft derrick to raise the other net and achieve a balance. The boat was a giant weighing scale. Andy went after him.

Andy had left the galley door open. Freddy made to shut it. The boat was tossed upwards. She clung to a bollard, her arms wrapped around it. Through rain and spray she saw the portside beam fly across the deck. It hit Andy and Ricky as if they were skittles. Freddy was ripped from the bollard and lifted on a raft of water across the deck.

A wave rose up, metres above her. She grabbed for something solid and found a plastic kit. *Useless.* The wave plummeted down. Before Freddy was dragged underwater, she saw her brothers washed into the sea. Neither wore a life jacket.

56

FREDDY

Freddy saw the ferry, vast as a skyscraper, looming over her against the mauve sky, streaks of dawn casting the slightest light. Not a ferry. It was the upturned hull of the trawler. Hampered by her life jacket, clinging to a crate, Freddy flailed against the burgeoning swell, gasping for air. Infinite cold seeped into her bones. Every attempt was futile. Miles out, she had no chance of getting to the coast.

She was hit by something hard. A wall. The current had carried her to the hull. Desperate, betting her all on it, Freddy let go of the box and swept her hands over the freezing metal. She caught something.

A trail of netting. Summoning the last of her strength. Freddy wrapped it around her wrist. The meagre purchase it gave her allowed her to feel for a footing. She found a hole. A freeing port. Everything was upside down. Or inside out. One of several holes in the hull for allowing water to escape, it was an ironic saviour.

Freddy resisted the tug of the undertow. It invited her, the lure of the sea-witch, to let go and float to the unfathomable depths. *Let go.* Something cut into her calves, unyielding, thin like a blade. *The warp.* One of the towing wires for the net. The net itself would be on the seabed. The cable, attached between the net and the drum, was taut. Using it as a brace, with the determination of a woman who does not want to die, Freddy hauled herself upward. Half clear of the water, each wave hit her with the force of a solid object. Each time, her tenuous hold on the freeing port and the warp weakened.

She saw an object. *A life raft?* Freddy blinked. Not a life raft.

A body floated along the line of the hull. Serene, in the eye of the storm.

Illuminated by the merest hint of dawn, Andy's face might be carved of stone, his expression impassive. He looked asleep. *Please God, make him only asleep.* His body bobbed and tipped on the waves. Desperate, Freddy caught at his oilskin jacket. She tugged. The movement made her slip. A sudden swell snatched Andy away. Freddy scrabbled with her life-jacket fastenings. She worked them loose and, twisting one leg around the warp like a tightrope acrobat, she ducked out of the jacket.

'I'll keep you warm. I'll keep you warm. It's all all right. I'll keep you warm. I'll keep you warm.'

She grasped the jacket in one hand and, letting go of the warp, reached further out. She grabbed at Andy's shirt collar. It tore. She lost him again. She stretched further and grabbed his upper arm. The warp was suddenly limp. It dropped away. She knew what had happened. It had become detached from the net. She clung to Andy.

The sea toyed with her, one moment rolling her closer to the hull then bouncing her away with a flick of spume. Freddy pushed Andy's arm through the neck of the life jacket and then shoved her own arm through. It was like when they'd arm-wrestled as kids. Was she to see her life pass before her? A gallery of faces and voices.

They were back at the hull. She kicked with her feet, feeling for a freeing port. The surface of the metal was smooth. It was like trying to climb a sheer glacier.

Above the roar of the waves, with Andy an inert weight, Freddy heard banging. *The hatch door.* The bangs were too frequent. It was a signal. *Ricky was trapped inside the wheelhouse.*

Freddy had no time to feel a semblance of relief. She was hit by another wave. The life jacket was snatched from her. She swallowed salt water and retched, and swallowed more. She surfaced, cramp crippling her. Andy had come to. He fought the jacket as if it was an enemy. He pushed Freddy back under the water. Distantly, fighting for breath, it occurred that Andy would kill her to ensure that his murders were never revealed. *He would risk his own life to end hers.*

As she surfaced, his hand clamped onto her ankle. He let go and grabbed for her again. His eyes were wild. He was scared.

'Andy, please.' Her throat was raw; no sound came out. Andy was grappling with her, not to kill, but to survive.

They both went under. Freddy felt herself give into the caressing swell. The fight had gone from her.

She swooped through the encrusted grotto, dipping and swirling until, with a swish of her fishtail, she came to rest on a seaweed leaf. She relaxed, warmed by ribbons of refracted sunlight from fathoms above. A flicker. Here was Mags, with Flounder too. Freddy was home.

57

TONI

'What's that?' Malcolm craned over her. 'There, down there.'

The helicopter dropped metres and swung around. Light caught a patch where the water was smooth. Something jutted from the waves, Toni saw lettering on the side. '... sa-Mary'. A snatch of a window. *The wheelhouse*. If Ricky had become trapped in there, he would not have got out.

'It's the trawler,' she whispered. 'Andy's scuppered it.'

'Possibly not. In this weather, it's as likely it capsized.' Malcolm was strangely calm.

The helicopter hovered, the clatter of the propeller lost in the crashes and bangs of the elements. Ricky's boat was paltry, insubstantial, no match for the contemptuous sea. The undertow would drag it down. What lay beneath was not the idyll of King Triton's palace and his mermaid daughters. It was fathoms of dark silence. Toni was numb, her eyes staring at the scene below with a terrible detachment.

'Oh God.' Malcolm tensed beside her.

The body was floating face down, arms outstretched.
Toni felt a scream fill all of herself.
'*Freddy.*'

58

TONI

Pentecost, 9th June 2019

'I solved my cases, Dad.' Toni felt the sun warm her back. A breeze flapped her hair. The sensation of contrasting temperatures was soporific; she was tempted to move to the bench a few metres from the grave and bask in the spring sunshine, but she had a pile of paperwork on her desk.

'Two girls I was at school with. Women now.' *Both murdered.* Toni faltered. She couldn't speak those words. If Dad could hear her, he'd know anyway.

A big solve. Three murders and one drowning. Terrific for the monthly stats, though Worricker had tempered his glee because Toni had known the victims. Two murder investigations running parallel were, he'd reminded her in a solemn tone, highly unusual for a medium-sized town on the south coast of England.

Toni had booked the pub in Tarring Neville again. This time she'd only stayed for one drink. The team understood.

They had got justice for Mags and for Karen and her son, but Toni got no satisfaction from the outcome.

Andy Power had created multiple tragedies and shattered lives out of greed and avarice. Andy had told Ricky fraud was a victimless crime. But it had escalated, it opened them to blackmail and to murder. She could have told Ricky there are always victims. There are always consequences.

Toni knew that Freddy and Ricky were heartbroken over Andy's death. Freddy didn't begin to condone Andy. She was in no doubt he'd have killed her when she refused to go along with his plan. But Andy was their brother and they loved him. Perhaps they were also missing the brother that Andy had never been.

For her part Toni was angry that Andy had escaped justice. Drowning didn't match his torture of Mags. Those moments when he had apparently struggled for his life in the sea were few. Toni wanted Andy to have suffered for longer. Mags would have forgiven him.

Toni would suffer the loss of Mags until the day she died. Freddy would never recover.

God goes up with shouts of joy

The Lord goes up with trumpet blast

That morning she had gone to Mass with Freddy. Apart from weddings and funerals, Toni had not been in a church since she'd left Our Lady of the Immaculate Heart. The responsorial psalm remained an earworm, lending rhythm to her thoughts.

Toni's brief flurry of prayer as she'd watched the lifeboat launch had not lasted. Surrounded by the dead of Newhaven, she remained rooted in the earth. She wanted to believe, like

Freddy, that Mags was in Heaven, but the idea was on a par with *The Little Mermaid*, a fairy tale.

Freddy, however, had rediscovered God. She consulted Julian's *Revelations* and regularly saw Father Pete. The Power family had been destroyed. Ricky was on remand in Lewes Prison, charged as an accessory to fraud. He faced at least five years, but his cooperation with the police and his obvious repentance might shave off a couple.

Freddy was running the fishery and the fish round. Kirsty Power had moved out of the townhouse on the river in Lewes and was living with her parents in Ringmer, a village on Freddy's fish round. She was changing back to her maiden name. The kids would not be Powers. When Toni had told Freddy, she'd said she was tempted get a new name too but, as God knew who she really was, names were irrelevant.

Toni envied Freddy her newly re-found faith. She was alone.

A Marine Accident Investigation was under way. The police had been shown preliminary findings. Watertight doors left open, freeing ports blocked by boxes, insufficient freeboard space and mishandling of derricks, resulting in significant reduction of the vessel's stability. An experienced fisherman, but exhausted by the increased hours at sea, Ricky had got sloppy. Toni didn't know if she could forgive Ricky for what he'd done. She told her dad that when Ricky got released she'd perhaps be there to meet him. Perhaps.

Toni had forced herself to contemplate the agonies Mags must have suffered in the battery and in the shipping container. She would suffer with her. If she had listened to Freddy that night at the pub when she insisted that Mags was missing, the search would have started sooner. She might have saved Mags. They had no body so she couldn't know exactly when she died. Freddy thought it was on Ricky's trawler. Toni suspected she hadn't made it out of the fishery alive.

Watching a glider cross the sky towards the sea, Toni ruminated that Mags had hidden the will and deprived Freddy of her inheritance because she feared that Andy would kill Freddy if she got her mum's whole estate. The boys got half each on Freddy's death. Toni guessed that Mags had felt guilty because she was also thinking of herself. She couldn't bear to have Freddy back in Newhaven. Mags had played God.

Andy had known Mags all his life. When it came to it, he'd been unable to kill her until, when Mags had tried to escape, he'd had no choice.

Andy's bloodied fingerprints were on the shipping container. The futon belonged to him. The pillow was traced to Kirsty's card. The container was on his property. He could have dumped the mattress in there. Desperate, Andy returned to Karen's after the police had finished and left Ricky's belt. With Daniel dead and therefore already harmless, it was a clumsy move to frame Ricky. With him out of the way – and eventually Freddy too – Andy would have had the business. Despite his crass effort, Toni wondered if Andy might still have got off. There were two witnesses to his confession on the trawler, but little else linked him to the crimes. With an adroit defence lawyer – like Sarah Wood – Andy could have walked.

Regardless of the warmth of the sun, Toni shivered. The shadow of a cloud crept across the headstones. Andy would not be buried in consecrated ground. Thank God for small mercies. Or thank someone.

In the month since Andy had drowned, Toni had become convinced that, had they met at the battery, Mags would have told Freddy she loved her. Freddy thought otherwise – she believed Mags had overheard details of the fishing scam from either Ricky or Andy and planned to tell her. But Toni had seen it in Mags's eyes when they bumped into each other outside the church. She loved Freddy. Mags would have told Freddy why she had hidden the will. She would have put it right. Fresh from confession, Mags had intended to absolve herself of sin.

Freddy cried when she saw the will: Reenie had left her everything. She'd never cared about the money; she wanted *The Little Mermaid* DVD, the fish and the animal hotel. She would share the estate with Ricky and with Andy's family.

Toni believed that Andy had gone to Karen's intending to kill her but found Daniel there with Daisy. Having discovered the faked logbook, Daniel guessed what was going on. Furious, he'd stormed out with Daisy in tow. Karen was left with Andy. That she was on the toilet suggested Karen had assumed Andy left with the youngsters. He had not. Why hadn't he killed Daisy when he saw her in the hospital? Toni could only guess that, faced with a teenager little older than his own daughter, even Andy had a limit.

Andy could have strangled Karen spontaneously in the heat of the moment when she'd upped the blackmailing stakes. But he'd taken elaborate precautions before he'd gone to her house. From Freddy's statement, Andy had said on the boat that he meant to murder her. He'd had no choice.

CCTV of the car park showed Andy plugging his car into

the electric point on the forecourt of his house and going inside. He changed out of his light raincoat. A wider trawl of cameras in the vicinity showed a man in a black donkey jacket getting onto a Vespa scooter ten minutes away from Andy's house. He'd ridden to Newhaven, murdered Karen and been back in Lewes within an hour. His wife accounted for the hour. Kirsty had heard Andy return, she said it wasn't unusual for him to go straight into his ground-floor office. Upstairs, watching TV, she'd believed Andy was there all evening.

If Kirsty had lied, she was good. During her interview with Malcolm she'd remained impassive and factual. Not spousal loyalty, Toni knew; although Kirsty had accepted a share of the fishery, she'd made it clear to Freddy she was done with the Power family. She'd done an interview for *Sun on Sunday*. Kirsty was a fierce mother, bent on keeping a roof over her children's heads.

That morning at Mass, Freddy had given the second reading, from the holy Gospel according to Luke. Father Pete had asked her to take over from Andy. Toni knew Freddy was in pieces, but she'd made it to the end. Like Ricky, Freddy was struggling with how to mourn a murderer.

'"...worshipped him and then went back to Jerusalem full of joy..."'

It would be a long time until Freddy felt true joy.

'My dad was gay.' Freddy had met Toni at the end of the service after she'd taken the host and sipped the wine, the body and blood of Christ.

'Why doesn't that surprise me?' Toni had been wondering when and how to broach the thorny subject.

'He had a long affair with a man called David Bromyard.'

They were strolling around Mary's garden at the back of the church. Mags's garden.

'I saw a file.' Toni had sat at the foot of Mary's statue and told Freddy all she knew.

When she finished, Freddy got up. 'I have to see someone.'

'Father Pete?' Toni wanted Freddy to be open about her faith. She couldn't share it, but she could walk alongside her. If she could talk to the priest, it might help her. Father Pete seemed a relaxed and open kind of man; he didn't strike Toni as a raving homophobe.

'David Bromyard. I owe him an apology. I think he is probably a kind man.'

A kind man. Freddy's own father had not been that.

Toni sat on the bench, her arms resting along the back. The cemetery sprawled away down the hill, the Downs stretching off for as far as the eyes could see. The gravestones shimmered in the heat. The day had begun misty and grey, but by the time they had come out of Mass the sky was blue, feathered with white clouds.

Toni let her gaze wander up the hill to where Reenie Power was buried. A lone wooden cross. If bodies did turn in their graves, Reenie's would be spinning. One son drowned before he could be convicted of three murders and the attempted murder of his brother and sister. The other son in prison. Only her daughter would be a source of pride.

From Newhaven, Toni heard a distant clarion call. Freddy's fish van. In a world where street callers had all but vanished, the milkman, the onion man, the rag and bone man and the window cleaner's chamois superseded by long-handled brushes and snaking hoses, in this town, the mobile fishmonger survived.

Freddy was building up the round. She had reopened the small animal hotel. She had declared she would remain single. Her relationships would be with her animal and bird guests. She was keeping Brad, Karen Munday's hamster. However, when Toni had gone to the house last night, bearing a bottle of Jack Daniel's, a woman called Rosie, who Freddy introduced – ridiculously – as a fish customer, was planted on the settee. Toni pretended Malcolm was calling and left. If there was an afterlife – which there wasn't – Mags could gain comfort from seeing that Freddy was doing OK.

Karen and Daniel were having a double headstone. Gold lettering, marble. The funeral was in a fortnight, the police having released their bodies. The Mundays were doing Karen and Daniel proud. Horse-drawn hearses with a wake to end all wakes at Seaford golf club. Toni would go with Freddy. Rejected in different ways all her life, Karen had always battled for a foothold. The Mermaids had administered another rejection. Karen's story was of betrayal and treachery. Toni owed her.

There was no grave for Mags. Only the sea. After Mags's Mass – they had that hurdle next week – Toni and Freddy would scatter petals on the shoreline at Newhaven. The petals would be carried out to sea. They were getting a plaque to go beside the grave of Mags's parents. In the shadow of the yew tree near the entrance.

Toni made her way back down the hill to her car by the bronze statue of the boy. She paused and looked back. The gravestones shimmered in the sunlight. Through the chapel arch she imagined a figure hurrying towards her. *Mags.*

Toni turned and, leaving the dead behind, drove along

the C7 towards Newhaven. Her phone rang. 'Guv, it's me. A body's been found in a house in Peacehaven. The death might be suspicious, Uniform want us to take a look. I can go if you'd rather—' Malcolm would think she couldn't face another death.

'I'm on my way,' Toni said.

Sunlight gleamed off the bronze boy. The headstones rising up the hill towards the Downs were white against the green of the summer grass. The *Seven Sisters* ferry glided out of the harbour and plied the English Channel towards France, seagulls crying its wake.

Acknowledgements

So many generously offered their knowledge and experience for *Death of a Mermaid*. I must emphasise that any factual errors are mine.

As ever, my heartfelt thanks to retired Detective Chief Superintendent Stephen Cassidy of the Metropolitan Police. Stephen has for years given me valuable help. His professional and informed description of the best policing inspires all my novels.

Jane Rivers of the Creature Comforts Small Pet Hotel outlined the ins and outs of running her fabulous establishment. I've tried to reflect Jane's high standard of care for her furred and feathered guests in Reenie Power's seaside guesthouse. Thank you, Jane.

I'm grateful to Steve Watts for a fascinating dawn visit behind the scenes of a Waitrose fish counter. Freddy Power's fishmonger skills and top customer service owes much to Steve. As does Freddy's love of Cullen skink, now my favourite dish.

My thanks to Chris Bish for sharing his thoughts on fish and crime fiction. Everyone at MCB Seafoods in Newhaven made me very welcome. (Mike Bish's murder idea involving the freezer tunnel is up my sleeve for the future...). Chris gave me a fascinating tour of his fishery. The rest I made up.

I've long wanted to write a novel featuring a mobile fishmonger. Every Wednesday this solitary writer flies outside for an exchange of fish and banter by Tim Woodward's van. Thanks to Tim for sharing the minutiae of his business and for suggesting I talk to Chris Bish.

Thanks to Miranda Kemp (Sussex Community Foundation) for putting me in touch with Steve Watts. And giving me information about Newhaven.

The team at the Newhaven Coastwatch station took me around their cliff-top tower overlooking the English Channel. The NCI save lives by monitoring our coasts. We need more of them. (www.nci.org.uk)

Thanks to Lisa Holloway for musical suggestions and specifically for *The Little Mermaid*.

The novel features the Newhaven lifeboat. RNLI crews risk their lives to rescue those in trouble at sea. (www.rnli. org/find-my-nearest/lifeboat-stations/newhaven-lifeboat-station.) They do so in this novel.

I used to live in Newhaven. I've spent hours exploring the Victorian streets and the harbour. Thank you to Stefan Storoszko for opening the Newhaven Museum on a cold January morning for me to ferret in the archives.

My gratitude to Jenny Bourne-Taylor for keeping me inspired.

My editor, Laura Palmer, is the best. I owe much to Laura's forensic, intelligent editing. My thanks to the special team at Head of Zeus for everything else.

Thank you to Georgina Capel Associates, specifically,

George, Rachel, Irene and Simon. And to Philippa Brewster for her steadfast encouragement.

Every novel I write depends on Melanie Lockett's love and support and her eagle eye. If it's rubbish, she tells me.

My writing day is nothing without a latte and a brioche from Libby's Patisserie. Thanks to Libby and Lola for keeping me sane around eleven a.m.

I'm always spurred on by my readers. Not least Shirley Cassidy (The Detective's Mother) and the novel-devouring sisters, Juliet and Helen Eve.

This novel features characters with varying relationships to Catholicism. I'm very grateful to Domenica de Rosa for her generous and meaningful introduction to the Catholic church.

Death of a Mermaid is for Domenica, my treasured friend and fellow crime-novelist.

Lewes, United Kingdom
2020

About the Author

LESLEY THOMSON grew up in west London. Her first novel, *A Kind of Vanishing*, won the People's Book Prize in 2010. Her second novel, *The Detective's Daughter*, was a #1 bestseller and the resulting series has sold over 750,000 copies. Lesley divides her time between Sussex and Gloucestershire. She lives with her partner and her dog.